Coming out with obstacles
or
two lovable men
and
the curious journey to the
jackpot with murder

W. T. Wallenda

Coming out with obstacles
or

two lovable gay men
and
the curious journey to the
jackpot with murder

Impressung / Imprint:

© 2025 – W. T. Wallenda

Titelbild und Rückseite / Cover and back cover:

Fotos/Bilder – Photos/Pictures:

bestsellers-1656185_1280
comic-characters-2026154_1280
crime-scene-29308_1280
fingerprint-649818_1280
man-2288176_1280
detective-4787272_1280

© and license by:
https://pixabay.com/service/license-summary/

Weitere Mitwirkende / other contributors:

Verlag/publishing:

BoD · Books on Demand GmbH, Überseering 33,
22297 Hamburg, bod@bod.de

Druck/print:

Libri Plureos GmbH,
Friedensallee 273,
22763 Hamburg

ISBN: 978-3-7693-7664-7

Article 3 Basic Law of the Federal Republic of Germany

(1) All persons are equal before the law.

(2) Men and women have equal rights. The state shall promote the actual implementation of equal rights for men and women and shall work for the elimination of existing disadvantages.

(3) No one may be favored or disfavored because of his or her sex, origin, race, language, country of origin and residence, faith, or religious or political beliefs. No one may be discriminated against because of his or her disability.

(Excerpt from the Basic Law of the Federal Republic of Germany)

"As long as we have not implemented this fundamental right in our society, we still have a lot of work to do. Everyone is allowed to love whom he wants to love. Everyone is allowed to believe in what or who he or she wants to believe in, and everyone is a *stranger* somewhere in the world because of his or her appearance, origin, and language.

We must overcome the last hurdles peacefully and hand in hand to achieve local and global harmony.

My dream: no racism - no wars - no hatred and no rejection just because you are different. Let's fight against it. This time with exaggerated humor to discreetly hold a mirror up to some people."

W. T. Wallenda

"I would love to have a mental duel with you, but I don't fight unarmed people."

Konny Wels
(stolen from an unknown person)

"His mind is his fortune, and poverty is no shame."

Berti Schwartz
(read the quote sometime)

"Give racism no chance!"

Daddy Schwartz

"Anyone who has the ability to laugh heartily at themselves can go through life upright. They are definitely strong, confident and happy people."

W. Wallenda
(Author's opinion)

Coming out with obstacles
or
two lovable gay men
and
the curious journey to the
jackpot with murder

Chapter 1
Coming out in suspenders

If there were a red thread in his life that was visible to everyone, the one of Herbert Schwartz, whom everyone calls Berti, would probably be pitch black rather than purple. And if the usual stumbling blocks on life's path were visible to everyone, Berti's path would be comparable to a pre-alpine terrain.

Wherever there was a stumbling block, Berti stepped into it. Whatever Berti started, it always went wrong. At first, the boy with an above-average caloric diet didn't even notice this everyday failure. After all, it was standard in his life that nothing went right on the first try.

Herbert Schwartz grew up in a safe suburban neighborhood. He was the baby of a family of four, and his personal destiny took its course. The overweight boy wore only the worn-out clothes of his siblings, in keeping with his childhood rank. But second-hand clothes were not the real problem. Instead, people at school laughed at the fact that Berti's outfit wasn't exactly up to date. This was because his siblings were a few years older than him.

Berti's father was from Franconia in northern Bavarian. He could never get rid of the dialect. He didn't speak normal slang, no, Daddy

Schwartz's pronunciation was very directly with a smart sound of sympathie.

"Where is my bombastic Berti? Come here, Berti! Let me have a look at you. It's still good, you can still wear it, boy," was his father's opinion, and it was the one that was decisive in the great court of arbitration when it came to sorting out and passing on clothes.

"Dad, they always make fun of my clothes at school," Berti tried to defend himself.

But Daddy Schwartz always had a solution ready. "Just tell them that you'll grow out of the clothes,and that they keep their ugly faces. We have to save money. This townhouse needs to be paid for. The stuff is still good," was Daddy Schwartz's usual closing line.

Then there was the matter of the glasses. Berti's horn-rimmed glasses weren't modern back then, they were more practical. They were so big and confusing that you could never really lose them. Despite his best efforts, Berti never lost his glasses. It was an impossibility, and not even Berti's general lack of talent had made it possible.

"We Schwartzs have been wearing the same model of glasses since grandpa's time! It is perfectly made for our heads," the overweight teenage boy used to say. Daddy Schwartz always had a bottle of beer in his left hand and a sandwich with Bratwurst in his right. Daddy's favorite food.

When the kids played pranks at school, it was always an incalculable risk if Berti was involved. Running away was not his specialty. It was always the same one who was caught in these so-called escape pranks. Berti! If you had one, you had them all. This increased the excitement for the other kids immensely. Only those who managed to pull off a stupid prank with Berti without getting caught were considered clever, brave, ingenious, and the coolest kid in school.

Berti believed that this constant getting caught was probably the key to his personal success. He had time to read during detention. He always felt more educated than his grades indicated. And in retrospect, he considered it pure luck that he was always the last to be picked for a team in sports. Not only did he learn to be patient, but he also had the opportunity to study the facial expressions and gestures of others while waiting.

Berti considered this phase of his life to be the cornerstone of his real training. Training to be a super detective. He wanted to be like

James Bond and all the other TV detectives in feature films, movies and TV series.

He just never wanted to be like Tom Cruise, the main character in the Mission Impossible movies. He couldn't stand the science fiction and all the posturing. Tom Cruise had double-A status with Berti. A so-called AA guy was nothing more than an arrogant asshole.

Berti wanted to be just like his screen idols and act the way they did in their movies. Superior, cool and smart.

When it came to choosing a career, there was only one option. At the end of his school career he applied for the police force.

After he collapsed during the physical education test, or rather somewhere between the starting block and the two-hundred-meter mark of a two-thousand-meter race, and woke up in the hospital room of the police barracks, he was advised to lose a few kilos.

"You can repeat the test another time," he was told.

He didn't retake the exam, but instead threw his hat into the lottery of career opportunities. Well, there weren't many tickets. In fact, there was only one ticket in the pot. It was a job as an office clerk at the nearby feed mill. Thanks to Daddy Schwartz's connections at the pub, Herbert Schwartz got the job.

"Berti, that's bullshit with the police. Don't go on a rampage now, but learn something good, then you'll get somewhere in life," his father said. "Look at Uncle Albert, he had a good job. Go to the boss or to the office."

Three years later, Berti had a business degree and was tired of being an office administrator. It was time to shoot for the stars.

"I'm ready now," he said.

Berti was absolutely certain that he was not cut out for the easy life. He needed more. He needed thrills. He was the adventurous type, the man with sunglasses in a linen suit, sipping a long drink at the bar with a smile on his face after solving a tricky case.

Berti was looking for adventure. He would need it in the future, like the air he breathed. That was a fact. To survive, he needed his daily dose of adrenaline. He needed a certain amount of danger, otherwise he wouldn't be happy. That, too, was as clear as mud. The police didn't want him, which he found absolutely ridiculous, so there was only one option left. He had to become a private detective. Not a private eye, but THE private eye.

"As if Sherlock Holmes ever solved a case after running 2,000 meters," he said to himself.

"Wait, Mrs. Tacklestone, I'll run another 2,000 yards before I find your missing husband. Dr. Watson, where are my running shoes?" he joked.

Sherlock Holmes was a private detective, not a sports star. This train of thought was the initial spark for Berti's future career. He was not destined to be a policeman, but a private investigator. With each passing day, week, and month, this idea became more firmly established. One day Berti woke up and knew that the time had come.

This is THE day, he realized immediately.

The decision was made. Berti fulfilled his life's dream. He became a private investigator.

The young man emptied his savings account, left home and sought adventure in the big city.

"If anything happens, call me. You know you can always come back," father Schwartz told his son, taking a bite out of his Bratwurst-Sandwich before adding an incomprehensible "Bye, Berti".

Separated from his parents, the self-proclaimed private dick moved into an apartment in the city. He had a door sign made, designed a homepage and placed banners on all sorts of websites. He also placed an ad in a daily newspaper to attract his first clients.

The private investigator still has appointments available. Investigations of all kinds. The ad was placed in large letters between the animal market and real estate search under the heading: Miscellaneous.

Berti proudly bought a copy of the newspaper, sat down on the sofa at home and waited. Two bags of potato chips and four 0.33-liter bottles of Coke later, he was still sitting there. The phone was silent. Nothing! Nada! Niente! Niente! Not a single call. He checked several times to make sure the phone was working.

It worked! He noticed every time. He never even received a phone call asking how much his fee was.

When the word "fee" crossed his mind, he slapped his thighs. "Exactly! How much money should I charge?"

Herbert Schwartz grinned. He would play it cool. As the Robin Hood of the big city, he would help the poor for free, and the rich would make him rich. He liked the concept. "Is 1,000 euros plus expenses a day okay?" he wondered aloud.

Berti went to the mirror and practiced. "My fee? A thousand plus expenses per day. What, you can't afford that? Look for a private dick in the toy store near the action figures. I only work for solvent clients. I'm a professional. Success is guaranteed with me. Problems exist only so I don't get bored. I solve them. Forever."

When he spoke, he disguised his voice, contorted his face, and imitated screen heroes. After Marlon Brando in The Godfather, he did Robert De Niro. He thought he looked better. In a hotter voice, he said to his reflection: "Hey, you wuss. Yeah, that's you, I'm talking to you. Either you come out with the photos or you're gonna wish the Mafia was here instead of me. I know you'd rather swim in the North Sea with concrete feet than see me here.

Berti was satisfied. Now he was prepared. The phone was ready. He waited again. Nothing happened. Silence. Agonizing, nerve-wracking silence filled the room.

Another phone test followed. Landline and cell. Both worked. He used the cell phone to call his own landline. The familiar ringing tone was heard. Berti waited for the answering machine. "Schwartz, Private Detective. Don't hang up. I'll call you back. Your problem is my problem from now on, and I don't have any problems, I'll take care of it."

More than satisfied, he sat back and waited for the first client to call. He waited and waited and waited.

In desperation, the detective began to read the newspaper. He spread it out in front of him, cleaned the lenses of his glasses, and scanned the headline. Rents are exploding!

"As if nobody knew!"
Berti read an article about the fate of an impoverished multimillionaire who received 50,000 euros in social assistance every month to cover her fixed costs.

He deliberately skipped the sports section that followed. After browsing through all the car listings, he came to the acquaintances page. Berti rubbed his hands together, opened a new bag of potato chips, took a sip of Coke and leaned back. He devoured the first ads with relish.

"Stallion seeks mare! Get in touch!"

"The animal page comes later," he commented amusedly and continued reading.

"Young-at-heart widow, mid-sixties, looking for a new partner."

Berti smiled. "All that's missing is the addition: cooking mushrooms as a hobby. She buried her first husband with that, now it's the next one's turn."

"W wants W to be affectionate. I'm slim, 35 and unattached. And you?"

"I'm not a girl," he chuckled.

"Looking for a fun group of friends for all kinds of activities."

"Buy a bone, then at least the street dogs will play with you if no one else likes you."

"New to town, late twenties, male, looking for a loyal friend. Also chubby if you like. Honesty counts! Likability is important. Get in touch!"

Berti read the ad three times. He felt hot and cold. His heart began to beat. The rising pulse made his palms clammy. A cell phone number was printed at the bottom of the ad. No cryptic crap, no dating agency, and no SMS scam. It was a regular cell phone number. Should he call? A man was looking for a loyal and honest boyfriend.

The guy is in his late twenties and likes chubby men. That's fate, Berti kept thinking. There's an ad in the same paper that's going to change my professional life because of my ad. He stopped thinking about it.

Everything was clear to Berti. He was gay and single. He also didn't have a client at the moment, which meant he had a lot of time on his hands.

So why not?

Excitedly, he typed the number into his cell phone. It rang. Beads of sweat formed on his forehead.

What could I say?

His index finger was about to hang up when someone with a very sympathetic voice answered the call.

"Hello, this is Konny."

"Hello, my name is Herbert ... better Berti."

"Hi, Berti."

"I read your ad and ..."

"Are you from here?" Konny interrupted the short pause.

"Yes. I thought we could ... well, I have time and ..."

Konny laughed. "You mean we could meet sometime?"

"That was the idea."

"You're really going for it."

"I have no ulterior motives," Berti gushed. He felt quite stupid.

"I didn't mean it that way. But as luck would have it, I don't have any plans for today either."

"You mean it works?"

"Shall we go out for dinner? We can get to know each other in a comfortable atmosphere."

"Dinner is great!"

"I'm new here. Do you know a good place downtown? I wouldn't know where to find it."

"Sure! How about Italian?"

"I'd love to."

From that day on he was with Konrad Wels. Konny was great. He was a perfect match for Berti. They got along right away. It was love at first sight. Konny was slim, athletic and visually the opposite of Herbert Schwartz. Perhaps that was the secret of their mutual affection.

"It can happen to anyone," smiled Konny when Berti tried to sprinkle some Parmesan over the pasta during their first dinner at the Italian restaurant, but the lid of the cheese shaker, including the entire contents, landed on his plate.

"I love parmesan," Berti chuckled, trying to put a positive spin on the mishap.

And even later, when he poured more red wine and knocked over the glass, Konny remained calm. Smiling and fascinated, he listened to the tough guy sitting in front of him.

"I can't stand white jeans anyway. They make me look like a doctor. I'll throw them away later," the new detective played down the embarrassment.

For Herbert Schwartz, his counterpart was a dream type. Konny had a degree in German. He loved to write novels and dreamed of becoming a great writer. As Konny Wels, he had already achieved his first respectable success. One of the big publishers occasionally published a manuscript by the up-and-coming author.

15

"They may be clichéd romance novels, or to be more precise, the weekly penny dreadfuls that women of a certain age devour, but with the stories about Dr. Kurt Lonedale, I hit the mark with this clientele," he said.

"Why Konny Wels and not Konrad Wels?" Berti wanted to know.

"Because women would probably rather read something by women than by men. The publisher changed Konrad to Kon-ny. It sounds more feminine."

"I don't understand."

"Never mind. I won't publicly present myself as a male author until I have my first bestseller in the stores. Until then, I can live with the fact that everyone thinks Konny Wels is a woman."

When the two men's legs accidentally touched under the table, her pulse immediately shot up. A tingling sensation ran from her little toe to the roots of her hair. Their eyes were glued together. Cupid had shot an arrow and pierced both their hearts at the same time.

Broke Back Mountain at the Italian Restaurant. Two cowboys were attracted to each other. They had only known each other for a few hours, but from the beginning they were as intimate as two friends from long ago. This was the jackpot for both of them.

Together they needed a bigger apartment. A car was to follow. The career plan was also perfect. Konny wrote his love stories. On the side, he was supposed to take care of Berti's office work while he was away on dangerous missions.

Unfortunately, the order situation was such that calls from potential clients did not materialize, and Berti ended up working as a department store detective for a large consumer temple. "Just temporarily, to pay the bills," he said.

"Think of it as a training program," Konny had said, and as he did every week, he gave his friend the postcard with the solution to the crossword puzzle from the TV magazine when Berti went to work. "Will you put it back in?"

"We can save the money for the stamp. We won't win anything anyway."

Konny's blink was enough. As usual, Berti took the postcard and put it in the mailbox in front of the department store. Then he entered the building, walked past the human resources department, greeted

Ms. Perla, and wanted to disappear into his four-monitor surveillance room.

"Mr. Schwartz, the boss wants to talk to you."

Berti stopped.

Damn it! What's going on now?

Just last week he had been told that the loss due to shoplifting in the last quarter had exceeded 20,000 euros. He was also sure to be told again that the company had hired him to prevent exactly that. All he had caught so far were a couple of teenagers who specialized in stealing girls' bras. "Hey bro', it was just a dare and all, to look cool in front of the chicks and stuff, you know. It's better than stealing a bag or destroying legumes, right?"

"Destroying legumes? What are you talking about?"

"Well, bro', where did you grow up and stuff? Hey guys, the dumpling with eyes doesn't know what legumes are."

The other two thieves laughed.

"This is canned beer. Can I go now, bro'? My producer faction will be terrorized if ... Shit, the cops!"

The three youngsters were picked up by the police and taken home. Berti celebrated his first success. He felt great. That was only two weeks ago. And now? Now the boss asked for him. He was hardly going to praise him for what happened two weeks ago. Berti took a deep breath.

"Thank you, Ms. Perla," he replied. At first, Berti wanted to go on, but then he spontaneously turned back. He returned to the secretary's desk. The store detective put on a particularly friendly smile. "You're wearing that lovely pale pink blouse again. Are you going out tonight?"

Mrs. Perla looked sympathetically at her outer garments. "Oh, you old charmer. It's nothing special," the aging lady replied, blushing slightly.

"Stop it, Ms. Perla. The way you look, I'm sure the gentlemen are lining up."

"Mr. Schwartz, you're one of them," she smiled.

"And you're nicely tanned, too."

"I've been in the solarium a few times. You know, I'm going on vacation soon," came the bubbly, flowery voice. "I don't want to get sunburned when we're sipping cocktails under the palm trees."

"Where are we going?"

Privately, he thought it was a shame about all the money Ms. Perla had brought to Mallorca. The artificial brown made her skin look more like wrinkled leather rags than a beautiful complexion.

"To the South Seas. I'm looking forward to it."

The anticipation of the trip was written all over the secretary's face.

"The South Seas. Isn't that expensive?"

"I've been saving for this for a long time."

Berti sat down on the corner of the desk to look relaxed. But when it creaked under his weight and the opposite part rose slightly, he stood up immediately. "What does Mr. Romer want from me?" he whispered softly.

The look on Frau Perla's face did not bode well. "I think it's about..."

"Schwartz, there you are," the branch manager's voice broke through the conversation. "Come into my office right away. Oh, Ms. Perla, I still need the purchase receipts from last quarter!"

Mr. Romer stood in front of Berti. The store manager that no one liked. As usual, the boss was wearing an ill-fitting suit, because the volume of his belly didn't match the length of his sleeves and the width of his shoulders.

Berti thought that Romer only knew the term Tailor as a family name. In his mind he saw his boss shopping. Everything off the rack.

"I'll take this one. It doesn't fit right, but it's reduced."

Surely he is known everywhere as the Rack-Romer.

Herbert Schwartz could no longer suppress a contemptuous grin. He had to concentrate to keep from snorting. His boss had just been given a new nickname. Berti would tell Mrs. Perla as soon as the conversation was over. She guaranteed that the news would spread very fast. Especially if you added the words: but please don't tell anyone.

Rack-Romer looked ten years older than he actually was. An optical parade. No! Not an optical clown, but the optical clown par excellence! A different suit every day, but the same look. Ash gray.

Berti's thoughts turned to his boss.

For him, everything goes according to plan. Lunch is served at twelve o'clock on the dot. Dinner at six. Shopping on Saturday. Sunday night, it's time for sex. Either before the news or after the crime show at 8:15. But it has to be dark, and it can't last more than ten minutes. In total. So with undressing, foreplay and climax. His climax. Moaning was undesirable, the missionary position was mandatory. Talking before, during and after the sexual act was forbidden.

Berti had to pull himself together not to laugh. This was exactly how he imagined the life of a Rack-Romer.

He couldn't stand that sack of shit from the start.

"What's up?" came from Berti's lips in a surprisingly friendly manner. Actually, he wanted to punch the guy, Jason Statham-style, but Romer was responsible for ordering Berti's money. So the store detective controlled himself.

The office was coldly furnished. Freezer-style Feng Shui. Emotionally, Berti would have placed it between his grandfather's long underpants and ochre women's bodices from the fashion catalog. Nothing lived here. In fact, the flies probably swarmed out of this sterile room. "Get out of here, houseflies. This is the forecourt of hell! Any spider's web is more comfortable."

The only splash of color in the room was a long-distance travel brochure lying around.

Berti felt a little uncomfortable. If you compared his performance curve with the results of other store detectives, you could say that he had had little success so far. His competitors, on the other hand, were racking up one catch after another. He was ridiculed. But since his last success, the store manager had put him in the center of the action, while the others eked out an existence in the PC department, the children's toy section, or the household goods section in the basement.

Berti was also annoyed by the way Romer kept introducing conversations. He couldn't listen to this Mr. Schwartz anymore. Romer's voice was certainly a model for many movie villains.

"Mr. Schwartz! We have another shortage in the women's lingerie department. I told you last week that I want results, otherwise we part ways."

"I ... hmhm," Berti cleared his throat, "... it's my turn."

"Whose turn? What do you mean, it's my turn?" he mimed with funny head movements. "I want to see the results!"

The detective's hands grew clammy. What could he say to Romer? Think, Berti! Tell him something. Only talking will save your head! Silence means loss!

"I was under surveillance and I can narrow down the circle of suspects."

"Narrow?" Roman's voice rose. He became loud. Very loud. "I want them arrested! I want charges filed! Arrests! I want the thieves hauled away in handcuffs by police officers!" The store manager stood up. His head was glowing bright red.

If he had hydrocephalus, he would start whistling. "Ready, the water's boiling," Berti mentally changed the subject, but it didn't help. Romer's words crashed mercilessly into his ears.

"You still have this weekend, Schwartz. Only this weekend! On Monday the regional director is coming for an audit. Either I show him the culprit or culprits, or you're out! You bear the entire responsibility for this enormous deficit!"

"No problem, Mr. Romer. As I said, it's my turn."

"Out!"

Badass, moron and ass-face were the most harmless insults that raced through Berti's mind. I'm going to show Rack-Romer who I am. First I'll catch the perverted suspender thief, then I'll buy this full-fledged ..., Berti thought of his own character and deleted the last word. He replaced it with, ... that armchair fart.

The day passed without results. We had high hopes for tomorrow, Saturday. Saturday was shopping day for the ladies. Rumble in the jungle! Like flies circling a dog turd, the ladies of the city stood at the lingerie baskets and rummaged until they found something to distract their husbands' eyes from their cellulite legs.

Anyone who knew Herbert Schwartz knew that he never gave up. Especially not when he was mad. Angry at Romer, angry at the thief, angry at the whole deadly situation.

But when the anger boiled over, so did the enthusiasm. He wanted to solve the case.

My first big case.

Berti suspected that there was a system behind the high number of thefts. It was no coincidence. A professional thief was at work.

The next day, he was already highly concentrated at breakfast. "I'll get it today," he thought.

Konny sat across from him as usual. He was in a good mood. His dark, almost black hair shone with the new wet gel as if he had just come from the sea. His brown eyes looked at Berti.

"Of course you'll get her," the writer smiled. The moment was perfect. Beaming with joy, Konny presented his good news, the hammer of the day. "Are you sitting well? I've got a great surprise for you. Maybe even the solution to our problem."

Berti put down his coffee cup. Solution to the problem? What problem? He was full of hope.

"This time I've solved the big crossword puzzle. You can win a weekend in a ski hotel. The second prize is 500 euros and the third prize is a 50 euro shopping voucher".

The hope faded. The bright light in the sky crashed. Konny's carefree, light-footed approach to life seemed to underestimate the fatal situation they were in. By problem solving, his friend meant the second prize. 500 euros was a small fortune for the two young men.

"We're not going to win anything anyway."

"Sourpuss!"

"What have you won so far?"

Konny frowned. "A knife block, a trial subscription to Woman's Health and ..."

Berti grimaced. "I know," he interrupted his friend, "and the red rubber ball to blow up."

"After all."

"Konny, we're broke. Your fee and my detective's salary are just enough to cover the rent and the first two weeks of our household needs. What are we supposed to eat in the second half of the month?"

"I'm a lucky mushroom, as the English say," replied the Penny Dreadful author, grinning irresistibly and holding up the famous weekly postcard. "I stuck on our last stamp. It's good luck. Will you drop it in on the way to the store?"

Berti gave himself a wide berth. The stamp was already on the card anyway. "Well, the second prize would be helpful anyway."

Konny got up, Berti poured more coffee. As always, something splashed out. The usual little brown puddle had formed on the saucer.

"Why don't you set a trap for her," Konny answered his partner's first comment.

"The suspender thief?"

"Of course! You have to be more cunning than your rivals and more devious than your opponents."

Berti picked up his saucer and cup. First he sipped the spilled coffee from the small plate, then he took a sip from the cup. Konny was right. "A trap," the detective repeated slowly. "I already thought of that," he interjected, not wanting to sit there looking completely stupid. "That's a very good idea. I just need to know how to do it. I can't draw attention to myself in the lingerie department."

"Disguise yourself as a customer," Konny suggested.

"Do you really think so?"

"Honey, don't be like that. You can do it. You're the best detective I know. Nobody's better than my fat boy."

"Don't always call me fat!"

"Fat. Fat."

"Konny," he literally blurted out. Berti was visibly angry.

"It's all right," the writer relented. "You have to go. And take the map with you."

"Give it to me."

"What has been stolen so far?"

"Lingerie of all kinds worth about 20,000 euros."

"A lot of stuff. That sounds more like a professional operation than random theft by frustrated housewives."

Berti got dressed. He opened the front door, greeted Mrs. Kapaunke, who was on stair duty, and turned back to Konny. "I'll get her."

"Okay, I'll see you later, sweetie."

"Konny! Please! Not when the door to the hallway is open," he grumbled back, but was secretly happy about the caresses. My Konny is already a big man.

The weather was as bad as Berti's mood when he thought about pole-vaulting. It was raining. The cold and wet weather had only one advantage. It cleared Berti's head. He was up a little earlier than usual today. The shelter at the bus stop was already full to bursting. He didn't feel like waiting for the bus anyway. Fuck it, he thought. I'll walk today.

He turned up the collar of his coat, pulled his mismatched baseball cap down a bit, and marched off. Rush hour. The streets were packed with angry drivers, but the sidewalks were clear. Hardly any pedestrians.

They stay home in the rain.

A plan matured in Berti's subconscious. The same words circled over and over again.

Professional action ... twenty thousand dollars ... I'm the only detective. Something's rotten. Totally rotten!

It went around and around in his head. After twenty minutes of walking, he was there. As always, the department store stood proudly in its place. The red brick building defied wind and weather. The mannequins stared impassively at the rain-soaked asphalt. Berti's coat and baseball cap were soaked, but not dripping. The yellow mailbox next to the staff entrance was already waiting for the weekly postcard.

"Here, eat or die," the detective breathed out as he slid the card into the mail slot.

Five minutes later, he was in his office. The store detective had another fifteen minutes before the front doors opened. The shopping-hungry crowd would pour in like vandals in ancient Rome. The first bargain-hunting she-wolves were already waiting to enter under dark umbrellas.

When the stores open, the thieves come. She is certainly the one.

Berti knew it. He suspected it. He felt it. Unrecognizable from the outside, they crept among Mrs. Müller, Mrs. Meier, and several other customers. They waited for a favorable opportunity to strike mercilessly at an unobserved moment.

Rack-Romer's face appeared in Berti's mind. Flushed red, he trumpeted the detective's name. "Mr. Schwartz!" He spat. The disgusting thought made Berti's skin crawl. The tingle of the Drake film stretched from his neck to his hips. He jumped up in disgust. A brief thought flashed through his mind. It was as if he'd taken his famous foot off the line. Berti had indeed had an idea.

"Brilliant idea," he shouted out loud.

Looking at the camera footage gave no real clues. He had watched it over and over again, but he could neither observe any theft nor clarify important questions, such as how the stolen goods were smuggled out. Or what faces kept showing up? Did they work alone or in teams?

That was the whole mystery. In this case, no answer was also no answer. Berti had no idea, but at least he had a vague initial suspicion. He thought he knew how the hot goods left the department store, and he just had to put it to the test.

Right now!

He left the office in a flash. He hurried down the corridor and into the sales room. There he hurried past the shoes and handbags, knocked over a basket of socks, and rushed forward to the women's underwear. The lingerie, or "sensual fashion for underneath," as the latest slogan on a poster read, was right across the street from the two dressing rooms.

The doors would open in a few minutes.

It didn't take long for the first customers to appear in front of the shelves, racks and baskets. Time was precious now. Berti had very little of it. Too little to be choosy. In front of the rack of tights and stockings, he reached for the largest size. Armed with a pair of XXL black fishnet stockings, he ran on. His right paw grabbed a pair of oversized panties, his left hand picked something out of the erotic basket.

Another seven minutes, he estimated.

Berti disappeared into the dressing room. The lights in the sales room went on. The countdown began. He had five minutes to carry out his plan. The detective quickly stripped down to his underwear.

"How do they do that?" he muttered as he pulled the black fishnet stockings over his impressive calves.

His initial apprehension was allayed. Surprisingly, he had no problem putting on the sexy underwear. Berti pulled the women's briefs over his underpants. The thong looked terrible. If he wasn't wearing his retro pants, the front middle section of the ladies' thong would barely cover half of his joystick. His testicles would inevitably be exposed to free fall to the left and right. He struggled a bit with the suspenders. The detective was satisfied when he had fastened the buttons on one leg.

"Thank God for Ruben's ladies. The regular stuff would never have fit me."

Berti looked at himself in the mirror. His dark blond hair was shaved at the sides and at the neck. He let the hair on top grow a little longer. That way he could wear it in different styles. Parted as desired

24

or wildly styled with hair wax in a wake-up style. The glasses looked sporty and elegant. The well-proportioned detective glanced down with satisfaction.

"For God's sake," he slipped out. "I look like a self-made faggot. I'm a drag queen with a welfare look. I'm a welfare-drag."

His free upper body with the huge belly was a familiar sight to him. The lower part looked wilder. Berti wore a pair of white retro-style underpants with a red lady's thong on top, the string of which had completely disappeared rectally, so that the retro pants in front of it could also be pulled into the gap. "Aep," Berti scolded. "Ass eats pants!"

The garters were wrapped around her plump hips. The erotic suspenders were tied to the fishnet stockings on the right leg. On the left leg they hung loosely like tendrils. Berti held a second pair of suspenders.

"49.99," he squeezed out, wedging the packaged department store lingerie under the buttoned suspenders on the right leg. They held.

"That's how they do it," he gloated. "That's one way to smuggle the merchandise out of the store."

The glee faded. He shook his head in disbelief.

No! Not possible! Anti-theft device! Damn it again.

Berti jumped when he heard footsteps. He looked at his watch. The countdown to the opening of the shop was exactly two minutes. Who was marching around here? The detective pushed aside the curtain of the dressing room. He peered cautiously through the small slit. Berti's heart began to pound. He couldn't believe his eyes when he saw Ms. Perla. The secretary was strutting past the lingerie. She deliberately grabbed one garment after another. Everything went into a cool bag she had brought with her.

That bitch, it flashed through Berti's head. She bypasses the electronic anti-theft devices. Mrs. Perla is a wolf in sheep's clothing. She hasn't been saving up for a vacation in the South Seas for a long time.

The secretary pulled out a piece of paper and nodded with satisfaction. The detective suspected theft for hire. He was boiling inside.

That old frigate! Now I know who's responsible for the 20,000 Euro damage. And silly me, I've watched hours of surveillance footage. Of course, I didn't notice anything out of the ordinary. The cameras are only turned on when customers come in. Automatically.

The brazen thief looked around to make sure. She was about to leave the lingerie department and return to the office when Berti jumped out of the changing room. He stood in front of Ms. Perla with a bare torso, a flabby belly and a pair of suspender straps on his left leg.

"I finally got you!" he squealed.

"Iiiiihhhiiiii!" screamed the surprised secretary. The bag of stolen goods fell from her hand. Shocked by the sight of Herbert Schwartz in his suspenders, she clapped her hands together in front of her mouth. Her eyes raced up and down Berti's body.

Just then, the first customers streamed into the lingerie department. As soon as they saw the half-naked garter belt, they too began to scream.

An elderly lady ran up to Berti in disgust. "You're a lecher," she shouted at him. The elderly pensioner kept waving her umbrella in the air.

From behind him he heard all kinds of expressions.

"Peeping Tom!"

"Castrate the pervert!"

"Stop that dirtbag!"

"I'm a detective! I've caught a serial thief in the act," Berti defended himself, but it was as if he was calling for help underwater. His sentence died unheard in the crowd of angry women.

Mrs. Perla's cries, on the other hand, were easily heard. Her shrill voice always found the right gap in the chatter of the women's squadron. "Help! He tried to rape me!"

Berti became afraid. The circle around him grew tighter and tighter. The faces of the angry women looked distorted, frightening. They seemed determined to kill him. They all stared at him with hatred in their eyes. From behind, the crowd opened up.

Berti was relieved. A movie scene flashed through his mind. Moses parted the sea. But it wasn't Moses walking through the parted sea of women, it was Mr. Romer and a member of the security service.

Both came running at a trot. The security guard's muscle-bound battering ram cut through the crowd like an icebreaker. Rack-Romer followed.

At least three of the customers punched 911 into their smartphones. "Emergency call? Police, please come quickly ..."

"Mr. Schwartz!" Romer shouted. He had stopped right in front of Berti and Ms. Perla. He, too, was staring at Berti's lingerie-clad body. It was a mixture of anger, horror and disgust that prevented him from cursing and left Romer speechless for a few seconds. "You ... are ... you're a ..." Romer couldn't get any further.

The security man shoved the manager aside. "I will get him," he shoutet.

"I arrested the thief," Berti shouted in defense.

The guard tried to get past the manager, tripped over his leg, fell forward, and grabbed Berti's retro underpants. He slowly slid to the floor with them. After the customers had been confronted with the naked facts of the store detective standing in front of them in his suspenders, the screaming in the lingerie department of the department store reached the top end of a gigantic noise level scale.

Probably even the wild howling of a Chippendales performance in a sold-out hall of man-hungry women was topped. Several photographs were taken. The scene was captured.

"I'm disappointed in you, Schwartz! I ... I ... hope you won't be released from prison soon," Romer half-stuttered.

"Damn it all! Ms. Perla is the thief! I caught her red-handed!" Berti's mood was like an erupting volcano.

"He was going to rape me," the secretary cried repeatedly.

"Never," Berti replied.

A police patrol ran up. "We happened to be on foot patrol and were right outside the door when the call came in," one of the officers explained, while the other tried increasingly desperately to keep the peace.

Berti pulled up his retro underwear. The two cops also ran their eyes over the man's body several times, clad in suspender belts and fishnet stockings.

"I'm a detective, I disguised myself and caught a serial thief."

"Well, well!" said one of the uniformed men.

"She steals to order. The freezer bag contains both the goods and a note on which she has definitely written down her customer's wish list. I didn't want to rape her," Berti gushed. He just wanted to get out of this embarrassing situation.

"Rudolf, do something," Mrs. Perla hissed at Mr. Romer.

Berti was astonished that the two were on a first-name basis, but they had known each other for years.

"Ms. Perla," Romer fended her off.

Berti wanted to follow up, but then the policeman began to speak.

"And we're supposed to believe that? It all sounds a bit far-fetched."

"Here's the proof! Look in Mrs. Perla's bag. It's got everything she got at the five-finger discount."

"And her outfit?" the officer pointed to the women's underwear.

"Camouflage! Or do you think I like walking around with the egg pincher and the stupid garters?"

"Who knows?" the officer remarked. "And the lady's details?" he added quickly.

"Lies!"

"And why should we assume she's not telling the truth? The way you look, it's quite possible you wanted to rape her."

A lot of stupid questions. Berti flew into a rage, he was about to explode. He was a hero, not a sexual predator. Besides, Ms. Perla was too old for him. And to make matters worse, she was a woman. That was enough. The detective angrily blew his top in front of Romer, the security guard, the two cops, and the entire audience. It had to come out. Here and now! The time was ripe.

"Because I'm gay!" he shouted at the top of his lungs to the mob. His voice was about to break. Some saliva shot forward. Berti's eyes danced wildly behind the lens of his glasses. His cheeks were blood red with rage and wobbled a little.

Silence. Icy, desolate silence. You could hear a pin drop.

Berti tried to think of something to say. His state of mind could easily be described as out of control. The detective tried to sound somewhat normal again, but still spoke with measured anger.

"I'm a homosexual, I'm in a committed relationship, I'm not interested in women, and I'm certainly not interested in Ms. Perla! Have you understood that now, or do you want me to confirm it in writing?"

That was a mental knockout. Berti had come out in public for the first time in his life. If Daddy-Schwartz were here, the Bratwurst-Sandwich would fall out of his hands. "My son is a warm brother, a Homo? Oh my God! I didn't know Berti was a back-side-lover."

The detective stared into open mouths. The crowd was still speechless. For the first time in several minutes, Ms. Perla was also silent. Romer and the guard looked at each other questioningly.

"I see," said the policeman, who was the first to regain his composure. "That's where the wind comes from."

A murmur slowly spread through the rows of spellbound spectators. It was replaced by whispers that escalated into wild cackling.

The day was over.

The headline in the local press was devastating. "Detective in suspenders catches suspected thief!" Berti's photo was emblazoned next to it. The worst of all pictures had been chosen. The guard was lying with Berti's underpants in his fists between the detective's fishnet-clad legs. The suspenders were hanging down, Berti's butt looked oversized. The case was the talk of the town, and cooperation with the department store was terminated.

"Mr. Schwartz, this has gone too far. The reputation of our company has suffered considerably as a result," said Romer.

Berti didn't care. He wouldn't have been able to work there anyway.

"Look at the bright side," Konny comforted his friend. "They can't see your face. The photographer was focused on something else. That´s good."

"And now the whole city knows my ass."

Konny smiled. "I think the stockings and suspenders don't look bad on you."

Berti blushed. For some seconds he forgot the desaster. "Do you really think so?"

Konny nodded, stood up, went to Berti and put his hand on his shoulder. "Do you still have them or did you have to give them back?"

Now Berti smiled. "Hm, if you ask me. I was allowed to keep them."

"Would you wear them again?"

"Konny ... it looks really stupid."

„Really?"
The blink was enough.

Chapter 2
Jackpot

There was only one thing that could beat the life of an extremely disgraced store detective. It was the life of an unemployed, disgraced store detective. No matter which store Berti applied to, he received rejection after rejection.

"Aren't you the one with the suspenders and ..." was how it usually began.

Everyone knew the photo from the newspaper, but no one mentioned the solved case. Berti still considered it his greatest success. He was sure that sooner or later he would be recognized for exposing this serial thief.

For now, however, the private detective had no choice but to spend all his free time at home with his partner. Konny spent the mornings working on a new Dr. Kurt Lonedale novel, while the afternoons belonged to them.

The internet and newspapers were scoured, ideas worked out, applications written, rejections collected. Day after day, the same procedure. Eventually, Konny Wels had enough. One day he brought home a surprise from the shops.

"Fatty, I've got something for you."

"Don't always call me fat."

"Look."

"Our checking account is almost full and you're buying clothes?" Berti wondered as Konny put a bag with various clothes on the table.

"I invested."

"In what?"

"In you! These are work clothes. We'll push your private detective agency in my direction. I've even got an invoice for the tax office," the author beamed. Konny continued to unpack. Beaming with joy, he laid a stack of business cards on the table. "Our first advertising campaign. You just hand out your business cards everywhere."

Berti stared at his friend in surprise. There was a certain gleam in the detective's eyes.

"That's a great idea! Clothes make the man. All I have to do is hit the city's high society, make a little impression, and hand out business cards. Konny, you're a genius! Let me see."

Konny handed his partner one of the cards. Gold background, black lettering. The author had chosen Verdana as the font. Berti read aloud: "Herbert Schwartz, private detective, your problem is my problem, guaranteed investigation," with the phone and cell numbers printed below.

"No address?"

"We can't receive clients here. The office has to wait. They call you, you come there, that's it!"

"Tell me, Konny. Isn't the guarantee a bit exaggerated?"

The writer grinned and shook his head. "Oh no, just the opposite. That's the difference between you and your competitors."

"And if I can't solve a case?" Berti's voice wavered a bit. "Not that I doubt it, I just mean ... well, it could happen ... well ..." He took a deep breath. "I'm only human, after all."

"It doesn't matter! You guarantee it to the customer! It's been proven that 99 percent of all cases can be solved. You can refuse the tiny percentage of unsolvable cases because of the workload," he winked.

Berti was on fire. "Why didn't we think of this before?"

"We just didn't think hard enough, or rather, we didn't see the forest for the trees, as they say. Now we just have to think about where to find the most solvent customers."

Berti snapped his fingers. "At the tennis club. That's where the rich and beautiful are."

Konny nodded. "Perfect."

"When we go to the tennis club, I put on some sports gear. I'll hang around the bar area a bit, leaving a card here and there."

"Good idea, but you have to show up in a suit, not gym clothes. They have bouncers."

"Bouncers outside the tennis club?" asked Berti. "Like outside the dessert?"

"Yes. Like outside the disco."

Berti was puzzled. "Why is that? Only members go there anyway."

"Stupid question. You know what kind of clientele goes there. They're there to protect them."

"Should we take that address off the list?"

Konny shook his head. "Never! Some of the big shots in the sports world are always cheating on their rich spouses. There's a lot of money to be made. Two or three conclusive photos, a few little notes, and you'll get a hefty bill."

"Maybe I'll go to City Hall and hand out business cards. The city council people have their fingers in all the pies. I think there are some surveillance jobs to be had."

"You mean poking around the big felt?"

"Logical. The bribery mafia, election scandals, and so on. In politics, private investigators are an effective tool in the ubiquitous party struggle."

"And we don't care from which dark channels we get the fee," Konny rubbed his hands together.

"I could go to the doctors. I have an appointment with Dr. Greenfoot this afternoon anyway."

"Has your back gotten worse?"

"Just a little, but I have endless time, so I might as well go to the doctor and get some massages. They always work."

"Look at your work clothes."

Full of enthusiasm, Berti reached into the large plastic bag with the advertising print of his last employer.

"They didn't have anything else at the thrift store," Konny apologized.

Two shirts, three ties, a bow tie, a suit that could easily compete with those of Rack-Romer, a Norwegian sweater with a moose pattern and a funky hippie jacket were already on the table. Then Berti reached for something hairy. Konny's eyes widened as his friend pulled out an Agnetha Fältskog wig.

"What's that?"

"Agnetha from Abba! Dancing Queen, you know."

"And this is supposed to be my work clothes?"

"Why don't you sit up?"

Berti was shy. "What nonsense."

"Go on," Konny urged.

Berti had had enough of dressing up. The thing with the suspenders had eaten away at the back of his mind. "Are you having a hetero fit or what? I'm not a chick."

The famous kissing wink followed and the weighty detective softened. "All right, then. Putting it on once is okay," he said and pulled the blonde, long-haired wig over his hair.

Konny looked at his friend and was thrilled. "Super," he exclaimed. "That thing really suits you."

Berti couldn't believe it and went to the mirror. "Hello friends. Agnetha is back. She's hardly changed. Maybe put on a pound or two," he mimicked.

Konny laughed heartily. "I know you're a big Abba fan."

"All right. I have to admit I like the wig. But it's not work clothes," she said energetically. "It's more for home."

"And if you're watching as a man, get discovered, disappear behind a wall and reappear as a blonde Rebel Wilson lookalike in a weird Hollywood role, nobody in the world would suspect the famous detective Herbert Schwartz under that wig.

Berti melted at the words. "How nice of you to say that."

Konny stayed on the subject. "So, where do you start? I mean with the business cards."

"As I said, with the doctor."

After Berti left the apartment a little later, Konny picked up the phone. He dialed a friend's number.

"Gerd? Hello, hello to you ... yes, I'm fine ... and how are you? ... Fine! Listen. I have a little problem. Are you still working for eBay? ... Great! I've noticed that a certain seller has been auctioning off all kinds of lingerie for a while now. The username is: Erotic Dream. Can you take a look?"

Konny waited. At the other end of the line, Gerd typed on his PC, found the account and gave the details to his friend.

"What?" Konny exclaimed in astonishment. "Twelve thousand euros in the last four weeks? Can you tell me who that is? ... Come on, you owe me a favor. After all, I was the one who brought you together..."

Again, it took a moment for the information to come through. When Konny found out who the owner of the account was, everything was clear to him.

"Thank you, Gerd. You can rely on my discretion."

Only two minutes later Konny was sitting at his PC. He created a letterhead based on the business card and started writing. "... I have investigated ... I must draw your attention to this ... Fee arrangements are with my secretary, Mr. Wels ... signed Herbert Schwartz, Private Detective".

Konny read the letter again, printed it out twice, signed it with the abbreviation pps and put it in an envelope. Then he went to the post office. The obstetrics for Berti's first solved case had been completed. As soon as he received positive feedback, he would present it to his friend. Konny leaned back in a good mood.

"Do you have the card with you?" asked Dr. Greenfoot's robotic receptionist. Of course, the question came without a hint of politeness. The monster behind the counter was the epitome of evil. She was the reason children were afraid of doctors.

"Come on, let's go see dear uncle doctor."

"No, that's where the evil dragon sits."

Berti could imagine the eternal struggle of the mothers who dragged their babies with mumps, measles, head lice, or gastrointestinal illnesses to this practice.

"Here you go," Berti replied politely, sliding his health insurance card across the counter.

The dragon took it, looked at it, and said: "Mr. Schwartz, you can take a seat in the waiting room. We'll call you in then."

It was the same stoic voice as before. The robotic style seemed to come naturally to the quirky woman. Sometimes Berti doubted that this woman was alive. She was somehow mechanical and worked the same way every time he visited the doctor.

"I'm number 5 ... I want to be a doctor's assistant ... please lubricate my vocal cords ... I need to recharge my battery in the evening ... please sit down in the waiting room".

Berti entered the waiting room. A young couple was whispering in the corner. Two older ladies were sitting to the right. They were obviously regular customers of the family doctor. Across from them, a mother sat on the bench. Her baby was coughing, and his three-year-old brother was rummaging through a virus-infected toy box. His nose was constantly running, which was relieved by constant sniffling. When the snot was a little longer, the sleeve helped.

"Yannik-Konstantin, please," was all his overwhelmed mother would say.

An overweight woman in her mid-fifties had sat down next to the little family. She was the living embodiment of the double-whopper and had to sit on the bench. She certainly wouldn't have been able to get up from an armchair. The sight of the woman awakened in Berti an immense joy of existence. He felt instantly slender.

Two men who belonged to the guards, who often got a special day off with a yellow slip, completed the patient program of the first hour. Berti sat down next to them.

"A nice little boy," the fat woman began. When she turned to the toddler, her cheeks wobbled like jelly. "What are you looking for?"

Yannik-Konstantin was startled. He looked at the mountain of meat, started to cry, ran to his mother and buried his head in her sweater. She smiled somewhat reservedly.

"He's in the alienation phase right now."

Nonsense! He's scared to death that the mountain of meat might eat him, Berti thought, imagining the scene. "I love little children! My favorite is sweet and sour or crispy fresh from the oven."

The couple next to Berti kept whispering something about children, but they both stared a little uncertainly at the three-year-old, who was pulling away from his mother. What remained was an unmistakable streak of nasal mucus that the mother tried to wipe away with a tissue.

One of the two men reeked of alcohol. Berti called him the Ensign. The other guy seemed absent-minded. Berti mentally called him Coke Head.

The two old men chatted all the time about their eternal illnesses and how old Dr. Greenfoot was better than their son.

After what seemed like thirty minutes, but was really only five, Robot #5 whined into the waiting room.

"Mrs. Schmitz, we need a urine sample! There are cups here, the toilet is over there," she pointed with her hand. "Put the sample in the window of the toilet."

It was unmistakably the tone of a military barracks. "Fall in, or I'll get a good beating," Berti thought. Before this job, the old woman must have been a warden in a women's prison.

The young woman blushed. She stood up and went to the counter. With an empty urine cup in her hand, she disappeared into the toilet.

"Mr. Niederreiner, we also need a urine sample from you, and while we're at it, Ms. von Emmering, you should also fill a cup for us."

Berti felt disgusted. The officer stood up. According to her reaction, the fat woman was Frau von Emmering. With a groan, she also got up and walked heavily back to the counter.

They both waited impatiently in front of the toilet.

The young woman came out. "Excuse me," she breathed as she made her way past the alcoholic and the cake fortress.

She took her seat next to her lover. The whispering started again. Now and then they both looked at Berti. When his eyes met those of the person sitting next to him, they quickly looked away. They were talking about him. That was unmistakable. They both laughed.

How can you talk so much about a urine sample, Berti wondered at first.

"So, how was it?"

"It's amazing! I hit it with the first jet."

"Oh, how great. I'm going to call you Robin Hood now," the detective mimicked in his head. Then he noticed the furtive look on the girl's face. Berti had unmasked her. He was sure of it now. They weren't talking about peeing in cups, they were talking about him.

Damn it! Now they're talking about me. Arrogant, hungry bastards! Snubbed, Berti stopped his friendly smile and turned his attention to a magazine.

And these two laughingstocks would like to be part of the fu-ture procreator faction and bring children into the world, the detective wondered. The drunk probably took a little longer to pee. He's been in there a long time. Well, he was probably shaking all over the place, Berti grinned. It's not like pouring grain into a shot glass.

His mental wanderings made him feel better. The visit to the doctor turned out to be quite funny.

You could hear the toilet flush right into the waiting room. The glowing nose appeared, Miss Double-Whopper squeezed herself into the toilet. Berti shut out his imagination. He looked at the wallpaper and tried to distract himself. Meanwhile, the mother was called into the treatment room with the children.

Did the toilet bowl survive? You have to turn off the movie in your head, Berti scolded himself and forced himself to calm down. To distract himself, one hand slipped into the breast pocket of his shirt. He felt the business card. Should he give it to the doctor or just leave it there?

"Mr. Schwartz! We need a urine sample from you as well!"

Berti jumped. There must be a mistake. He'd better clear this up right away.

"I have back pain," he replied.

He felt color shoot into his face and stood up. He had to clear this up at the counter. A fart came from the toilet. Three times. The fat woman had endless flatulence. But-tock coughing in the final stages.

"I'm sorry, there's nothing more we can do for you. Your rectal disharmony is incurable. By the way, we recommend an oversized air-tight coffin. Unfortunately, cremation is not possible due to the acute risk of explosion. The UN would sue us for unauthorized nuclear bomb testing."

"I have back pain," Herbert Schwartz repeated as he stood in front of Robot #5.

"We need your urine," came the ruthless reply.

The cup was placed right in front of Berti. "Schwartz with tz?"

"Yes! That's what it says on my card, but ..."

"No buts! Dr. Greenfoot knows what he needs. He always does full body and complete examinations."

Robot #5 had won.

"Even ... of course," Berti stammered, somewhat embarrassed.

The dragon was so determined that any opposition was nipped in the bud. Why did they have to hire that snipe? Her predecessor was really nice.

The old doctor had passed his practice on to his son. From time to time, he filled in for the doctor on vacation. During that time, Berti avoided going to the doctor.

When the door to the consulting room opened, Yannik-Konstantin ran out crying and Dr. Greenfoot senior called: "Three times a day", Berti knew that today was a bad day to go to the doctor. He'd better leave his business card in his pocket. Old Kleefuss didn't need a detective. If he did, it was his son, the young doctor. Berti was no longer surprised that he had to give a urine sample. Kleefuss Sr. was just Kleefuss Sr.

"Better urine than blood," he said to himself.

"Excuse me?" asked Robot #5.

"Oh, nothing."

The toilet door opened. Mrs. von Emmering stepped to the counter, beaming. "It worked."

"Good, then you can sit down again."

Did No. 5 just have a touch of politeness?

"What are you waiting for? The toilet is free," she threw at Berti in the same breath.

No, that wasn't politeness. That would also be utopia. Robots are robots and patients are patients. A necessary evil to get paid at the end of the month.

Berti entered the toilet. He was greeted by an invisible cloud of scent. He immediately held his breath and then breathed through his mouth with his nose closed.

In front of the window were three urine samples. The screw caps were labeled with the names of the do-nors. Once Berti got used to the smell of the toilet, he got down to business.

"Medium stream," he said, filling the cup and setting it down with the others. He flushed, washed his hands, and screwed the lid on the cup. He turned to leave. Then he had another one of his bright ideas.

Miss *Cakewonder* leaves a trail of scent that turns any cowshed into a perfume temple. Mr. Whiskey-Barrel spread more urine on the floor than the inmates of an old people's home lose during a polonaise, and Miss Nonstop-flow-of-speech made fun of me. Enough reasons for a little revenge, he decided spontaneously.

"Just wait," Berti muttered. "I'll turn the young turkey into a cirrhosis patient, I'll put a child under the double-whopper, and the alcoholic will have diabetes from now on."

The detective replaced the caps on the urine samples. Satisfied, he returned to the waiting room. Later, when Dr. Greenfoot said goodbye to him: "Ten massages will have to do. Otherwise, exercise, exercise and more exercise," Miss Cakewonder nagged at the counter. The results of the urine tests were apparently available.

"Pregnant? I haven't had sex in years. I must have been raped in my sleep. The new janitor seemed so weird to me from the start .... ," the fat woman gushed.

"Avoid alcohol as much as possible. You have to give yourself a shot of insulin every day..." the alcoholic could hear. His red nose had turned white.

"Too much alcohol, my ass? I don't drink any more than you do," the young woman argued with her partner. "You're drunk more often than I am. Why don't you get yourself checked out?"

Berti felt great. As a precaution, he didn't leave any of his business cards behind.

After the failed business card campaign at the doctor's office, the friends decided to try their luck at the tennis club. Their destination was not just any tennis club, but the crème de la crème of tennis clubs in the entire region. Here they would play the yel-low ball with an annual income of five million euros or more. Aston-Martin, Bentley, Rolls Royce, Ferrari and the like were parked in the fenced parking lot in the exclusive residential area on the outskirts of the city. The most expensive Mercedes, Porsche, Audi or BMW models were just barely acceptable as second cars for the wives. If you drove a different car, you were immediately targeted and talked about.

Konny and Berti arrived by public bus.

"Do you think we're in the right place?" asked Berti as they approached the temple of luxury.

"Absolutely right! Here's the clientele we need. The people who come in and out of here will laugh at your dream fee of a thousand a day."

Berti swallowed. He didn't feel very well. From the street he could already see the monstrous entrance gate. It was guarded by two golden lions enthroned on marble portals to the left and right. Next to them stood a bull-necked man in a suit. He blocked the entrance to the tennis club like a rock.

"This guy's probably killed a lot of people for the Russian mafia," the detective breathed to his partner.

A fat limousine pulled up. The driver jumped out, opened the back door, and seemed to bow his head.

"Look at this Punch and Judy," laughed Konny. "He's making a fool of himself for the money bag."

An older gentleman with a beer spoiler got out. Then a lively blonde jumped out of the luxury car. She was carrying a gym bag. The chauffeur closed the door, got in and steered the car into the parking lot. He stayed in the car.

"Watch out! Now we'll see how to get in."

The bigwig in the designer suit nodded to the doorman. He rang the bell. First a window was opened, then the door.

"There's a second gorilla!"

"Never mind."

Berti no longer felt comfortable in his suit. He felt more like a vacuum cleaner salesman than a private detective.

"I should have worn the baggy Hawaiian shirt, even though it's out of season."

"But then you would have had to drive a Ferrari."

Konny was right. Luckily he had come along to help Berti. Konny also wore a suit. The Penny Dreadful novelist was sporty and was supposed to take on the role of tennis player if necessary.

They entered the property. The point of no return had been passed. The living tree trunk had them in its sights. The two newcomers were scrutinized with down-turned corners of the mouth.

"Good day." Berti was especially polite. If you imagined slime on a scale of ten, Berti's greeting had already passed point eleven.

"Members only," the guy at the door accused them gruffly.

It was already clear that they were not welcome.

Berti wanted to turn back at once. "Well then," he smiled, but Konny took over the conversation.

"What if I want to become a member?"

"Our club is not an ordinary tennis club. It is a private tennis club. Our members belong to a select social class. You don't just walk in and become a member."

His pronunciation was harsh. Eastern European inflection. The sentence seemed to be memorized. There was nothing to be gained by negotiation. Konny had a good understanding of human nature. If he couldn't come up with an argument now, they were doomed. He searched his vocabulary. He wouldn't be dissuaded from his plan that easily. Konny's verbal counterattack had already been prepared at the first members-only meeting. Change of plan. He introduced himself in a stilted, snobbish voice. "Good sir, I don't want to become a member. My name is Wels. Konny Wels. I'm sure you've read about me. I'm an author."

"No! I don't know," came back numbly.

Berti immediately realized what Konny was up to.

Okay, let's go into the ring, he thought and changed from retreat to attack. "Mr. Wels, you don't think this individual reads, let alone your novels. His mind is his fortune, and poverty is no disgrace."

The young Schwarzenegger lookalike was taken aback and couldn't quite place the words.

"The mayor, the prime minister and Dr. Greenfoot will be very interested to hear that Konny Wels was turned away at the gate. I told you right away that we should accept Mr. Putin's invitation."

Konny thought Berti's feint was first class and immediately went for it. "Mr. Schwartz, we were invited first. A gentleman keeps his agreements. We'll wait exactly fifteen seconds, then we'll leave. Go ahead and call the minister."

"What can I say?" Berti shrugged.

"Tell them I couldn't prepare the reading for the tennis board at the club because some rude lump of a man wouldn't even let us into the foyer."

"Right away, Mr. Wels. You can be sure I'll make sure there's someone else at the door tomorrow."

They both turned and pretended to walk away.

The doorman's head was spinning. "Sorry! I didn't know who you were. People come in here every day who just..." the giant started, but was interrupted by Konny.

"Thank you! That's enough! I'd love to have a mental duel with you, but I don't fight unarmed people."

The muscle mountain frowned again.

"Well, what is it now?" Konny added.

The clumsy hand, as big as a soup plate, rose. He rang the bell. The window opened. The second bouncer looked at Konny and Berti. The mountain of meat in front of the club barked a few Russian words, then the door opened.

"Excuse me, gentlemen, our guest list seems to be out of date. I'll call the office and check." The second security man picked up the house phone, waited a moment, hung up in total annoyance, and apologized again. "There's no answer! Please come in."

The biggest hurdle had been cleared. They both pushed past the bouncers. They had made it.

"Noble shed. Even the hallway looks pompous," the detective said.

A stuffed tiger showed its teeth. Sports trophies were displayed in a case. The teeth of a narwhal, the shell of a giant tortoise, and a few stuffed animal heads suggested that, along with tennis, big-game hunting was very popular.

"How did you come up with the mayor and Dr. Greenfoot? You can't mention them in the same breath as the prime minister and Putin."

"I couldn't think of anything else."

"And the prime minister doesn't make a million a year!"

"You mean without additional income."

Thinking of Dr. Greenfoot, the detective wondered if the young bride would stop drinking prosecco and if her boyfriend would take a fertility test. The cake fairy would definitely look for the alleged father of the child, and the alcoholic would have himself checked for diabetes. Berti had to laugh.

They walked down the corridor. On either side were doors made of fine mahogany wood leading to the various areas.

"I wouldn't be surprised if the lettering was made of solid gold," Konny whispered. He read the signs: "Changing rooms, Sauna world, Tennis hall, Racket rooms ..."

At the end of the corridor an arrow pointed to the right.

"Outdoor tennis courts, those show-offs. Where else would they be? Underground maybe?" Berti scoffed.

"This way," Konny pulled him in the other direction.

Another sign pointed to the recreation area.

Relaxed seats made of the finest leather invited to linger. Flat screens as big as movie theaters hung on the walls. Staff dressed in old-fashioned butler and maid costumes served the guests. They brought freshly squeezed fruit juices and deluxe mineral waters such as Bling H2o from Tennessee, 420 Below from New Zealand, or Japanese Finé to the tables. Chess was played in an adjoining room that seemed hermetically sealed. The two players smoked big cigars. The blue cloud of fumes hovering above them wafted leisurely toward a kind of extractor hood and was gently led out through a filter.

"Those cigars must cost as much as my monthly fee," he pointed to the two smokers.

They followed one of the butler-waiters into the restaurant. The first glances were at the newcomers to the club. An older lady with a young companion looked at Konny for a conspicuously long time. She didn't waste a glance at Berti.

After two employees also noticed the visitors, they sat down at one of the empty tables. The grandfather in the designer suit from the limousine and his blonde sports bag sat at the next table.

"A glass of champagne for me. What would you like?" he asked his companion in a smoky voice.

She ordered the most expensive water on the menu in a manner that could hardly be surpassed for arrogance. A bottle of Bling H2o. "A glass before exercise. My tennis teacher won't be here for another quarter of an hour. I told you Joshua shouldn't drive so fast," she drooled into her companion's face.

He mumbled something unintelligible, and the blonde put on her chameleon smile again. "Darling, I didn't know you wanted to go to the jeweler's today. I wasn't ready to go shopping. I didn't bring anything to wear."

"Then we'll go to the boutique here at the club after the tennis lesson."

"Honey, they only have sports clothes here. When I go to the jeweler's, I need something decent to wear."

"Then let Joshua make a detour. As long as you're dressed up tonight. I have a business dinner."

"First class dress?"

"Fine by me," came the bored reply.

"Yuppiiehhh!"

The waiter wanted to finish the order. In a slightly exaggerated manner, resembling a stately penguin on the outside, he asked in a nasal voice, "Would you like anything else? Perhaps an hors d'oeuvre? The first fresh oysters of the season arrived today. The chef also recommends carpaccio de saumon frais with a touch of créme de tuffe."

"Nothing for me, the tennis instructor is just coming in," the blonde waved off. This time there was no feigned arrogance. This time, the brain relayed the voice command in its original state, reflecting the actual IQ that lay beneath the blond mat. With the grace of a comedic peasant girl, she jumped up, grabbed the gym bag, and walked quickly to the entrance. "Giovanni! Here I am!"

The rich beer-drinker remained seated. "Bring the water anyway. And I'll have both appetizers!"

"As you wish."

"This is your first customer, Berti. The old woman is screwing him over with the tennis instructor."

"Do you really think so? She's dumber than a bag of salt. The guy with the champagne barrel under his shirt has a lot of money."

"And the tennis gigolo has the body to match," Konny winked.

Berti beamed. "You're a genius."

The waiter moved a table over and stood in front of Konny and Berti. That disparaging look again. "The menu?"

"That's not necessary," Konny thanked him politely. "I'd like a glass of water."

"Bling H2o? Finé or 420 Below?"

Konny didn't understand. "Naturell," he answered carefully.

"A beer for me."

"How was it in the middle?" Konny asked.

"Finé. This is a Japanese specialty and comes from an underground hot spring 600 meters under a mountain. It is completely protected from outside influences by a pressure chamber, which completely excludes pollutants of any kind. Contamination can never occur here. Finé also has a very high silicon content".

Konny swallowed, Berti stared at the waiter in amazement.

"Yes, please. I'll take that," the writer breathed.

"One fine, very good."

"And I'll stick to my ... uh," Berti pondered. He had read an article about brewing pilsner in one of the magazines in the doctor's waiting room. It was time to confront the waiter.

"Please bring me a pilsner. Bottom-fermented, of course, with a high hop content and a maximum original gravity of 12.5%. It should have a regional reference and be golden yellow in color. The head should be thick, but not too thick, because that always leaves a rim around the corners of your mouth when you drink it. It shouldn't be too flat either, because that makes the beer too stale."

The waiter was a little taken aback, but made a note of it without asking. The hors d'oeuvres followed. Both declined with thanks.

"You should have had the appetizer. The chef here is an artist," the beer spoiler from the next table started a conversation.

"We just wanted to look around. We're thinking about membership," Berti fibbed.

"Why don't you sit with me? I'll be alone for an hour anyway. My wife has tennis lessons."

Bingo!

"Hindelang. Bernhard Hindelang, builder," he introduced himself.

"Konrad Wels, writer."

"Herbert Schwartz, private detective."

The construction lion shook their hands. A gold signet ring with a brilliant and a Breitling watch stood out. The tan on his skin wasn't from the tanning salon. It was pure Caribbean sunshine. Sitting in front of them was someone with a lot of ashes in his back pocket.

"A writer and a private dick," laughed Hindelang, who seemed to be in good spirits with the company. The boring hour was saved for him. "Finally some power in this old people's home."

Konny and Berti exchanged looks.

"When I built this thing, I thought there would be more momentum in the city, but I was wrong."

"You own the club?"

Hindelang laughed again. "No, I just build it. I build everywhere. I'm the Donald Trump of Germany," the contractor told him ostentatiously.

The waiter brought the drinks. Berti took the menu that was still on the table. When he saw that the Bling H2o cost a whopping 150 euros, he turned pale. He quickly searched for the finé. "50 euros for a water," he slipped out.

Hindelang grinned. "That Japanese swill isn't worth more than a penny."

"Of course."

After the usual small talk, Konny turned the conversation to the tennis instructor. Meanwhile, Berti was doing some mental arithmetic.

His hands got a little clammy when he realized that the bill already exceeded the cash they had brought with them.

"Giovanni is an excellent tennis player. He has a good feel for the racket. The women in the club like him."

"I can imagine. He looks at them so... how can I put it? He looks at them so differently."

"You think he's a faggot?"

Berti swallowed. Konny remained calm. "No! I think he's more in love with the weaker sex. Giovanni gives the impression of being an unpredictable heartthrob who doesn't miss a beat," he winked. "You know what I mean?"

The waiter served the oysters. "Bon appetit," he said, still eyeing the two friends suspiciously.

When he was gone, Hindelang leaned forward a little. "He's from the other side, too. The guy's so warm, he really burns. When he passes a candle, only the wick is left, the rest is melted," whispered the builder, laughing at his own joke. Tears welled up in his eyes.

Berti and Konny smiled out of politeness so as not to draw attention to themselves. Secretly, the author had already prepared a suitable counter-attack, but that wouldn't have been good for business. So he let the old horned sack have the laugh.

Berti would have loved to play Jason Statham and tear the place apart. But when he thought of the bouncers, he changed his mind and decided to do nothing.

The elderly lady and her thirty-years-younger lover looked over at them, a little snubbed. Apparently, the laughter was too loud for them.

"That's a good one, huh, ha ha. I overheard him at a board meeting the other day. The Minister of the Interior, he has a chair in my company, he's on the board because of the contracts and so on," he explained briefly. "He threw himself away. Politically speaking, my friend just said don't make waves," Hindelang laughed again. "Making waves ... he meant the guy from the other party ... he he he! That was a cheeky reference! Hi, hi, hi," he changed his tone as he laughed.

Hindelang began to calm down. His eyes slid over the appetizer. Seven oysters lay on a block of ice carved to resemble the massif of Mont Blanc. Slices of lemon and lime were placed on the edge of the plate of the finest porcelain. Naturally cut with a pattern and not simply halved. The oysters themselves were already open. Hindelang took one of the shells, sprinkled a little lime juice on it, removed the meat from the sphincter with the oyster fork, and slurped the delicacy from the shell with relish. "Mmhh, the first oysters are especially tasty. Would you like to try one?" he offered, reaching for his champagne and taking a sip.

"No thanks," Konny declined. "I prefer animals with four legs. I don't like anything out of water."

Hindelang laughed. "Sure," he said, grabbing one of the oysters and holding it out to Berti. "You look like a gourmet. Here you go!"

Berti tried to act as normal as possible. Completely disgusted inside, he tried to refuse. "You were so looking forward to it. I ..."

"I'll get the salmon with truffle cream. Now take it before my arm falls off."

For better or worse, Berti grabbed it. The oyster lay peacefully in the saltwater bath of its shell. White, living goo. At least it hadn't been dead for long. And if it was, it was definitely raw! Berti faced his own personal jungle test. A thousand images flashed through his mind. He saw celebrities from C to Z making fools of themselves on private television. Once he had watched a camp resident eat something alive. Afterwards, he had run his chips through his head. Pure food orgasm! Since then, Berti had been one of the show's boycotters. Now his fate was in his own hands. His first potential client was waiting for him, Berti, the master detective, to eat an oyster.

The stomach spoke. "No! If you do that to me, I'll spit!"

The brain warned: "Silence! I order you to keep the morsel! Our future depends on it!"

Stomach: "What do you know about the disgusting things I am served from time to time?"

Brain: "Either you keep the oyster, or we'll starve to death because we'll go bankrupt!"

"A little lemon? Or would you prefer a little more zest and a few drops of lime?"

The lemons were bigger. Berti grabbed the largest citrus fruit on the plate. He held it over the wobbly thing and squeezed it. His fist was so tight around the lemon that the white part protruded from his knuckles. Hindelang watched with interest. "Isn't that a bit much?"

48

"No," Berti smiled mischievously. "I have a very mild case of angina anyway. I mean, it's coming on, as they say. So I thought a shot of vitamin C might help."

"Now eat the oyster. I want to know how you like it."

The shell approached his mouth in what seemed like slow motion. Berti smelled it like a glass of wine. He inhaled a whiff of the sea mixed with citric acid. "Smells delicious," he grinned forcibly.

"Schwartz, I like you. I thought you were a first-rate gourmet. I must invite you to dinner sometime. People nowadays have no idea what tastes good. How about a barbecue?"

"Barbecue sounds good," Berti raised his thumb.

"I especially like mutton testicles and sheep's kidneys. Finally, someone who can keep up! I really like them."

Berti broke into a sweat. Armpit terror without end. His 48-hour deodorant had only lasted an hour. When will they invent a 480-hour deodorant?

A kingdom for a cheeseburger! The guy was a pure cannibal. How did he grow up? "Mom, is there any tasty offal for dinner tonight?" Berti had to get out of this barbecue business immediately if he wanted to win the construction magnate as a client.

"Don't you think the barbecue season is over?"

Meanwhile, Hindelang had slurped down two more oysters. "We'll find a suitable menu together. I haven't had a cuddle in a long time. Do you have your own menu?"

Berti still held the oyster in his right hand. His left hand went into the breast pocket of his shirt. He took out one of his new business cards. "Here you go."

Hindelang took the card and read it. That was the saving moment. Berti sipped the water from the clam shell, then his hand shot up and back in a flash. The law of gravity kicked in and the dried oyster flew across the dining room. Konny followed the trajectory, white as a sheet. For a split second he saw its sudden death, brought about by the two bouncers.

They spurned the oyster. We had to break all their bones. The fat one is already on the grill, he thought.

The oyster made its way to the rich snipe, who couldn't stop blaspheming.

Please don't, please don't, the author whimpered in his mind.

The flying clam started to land. Whoosh. The space shuttle arrived safely. The open Louis Vuitton handbag of the living mummy served as a landing strip.

Thank you, Konny groaned inwardly.

He looked up. Heavenly justice. His second was for Berti. He shrugged briefly. Chewing, he praised the imaginary oyster he had eaten. "Very first cousin. Excellent, but unfortunately I can't eat any more. I have to go to the doctor today. I have a very rare blood group. An emergency patient needs some of my lifeblood. A diplomat from Nepal. I have to appear sober."

"Your problem is my problem! That's good. I like the guarantee too. If I ever need a detective, I'll call you! Where is your office anyway?"

Woof

All three turned around. The head of a dog that had been bred back to rat size emerged from the luxury purse. The mutt licked its snout with relish.

"Sir Nelson, are you all right? Are you all right, my little darling?" asked the Money Grandma. Her wrinkled fingers stroked the purse inhabitant's head. The hairy salami sniffed and jumped out of his portable luxury dog camper in joyful anticipation of more oyster bites.

The friends had found an ally. The oyster was gone without a trace. Sir Nelson ran to Berti, making little faces and begging for more.

"I have nothing for you, puppy." He stroked the puppy. "Wouldn't that be something for us?" he breathed to Konny.

He did not hear his friend. He was deep in conversation with Hindelang. "We're still looking for suitable office space here in town. So far, we've been leaning towards this," Konny made a thoughtful face to appear more interesting. "Let's say we operate internationally."

Sir Nelson was picked up by the servant of the dressed-up grandmother. "Come with me! You need to get back in your bag." He grabbed him roughly. The lapdog looked frightened and stared at Berti with his beady little eyes.

The detective watched as the pet was put back into the Louis Vuitton bag and felt sorry for the nice little dog. Then he joined the conversation between Konny and Mr. Hindelang. Konny had just mentioned the matter of the office. Berti nodded. "You could put it that way."

"Wonderful. Here's my map. I have a few empty office buildings. How many employees do you have? How much office space do you need? 500 square meters? 1000 square meters?"

"I don't know?"

Hindelang waved him off. "Don't worry about the rent."

Berti drank his beer. The salt water lemon taste had to go.

"I don't take more than half a million for office space."

Berti choked. Coughing, he gasped for air.

"Is everything okay?"

He nodded. "I ... I ... so .... the angina has set in."

"We were thinking of something simple to start with," Konny said of the offer.

"Simple? Well, get in touch with my secretary," came the slightly disappointed reply.

The oysters were devoured and the salmon served. Konny apologized. "I just need to powder my nose."

Hindelang's eyes widened. "What?"

"A joke," Konny grinned.

"Ha, ha," that was a good one. "Today is *Gay Joke Day*!"

The gay jokes annoyed the author. He was glad to leave the table for a moment. On the way to the toilet he searched his brain for fat jokes.

Even though I feel sorry for Berti, I have to rub the construction worker's nose in it. He passed a large window. From here you could see all the outdoor tennis courts. All the outdoor courts were empty. Nobody was playing.

Strange. The chick from Hindelang was supposed to be training here, Konny thought.

He found the toilet. Here, too, pure luxury was the order of the day. Golden faucets in retro style. Separate cubicles. The urinals were generously spaced.

Privacy was a top priority.

He did his business and washed his hands. A soft moan drew his attention. Curious, he walked along the stalls. The moaning got louder. He could also hear high-pitched squeaks between the low sounds.

"Ehh ... ahh ... yaaa ..."

"Ti amo," a man muttered.

51

I can't stand it! The dago is screwing the old lady from the building lion on the golden toilet.

Konny pulled his cell phone out of his pocket. He immediately wrote a message to Berti.

Berti's cell phone buzzed and vibrated slightly. "Sorry, a customer."

Hindelang nodded and shoved a salmon into his mouth.

Berti scanned the message twice. He could hardly believe his luck. Situations like this were a godsend. The case was solved before it even got started. The blonde was indeed having an affair with the tennis teacher. Berti tried to remain cool and calm.

Hindelang gratefully assisted. "Problems with the case?"

"Yes, unfortunately I have to go! It's incredibly important."

"Too bad, it was a pleasure. I'll take care of the bill. We'll stay in touch. I'll call if I need to. And two things are crystal clear. You'll move into one of my offices and accept my invitation to a barbecue."

Berti was relieved. The matter of the bill was settled. "That's settled. And thank you for the invitation."

"That's not an invitation," Hindelang waved off. "A water and a beer is nothing to write home about."

"Thanks anyway."

"Oh, what else I wanted to know, how much is your fee?"

Berti put on a confident expression. "A thousand euros a day plus expenses."

"Respect! Only someone who guarantees success can really afford that."

Berti stood up.

The voice of the old dressed-up lady could be heard. "Ugh! Sir Nelson! What have you done?"

An accident had happened to the dog. He couldn't eat the oyster. Berti strolled leisurely into the hall.

"It smells like fish in here! My dog gets diarrhea if he eats fish. Who fed Sir Nelson? Was it you?" the dog's owner called after Berti.

As the old woman's gaze lingered on Berti's back, he hurriedly left the guest room and made his way to the toilets.

"Careful, he's crouching," the young companion warned the lady.

Too late. The screaming that followed could be heard down the hall.

"My new handbag."

Hindelang drowned out the lady. "Filth," the contractor whined. "It smells disgusting!"

"What took you so long? They're almost done," Konny whispered. At the same time he raised his index finger to his mouth. "Shh, be quiet!"

"I couldn't get away any faster."

"They're in here."

"What are we going to do?"

"I'll see if I can film them with my cell phone," Konny suggested.

The author pressed the appropriate app on his phone. "Run! Tennis club. Toilet," he said, giving the address, date and time. Then he stretched to hold the phone over the top of the stall door.

Berti knelt down. "The keyhole is damn tight. All I can see is a naked ass wiggling back and forth. It belongs to the tennis spaghetti," he breathed barely audibly. "Wait. Now I recognize the chick's shoes. You were right. They're doing it right now."

Konny rolled her eyes. "Of course they're doing it. They're probably not here together in the toilet because they suddenly got diarrhea and there wasn't another free stall in the whole house."

"Could be. Suddenly, a common spray sausage comes in."

"Get back to work and don't make jokes."

The fat detective had to stifle a laugh.

A door opened and fell back into the lock. Footsteps were heard.

Konny warned, "Make sure no one comes in.

Meanwhile, the bouncers had begun to have doubts about the two new guests. They called the office again. This time the busty but somewhat simple-minded secretary was at her desk. She looked at the PC. Careful not to damage her newly painted fingernails, she pressed a key. A list opened.

"What's the guy's name?"

"Catfish," the Russian doorman growled into the house phone. "A writer. He's supposed to do a reading."

"No, I've got nothing here."

"Ask the boss! The writer wasn't alone. He had a fat guy with him. His name was Schwartz."

He waited. He heard the secretary chuckling. She was talking to someone. Then she picked up the phone. "It stays the same. No reading, no author, no catfish, no Schwartz."

"There's no reading?"

"I told you."

"Sure?"

"Sure! Is there a problem downstairs?"

"No! No problem." He hung up. "We'll handle it discreetly and quickly." A smile crossed the meat mountain's face.

Konny was still standing in front of the toilet door, while Berti was kneeling in front of him, moving his head back and forth to get the best view through the keyhole. He wanted to take some proof photos from his perspective in addition to the video. "Man, this is something. I think I've got her face," he said happily, trying to get another conclusive photo.

"I got it. Yeah, that's good," the detective said happily.

"Ah, everything hurts already," groaned Konny, who was still holding up his cell phone for the video recording with his outstretched arm.

In their eagerness to work, neither of them had noticed that someone had entered the bathroom. It was one of the two bouncers. He saw Berti kneeling in front of Konny, heard a groan and assumed the worst. "You rotten little pigs," he thundered in a fighting mood.

The trapped friends froze in shock. They immediately realized the embarrassing situation they were in. "It's not what it looks like. Look," Konny said with a smile and turned around to show that his snake was in the nest.

At the same time, a fist shot forward. Konny felt a mega impact, saw stars and fell over.

Berti jumped up in panic, slipped on the smooth polished floor and stumbled forward. His head landed in the middle of the 160-pound muscleman's genital area. The Russian rolled his eyes and collapsed. His face contorted in pain, he came to rest right next to Konny. Berti jumped around frantically.

"Eeijeijeijeijei! Shit! Bloody hell! He's going to kill us when he recovers. We're doomed!"

The guy and the blonde remained silent. Not a sound came from their cabin.

Berti bent down. He shook his friend's torso. Morally afraid that the Russian would recover faster than Konny, he patted the writer's cheeks. "Wake up. Quickly!"

The stricken giant let out a guttural rutting cry. "Uaahh! That hurts. I'll cut you in half!"

Berti stood up. In his desperation, he kicked the Russian again in the middle of his privates. "Urarrgh," he could hear.

Konny opened his eyes. He knew immediately what was happening.

"Get out of here," Berti shouted.

The writer jumped up. They both ran to the door. Ripping it open and jumping out of the toilet room was one movement. They ran down the wide corridor. Customers were streaming out of the restaurant. Something had startled them.

"What happened there?"

"I'll tell you later," Berti blurted out.

They reached the part of the corridor that led to the exit. The toilet door opened behind them.

"I'm going to eat you for breakfast," roared the angry bouncer, who had recovered from the last genital kick faster than Berti had hoped.

The second Russian appeared. He had been looking for the two friends in the restaurant and was one of the guests who had fled the room. The way to the exit was still open. They ran for their lives. Konny had a small head start and reached the door. He pulled it open and held it for Berti. "Run! Run!" he urged him.

Berti put one foot in front of the other. Beads of sweat ran down his forehead. His fainting spell from the police recruitment flashed through his memory.

This time I won't faint. I'll make it!

His lungs pumped. It burned. He vowed to go on a diet. He would start tomorrow. Konny saw that the key was in the lock. He had the presence of mind to pull it out and put it back in from the outside. Berti

55

arrived. Behind him, the monster wrestlers came at them mercilessly. They approached damn fast.

"Run! Protein one and protein two are catching up," Konny cheered his friend.

The front living muscle cord was already reaching out for Berti. He reached the exit and slipped through the door frame into the open. Konny slammed the door and turned the key. Something hit the wood inside. Curses were uttered. Banging, knocking. The window opened. "We've got you!"

As the corners of Konny's mouth twisted into a grin, the spot where the talking prehistoric monster's fist had struck hurt. He felt the typical throbbing of an acute swelling. "But not today, you ass," he snapped at the tortured looking face in the doorway. At the same time, he raised his hand and extended his middle finger. He threw the key in front of the door. "Go get it."

They had done it. Of course they had. But this address was off-limits to them for the time being. Another encounter with the two bouncers could be fatal, or at least result in a few weeks in the hospital.

The fact that they might have caught their first customer was seen as a positive. Berti recovered on the way to the bus stop. His gasping became shallower, the pumping of both lungs slower. When they finally boarded the ambulance, the heavyweight detective was still drenched in sweat.

Two days later, Konny lay on the sofa. The large area between her cheekbone, nostril, and ear changed color for the third time. This time the dark purple faded to a dirty yellow-green. The warm cherry stone pillow on the back of his neck still felt good. He did not use the ice pillow today. The swelling had gone down. Berti had put some tea water on the stove. A classical radio station was playing Smetana's Moldau. The flute and clarinet sounds of spring were replaced by the horns of the hunting scene.

"Yasmine tea, mint elderberry, herbal mixture, or would you prefer a strong East Frisian?"

"I could really go for a splendid lesbian count," Konny joked.

Berti laughed. "I see you're feeling much better already."

"Bring me some jasmine tea, please."

"Ten minutes later they were sitting in front of steaming teacups. A scent of jasmine hung in the air. They both listened to the sounds of the orchestra. The strings came to the fore. They were supported by harps. The moonlight scene.

"This is the best part."

"I love that part too."

Konny hummed along.

"Have you thought about it?" asked Berti.

"About what?"

"The one with the dog."

"I don't know."

"A little puppy would be nice. Maybe like the one from the restaurant."

"I don't know."

Berti probed further. "Did you see the way the dog looked at me? It was love at first sight! I can feel something like that."

Konny tried another approach. "Dogs from a good breeder cost a lot of money."

"Maybe for Christmas?"

"We'll treat ourselves to dinner and a good bottle of wine. That's all our budget can afford. We've already agreed on that."

Berti poutted at first, but when that didn't work, he put on his "don't look now" look.

The effect was not long in coming.

"Don't look now."

"A little dog like that hardly eats anything. And it's healthy, too. You have to go out in all weathers. Every day!"

"I'll think about it."

"Really?"

"I promise!"

"Well, let's see what breed Sir Nelson belongs to."

"You bought a book on dog breeds?"

Berti smiled. "Borrowed it from the library."

"Why is that?"

"When you go for a walk, you can identify the breeds of dogs in the park. There's something like that for trees, plants, insects, and so on. And suppose a dog is kidnapped and I have to save it. I need to know what it looks like when you tell me the breed.

"You don't walk through the park and say, 'Look, there's a Pe-kingese.'"

"Right, you can also use the book for the Chinese restaurant. As a menu, so to speak."

Konny laughed. "All right, have a look."

Berti began to leaf through the pages. He found what he was looking for at the letter C.

"I've got it, I've got it," he exclaimed happily.

"Let me see."

"It's a Chihuahua, it comes from Mexico, it's the smallest dog breed in the world and..."

"Let me see," Konny repeated. "I can read for myself."

Berti handed Konny the dog book. He reached for his teacup. "Great features, aren't they?"

The bell rang. Normally this was a perfectly normal occurrence, but since that day at the tennis club, Berti was a little afraid. He was afraid of Russian revenge in the form of a visit from Moscow Incasso. His body sent out warning signals. Goose bumps and a sinking feeling in his stomach, accompanied by trembling, were the warning signs this time.

"They've got us," came out of Berti's mouth. He put the teacup back on the table.

"Don't talk nonsense. How do the buffalo know where we live?"

"From Hindelang. He has my business card."

The seconds of anxiety intensified.

"That can't be. We don't have an address on the card, just phone numbers. Since Eiweiß und Eiweiss didn't call us, Hindelang put the card in his pocket and didn't pass it on."

The doorbell rang a second time.

"Aren't you going to answer it?" asked Konny.

"Why me?"

"Because I look like I've been in the ring for ten rounds against a world boxing champion! And besides, none of them really know where we live."

Berti looked at the variety of colors on Konny's face.

"All right," he admitted defeat. Although he still felt a latent fear that the thugs might be at the door, he stood up. "See, it stopped ringing. Someone must have made a mistake with the bell. Or it was a child's prank," he said with relief, wanting to go back into the living room.

"Please check."

"I'm already on my way."

Berti looked through the peephole. At the same moment there was a knock. The detective was frightened to death. At that moment, the security chain hanging from the door looked more like the plastic links of Berti's former child handcuffs.

"Mail," someone called from the hallway.

A sure second glance through the peephole. An annoyed postman in a yellow-blue uniform was about to leave when Berti opened the door.

"You're home after all!"

"Um, yes. I had ... headphones on."

The Moldau could be heard in the background. Soft strings. The mouth had been reached.

"Headphones? For what? So you can't hear the music?"

"And I'm alone," Berti fibbed.

"Who's that?" shouted Konny.

The postman was surprised and smiled at the same time. "Did I disturb you?"

Berti blushed. "No! You didn't, and it's none of your business."

"Calm down, young man. I have a registered letter for a Konrad Wels."

"I'll take it."

"Who are you?"

"It's at the door," Berti hissed gruffly at the postman.

"Schwartz, Herbert," the postman noted, made Berti sign, handed him a thick envelope and left. "Strange fellow, that Schwartz," he muttered.

"Pushy guy," Berti said after closing the door. "You've got mail from a magazine company. Probably another trial subscription."

"Give it to me," Konny took the envelope in surprise. He opened it carefully. Curious, the writer risked a glance. "Surely a letter and a brochure," came the disappointed reply.

"You don't send things like that by registered mail."

"You're right again."

"Just take a look," Berti urged.

Konny took the contents out of the envelope. "The letter is from a notary," he wondered and read. "Dear winner ... we inform you that you have won the first prize .... Luxury ski hotel ..."

They both looked at each other with big eyes.

"We won!"

Konny hugged Berti. They cheered and danced in a circle. "We won," they sang in unison. "We won."

After three rounds around the living room table, Berti let go. "What did we win?"

"Do you remember? The big crossword puzzle?"

"The last stamp? Of course, how could I forget that day?"

"Sorry!"

Berti waved him off. "So, what did we win?"

Konny read the letter a second time. More accurately this time. "I won the first prize, a weekend for two in a luxury mountain hotel worth 5,000 Euros."

"Can you ..."

"The prize cannot be exchanged for cash. If you accept the prize, please contact the notary's office of Dr. Gregor Bayerlein within three days of receiving the prize."

"Too bad, I would have preferred the money."

"Look at it practically, fatso."

Before Berti could protest his pet name again, Konny continued. "First of all, we can finally go on a great vacation, and secondly, we're staying in a luxury hotel. That means we'll meet lots of potential wealthy clients."

"Konny, I never thought of it that way."

"I'll call right away."

Konny picked up the phone and dialed the number of the notary's office. It rang.

"Notary Dr. Gregor Bayerlein. This is Mrs. Eberhartinger, what can I do for you?" a notary's assistant answered.

"My name is Wels. I received a letter from you. The competition."

"Which one?"

"The ski hotel!"

"One moment, please."

Konny was on hold for about two minutes, then a man answered. "Bayerlein, notary," he said dryly.

After the writer explained the reason for his call, the notary's voice brightened.

"Congratulations. You have won the first prize. Do you agree to a photo? The newspaper publisher would like to publish it in the next issue."

Konny thought of his oversized shiner. "Do I have to?"

"No, if you don't want to, then ..."

"Then I'd rather not."

The notary congratulated the winner, noted down a few details and concluded: "Then nothing stands in the way of a luxurious weekend. The hotel suite has been reserved for you, the documents will be sent later. The date of travel is known, and the train tickets will be in the mail soon. All that's missing is the name of your companion."

"Herbert Schwartz."

"Same address?"

"Right."

"Wonderful. As I said, the hotel vouchers and train tickets will be here shortly. Congratulations again on winning first prize."

people-6326306_1280

Chapter 3
House Community

The apartment building Berti and Konny had moved into was located in a quiet side street. The old building had been built at the turn of the century. In the meantime, the building had been completely renovated. The brickwork, the wood-beamed ceiling and the box windows shone in new splendor. The house was an architectural jewel. Passers-by would stop to admire the facade and the architectural style. Recently, an art student even sat in front of the house and sketched it. You had to park somewhere on the street as there were no parking spaces, let alone garages, but the house had a beautiful garden that tenants could use.

Schwartz and Wels was written on a sign on the door of their apartment on the second floor. It was a very spacious two-bedroom apartment with a nice balcony. Her next-door neighbor, a divorced salesman, had three rooms. His two children often visited on weekends.

The Kapaunkes lived on the floor above them. They had the whole floor to themselves. Mr. Kapaunke was a grumpy guy you didn't want to run into in the hall. He still looked incredibly fit for his nearly fifty years. His wife was at least ten years younger and incredibly beautiful. Karl-Heinz Kapaunke, their ten-year-old son, was a real ray of sunshine. Konny once compared him to Astrid Lindgren's *Emil from Lönneberga* and hit the nail on the head. The Kapaunkes' younger daughter was called Gudrun and was still in kindergarten.

A young couple from eastern germany and a Turkish family lived in the two apartments on the second floor. Hasan Özdemir ran a small vegetable shop two streets away. Konny and Berti had been regular customers since they moved into *Hasan's vegetable shop.*

The large apartment on the ground floor was rented to the elderly Mrs. Mint. She was well into her 80s, a widow and always friendly. The smaller apartment next to her was mostly empty. It was used by the landlady's son when he was in town.

The two friends felt at home there. Five weeks ago, Konny came home from shopping. Karl-Heinz was sitting outside the front door crying.

"What's wrong?" the author inquired.

"I still have five in German. My dad is going to be really angry."

"What's the problem?"

"I just can't remember all that grammar stuff."

Konny put down the basket, pulled out a tissue, and handed it to the boy. While Karl-Heinz dried his tears, the writer sat down next to him on the doorstep. "What grade are you in?"

"The fourth. This year will decide which school I go to later," Karl-Heinz sniffed and blew his nose.

"How are things at school otherwise?"

"Pretty good. Very good, actually."

"Then it doesn't look so bad."

"But that stupid German."

Water shot into the boy's eyes again.

"I wasn't that bad at German. To be honest, I was so good that I studied German. I could tutor you."

"I had tutoring once, but it's too expensive. Mom said we couldn't afford it."

Konny laughed. "I'd do it for free for a neighbor."

When the handkerchief was completely soaked, the boy wiped the last tears from his eyes with his shirt sleeve. Hope began to germinate. "Really?"

Konny's answer seemed to light up the horizon. A ray of light shot into the sky. "Sure. I suggest you go up to the apartment first, talk to your mother, and then the two of you come down to my place for a cup of tea. We can sort everything out then."

"Great!"

Since then Karl-Heinz Kapaunke has been tutored by Konny twice a week. Only Mr. Kapaunke did not know about it. His wife thought it was better, because the old curmudgeon, as she put it, was always blaspheming about the two clowns who had moved in below them. She was embarrassed.

Karl-Heinz was back in the living room with his tutor. The notebooks were on the table. Konny sat across from them, giving tips and explaining this and that.

"I'll be off," Berti called to them.

"See you later."

64

"Bye."

Berti left the apartment. However, he accidentally left the door unlocked and ajar.

Mrs. Kapaunke was in the kitchen preparing dinner. Little Gudrun was playing. The front door was unlocked. Since it was too early for her husband, her mother asked: "Karl-Heinz, are you ready?"

Her husband's dark voice was heard. "It's me, darling. The scheduled meeting was canceled. Our boss got sick and sent us home."

Mrs. Kapaunke jumped. She hadn't expected Ulf to come home right now. She felt caught out.

"Why should Karl-Heinz be ready already? Where is the boy?" asked Ulf Kapaunke with a touch of curiosity.

"With the clowns," exclaimed four-year-old Gudrun. She was rolling a doll carriage through the apartment.

"What? Where is he?" Mr. Kapaunke asked. The friendliness had vanished in one fell swoop.

"Ulf, calm down. I wanted to tell you a long time ago, but ..."

"Tell me what?" he interrupted her.

"Karl-Heinz is getting from Mr. Wels ..."

"Stop! Don't go on." He turned to his daughter. "Go to your room, Gudrun!"

The girl turned back. Bored, she pushed the doll's carriage back into her little princess kingdom. Ulf Kapaunke closed the door to the nursery. With a flushed face, he went back into the kitchen. His wife dried her hands with a dish towel.

"You let our boy into the apartment with those faggots? Are you crazy? Who knows what they'll do to him! I'm going to go downstairs and get those two pipes. I'm going to kick down the door, and if I catch them doing anything, I'm going to break every bone in their bodies and throw them out the window. I'll talk to you later!"

"Ulf!"

"Shut up!"

The father of the family left the apartment. Furious, he threw the door into the lock. The bang echoed through the stairwell. As Mr. Kapaunke hurried down the stairs, he took two steps at once. Seconds later, he was standing in front of Konny and Berti's front door. The sign was inconspicuous. Silver background, black lettering. Two surnames, written in block letters. Schwartz and Wels.

Mr. Kapaunke was about to lunge in and ram the door with his body when he noticed it was open. He rolled up his sleeves and quietly entered the apartment. The small hallway was very neat. In fact, it was meticulously clean. There were photos on the wall. Berti and Konny walking in the park, two swimming in a lake, and a third showing the friends at a party. They were laughing and radiating happiness.

Kapaunke choked out a barely audible: "Sick faggots," and clenched his hands into fists. The moment of truth was at hand. Now! It was time for someone to clean up this house. And that someone was him. The two were bothering him anyway. He heard his son's voice.

Karl-Heinz was reading an essay. "Dad looked for me everywhere. I had lost my way. The forest was dark..."

"Pay attention, Karl-Heinz," Konny interrupted. "We got the grammar right. But it sounds better if you write that it was dark in the forest, doesn't it?"

"Yes, that's right," the boy replied.

"Tell me, what grade did you get on your last class test? You haven't told me yet?"

"A D," came the cheerful reply. "We got the test out today."

"That's great. So we've already got a good handle on the two E's. Next, you'll write an experiential essay. What you've just read to me is a good basic structure, but it sounds yawningly boring. If you put more effort into it, you might even get an A."

"That would be great, Konny. Dad would be so proud of me. I'd like to make him happy. How do I put more power into the essay?"

Konny laughed. "Your parents can be proud of you already. From a E to a B in such a short time. That shows you're a smart guy."

"I'd like to give you a big hug," Karl-Heinz said.

Ulf Kapaunke was about to storm off, but he just managed to stop himself. He heard Konny's answer. "No, you! Leave me alone. Here we learn, learn and learn again! You hug your parents and your sister, but not me."

"Sure! So tell me. How do you get power into the essay?"

"Write about your feelings. Write that you got goose bumps, that you felt the tingling down to the tips of your toes. Use literal language.

And write down what you see when you picture the scene in your mind. Then you've got a killer essay."

Ulf Kapaunke began to think.

The guy is really good at explaining things. I have to admit that. I had no idea that my boy had improved so much. Respect, that's great.

The anxious father spent another ten minutes in the hallway, then heard the front door downstairs open and close. As Ulf Kapaunke left the door wide open, a gust of wind swept through the apartment.

"There's a draft in here. I'll go and see if Berti hasn't locked the door properly again. He's always so scatterbrained."

Konny had gotten up. He was startled when Ulf Kapaunke suddenly stood in the doorway. At first he was speechless, then he said: "Oh my God, I was startled. I didn't even hear you come in."

"I, uhh, well, the door was open," the neighbor stammered.

Konny held out his hand. "Konrad Wels, but everybody just calls me Konny. It's about time we get to know each other and introduce ourselves. After all, we've been living in the house for a few weeks now."

"Ulf Kapaunke."

"I am a writer. Before that I studied German and of course I graduated successfully. When I heard about your son's problems at school, I offered to tutor him. From neighbor to neighbor. As a writer, I work at home anyway, and it's fun to help someone.

"Dad," Karl-Heinz called, running into the hallway. "I got a B on my last grammar test."

Ulf saw his boy's beaming face. His fists had long since relaxed. A guilty conscience spread. "Great."

"Berti must have forgotten to close the door completely. He's often a bit scatterbrained," Konny repeated.

"Where is he?"

"He's downstairs doing some shopping for Frau Mint. The old lady can't leave the house in this weather."

"Very helpful," Kapaunke marveled.

"Would you like some tea?"

"Thank you, Mr. Wels, I mean ... Konny ... but I ..."

"It's already on the table. Karl-Heinz can finish the exercise paper in the meantime."

Now Ulf Kapaunke felt completely miserable. The two clowns, as he called Wels and Schwartz, were nice, helpful and friendly. This Konny was even a very good tutor. Karl-Heinz seemed to like him and his success was phenomenal. Ulf gave himself a jolt and accepted the offer. What was the big deal? And he also had to consider whether he could continue to send his son here for tutoring.

"I'd like a cup of tea."

"Why don't you sit down?"

Konny got a third cup.

"What, how much do you charge for an hour?"

The author poured tea. "You mean do I charge for it?"

Mr. Kapaunke nodded, choked out a short. "Yes," he choked out.

"No, of course not. That would be more than unfair. The boy needs some help. My reward will be to see Karl-Heinz running happily through the stairwell again. I'm really glad that I can help at all."

A little later, Karl-Heinz was done. "Here Konny, my essay. I'm going to play now."

The boy left the apartment, Ulf Kapaunke stayed. Berti came home. He sat down with the two of them in the living room. Ulf Kapaunke also found him quite likeable. Berti was funny and entertaining. After tea they had a beer, then a bottle of wine. They laughed, got to know each other, and just two hours later, Ulf Kapaunke invited his neighbors over for dinner that weekend.

When the wine and a little brown, as Berti called his Aldi cognac, were empty, Ulf said goodbye. "But now I have to go," he stood up, slightly tipsy. "And the goulash dinner at the weekend is on, isn't it, boys?"

"You can have it, Ulf. I never say no to good food," Berti laughed and rubbed his bulging belly.

"I want to invite the whole house. The new goulash pot has to be inaugurated with a house party."

"Great idea."

Berti and Konny's new friend stopped in the hallway. He turned around again. "I have something to confess," he said ruefully.

"It's okay."

"No, it's not. I always thought you were a fag..., uh... homo..."

"Go ahead and say it, Ulf. Gays, homos, warm brothers, whatever," Konny smiled.

"My father always says breechloader," Berti giggled, and all three of them laughed.

After this burst of laughter, Ulf's expression became serious again. "I thought you were stupid, sick clowns who sometimes prey on children. I thought you were perverts and ....", the man's face looked sad. "I was so stupid! I am so sorry. From the bottom of my heart!"

"Thank you Ulf. Thank you for letting us be who we are. Completely normal. Your honesty honors you."

The laughter returned. "Friends, the goulash party is going to be a hit! And now I must see my wife. I think I'll apologize to her too ... you know. I tried to beat you both up. Instead of a beating, I met two nice buddies. And if Karl-Heinz makes it to high school, we'll have a bottle of champagne!"

"Done!"

Except for the salesman, all the residents had come. Berti and Konny's neighbor could not attend. He was spending the weekend with his children at his grandparents' house. There was an important birthday to celebrate.

Ulf had set up beer tables. Karl-Heinz and Emre, the son of the Turkish greengrocer Hasan, were putting logs in the fireplace. A chain hung from a hook at the top of a metal tripod. A large enameled goulash pot dangled from it over the open fire. It smelled wonderful.

"I reckon it'll be another half hour," Mrs. Kapaunke said, stirring with an oversized wooden spoon.

"I'll get plates for everyone," Fatima Özdemir decided. "Hasan brought a lot of salad from the store. Can somebody help with the washing up?" she added.

"I'll help," replied Vivien Hobelsberger, a bride from Eastern Germany.

Berti fetched a blanket for Mrs. Mint, who was shivering despite the sunny early winter day.

Ulf Kapaunke, Konny and Maik-Robin, Vivien's boyfriend, opened the first bottle of beer.

"To our house fellowship," trumpeted a very cheerful Ulf.

"Cheers!"

The sound of bottles clinking together suggested a wonderful afternoon.

"Wow, that'll be a feast! Since they've been living there, there's nothing to do."

While Vivien had largely dialectically blurred her Saxon origins, Maik-Robin did not deny his regional mother tongue.

"Let's have a drink until we all calm down."

"Dad, shall we play another round of soccer?"

"Please," urged Emre, who was about two years younger than Karl-Heinz.

Maik-Robin stood up. "I'm here, Sparwasser. That was my idol! He shot us down in 1974 with a score of zero. Do you remember the Soccer World Cup 1974?"

"Then I'll show the old GDR striker who was the best defender of my time."

Berti came in. He put the blanket over Mrs. Mint's lap. "Berti, you have to play soccer. Ulf, Karl-Heinz and you against Konny, Emre and Maik-Robin," the old lady said.

"Wow, is that really necessary?"

The staunch anti-sportsman was anything but enthusiastic.

"Berti, get in goal," Ulf demanded.

"All right," the heavyweight said broadly.

"It's great that you haven't dismantled our soccer goals yet, Dad," Karl-Heinz and Emre said happily.

Konny had kicked off. Maik-Robin ran forward.

"Ball," he called loudly.

Konny passed to Emre. He ran around Ulf and passed the ball to Maik-Robin. The *Jürgen Sparwasser* impersonator took the shot. Berti stood motionless in the goal. The ball flew towards him. Memories of school sports came back. Soccer. 5th grade. Back then, he managed to save one out of an estimated 120 shots on goal. Today was the day of revenge. While the goalkeeper was still deciding whether to kick the ball away or catch it, the ball struck Berti in the face. His glasses fell from his nose.

"Right in the face," laughed the star striker in disguise.

"Well held," Karl-Heinz blurted out, only to immediately turn his attention back to the front.

Berti adjusted his glasses, then raised his fists. He stood there in a triumphant pose. It was an unthinkable pose in his life. "Yay," he cheered at the top of his lungs.

Everything had changed. He lived much more freely than before. Nonsense! He was living his life. That was a better way of putting it. In short. He was happy. He would never leave here again. Everyone in this house was the way it should be everywhere. All Germany should take this house as an example. He even stood up to his archenemy, sports, in the me-time.

Ulf got the bouncing ball right at his feet. He took the shot. The leather fluttered in an arc towards Konny, slipped past the goalkeeper and landed unstoppably in the corner.

"Goooaaaal!"

Berti was ecstatic. Something unprecedented had happened. A novelty, a world premiere, the novelty par excellence. His team was in the lead. Today was a good day.

Maik-Robin cursed. "No, you. That's not true!"

Kick-off. Next attack. Emre stormed past Ulf, skillfully outpaced Karl-Heinz, who was just a step too slow, and shot the ball into the bottom corner of the goal. Berti fell back, but had no chance against the well-placed shot.

"Goooooaaaaal! Emre, that was great. Berti, the Bottom has to come around quickly! The hands should catch the ball," he joked to the beaten goalkeeper. "One to one!"

Kick-off for father and son. An attack on the opponent's goal followed. Shot and ... Konny went flying. Berti saw his friend in a cross position. The goalkeeper's hands grabbed the leather.

"Held," said a delighted Emre.

The counterattack began. Maik-Robin took the ball. This time he managed to get past Karl-Heinz and Ulf. He ran alone towards Berti. He stopped. The goalkeeper's gaze was crystal clear. Highly concentrated, he watched the striker step by step. Maik-Robin stopped the ball. Ulf came running up from behind. The East German hurried to shoot. He didn't hit it properly. The round leather fluttered halfway to the goal. Berti didn't move an inch. When the ball hit exactly where no one wanted it to, there was no cheering. It was more like an exclamation: "Grpffmmt"

Berti rolled his eyes. "G..g...got ... it," he snorted and dropped to his knees.

"Still undecided," Karl-Heinz said.

Maik-Robin ran to Berti. "Sorry! You have no intention."

"Never mind," Berti struggled out. "I've held two big ones. I've never been so good."

"Hey, hey," came the shooter, "you're still holding those two fat ones," he pointed to Berti's loins.

"It's still a tie. Everybody to the table," Vivien called. "Dinner's ready."

While the neighbors sat down, Maik-Robin went back into the house. "Quickly change clothes. They're really weird."

Five minutes later he returned. "Berti and Konny," he called to the two friends.

"What's going on?"

"There are two plugs standing there. They're looking for you. A wide, long mountain and a dam wall."

"Please who?" Konny asked and stood up.

Berti was also curious. When they both went to the front of the house and saw who was asking for them, they stood rooted to the spot. Protein one and protein two had settled in front of them. The Moscow collection of the Nobel Golf Club had found them.

"Hello, friends," one of the two Russian bouncers said to them.

"Greetings," the second broad-shouldered mountain of flesh bellowed. He slammed his right fist into the open palm of his left hand. He let his knuckles crack audibly. "Come here! Pay the bill. Where's that middle finger you showed me? I'll break it for you, you little louse."

Konny turned around, screamed loudly, and started jumping back into the garden. "Ahhh! Heeeeelp!"

Unfortunately, Berti was too slow. The chunky hands of one of the 160-pound men grabbed him. It was the one Berti had knocked out in the golden toilet with a head butt and a kick to the genitals.

"Do you know how long my balls hurt, fatty?"

He pinned Berti against the wall of the house. He shook his head. "How could we, we just left," he groaned, knowing full well that this wasn't a good answer. He thought feverishly what else he could say. "But I just got hit in the balls with a soccer ball. That could have hurt," he added. "From that point of view, we're actually even."

Unfortunately, the pity ploy didn't work.

"Ivan, go ahead! We'll break his fingers first, then his arms, then his legs!"

"Kooonnnyyyyyyyy," Berti screamed in panic. "Heeeelp! Save me!"

Konny stood before his neighbors. His face was as white as a sheet. His whole body was shaking. Mrs. Mint was spreading the goulash with a ladle. Ulf had sat down, Hasan was cleaning the big kebab knife with which he had cut the goulash that morning. Maik-Robin drank beer, the women distributed bread and cutlery, the children added wood. All eyes were on the writer.

"Russian sh-shthugs," Konny stuttered in agony.

"Moscow debt collection or something? Are you in debt?" asked Ulf Kapaunke. He stood up. Ulf got that disgusting look on his face again that had kept the two friends from liking him for weeks.

Konny shook his head violently and gesticulated wildly with his hands. "No! They're bouncers from the luxury tennis club. We were there to solve one of Berti's cases and they got in our way."

Ulf Kapunke stood up. "Luxury tennis club. Those rich assholes," he grumbled.

Berti's bloodcurdling cry for help could be heard. Konny closed his eyes. "My Berti," he groaned. The writer turned and ran back to the front door. "Berti! I'm coming! We'll die together!"

The second Russian took Berti's right hand and pressed it against the wall of the house, while the first Russian still held the detective by the collar. Berti was helplessly at their mercy.

"You'll soon lose the feeling in your fat fingers," Ivan laughed. "I'll break them one by one."

Konny realized the threatening situation. "Bertiiii," he shouted. It was a cry of fear, anger and helplessness. The writer got the better of him and jumped on Ivan from behind. He covered his eyes.

Ivan let go of Berti's hand. "You dung fly," came in a harsh Eastern Bloc dialect.

He shook himself, which probably looked a bit like a cow chasing away an annoying gadfly. As the massive body moved rhythmically, Konny could no longer hold on. He slipped down.

"Now we both have. This is going to be fun. It wasn't easy to find you zeros, but there aren't many Konny Wels writers in town, ha ha ha," he laughed maliciously. "Dr. Long-Snouted Shit Writer, I'm going to crush you."

"Stay away from my friends, you potato sacks with eyes," Ulf Kapaunke's voice drowned everything out. He was standing behind the two Russians, taking off his jacket and rolling up the sleeves of his sweater.

"What do you want? Go home, old man," Ivan sneered at him.

As soon as he spoke, Ulf took a step forward, grabbed the Russian, spun his own body around in a flash, bent down, and 160 kilos of human flesh flew through the air.

The Russian hit the floor hard. "Whew!" came out of the bouncer's mouth with a gasp. He gasped for air and lay there like a fish out of water.

"Leave Berti alone," scolded Mrs. Mint, who had rushed up with remarkable speed for her age. She still held the goulash skillet in her hand. The enameled kitchen utensil was lifted, swung and landed on the head of the Russian, who still had Berti firmly in his grip. The old lady smashed the ladle repeatedly against the thug's nearly shaved skull.

"Ouch! Stop it, you old bag!"

"You don't insult old ladies. Have you no decency?" asked Hasan, not very kindly. The blade of his kebab knife pointed at the tip of the meat pile's nose. "I can make a lot of kebab skewers out of you!"

"Don't be silly," the Russian hissed, looking respectfully at the blade.

"Vivian! Get me a jack! I have to go!" Maik-Robin shouted belligerently.

"I didn't understand you. What did you say?" Ulf threw himself at the bouncer, whom he had knocked to the ground.

He still groaned a little, but seemed to have recovered from his shock. "Hang on," the shaven-headed Russian grumbled, turned around and jumped up quickly despite his sturdy physique. Ulf reacted in a flash. Before his opponent could get to his feet, he had grabbed him again. He spun around and pulled the bouncer with him until he lost contact with the ground. Then he let go with a full swing. "It's called swinging, you warm meatloaf. It's a Swiss national sport. Similar to our wrestling. I practiced it a little on the side."

Centrifugal force struck. This time, the Russian's 120 kilograms of muscle mass crashed into the wall of the house. After an indefinable thud, the body glided leisurely downward.

Now it was Ulf who grinned. "What did you say? I didn't quite hear you. What am I supposed to wait for, you bloated bagpipe?"

"Don't be silly, guys," the second Russian groaned.

Hasan was still imitating fast cutting movements. "Kebab," he said unmistakably.

The bouncer let go of Berti and took a step back. Ulf Kapaunke stood there.

"Another overfed, ugly, brainwashed wannabe thug from the asshole club of the super rich. Come here! I'm in the mood! Fancy a round of judo or swinging?"

Ulf did not wait for an answer, but went for it. The arm lock, the body twist and the throw were a single movement. The Russian, taken by surprise, crumpled to the ground next to his partner.

"Now let me try, Ulf. I'll cut up the troublemakers," Hasan pushed his way to the front row.

"You ruffian," Mrs. Mint scolded. She pushed Hasan aside and continued to beat the Russian bald heads with the ladle. It was like playing the xylophone without the melody. Except for the dull tock tock tock when the ladle hit the heads. "You want to hit my Berti? Take this!" Zack again, she hit them with the trowel.

tock tock tock

"If my Rudi were still alive, he would have given you a load of shotgun pellets by now!"

Vivien came running. The stress threw her back into Saxon. "Maik-Robin, here ist the jack! But be careful, it's new. Just hit gently."

The assembled household frightened the two musclemen. "Ivan, let's get out of here, they're all crazy."

"Just get out of here! They'll kill us. We wanted to give the two faggots ... ouch ..."

Mrs. Mint struck again, "You don't say that about my Berti. He's a gentleman. And Konny is a very smart man."

The octogenarian seemed to have been a master of the ladle in the past. Again and again the enameled piece landed on the heads of the two Russians.

"Let's get out of here," Ivan grunted.

The two bouncers got up and ran out into the street. They turned around anxiously. They were not being followed. Chatting animatedly, they ran off.

"I said right away, forget those two weirdos! No, they wanted revenge. For professional honor and loss of face and all that, you said. Now we've embarrassed ourselves. All because of you! You're a wanka - a village idiot," Ivan scolded.

"I'm not a village idiot."

"You are and always will be the village idiot. Wanka, Wanka!"

"Never show your faces here again," Hasan shouted after them. He held up the kebab knife threateningly. "Kebab!"

"Has something happened to you?" Vivian asked.

"No. Everything is fine. Thank you," Berti groaned.

Konny was relieved. "Thank you, you saved our lives."

"We are neighbors. Good neighbors always help each other," Ulf grinned. "And it was fun, too. You know, I'm a Judoka. Second Dan. I used to train for the Olympic heavyweight team. I didn't quite make it, but we really beat those two walruses."

"It's a pity, I would have liked to hit the guards on the head so hard that they would have grinned," said Maik-Robin disappointedly.

"You are the best and dearest neighbors I could wish for," Konny said happily and hugged Ulf.

"Well, well, let's leave the church in the village," he joked.

"How about a beer and some kettle goulash?" Mrs. Kapaunke asked the group.

"But I'll wash the pan first," decided Mrs. Mint.

Everyone laughed.

"Grandma Mint, I don't want to mess with you," said Berti affectionately.

"You know, my boy, a lesson learned is a lesson learned."

"I don't want to know how your husband died," the detective added.

Everyone laughed again.

Mrs. Mint pinched Berti's flabby cheeks with a grin and said affectionately: "You cheeky rascal."

Konny was overjoyed. The Russian danger would be averted forever, his XXL purple was more than avenged.

"Dad, that was mega cool. I filmed the whole thing with my smartphone."

"Great," said Fatima. "Then let's put it on YouTube. Finally I can use something from my computer class."

"Yes," rejoiced Berti, clenching his triumphant fist again and raising it for the second time. "Today is a good day after all."

The food was hearty home cooking and tasted better than anything Berti and Konny had ever eaten in their lives. It tasted of equality. It tasted of friendship. It tasted of security, love and idyll. They were happy.

"Why can't it always and everywhere be like it is here with us?" asked Berti, smacking his lips. "We're gay..." he paused and looked at the two children.

"You can say that. We know what gay is," Karl-Heinz laughed.

"Boy," said Uschi Kapaunke.

"Emre," Fatima groaned.

"From school. Or what do you think the grown-ups talk about at recess?"

"Well, when you think that horny used to be a so-called frowned upon frivolous word and now every kindergarten child says horny to something nice," Ulf helped the children.

Uschi Kapaunke didn't recognize her husband. He had become extremely liberal in the last few days. That's why I married that scoundrel, she thought and was happy.

"So a couple of men, a single old lady ..." Berti started again.

"Thank you for not saying old crotchety woman," Mrs. Mint winked at him.

Berti grinned wryly, but continued despite the old lady's interjection. "... a divorced man, a Turkish family, a normal," he stretched the word, "a German family and an east-german couple living under one roof."

"You forgot the Christians and the Muslims," Hasan added.

"That's right! And that's not all. Christians and Muslims live together peacefully," Fatima beams.

"Well then, cheers! That's international," said Maik-Robin and raised his glass.

They clinked glasses. Then Berti had to talk about the case of the golf club. He left out some details. For example, some things that happened in the luxury toilet. On the other hand, he gave a detailed account of his acquaintance with the construction magnate Hindelang and his eating habits. He also talked about the flying oyster and the cute dog that had emptied itself into the sinfully expensive handbag.

"So, did you get any money?"

Konny saved the answer: "We're still thinking about it. About the amount of the fee, because the developer really wants Berti to rent office space in one of his buildings. Let's see how we can come to an agreement."

"How about a little shot?" asked Mrs. Mint.

"Give me the bottle," Maik-Robin slurred.

Vivien whispered to Fatima. "He'll have to go through it alone. He'll probably be sick tomorrow."

Two hours later, Maik-Robin was carried into the apartment by Ulf and Hasan. He had fallen asleep drunk at the table.

The party had been a success.

locomotive-2027702_1280
© license by:
https://pixabay.com/service/license-summary/

Chapter 4
Traveling acquaintances

"Let's go through everything again, darling."

"Oh Konny, we've already checked the list twice. We definitely haven't forgotten anything," came from a visibly annoyed Berti.

A dusty Rolling Stones hit was playing on the radio. Konny started to sing along. But he kept skipping passages. "Paint it black, I see ... every day ... your whole world is black ..."

"If you're not sure of the lyrics, don't sing along. Old Mick Jagger can do it without you," Berti grinned. At the same time he danced around the apartment in a good mood.

"And you're not a natural dancer. When I see your body dancing like that, it reminds me more of surfing than dancing."

"You're just jealous," Berti laughed out loud.

The song was over. The voice of a newsreader could be heard. Berti went to the bathroom. "Should I put on the Norwegian sweater for the trip?"

"Please be quiet for a moment. I'd like to hear our travel weather."

"The German weather service has issued a warning for the Alpine region..."

"Or should I save the sweater for a walk and wear the flannel shirt instead..."

"Berti, I don't hear anything!"

"... heavy snowstorms ... partly down to the lowlands ..."

"So you prefer the Norwegian sweater after all?"

"... temperatures drop to minus .... at night"

The detective continued. "Oh, that's kind of stupid. You can't wear a moose pattern on the night train. I sweat so easily anyway."

"Jeez Berti," Konny sulked, "now I haven't quite understood the weather forecast."

Berti came out of the bathroom. "What will the weather be like?" Konny frowned.

"What's going on?" Berti asked, looking into a slightly desperate looking face.

"Oh, nothing," Konny waved him off. "Nothing at all. I just didn't understand the weather forecast."

"You should have listened better. You always talk so much. So, what should I wear?"

The author took a deep breath. Well, Berti was just Berti. "At least I understand that there will be snow this weekend. Lots of snow!"

"Konny, we are lucky kids. We've got a dream weekend in a luxury ski hotel and the weather to match."

"You're already dreaming of log fires, sleigh rides through a dreamy snowy landscape and..."

"...and a marriage proposal."

Broke Back Mountain Part Two. More thrills, chills, chills, chills and everything that goes with it.

"Let's get there first. When do we have to be at the station?" Konny dodged the question. He was pleasantly surprised by Ber-ti's words.

"At 21:00. Our train leaves half an hour later than we thought."

"I think they did a good job. In a sleeping car to Munich, from there by luxury bus to the ski resort and by taxi to the mountains."

"What mountains? You mean to the hotel, right?"

"Berti, our luxury hotel is far away from any civilization. Here," Konny pulled the travel documents out of the side compartment of the car again. "Take a closer look at the brochure. *Berghotel Alpentraum.* The secluded five-star hotel for the discerning vacationer," he read.

"Sounds expensive."

"It is expensive! The hotel has only ten rooms. All with fireplaces, balconies, large marble bathrooms with Jacuzzis, and so on. There is a swimming pool, sauna and gym in the basement. The small restaurant has 1 Michelin star. A private ski instructor is also available."

"Now I understand why a weekend like this costs 5,000 euros."

"As befits a Michelin-starred restaurant, a Michelin-starred chef prepares the menus. The wine, by the way, comes from selected winemakers."

"The hammer."

"And it's all inclusive for us."

"As for skiing, I can't... I'm not ... so I can't do that."

Konny laughed. "Me neither. But we can take a trial lesson. The hotel rents out the equipment."

"And if I don't want to?"

"Then we go sledding, take a walk, or swim a few laps in the pool. Then we sweat it out in the sauna."

"Is that a mixed sauna?"

Konny shrugged. "I have no idea. Would that be a problem for you?"

Berti fumbled around. "That would be a first."

"With women?"

"Yes. I don't know how I feel," he made a gesture with his hand. "Oh, it's just annoying."

"Not that you'll turn into a normal straight guy."

"Don't worry about that. I'm normal as far as that goes."

"Thank God."

"Konny, we'll let it rip."

"What you can get, baby."

The time had come. The last steps were discussed again. "Uschi Kapaunke will take care of the flowers. Does she have the key?"

Berti nodded. "She does!"

"Fatima takes the mail out of the mailbox so it doesn't overflow with requests from rich clients."

"Or something from the publisher for you," Berti countered. "Does she have a key, too?"

He nodded.

"Why doesn't Uschi Kapaunke do both?"

"Because everyone wanted to do something for us."

"And Mrs. Mint?"

"I told her to watch out for burglars."

"Konny, that was brilliant."

"Did we get everything in the suitcase?"

"You had the list."

"Let's check again."

"I'm ready."

"The laundry?"

"Yes."

"Underwear and socks?"

"We packed them."

"Warm clothes for the day, suit for dinner?"

"All in."

"Detective gear for emergencies?"

Berti was taken aback. "I've only got the Agnetha wig and the suspenders."

"That's enough," Konny grinned. He used that look again.

"All right."

"Then we have everything. Will you call the taxi?"

All train stations in the world have one thing in common. They attract people from all walks of life. You will find everything from thrifty millionaires, civil servants, pensioners, families and students to homeless people, junkies, social parasites and shady characters of all kinds. Train stations are a mirror of our society. All kinds of characters from all over the world can be found in this small place.

The smells of the stations are also very similar. In addition to the oily metal smell on the tracks, the stench of French fries and grease, reminiscent of used oil, lingers in the air. A few meters further on, the smell of bratwurst or currywurst rises to the top and immediately triggers a ravenous appetite. Just a few steps away, a kebab skewer rotates, and right next to it, the aroma of freshly baked goods wafts.

Around the corner, the acrid smell of urine, at best reminiscent of a carnival toilet, creeps into your nostrils.

The magazine stores smell of the wider world. The freshly printed press offers a pleasant taste. The tobacco shop next door has its own smell, as do the overpriced sweets at the kiosk.

Berti and Konny followed the aromatic scent of coffee. A freshly brewed, hot espresso at Starbuck's would shorten the wait. The train was already at the platform. A voice reminiscent of Maik-Robin echoed through the station hall. "The Intercity Marco Polo is arriving on track 18 ..."

"This is pure travel fever. I'm totally excited."

"Berti, how many times have you traveled?"

"We always took the train to Würzburg. We visited dad's brothers and sisters there."

"And where else?"

"Nowhere, but what do you have against Würzburg?"

"Nothing, I just wanted to know where you were."

"I see. In Würzburg."

Konny closed his eyes for a moment. "Würzburg is okay."

Berti laughed as he remembered the holidays with his relatives. "Uncle Ernst was always funny. I'll tell you his standard line. But I have to do it in Franconian, otherwise it won't work."

"You can speak Franconian?"

"My father is from Franconia."

"Let's go then."

"Well, I'm Uncle Ernst now. You should know that he lived up to his first name in his facial expression and also wore the typical Schwartz horn-rimmed glasses."

"Go ahead, start."

Berti tried to imitate his uncle. "I'm going to rip your head off and throw it in your face!"

Konny forced a pained smile on his face.

"Or at dinner," Berti added. "Our uncle always told the same joke."

He imitated Uncle Ernst again. "Why do you stick your nose in everything?"

Konny grimaced. "Hilarious. Really," he exclaimed ironically.

"My God, I was a kid. I thought it was funny and I still think it's funny."

"Then I'm no longer surprised at the Franconian merriment."

"I thought you liked the Comedians Erwin Pelzig, Urban Priol and the Franconian carnival."

"You forgot Michl Müller. This yellow sausage song is also quite funny."

They both laughed.

The espresso was invigorating. The hands of the station clock moved forward.

"Leave and pay."

The reserved Comfortline sleeping car on the City Night Line train from Amsterdam to Munich was ingenious. A friendly train attendant checked the tickets and showed the friends the way to the compartment. Which wasn't too difficult, given the choice of left or right. "Here you go. Have a nice trip."

When the friends entered the double compartment, they were amazed.

Konny was more than pleased. "Comfortable beds, duvets, my own toilet with sink. What more could you want?"

"We even get breakfast delivered to our room," was Berti's first sentence.

"Compartment, darling. It's called a compartment on the train!"

"You could be a knee-dragger."

They made themselves comfortable. As the train pulled away with a slight jerk, there was a tinny clack above them. The engineer greeted them over the loudspeaker. "My dear passengers, I welcome you aboard the ..."

"Are you tired already?"

Berti shook his head. "The espresso really woke me up, and I'm so excited that I couldn't sleep at all."

"Shall we go to the dining car for a nightcap?"

Berti jumped up. "I didn't dare ask. Of course you did! And I'm a little hungry, too."

"That's why I brought slices."

"Slices?"

"Sure. The fresh sausage in the fridge had to go, and we still had toast. So I made us a sandwich."

"Yum. First we'll finish the sandwich, then we'll go to the dining car and wash it down with a beer. There's a glass or two in there, right?"

Konny grinned a little mischievously. "Even a little more. We have a dining car voucher for 50 Euros."

"Yay! I knew you'd win a prize one day."

"Well, well..." Konny grinned.

The dining car was full. Most of the guests were a group of spiritualistic followers of an itinerant preacher. Some things were reminiscent of the days of Bhagwan's long gone disciples. Missing, however, were the orange and red Buddha leaves, Indian musical instruments, incense candles, and the annoying Hare Krishna chanting.

"Come on, let's sit here," Konny suggested. He deliberately chose a table as far away from the religious freaks as possible.

"Okay."

84

Berti squeezed himself onto a bench for two, which he easily filled himself. "Look, you can light tea lights. Do you have a light?"

"Stupid question. Where from, we don't smoke."

"That's right," Berti smiled.

A train attendant fought her way out of the crowd of enlightened people. She stood in front of the two friends. You could tell she was upset. Still, she made an effort to appear friendly.

"Good afternoon," came the greeting. "Would you like to come?"

So the origin of the lady is clear, Konny thought. Maik-Robin and Vivian came to his mind. What would be the first name of this well-proportioned train attendant, whose nameplate read Kastenbauer? Jeanette-Cordula? Jacqueline-Annemarie? Cheyenne or just plain Mandy?

Konny doubted that more than 50% of the Ostrogoths whose names had been desecrated would be able to spell their given names correctly by the time they came of age.

"Two beers, please."

"Two beers, and you?" she turned to Konny.

"The two beers are for both of you," he grinned.

The conductor noticed the little faux pas. "You have to finish. The clothes on the Danes' backs are up to their necks."

"They're a bit annoying, aren't they?"

"That's how it is. That's the way it is."

"Do you have a light?"

"Here is smoking forbidden!"

"For the tea light," Berti pointed out politely.

A small smile flitted across the train attendant's lips. "Oh, well, no problem. Here," she said, handing Berti a pack of matches. "You can keep them."

"Thanks."

"Would you like something to eat?"

Berti hesitated, Konny nodded. The sandwich had whetted his appetite. "Maybe a little something. After all, we have a 50 Euro coupon."

That was the decision, the hint with the fence post. Berti immediately seized the opportunity. "It smelled so delicious in the station hall, like currywurst. Do you have something like that?"

"With French Fries? With a roll? With Baguette?"

"Two with fries," Konny ordered.

"You two are probably always of the same opinion. That explains it." She was about to continue when she thought of something else. "Is the food here? Or should I take it to the room?"

"We'll eat here, thanks for the offer."

"Good."

She was gone. Berti grinned broadly.

"What's wrong?"

"It's called a room."

"It's called a compartment. We're on a train and it's called a compartment!"

"The train juicer must know."

"Either she was trying to be casual or she comes from one of Germany's intellectual deserts."

The freaks got louder and louder. They laughed all the time.

"You're one of the good-humored people," Berti whispered.

Konny nodded and said: "Don't look at them so insistently. You know the old pub rule."

"Which one?"

"When an idiot comes into the pub, you always have to look a-way. If you look at him and you look back at him, it has a magnetic effect and he sits down with you. Then the evening is ruined."

Berti looked away immediately.

The beer was served. "Curry-Sausage is ready soon."

The candle was lit and Berti put the matches in his pocket. Nothing stood in the way of a romantic evening. They both felt like two guests on the famous *Orient Express*. They wouldn't have traded the weekend trip they had won for anything in the world. The only annoying thing was the partying mongooses behind them.

Meanwhile, the head guru had taken the floor. His flock listened intently. "Dear friends of faith, brothers and sisters, I greet you on your way to our independence. We are expected in our new community. Since my name is Knut Hofmann, you can be sure of enlightenment. No one but us knows that the old established churches are on the wrong track and lost. We know the way of salvation. Hallelujah!"

The audience responded in unison. "Hallelujah, praise the Lord of the sun, moon and stars. We are the children of light and follow the Enlightened One."

Berti covered his face with his right hand. "Konny, we have to get out of here."

"I know. Let's finish our drinks quickly."

"And our food?"

"We'll take it to the compartment."

They quickly finished their beers. The waitress trotted over. Instead of the curried sausage, however, Mrs. Kastenbauer brought two new beers. "I know my guests and have a look fort hem," she exclaimed proudly. "I used to be a waitress. And for the fifty euros, you can all have two more beers."

"Th-Th-Thank you," the writer stammered, caught off guard.

Before the next pint of beer could be ordered for the compartment, the conductor scurried through the crowd of enlightened passengers.

The hallelujah was repeated. Three times. Then came the recorder and guitar. The two friends knew the tune. It was clearly: "Thank you for this beautiful morning.

"Thank you for this ray of sunshine... Thank you for this journey into the light... Thank you for saving us from the bang ... Thank you and don't hide..."

The self-congratulatory superstars enthusiastically bobbed their heads back and forth as they sang.

Berti and Konny finished their beers in record time. Mrs. Kastenbauer brought the curried sausage and two more beers, but in glasses and not in bottles to take home as we had hoped. The term "worst case" took on a new meaning. Berti had the solution. "We'll have a light meal and the beer in one go."

Konny rolled his eyes. "That's the third beer."

"Beer," Berti improved. "O.33 liters. Think of it as half-liter glasses. Or glasses as big as the ones the Bavarians serve in their beer gardens."

"It's called a Mug. And I can't get the beer out of it."

"Never mind. Get rid of the stuff. And we'll drink the beer in sips. Let's go," Berti gave the order. "Go!"

The sausage was not eaten, it was devoured, each bite washed down with a gulp of beer.

"I can already feel the alcohol," Konny breathed.

"I feel it too. We probably drank the first two glasses a little too fast."

Mrs. Kastenbauer brought two more pilsners without being asked. Berti wanted to refuse, but the determined ex-FDJ standard bearer refused to negotiate. "This one's on me. You're both so drunk, and I'm talking here in the car."

"We'll give her the rest of the coupon as a tip," Konny decided as he emptied his third glass, noticeably tipsy, to start the fourth. "Toast," he laughed.

Berti hummed the melody of the song that had just been played. For some time now, the out-of-touch lunatics had been belting out the prominent part of the Beatles' song Hey Jude. It was the last part of the mega hit.

"La la laa lalalalaaaa ... hey Knut .... la la laa lalalaaaa ... hey Knut ..."

"Yes, dear brothers and sisters," Knut Hofmann drowned out his warbling brothers in faith, who were singing themselves into ecstasy.

The guitarist had gotten up in the meantime and had long since overtaken the colorless flute player. He struck the strings of his guitar furiously. He waved his sparse long hair wildly back and forth like a headbanger. His voice was boozy and smoky. Joe Cocker would have been jealous.

"Knuti ... Knuti ... oh Knut .... La la laa lalalalaaaaa ... hey Knut..."

"Our aura flows through this train. It has already reached two new brothers. I can feel the power you are summoning, dear friends. It is flowing through my ears into my body. Oh yes! This is it. This is salvation."

Berti and Konny had eaten the curried sausage. Mrs. Kastenbauer cleared the dishes, but first she put two double ramazotti herbal schnapps on the table.

"For digestion, you two eaters," she winked. "What compartment are you in?" she asked Berti, gently stroking a hand across his shoulders. Only now did he notice that the train attendant's blue blouse was more open than it had been when the second beer had been served. "I'm Erna, by the way."

"B-B-Berti," stammered the detective, whose eyes couldn't tear themselves away from Erna's double-D unloading. The conductor seemed to take this the wrong way. While she was looking forward to a hot break between two and four in the morning, Berti was shocked.

"He's lactose intolerant," Konny muttered. He thought the statement was gentlemanly enough not to offend the hot eastern bride in view of her advanced age. Chuckling, he repeated. "Hi hi ... lactose intolerance ... because of the big milk cartons."

Erna didn't answer. She probably thought lactose intolerance had something to do with shyness. "We'll get that out of him. I've got toys for two." She wiggled her upper body briefly, causing her breasts to bounce considerably.

Berti was speechless. He had never seen dancing pumpkins before. Konny had to drink the Ramazotti immediately. "Tipsy is ok, drunk shouldn't be there. Otherwise nothing will work. Your number?"

"Nine."

"See you later!"

"Are you crazy, Berti? The old woman wants to eat us," Konny hissed. He seemed to sober up for a moment. But that disappeared in an instant. He laughed. "Disgusting."

Berti was somehow still in a state of shock. He shook his head and stared at Konny. "You can't do that."

"What should we do?"

"We just don't open."

In the background "Hey Knut" was sung for the hundredth time.

Konny found it hard to think, but he desperately searched for a solution. Suddenly he felt a hand on his shoulder.

"I didn't look at him," Berti said defensively.

Knut Hofmann sat down beside the author. "Hello, friends."

"Good evening," Konny slurred. Shocked by the thought of having to lie in bed with Erna Kastenbauer, he had also drunk Berti's ramazotti.

"May I invite you to join us?"

"We ... uh ... actually, we wanted to celebrate a bit on our own here," Berti huffed.

"Exactly," Konny added. "Ride in there ... hi hi."

"Wonderful. We're also celebrating, as you can hear."

"Knuti ... Knuti ... Knut ... la la la lallalalaaaa ..."

Knut Hofmann extended his hand. "I'm Knut."

"Herbert."

"And I am Konny Wels. I write the Dr. Lonss, uhh Lonesdale, hi hi, Ramzotti... novels."

"That's interesting. Where are you going?"

"Munich. We'll change there," explained Berti, who was beginning to worry about the babbling Konny.

"What a coincidence, so are we."

Gradually, more and more sect mongooses joined them. "Are you having problems?"

"Uh... no," Berti shook his head.

"Just think about it. Everybody has problems."

A second freak followed. "I used to have problems, too. I was a punk. Now I'm cured. Knut has it."

"Good," Berti smiled. He felt stifled and anything but comfortable.

"Great romantic evening," Konny giggled.

"He probably means romantic evening," Knut improved. The way the cult guru pronounced the word romantic sounded ironic.

Berti wanted to get up, but the ex-punker from Berlin squeezed himself into the narrow gap in the bench that Berti's body didn't fill. The uninvited guest rolled himself a cigarette that looked quite wide at the back. He put the cigarette, which looked like a satchel, into his mouth and lit it. A strange odor spread. Berti was sure that this was anything but normal tobacco.

"Do you want something from the bag?"

The detective shook his head, but the joint was already in his mouth. For some inexplicable reason, the notorious non-smoker took a drag on the joint. The smoke was supposed to be blown out immediately, but during a coughing fit, a considerable amount of it got into the detective's lungs. It hurt. The coughing got worse. Berti's eyes twisted.

"Good! That was really good! You know, we go to Holland with Knut every two weeks. That's where the action is."

Berti felt strange. Everything became surreal. He had to laugh. The Group weren't that stupid. Konny seemed to like them too. He sang the *Maya the Bee* song with the guitarist.

Berti watched for a while. Someone was taking pictures. Everyone was in a good mood.

"Great party," said the guitarist.

Eventually, Berti had enough of the party. He whispered to Konny: "Shall I take you to the room... uh, the compartment?"

He waved him off. "I think I'll have another beer."

Oh God. He hadn't even thought of Erna. In his mind the mega boobs appeared before his eyes. He felt another joint on his lips. Berti inhaled again. This time he sucked the smoke deep into his lungs, only to blow it out again like a fountain with another coughing fit. He felt great.

"Which compartment have you got?" asked Knut.

"Nine," Berti laughed.

Konny also joined the conversation. "We're getting ... a visit today ... hi, hi ... from a wonderful country ... Erna the bee is coming ... hiccup".

"There must be some mistake. I have the number nine. Your number on the door must have come loose and turned. You must have cabin number 6. We booked compartments one through five and seven through eleven."

"That was number six when we went in, and number nine when we left the compartment to go to the dining car. That's right, now I remember," rejoiced Berti. He still couldn't believe his luck. "Konny, we have six."

"Of course we have sex. We are ... hicks ... young and hot."

"Non Somkers," Erna Kastenbauer's voice rang through the dining car. Some of the smokers immediately put out their joints. Berti seized the opportunity. "Can I get out?"

"Sure."

Berti's head turned slightly toward Erna. "Konny. You wanted the coupon..."

"Voucher? Ah ... we'll pay, please."

Berti could tear up trees. He was on cloud nine. Was it because of the stuff?

Konny slipped the coupon into Erna's plunging neckline. The look he caught was lustful. The conductor winked repeatedly at the two friends. "Nine," she breathed barely audibly. She played with her tongue. She pressed it from the inside against her right cheek, making it bulge. "See you soon, you bastards."

"Come on," Berti squeezed and tugged at Konny's sleeve.

The completely dazed writer clung to his friend. "Berti," he whimpered. "Berti, take me to bed."

"Let's go to bed slowly, too," Knut's voice drummed through the dining car. "Let's accompany our new friends to their sleeping places with a song."

The guitar mongoose jumped up and strummed the strings. "Thank you for the new friends ... Thank you for a great day ... Thank you ..."

Konny joined in. Berti laughed all the time. When they finally reached the sleeping car, Berti looked for the right compartment. When he stood in front of it, he looked at the crooked nine with great scrutiny. At the top of the six was a rubber nipple that had slipped out of its hole. Berti pushed the fallen six up and clamped it back in place. They were saved. The airbag carrier would not hit them.

Should I warn Knut?

Konny coughed.

No! I'll let the chief mongoose go to his doom.

Half an hour later, the feeling of weightlessness subsided. The euphoria slipped out of Berti's body and disappeared. It was replaced by an indescribable feeling of emptiness. The detective suffered from a queasy stomach, dizziness and a taste in his mouth as if he had bitten into a rotting marijuana plant.

Konny groaned. He had just thrown up for the second time. He crawled back into bed on all fours, pulled the covers up to his chin, and fell asleep. A few minutes later, Konny began to snore softly.

The romance was over. The dream of an exciting, erotic night in a Deutsche Bahn sleeping car was over. Berti pulled on his sky-blue pajamas. The dizziness had subsided somewhat. As he lay down, he vowed never to smoke a joint again.

Berti heard doors slamming. More than one slammed open and closed. Loud giggling. Hurried footsteps outside the compartments. Somewhere someone was moaning louder than usual. The guitar mongoose was playing Bob Dylan's Blowin' in the Wind.

The big partner-swapping action at the Joint-Faces has begun, went through Berti's head. He thought about the evening and the individual scenes that played before his eyes. Suddenly he jerked up. Two pumpkin-sized breasts appeared in his imagination and bobbed up and down in front of him. Sitting up in bed, the thought of Erna Kastenbauer sent shivers of fear down his spine. Goose bumps formed on his neck and crawled down his back. Berti's fingers felt along the wall. He found the light switch.

Click.

He stood up anxiously. Two small steps brought him to the door. He looked at the clock. There were two minutes left. She had announced her visit for two o'clock sharp. The detective carefully opened the door to the bedroom. He was relieved to see that the six had stopped and had not slipped back down and turned around.

The guitar man was missing the right notes. It sounded like he was raping his guitar. The lyrics were reduced to a single word, the voice swaying back and forth uncontrollably. Sometimes he sang high, sometimes low. "Blowin ... blowin ... blo...blo...blowiiiiinn ... jaaaa baby ..."

Someone opened the door to the sleeping car. Berti pushed his door into the lock, but immediately put his ear to it, curious. Soft footsteps could be heard. The song was over, imitation-Santanas guitar had fallen silent.

Silence.

Berti trembled. Hopefully she would pass his compartment. A sweat of fear formed on his forehead. Single beads of sweat already broke off and ran down his temples. Erna passed their compartment. She knocked on one of the doors. "Hello, sweetie."

"Come in."

Berti heard the opening and closing of a compartment. This was followed by words like: "No ... I want to go to the two ... ohh ... that's a thing ... well then ... yes ... yes ... yes ... . Knut ... Knuuuut."

The guitar man spoke again on cue. He immediately started to play his old hit. "La ... la ... la ... lalalalaaaaa ... hey Knut."

A door was flung open. "Shut up," yelled Knut.

Erna could be heard: "Come on, sweetheart. Now on the straight silk and now on the loose silk .... ohhh good Knut".

"Hey Knut ... la ... la ... laa ..."

Satisfied, Berti lay down in bed. The danger was averted. The sweat of fear dried. The soft rattling of the iron wheels as they passed over the sleepers lulled him to sleep.

"How are you?"

Berti opened his eyes. Konny was standing in front of the bed, fully dressed. For the next three seconds, the detective had a mental movie of last night. He didn't feel a headache, sat up quickly and looked at stars. His circulation didn't seem to be running smoothly. "Great," he gushed. "And you?"

"I don't feel good at all. My head is buzzing like crazy and I feel sick. How many times did I throw up yesterday?"

"Twice."

Konny's face was pale. "No wonder. I don't have a hangover, I have a whole race of cats."

"You also ate both ramazotti. And quite a few beers, too."

"Please be quiet. I don't like to be reminded." The author grabbed his temples and massaged them gently. "Rise and shine."

Berti got up and washed. As he put on his Norwegian moose-patterned sweater after his morning toilet, there was a knock.

"Breakfaaaaast," Erna squealed in high spirits.

Konny opened the door.

"Morning, together." The conductor grinned broadly. "You two are probably snotlout spoons."

Berti and Konny took a step back.

"What fun you are having. Well, it was really good with Knut. Man, he could have ..."

Konny lifted his index finger and put it to his mouth. "Shh. We don't want to reveal any secrets."

Erna grinned. "Okay. Here, I've got a Coffee for you."

The deeply relaxed and happy looking train attendant handed over a tray with two cups, a pot of latte and two croissants.

"Good trip."

"Goodbye," Berti replied and closed the door.

Whistling, Erna went to the next compartment and knocked. "Hello you Song-Starlet. Blowin in the wind and so on, he he," she laughed.

Berti took a deep breath. "Phew, lucky you."

"Hopefully we'll have different personnel on the way home," Konny groaned.

"I directed them to Knut Hofmann's compartment," Berti announced proudly. "Because I got our room number right again."

Konny laughed. "The old lady would have crushed us."

"Stop with the horror stories! Look, I'm getting goose bumps again."

The loudspeaker crackled. "Dear passengers. We will be arriving at Munich Central Station in about thirty minutes. We thank you for your travel and wish you a safe journey." Crackle. The announcement was repeated in English. "Ladies and gentlemen ..."

Konny was satisfied with a sip of coffee and half a croissant. That was all he could manage at the moment. Berti devoured the rest. The friends arrived in Munich with a slight hangover.

"Let's find a pharmacy and buy some aspirin."

Both strolled down the street. Behind the two men, the members of the illuminated group of stoners got off the Amsterdam Express. Their faces looked tortured, too. Knut Hofmann's face was briefly visible. He seemed to hide in the mass of his congregation. He kept looking back. The leisure preacher always deliberately stayed in the middle of his flock.

"Look," Berti giggled. "Cool Knut is trying to get away from the man-hungry Erna and is hiding among his disciples."

Police Chief Rudi Radtke had an eye for dealers, illegals, and all manner of scum, as he liked to say. Whenever the night train from Amsterdam pulled into the Bavarian capital's station, the civilian investigator would stand on platform 23 and keep an eye out. Radtke loved the bustle of the station. He liked the mix of people he encountered here, the greasy smell of the fryers as much as the sweet aroma of the almond distillery or the exotic flavor of the Chinese fast-food restaurant. He had worked here for more than twenty years.

"A day without an arrest is a day lost," was his motto.

Over time, Radtke made many enemies, as well as a few friends. One of them was Jens-Udo Erdmann, the cook on the Amsterdam train. Erdmann would wander through the carriages during his breaks. He was looking for drug dealers. His nose led the way often enough.

One day, he was sure, he would compete against a police drug dog on Supertalent or some other TV show and win. They had made it easy for him that night. They were all completely stoned when he walked through the dining car. He had even photographed two of the stoners smoking a joint with his smartphone. The photos had been sent to Master Radkte via MMS.

The policeman studied their faces over his morning coffee. One of them was an old punk, the other had a flabby face. He would pick them both out of the mob. The leader of the whole gang was a religious nut. A typical cult guru. Radtke had been sent his picture, too. His people were everywhere. Nothing could go wrong.

"Konny, Berti! Wait a minute," Knut Hofmann's voice boomed through the station hall. The charismatic man in his mid-fifties caught up. He put his left hand around Berti's shoulder and his right around Konny's. "Speak up, do I have to thank you two for Erna's visit?"

Konny looked down and cleared his throat. Berti blushed.

"It was a cool event. I had a lot of fun, but she got really pushy towards the end. She doesn't know the word 'end'."

"I don't know..." Berti started, but Knut interrupted him.

"Give it a rest. It will take a few days for my noodle to work again. In the meantime, I have to take care of other things. There's my business, for example."

"I think you're a ... a vicar, priest, pastor or something like that?" Konny was confused.

"My congregation is generous, but you can't live on it. I work full time in the forwarding business. I transport and move goods from here to there."

"Interesting," Konny said, trying to end the conversation. "Berti, do you know by heart where our bus leaves from?"

"No."

"You were a bit quick to get out," Knut Hofmann smiled. "To be honest, I thought you were going to have breakfast in the dining car."

"Why?"

"Because," the guru continued, "I left something with you and I wanted to get it while you were having breakfast."

"You what?" Berti interrupted him.

96

Hofmann's expression changed. The friendliness disappeared. His look became cold and unpleasant. The tone of his voice changed as well. There was no kindness at all. "You two bastards are in possession of something that belongs to me. It's in your car. We're all going to the next bathroom together. I'll get my package there and you'll forget what you saw."

"Are you crazy?"

Knut's right hand went into his jacket pocket. Something long stuck out. It was hard. The guru pushed it into Konny's back. "That's a gun, you homo. Either I get my package back or your wandering roast pork will be alone in the future! You bitches have a lot of snow in your suitcase. My snow."

"Konny," Berti exclaimed anxiously. He was on the verge of a cardiac arrest from fear.

"It's all right," the writer reassured him. "We'll give him whatever he wants. Then we'll go to our ski hotel. I have a fucking headache."

"That's what I wanted to hear," grinned Hofmann.

"Welcome to Bavaria," came the unexpected greeting from police chief Rudi Radkte. It was probably the puzzled faces that made the policeman decide on a more or less understandable German. "Police! Welcome to Munich. Your IDs please!"

They froze. A police check was the last thing they needed at that moment. Berti was speechless, Knut had a big grin on his face, and Konny wondered which evil was the least of it. Being shot by Knut or being arrested for drug possession. The situation was catastrophic. A suspected drug smuggler had hidden his package in her suitcase. This would probably be discovered by the plainclothes officer in the next few minutes. The owner and drug smuggler still had a gun in his back. If he or Berti said the wrong thing, it could have been the last sentence in Konrad Wels' life. Konny knew he had seen better moments. Berti was used to getting into unusual situations, but him? Konny Wels, the quiet author, didn't know such things? Konny searched for a few seconds for the hidden cameras. He checked if he could see a camouflaged celebrity in the worn-out face of the policeman who was about to shout "hidden camera". Nothing. Nothing of the sort happened. Konny had seen similar scenes in some Hollywood movies. First there was a big confusion and then everything turned out fine in the end.

I hope Berti stays calm. Damn it! If the cop finds the idiot's package. Konny was about to go crazy. The throbbing in his temples was now spreading to his neck. Headache and stress. This was hell on e-arth.

"Fatty, you're coming with me."

Berti thought he hadn't heard right.

"Nobody calls you fat, you dried-up plum. How dare you talk to me? And what makes you think you can control us?" Berti interjected. "We are decent people. See those people over there?" he pointed to the back. "Why aren't those people checked?"

"Because you're a pothead, fat boy!"

Berti froze. He felt hot and cold. "What? Should I be? I don't even smoke, so I'm a N-N non-smoker," the detective rasped. His circulation started up again.

"If you're a non-smoker, then I'm not a policeman, I'm a whale-catcher," growled Rudi Radtke, showing the printed photo of Berti. He had an unmistakably fat joint in his mouth. "Or is that not a bag, but candy floss? Burning candy floss?" the policeman asked.

Berti was speechless. Were there satellite monitored train compartments?

During the conversation, Hofmann pressed the gun noticeably into Konny's back and whispered: "Not a word, or you'll be living in the cemetery!"

The cult leader's followers closed in. Radtke raised a hand. "The one with the sunglasses," he pointed to the old Berlin punk.

Two policemen disguised in janitor's overcoats immediately rushed up to the punk. They handcuffed him in an instant.

"I am innocent. I have nothing to do with this. I don't like it!"

"Knut? What's going on?" asked one of the girls.

The trader turned his head to the side for a moment. Konny used this moment. The writer turned around. His right hand was clenched in a fist. It whizzed forward and caught Knut Hofmann on the side of the chin. The guru staggered. Rudi Radtke's jaw dropped in astonishment.

"This is a criminal. He threatened me with a gun," Konny shouted loudly.

Radtke drew his weapon. "Freeze!"

Two other policemen, dressed as tourists and pushing suitcases back and forth, also drew their guns. "Police! Freeze!" they shouted as well.

Berti felt dizzy. "I have to sit down. My eyes are going black," he breathed, staggering.

Hofmann felt the blow to his chin. It hurt. The attack came too unexpectedly for him to block it. He had to take his right hand out of his jacket pocket to keep his balance. Unfortunately, he forgot to let go of his revolver.

"Guuun" Radtke warned.

This was too much for Berti's frayed nerves. He could no longer stand on his feet. Stars danced before his eyes. He suddenly became light. Very light. It was the same feeling as when he took the police recruitment test. He fell backwards.

When he opened his eyes this time, he was not in a hospital room. He was still by the train tracks at Munich Central Station. Berti heard voices.

"I've got him!"

"The weapon is secured!"

"He can't breathe. His face is already completely blue."

"The fat guy has to go down! He's crushing the guy!"

Berti's brain was working at full speed. He immediately realized what must have happened. With the presence of mind, he pushed his upper body up, rolled over and slowly stood up. "Did you get him? I knocked him out with my famous backflip. It's an old trick from my sumo days. By the way, the stuff you're looking for is in this case. We had the guy put it there to make sure the police got it. They can check it out."

Konny was perplexed. Radtke stared at Berti with his mouth o-pen.

"You have to get it out yourself. We, my assistant Mr. Wels and I, did not touch it. Fingerprints, DNA samples and so on are only on it from this itinerant preacher Knut and not from us."

Chief Master Rudi Radtke lost track of the situation. "We'll sort everything out at the station."

"By the way, the bag on my face is just a disguise. I'm actually a non-smoker. Allow me, Schwartz. Berti Schwartz. Private detective."

"That's good. What the man says is right," whispered the Berliner. "I only took the bag to disguise the fact that it wasn't a bag."

"Slowly, slowly," pleaded Rudi Radtke. "I'm overwhelmed at the moment. Get everyone to the station!"

With nicotine-stained fingers, the undercover cop swung the filter container of the aging coffee maker to one side. He picked up the glass jug and poured the brown brew into a cup whose dark rims showed a certain laziness when it came to washing up.

"I've checked out the whole squad," said the young police inspector Angela Adler. She looked out from behind a flat screen. "This Konrad Wels and the fat private detective are completely undocumented. They're both fugitives."

"Or have never been caught," Radtke grumbled.

"The other one is a big fish. Knut Hofmann is an alias. His real name is Detlev Ranzinger. He's wanted in three states. His rap sheet is longer than my weekend shopping list. The guy makes his money mainly as a drug smuggler, but he also has all kinds of other crimes under his belt," added Angela Adler.

"The scam with the crazy enlightenment freaks is really good. They're so conspicuous that they're inconspicuous again," grinned Radtke. "Until they cross my path, of course," he added smugly.

Another plainclothes officer burst into the office. "There was a kilo of coke in the car. Neatly tied up."

"Now the two dummies have a problem."

"Rudi, they came in later. 99.99 percent of the coke comes from Amsterdam. It's wrapped in a Dutch newspaper with yesterday's date on it."

"I'm going to get those two queers anyway. Where are they anyway?"

"In the open cell."

"All of them?"

"Except Hofmann, better Ranzinger. He's already in a so-litary cell. We thought it would be better to keep him away from the others."

Radtke grinned. "Good idea, after all, they literally flattened him."

The cell was about as uncomfortable as you could imagine. Three walls were tiled white all the way to the ceiling, the fourth was made of steel bars. The floor was nothing more than cold poured concrete painted with a washable paint. A long bench seated about twenty people.

The two main winners of the crossword puzzle sat close together on the wooden bench. They had taken the seats on the far right. Next to them sat all the Freaks of Enlightenment. The guitar man was already humming another song. However, his instrument was in front of the cell. One of the chicks was babbling endlessly about salvation and miracles. At some point she opened her handbag, took out a Direct Aspirin and swallowed the tablet. Konny approached her and asked for help. She smiled and gave him and Berti a headache tablet each.

"Thank you."

"We have to stick together. That's something. Who would have thought that our Knut was a courier? He must have done it for us. And he'll get us out of here. He can work miracles."

"Sure," grinned Konny. He switched to "pull-through" mode. The old woman babbled and babbled, but he just didn't listen. Instead, he read the inscriptions carved into the wooden bench by her imprisoned predecessors. Sometimes he had trouble deciphering the scribbles, which often resembled ancient cuneiform.

"Cops are dirty!"

"Mehmet is an asshole!"

"Bitch Cops are all grooves!"

"Such intellectual losers," he said quietly and read the slogans on the right. Someone had written "ACAB" in large letters. Underneath it read: "Eight Beers, Eight Cokes," and next to it: "All cops are baseball players."

In turn, another prisoner mocked his stupid fellow inmates. "All cops are bastards, you bastards!"

By the time the headache finally subsided and some color returned to Berti's face, Konny had found the word fuck twenty-seven times. There were eight different ways of spelling it. The regulars in this room must inevitably have an innate tendency to live stupidly.

"What IQ do you have?"

"Me? None at all. I've never bought anything like this before."

"You can't buy that."

"Is that a disease?"

"Are you sick? What did the doctor say?"

"He babbled something about a diagnosis."

"For God's sake. I had that once too. Don't worry about it. The diagnosis is curable."

This is how Konny imagined the usual conversations here in the cell.

A policeman came to the gate. "Schwartz and Wels?"

"Here," said Berti.

Konny raised his hand.

"Come along!"

As they were led into the interrogation room, Berti felt a certain nostalgia for Rack-Romer's dungeon. Until now, he had always thought that there was no colder place on this planet than Romer's office, including the two poles. But today he was proven wrong. They were in a bare room whose formerly white walls had been stained nicotine yellow for eternity in the days when smoking was still allowed in government offices. A cheap lamp hung from the ceiling, its energy-saving bulb emitting the harshest, most eye-straining light in the world. The chairs they were offered to sit on had an estimated 100 years of police service behind them.

"Napoleon sat on them when he marched through Bavaria," Berti whispered.

The large desk in front of them looked completely worn out. A PC, a completely dusty flat screen and a few files completed the office design. On the windowsill was a coffee maker, some filter papers and a packet of coffee. Cheap brand. No plants, nothing personal, bare, bare walls.

Radkte sipped the coffee. He offered none to his two suspects.

"And now one thing at a time. When and where did you board the train? Where is the journey taking you? When did you book it? How do you know Ranzinger? And why do you have a kilo of coke in your suitcase?"

Konny immediately asked a counter question in astonishment. "Who the hell is Ranzinger?"

"What was in the suitcase? Oh, you mean Knut's snow."

"The stuff was in a lady's wig. Long blond hair," Radtke said in a monotone. For the time being, he kept quiet about the Amsterdam newspaper.

"It's an Agnetha Fälstkog wig," Berti improved. Radtke's stupid face made him quickly add: "She was part of ABBA and I'm using the wig for camouflage.

The interrogation went on for more than an hour. Then Radtke checked the travel documents. His next step was to call the notary and talk to Erna Kastenbauer. Both were unnecessary. The young inspector had burst in on the interrogation. "He made a full confession. The two of them were only casual acquaintances. Ranzinger is willing to tell us who was behind it. He's hoping for a lighter sentence.

Rudi Radtke's features slipped, jumped back onto the tracks, and took a turn on the roller coaster. "Is the confession signed?"

"Yes."

The policeman took a deep breath and turned to Berti and Konny. "All right, you two comedians. Then I wish you a safe journey. You can go now."

Konny was angry. With the redeeming news of their proven innocence, he felt he had the upper hand. "Thank you very much! And I'd like to point out that we're not comedians. If anyone has made a fool of themselves here, it's you. You walk around in clothes from the last millennium, you keep saying lines you've stolen from old-fashioned TV shows from the 70s and 80s, and you think you're cool. Your brain is nothing more than a leftover TV Guide from 1979. One more stupid word to us and I'll slaughter you in the press like a fattened sow!"

Radtke was speechless for the first time. He stared at Konny Wels in astonishment.

The author cleared his throat. "Please remove that last statement from the minutes. I just wanted to put the facts on the table, not be insulting."

"Alwright ," he said in dialect. The cop from the station hadn't expected such a verbal attack. He tried to turn the tables. He didn't want to put up with this attack. "Then we'd still have the documented joint in Mr. Schwartz's mouth."

"Consumption is not punishable," the inspector interjected.

Schwartz closed his eyes. He admitted defeat. Had Angela Adler's stupid turkey, straight out of the police academy, blown his last joker?

Konny reacted immediately after a moment of shock. "So I have to inform the press? My friend, Mr. Schwartz, risked his life to overpower an armed drug smuggler. This smuggler threatened me with a gun and they just stood around making stupid comments. And I'm damn proud of Mr. Schwartz for doing your job!"

"Alwright, alwright," Radtke rowed back. Right now he couldn't pin anything on the two guys. It didn't really matter. He had a big fish on the hook in Ranzinger. That was enough for now. He could easily take a little defeat like that. Radtke opened a desk drawer. It rattled as the bottles inside tapped lightly against each other. The cop pulled out a business card. Noticing the frown on the other man's face, Radtke gently pushed the drawer closed, but he couldn't stop it from jingling again. He handed the card to Konny. "Your statements have been taken, there are no charges against you. You're free to go. Take the card with you. If you think of anything later, call me."

Konny took the card and put it in his pocket. "Come on, Berti, let's go."

They both got up. There was no goodbye.

"Give them their luggage back," he said to Angela Adler. "I'll get this Ranzinger and button him up myself."

"Mr. Radtke," Berti said as they stood in the doorway and turned briefly.

Radtke raised his head. "Yes."

"Cheers!"

That was satisfaction. Konny, Commissioner Adler and Berti grinned as they left the office.

"Follow me," the young inspector said. She walked down the corridor. "I'll take you to the evidence room. That's where your luggage is."

"Thank you, you're kind."

The young policewoman smiled. She marched down the corridor once and followed the winding passageway. Finally, she stopped in front of one of the doors and knocked.

"Come in."

She opened the door and stepped into the office. It was large and looked like a lost and found office. An older, bespectacled policeman sat behind some kind of counter. In front of him was a newspaper. "Please?"

The policeman got up and returned with the trolley. He set it down on a table and opened it. "Schwartz and Wels?"

"Yes, we are."

"Then I have your suitcase here. Including the contents, of course. Hi hi," he chuckled and placed a list next to the suitcase. "Then we have four pairs of underpants in XXXL, four pieces in size L, four T-shirts in size ..."

Berti whispers to his friend: „I feel like the Blues Brothers. Do you know that great movie? I mean, whan Jake got out of the prison an Elwood …"

Konny gave Berti a little smile. „Yes, I know the movie. But now we have to hurry up."

„Jep".

Konny looked at the officer. "We have to catch our bus. I see that everything is in the suitcase. You don't have to read the list."

"You have to sign that you've got everything back."

"It's complete. Where do I sign?"

"Both of you," the officer demanded, waving them over.

Two signatures later, they pushed the cart down the long corridor toward the exit. The inspector led the way again. "Don't hold it against Rudi. He's a good policeman. His methods may be strange and he himself is a bit rough around the edges, but Rudi is quite successful."

Konny pressed his lips together for a moment. "He needs to work on himself. I mean, the way he behaved towards us, that's not right. That was dancing on the edge of a huge lawsuit."

"What do you think he should have done? The cocaine was in your suitcase, he had a photo of Mr. Schwartz smoking a joint, and you, Mr. Wels, were standing next to Ranzinger celebrating in the photo."

Konny and Berti looked at each other. "All right," he came back. "You're right again. This can be misinterpreted. We certainly won't complain."

They were at the exit.

"Have a good trip."

"Thank you very much, goodbye."

ai-generated-8802675_1280

Chapter 5
Bonnie and Clyde

They were outside the station building in the bus parking lot. Their bus was gone and Konny was desperate. He paced up and down angrily. He kicked an empty Coke can that was lying around. It clattered to the side and rolled to the curb across the street. For the third time, he read the departure times of the hotel shuttle in the travel documents.

"Missed it! Only because of that cult guru. The bus is gone," he groaned in disappointment.

"I can see that too. When does the next one leave?"

"On Monday."

Berti was perplexed. "M-M-Monday," he stuttered. "Crap! And all because we went to the stupid dining car."

"Why did you smoke that stuff? Without that session and all the stuff that followed, we would have made the bus easily."

"Why did you shoot yourself up with Ramazotti and a couple of beers? Which one of us was attached to this guru and was singing songs with the cult groupies?"

Konny frowned. What Berti had said was true. None of them was really innocent. Arguing didn't help either. With a slightly sad look he asked: "Quit?"

The corpulent detective replied with a grin. "Yes, even! I can't stand this bickering. We'll get to the hotel somehow."

"Good, then let's think."

Berti had a good idea. "It's quite simple, Konny. We just have to catch the bus. Are there any more stops?"

The author took another look at the travel documents. He found the sheet with the route of the shuttle bus, read the stops and then looked at his wristwatch. "It left Starnberg eleven minutes ago. According to the schedule, it should be in Garmisch-Partenkirchen in an hour. After that, it stops twice more in small villages whose names I've never heard before."

"How far is Garmisch from here?" Berti pondered.

"I don't know."

"In any case, Garmisch is damn close to the mountains."

"I'll go to the taxis and find out."

"And I'll run to the information desk and ask how we can get to Garmisch-Partenkirchen by train as quickly as possible," Berti suggested. Although the word "hurry" sounded funny coming from him.

"Another train ride? No thanks, the night trip was enough for me. I really don't want to take the train anymore. Wait for me here."

Berti grimaced a little, but he could understand his friend's motives. "If you insist."

Konny went to the taxi stand. The ivory-colored cars were parked from the side entrance of MunichCentral Station to the adjacent Arnulfstraße. The writer went straight to the first cab in the row. When he opened the door, he was greeted by a mixture of donkey salami and garlic bread. An Arab with a full black beard was biting into a three-story sandwich with relish.

"Where to?" he asked, chewing and barely intelligible. A few pieces of bread crumbled onto a white caftan, while light sauce ran down the side of his mouth.

"Excuse me. I just wanted to know how far Garmisch-Partenkirchen is from here."

"A trip to Garmisch?"

"No thanks, just some information for now."

The taxi driver's face suddenly darkened. "I don't understand anything. I'm a taxi, not an information desk!"

"Where Garmisch?" Konny tried again.

A passenger opened the back door. "Free?"

"I'm free."

"Garmisch?" asked Konny.

"Close the door! It's cold outside," came the gruff reply.

Konny slammed the car door in annoyance. "Asshole," he whispered softly. He didn't want to say it out loud. He was too afraid the guy might be a thug.

"These Southerners freak out at the slightest thing. It's often enough just to look at them," he was told recently by an acquaintance who had gotten into an argument with some Arabs over such a small thing.

"In the worst case, it could be a terrorist in disguise who blows himself up immediately after an insult. Out of revenge," the acquaintance had warned.

"Our brother had to kill him, the infidel called him an asshole.

And on the news you would also hear: "The German writer Konny Wels was the victim of a suicide bomber. The novels of Dr. Kurt Lonedale are being burned all over the world..."

As luck would have it, two Arabs passed Konny. One of them bent down and picked something up. "Excuse me," he said with a heavy accent. "Your wallet fell on the street."

Konny picked up his wallet and silently scolded himself. A guilty conscience began to spread. These two men of Arab descent were very friendly. "Thank you."

"Salem aleikum," they both replied and walked on.

"Thank you very much," the writer called after them again and walked to the next taxi. The driver looked like a typical picture-book Bavarian. He looked like he had just stepped out of an advertising poster for the Oktoberfest. A monstrous beer belly pressed against the steering wheel, his round face adorned with a twirling mustache. The cab driver was dressed in some sort of traditional costume. White shirt, bavarian leather pants, brown jacket. Konny repeated his question.

"To Garmisch? That's a lot of kilometers! The trip is too long for me. I have to get back to my old lady! I worked the night shift and have to get home. I'll have a good pork sandwich for lunch. I'll be fit again by then."

Konny didn't understand a word. From the friendly man's gestures, however, he concluded that the trip was out of the question for him because of the distance, as he had an appointment in the near future. There was no mistaking the wave. At least the linguistically alien Bavarian smiled. The taxi driver looked into a face full of question marks and tried to repeat the sentence in understandable German. "I had the night shift and I'm going home right now because my wife is cooking a roast pork this afternoon. I don't want to be fit by then." He also used his hands to give helpful hints.

Long live sign language.

Konny now realized that even in the middle of Germany, he would need a dictionary if he wanted to communicate with the locals. German-Bavarian was the first step.

Berti joined them. "It's getting fresh. Shouldn't I go to the information desk instead?"

The taxi driver glared at Berti. "Is the beer barrel coming back to you?"

"Excuse me?"

"Are you two getting together?"

A Japanese tourist interrupted the one-sided conversation. "Taxi? Airport?"

The Bavarian nodded. "I have to go. Bye and servus," the native said goodbye with words the former German student couldn't even begin to interpret. Only one thing was certain. It was a polite farewell. Smiling, Konny and Berti raised their hands and waved.

A black African grinned from behind the wheel of the third taxi. Expecting another breakdown, Konny opened the passenger door again.

"Garmisch?" he asked with only one word, so as not to overwhelm the migrant from Africa too much. He was all the more surprised when he heard the answer in good and above all understandable German.

"Hey, that's good, man. I'll give you a fair price, guys."

The man with the Rasta hairstyle was listening to Bob Marley. The song *Buffalo Soldier* was playing. Konny was no longer sure if the guy was from Africa or Jamaica. Either way, he tapped his fingers on the steering wheel to the beat.

"The normal price is way too high, yo. I'll turn this thing off and drive you for 100 euros, man," he said, then sang along. "Sto-len from Africa ... brought do America ..."

Berti nodded. "It can't get any worse than the train ride."

"All right, then. It's the last of our money, but if we get the bus, we won't need any more money for the weekend anyway."

"Exactly! We won't let them ruin our vacation."

"I'm Eddie, man. Well, my name is not Eddie Mann, I just always say ey and man, ey. So my name is just Eddie. Well, not Eddie Just. So just call me Eddie. Really simple, ey, man. All right?"

"Do you smoke weed?" Berti asked unabashedly, shaking his head.

"Not while driving," Eddie grinned.

They both got in the back. Berti was just about to slam the door when a commotion was heard from the concourse. A shot rang out. Shrieks and screams mingled to make a terrible noise. A crowd of people rushed out and spread out in front of the station building. One person ran straight out of the crowd in the direction of the taxi stand.

"Hey, there's action back there. Cool. It's full of action here," Eddie grinned. "Munich is a cool town, yo. Everything here is kind of crazy, man."

Konny turned around. The commotion was gigantic. Only with the famous second glance did he realize who the person was who had broken away from the crowd and was running towards them at lightning speed. He turned white as a sheet. "Hurry, Eddie. Get going!"

Berti slammed the car door. "What's going on?"

Konny's voice cracked. "Hurry, fast Eddie!"

"That's right, man. I'm the Fast Eddie. How do you know my nickname?"

The taxi driver didn't understand what Konny wanted from him. By then it was too late. The guy who was coming straight at them from the station was none other than Detlev Ranzinger. He held a gun in his right hand. It wasn't the silver revolver from before, it was a black pistol. And it was exactly the same model that Rudi Radtke had used when they had been arrested. Konny suspected the worst. His thoughts were not finished when Ranzinger threw open the passenger door, swung onto the seat and pointed the gun at Eddie. "Step on it, you ape!"

The colored man's white teeth gleamed, his eyes rolled once. "Holy shit, yo." Legs moved automatically. Kicked down. Eddie's Mercedes shot forward in one bound. Tires squealed as he turned onto Arnulfstrasse.

Ranzinger gave instructions: "Quickest route to the highway, then south!"

"Hey man, that's cool. I have to go there anyway. What do I get if I set a record time?"

"Don't say anything, bimbo, or I'll put a bullet between your ribs and drive myself."

"Hey man, hey. Always slow down. Just because I'm black doesn't mean you have to insult me."

"White bread ... ha ha ... white bread is really good," Ranzinger laughed. "And if you insult me again, you'll wish you'd never left your Negro kraal." He emphasized the word "me. The kidnapper's voice was serious and unmistakable.

"Hey, that's not fair either, man."

The drug smuggler looked out the window. The chaos at the station was still going on. The fugitive grinned with satisfaction. "I guess I was too fast for the cops. They didn't realize I'd jumped into a cab."

Eddie had turned the cab around and was now heading out of town on Arnulfstrasse towards the highway. "Is Garmisch okay?" he asked, just to be sure.

"Garmisch is great. And don't do anything stupid. If I see you pull the alarm, I'll give you a third nostril with this gun."

"Hey man, don't worry. I have to go to Garmisch anyway. My other passengers want to go there. It's really okay with me."

What had to happen happened. Ranzinger turned around. When he saw who the two passengers in the back seat were, he could hardly believe his luck. "Well, well, well. My two buddies from the dining car. Good to see you again. Kiss my ass, what a lucky guy I am. I'm taking a taxi and there's the Laurel and Hardy of modern times in the back seat."

"Hello Knut, or whatever your name is now," Berti said grumpily.

"Hello," said Konny and raised his right hand. He wiggled his fingers in greeting.

"You know each other? Hey man, what's going on?"

"Muhamed Ali, concentrate on the traffic! If you screw up, I'll kill you. That's a very simple rule. Got it? I'm the boss, you're the worker!"

"Hey, man, I'm black, not stupid! You've shot me almost three times now and insulted me twice as much. Of course I understand."

Ranzinger turned back to his friends. "You two idiots owe me a kilo of coke. Or you could give me 40,000 euros. Or let's say 50,000 Euros. It's just a little extra because of the circumstances. I'll probably have to go on forced leave for a while. That's about the same as short-time work for you".

Berti broke out in a sweat, and Konny closed his mind to life. He believed that the crazy criminal would shoot them sooner or later. "Wh-where are we going to get the money?"

"I don't know, you bums! You two had the great idea of beating me up. You'll get it back anyway."

Ranzinger would have liked to hit the back of the cab, but he had to watch out for both the driver and the two hostages in the back seat. They were not going to surprise him again.

"We're about to hit the highway, ey man."

"Don't always say ey man. It's annoying, you garbage can."

"I'm a cab driver, not a garbage can, man. If you don't like it, find another taxi."

Konny and Berti closed their eyes. They were expecting a gunshot. Instead they heard Ranzinger's voice. "For the last time, you chimpanzee with a driver's license, drive and shut up. Otherwise..."

"Yeah, right, man yo, otherwise you'll put on your Ku Klux Klan hat and whip me to death."

"Hood. The Ku Klux Klan wears hoods, not caps," Ranzinger corrected.

"Cap."

"Hood," he confirmed. At the same time, he aimed at Eddie's head again.

The cabbie rolled his eyes again. "Whatever you say. Hood works too."

"There you go." Ranzinger was satisfied and adjusted the right side mirror. This gave him a better view of the traffic behind him. "Good, no cops in sight. Punch it on the highway, blacky!"

"Call me blacky again and I'll back this car up against a concrete pillar, you cheese fondue."

"You're risking a pretty cheeky lip. I got a good mind to put a bullet in you right now."

Eddie pulled onto the highway and accelerated. Despite the speed limit of 80 km/h, the speedometer needle went up to 160 km/h. "Shoot, stupid!"

"Slow down!"

"Kiss my black ass!"

"I'm warning you!"

"It's me behind the wheel! Now you've fucked up, big mouth!"

Ranzinger buckled his seat belt.

"Scared, ey man?"

"If you really want a mess in your junk car, I'll shoot the fat bastard! I've got a score to settle with those two shooting gallery characters anyway."

Berti suddenly went white as a sheet.

"Just calm down! Nobody benefits if something happens to one of us," Konny tried to calm the situation down.

Berti started to sweat.

"Ha, ha," laughed Ranzinger. He imitated Konny: "...if something happens to one of us." He pointed the gun backwards.

"No," Berti screamed.

"Please don't," Konny shouted.

"Hey man, I'm already slowing down," Eddie relieved his friends and reduced the speed.

"There you go," the hostage-taker said triumphantly. "You three bastards want to gang up on me? I'll beat that out of you. Now, where were we? Oh, yes. With my money. The thing is ...", the drug smuggler explained unabashedly, "... if I don't hand over the coke, or at least the equivalent in cash, to some people by this afternoon, they'll cut me up. Besides, I have a reputation to lose. I'm considered a reliable businessman in the milieu."

"Of course," Konny grumbled, shaking with fear.

Bob Marley's *Kaya* was played.

Ranzinger was visibly annoyed by the reggae. "I can't listen to this monkey music anymore. Do you have anything else?"

"Nope!"

"Is there some USB shit going on?"

The colored cabbie gave the kidnapper a quick look of horror. "No! Hey man. USB stick..." he replied with an appropriately derogatory emphasis and grimace. He pulled both corners of his mouth down extremely. "How do you come up with such garbage? Does your brain actually get unemployment benefits, man? Look around you. This is a real retro cab. I've got a CD player. I want my passengers to arrive cool".

Ranzinger toyed with the idea of just pulling the trigger, but that was too dangerous while driving. "You're risking a pretty big lip. You better think about what you're saying next time, or it's gonna be a bang.

I've never been on unemployment before." Then he hit the eject button. The CD was ejected. "Bob Marley?" the criminal grimaced. "He's already with the voodoo angels teaching them how to smoke weed," he laughed, thinking his joke was good. "Where are your disks?"

"This is my only record! Yo, man, Bob's the greatest."

Ranzinger grimaced. "The greatest was first Al Capone, then Hitler, and then Muhamed Ali. Just to be clear."

Silence.

"What's in the glove box?" the kidnapper asked.

Eddie gave the passenger a quick look. "Yo man, you are a Nazi."

"I'm not a fucking Nazi! I'm an honest freight forwarder. I'm a specialist in special things and stuff."

"You said Hitler was good."

"I didn't!"

Eddie looked briefly in the rearview mirror. "Hey man, guys, why don't you say something?"

Berti was still speechless with fear. Something bad was happening. He was getting hungry.

Konny cleared his throat. "Knut, you, uh, you said that Hitler was one of the greatest."

"Generals! I meant that he was one of the greatest generals. Got it? After all, he defeated Napoleon and Alexander the Great."

Oh my God, it flashed through Konny's mind. How many of these sayings carved into the wooden bench of the cell were probably written by Knut Hofmann, alias Detlev Ranzinger, as he was actually called?

"Okay, he must have been one of the greatest ... geniuses," the author groaned.

"If that's the case, man, then I won't say any more," grumbled Eddie, who now frowned as he looked in the rear-view mirror, this time to watch the traffic behind them. They were still not being followed.

Ranzinger opened the glove box. "What's in there?"

Eddie squinted over. "Stuff from the other drivers, ey man."

The criminal rummaged around. "Chocolate, papers, oh, what have we got here? There are still some wafers here. Let's see what the Munich taxi drivers are listening to. Anyone want chocolate?"

"I'd like a piece?" Berti spoke up. He felt slightly hypoglycemic.

"I thought so. Fetty wants to eat. All right! Here's a piece." Ranzinger handed it to him. At the same time, he didn't let Eddie out of his sight. "You're not getting any," he said to him. "It's not white chocolate, you'll just bite your fingers off. Ha ha ha," he roared, laughing at his great joke. But once again he was the only one.

Eddie was mad. Really mad. "That's enough, you poseur asshole with a gun. You can kill whoever you want, I'll crash the car into the next obstacle," he grumbled. At the same time, the taxi driver slammed the accelerator down. The engine roared. The speedometer needle danced steadily to the right.

Ranzinger, still laughing at his joke, suddenly became deadly serious and pointed the barrel of his gun at the driver. "I warned you, blacky!"

"My name is Eddie, and I don't care which one of us you shoot. We'll all be dead after the accident anyway."

"Eddie, he doesn't mean it. He's probably a Tourette's patient. You know that disease where you have to use swear words all the time? It's called Tourette's Syndrome."

The road ahead of them was still clear.

"Hey man, I warned him!"

Ranzinger was furious. "What am I supposed to have? The toupee disease? You've got a massive bird, you wise guy. I'm perfectly healthy. And my hair is real. It's not a cap on my head."

"Eddie, don't you see? Knut is different from us. His problem lies behind his forehead."

"How am I different, you brainiac?" It worked in Ranzinger's head. "Yes, maybe I have this thing syndrome. But when I went to the doctor the other day, he didn't find anything. It was a urologist, though. I had to get some medicine for my pipe. I must have fucked the wrong girl.

No one responded.

"I see a nice bridge pier," Eddie remarked, maintaining his high speed.

Ranzinger turned around. "Hey, smart guy, is this thing bad? I mean, if I have it, am I going to die?"

"Hey man, what kind of disease is this?" Eddie also asked.

Konny tried to explain it differently. "If someone dies, it's bad for the others, but not for them. If someone is stupid, it's exactly the same."

"Exactly," Berti squeezed out, for whom the pace was much too fast.

"I see," the taxi driver nodded. "Tell him to apologize and I'll drive on as normal."

"I'm not doing anything. Besides, I don't get it. What if you die and you are stupid?"

An old VW Beetle appeared in front of them, desperately trying to pass a truck. They approached the vintage car at a menacing speed.

"Eddie," Konny warned.

"First the apology," the colored man grumbled in the style of an affected movie diva.

"Fuck him," grinned Ranzinger in a fit of suicidal madness. "And so can you with your sick, dead and stupid talk.

"Well, bye guys, it was great to meet you," the cab driver screeched. "Hey Mr. Bob Marley, man, build me a welcome bag up there."

The distance to the Beetle was getting smaller and smaller. The point of no return - the point at which an accident was unavoidable - was soon reached.

Ranzinger watched the driver closely. Eddie kept a straight face. He kept his eyes on the VW Beetle in front of him and got a kind of tunnel vision. His right leg remained on the depressed gas pedal. The speedometer needle had reached its maximum deflection. Now he realized this was no bluff. This crazy cabbie was deadly serious. Ranzinger swallowed. His Adam's apple was moving up and down. He wondered if a shot in the colored man's leg would help.

Nonsense, he has to brake with the same foot.

It didn't help.

The two comedians in the back seat have their eyes closed and are holding hands. The monkey behind the wheel is serious. Fuck!

"Okay, I'm sorry," the criminal breathes out, barely audible.

Eddie kept up the pace. "I didn't hear it."

"Sorry, man," the hostage-taker repeated at a normal volume.

"Eddie! My name is Eddie!"

Now Ranzinger panicked. "Bloody hell. Sorry, Eddie! I'm so sorry, Eddie! Now slow down," he shouted.

The cabbie took his foot off the accelerator and slammed on the brakes with all his might. The centrifugal force pushed the passengers forward and backward. The vehicle in front of them grew larger and larger. They were still approaching at an alarming rate.

"Can you slow down any more?" shouted Berti.

"No way!" Konny shouted.

"Shit," came out of Ranzinger's mouth. He was about to lose his life. I wish I'd apologized earlier.

Eddie gripped the steering wheel, literally pushing himself into the seat as he continued to press the brake pedal. The spacing of the anti-lock brakes had been noticeable for some time. The distance from bumper to bumper was less than ten centimeters before the speed of the two vehicles was finally equalized and the cab slowly fell back.

We made it!

The truck driver honked. The two occupants of the VW Beetle gesticulated wildly with their hands.

"Ey man, ey, what a horny driver I am. I'm in complete control of my retro cab," boomed Eddie. "For a moment I thought I was going to hit Bob Marley and we were going to pull a mega-big bag."

"Are we dead?" asked Berti, opening his eyes.

"Everything's fine," Konny reassured him.

"You can be really annoying. Were you once a woman?" Ranzinger asked the driver.

Eddie wanted to speed up again, but the fleeing police officer immediately calmed him down.

"Well, that was a joke. I'm allowed one more joke, right?"

The traffic beep sounded. We interrupt this program to bring you an important police bulletin. Twenty minutes ago, armed felon Detlev Ranzinger ..."

"Criminals, they've got their asses open," grumbled the gangster. He rummaged through the music CDs, picked out a Tote Hosen record and popped it into the CD player. "Finally something groovy. Makes the bear dance."

There was silence for a few miles. When the song *Bonnie and Clyde* came on, Ranzinger turned up the volume.

"Great, that's my song. From the Band *Tote Hosen*."

Though he was anything but sure of the lyrics, the drug runner sang along in part. "... *we'll kill three, four cops... put your head on my shoulder... cause we're Bonnie and Cly-de...*"

"Bob is better! Hey man, who listens to songs about bank robbers?"

"Shut up! I want to hear the song."

The smuggler fell silent. He looked at Eddie, looked back at the back seat and thought. Wrinkles had formed on his forehead. Suddenly he cheered: "That's it! Eddie, you're wonderful! We'll send one of the two warm brothers to a bank. Then I'll have my ashes and you can go."

"What?" exclaimed Konny in amazement. "We don't have that much money."

"I'm not talking about robbing accounts, you cotton ball thrower, I'm talking about robbing a bank."

"Without me," Berti sulked. He crossed his arms demonstratively over his chest and turned to his left to stare out the window.

"It's either a bank robbery or I kill one of you brain farts."

"This is blackmail!"

"You're a real smart guy. I wouldn't have thought of that," Ranzinger remarked. "So what are you going to do? Turn me in? Hey hey hey," he laughed. "You zeros heard what I said. There's nothing to discuss. I don't talk, I act."

"I noticed that on the train yesterday. About dear brothers and such," Berti commented. He was still speaking in a sulky tone.

"Hey fatty, that was my job. This is different."

"Hey man, how is that supposed to work with the bank? They're going to run when they get to the bank," Eddie interjected.

"Thanks Eddie," Konny said sarcastically.

Eddie checked his mistake. "Sorry man. I didn't mean it."

"You must think I'm an idiot. Of course you're going in there alone," Ranzinger said to Konny. "Your buddy can't really step on the gas when it comes to towers. He'll stay here as a hostage. If you don't come back, then..." Ranzinger pointed the barrel of the pistol at Berti.

"Ahhhhhh ..." he screamed in panic. He had imagined the hard detective life differently.

"Drop the gun," Konny demanded.

Ranzinger pulled the gun back. At the same time he looked at Konny. "And now what? Make up your mind! But quickly! I'm getting a stiff neck from turning around all the time."

Konny was desperate. "I can't do it."

"Boom, he's gone," laughed Ranzinger.

"Okay, I can try."

"Konny, that's way too dangerous. And then you'll have to go to jail."

"Berti, what am I supposed to do?"

Ranzinger laughed. "Simple, you go to prison with me. You can share a cell and it doesn't matter who drops the soap in the shower. Ha ha ha."

Eddie also laughed and casually tapped the steering wheel. "Cool banana, guys. This is a really fucked up cab ride, man. Nobody believes us."

"Next exit, you'll bug of from the highway. We'll leave a hole in the highway. There's got to be a bank in some small town. We'll rob it, then continue on to Garmisch."

Silence.

Konny pointed to Ranzigner's gun. "Will you give me the gun then?"

"My gun? Are you crazy?"

Shrugging in the back seat. "How am I supposed to rob the bank?"

"Don't you have any brains? Put your hand in your pocket, pull your finger out, and the little man's gun is ready."

"That'll never work," Konny doubted.

The criminal raised his eyebrows. Then he looked at Berti, pointed the gun at him and said: "Boom, he's gone."

Berti jumped and Konny raised both arms and waved them away. "All right, all right," he huffed. "I'll try."

Eddie had an idea. "Hey man, you can write notes like that too. I saw it on 'Cold Case XY Unsolved'. With a threat on it. Then you'll get the money."

Ranzinger agreed. "Yes, this option could also work. Might be better for you, Sissy." He rummaged in the glove compartment and found a receipt pad and pen. "Here. You can practice your lines. You're a writer, ha ha ha."

Konny walked over to the cab driver. "Very funny, Eddie. Why don't you go inside if you already know such clever tricks?"

"Hey man, sorry. I have to drive, besides I can get away. Because I don't care if it goes boom, ey man."

Ranzinger grumbled again. "Don't you have a sense of humor? Why don't you leave the chick alone?"

Eddie shook his head. This guy is incorrigible, he thought, and put on his blinker. They left the highway and drove through two small villages, followed by a long stretch of country road. As they rolled through the center of the next community, they spotted the offices of a *Raiffeisen Bank* branch.

"We'll take it," Ranzinger decided on the spur of the moment.

Eddie stopped and parked across the street from the bank, in one of the three free guest parking spots at a closed pub.

Konny looked at his watch. "The bank probably isn't open yet. It's just..."

"Shut up!"

Albert Wagenbauer was born here, went to school here, and after graduation started his apprenticeship as a banker in this branch. Three people applied for the job. He was hired. Today he is 52 years old and a year ago he was appointed branch manager of *Raiffeisenbank*. He is chairman of the shooting club, treasurer of the choir and deputy chairman of the community gardening association. By the time he was 28, he lived in his own house, by 30 he was married, and by 36 he was the proud father of three children.

He was the quintessential village professional. Next year, he would go for the crown and run for mayor.

At the moment, he was working on something else entirely. He had his eye on his new employee. Her name was Anita Miller, she was slim as a rail, had a tight ass, and had been working in his store since September. He had taken a shine to the blonde thoroughbred. He had asked her out so many times in his head.

Nowadays it wasn't a problem for a successful man to cheat. Everyone does it, he thought, comparing himself to pop stars and politicians.

Sure, she was more than twenty years younger than him, but he was still good-looking and convinced that he was a heartthrob. He and the man in the Coke commercial were on the same level. Except for his figure, of course. But he was a bank manager and the Coke man was just a beverage delivery man. One point for him.

Today was the day. Albert Wagenbauer had chilled a bottle of champagne especially for him to drink with his employee after work. He was going to blow her away with his charm.

When I pull down the knot of my tie, undo the top button of my shirt, and stand in front of her with two glasses and the bottle in my hand ... wow. She will melt. A glass of champagne is half the battle. Guaranteed!

He didn't skimp on the champagne either. The store manager thought five euros was reasonable.

I don't have to come up with the cheap stuff, he was convinced.

His anticipation was great. Anita happened to be wearing her dirndl. Wide cut.

Her bust is a dream.

Wagenbauer wasn't quite sure whether it was her feminine intuition or just a twist of fate. After all, he hadn't told her about the planned drink. Why should he? He looked stunning and was the best match in the community.

His eyes kept falling on Ms. Millers curves. He walked into the counter room and sat down at the desk while she opened the front door of the store for customers.

Wagenbauer leaned back.

This is the start of a good day. Something great is going to happen today. I am a hero, a star, a Casanova, a dream man.

"Done," said Konny. His hands trembled slightly.

"Let me read it," demanded Ranzinger.

"No!"

"Give me that piece of paper, you fart face!"

Konny handed the receipt pad forward out of necessity. Ranzinger took it and read it aloud. "Dear bank employees, please don't be alarmed. Unfortunately, I have been forced to rob this branch. A man named Ranzinger has taken my partner hostage."

"Hey man, what about me?" Eddie grumbled. "I'm a hostage too."

"I had limited space," Konny defended himself. "This isn't A4 stationery, it's a small receipt pad."

While the two argued, the hostage-taker's cheeks and ears turned bright red. A bad sign. "You must be trying to trick me, you rubber finger," he said indignantly. "Trying to sell me out, huh? I'll put a bullet between your ribs in a minute, you flat-head."

Eddie cleared his throat. "It's called a flat-nose pliers. If you use the tool as an expletive, it's flat-nose, not flat-brush."

Ranzinger exploded. "You donkey driver. I'll say what I want! Got it?"

"Ey man, ey. You can call the Turks or the Balkan pepeople donkey-drivers. Camel drivers are the Arabs, and I'm a ..."

"Cotton picker," the criminal added.

"My ancestors are not American slaves. I come from ..."

"I don't give a damn what kraal you come from. As far as I'm concerned, you're a donkey-driving cotton picker and nothing else. Now shut your mouth or it'll fall down and I'll drive myself, you chocolate Santa Claus."

Eddie was seething with rage. His hands clenched into fists. He would like to punch this right-wing racist out of the cab.

Berti intervened. "Touret! Always remember that. It's a handicap."

Eddie relaxed. Ranzinger gave Berti an angry look. "You dumbling on legs want to take a bullet too, do you?"

Konny intervened. "I'm an honest man. I can't rob a bank. What else should I write on the note?"

Ranzinger was about to go crazy. "Man oh man, what kind of wimps are you three? You have to do everything yourself."

"Hey man, should I go again? To Garmisch to finish the job?"

"Just shut up, blacky! Can't you see that?"

It was too much for the taxi driver. "That's enough. I won't take any more insults. One more bad word about me or a racist remark and I'm getting out. Then you can shoot me for all I care."

"It's all right," the hostage-taker soothed. "Chill out."

The *Toten Hosen* blared in the background: *"... I don't want to go to paradise if the way there is so stony ..."*

"I see," said Ranzinger, "I have to do it myself. If I send blac ..., Eddie," he quickly improved, "to the bank, he'll run away. The fat nose is too fat and can't run fast enough, and the gadfly novelist is a complete wimp. He can't even write a threatening note. If you had to write a James Bond novel, they'd throw cotton balls at you."

"Hey man, you want me to drive again?"

"Shut up, Eddie!" Ranzinger corrected himself and shifted down a gear. "Now, ... I mean ... please shut up."

All three hostages looked at the criminal. Ranzinger waved his gun around, pointing at all three men in turn. "I have an idea. We go in together. You three bagpipes will walk in front of me and enter the bank in a well-behaved manner. Once inside, you will stand neatly to one side. I'll take care of the robbery, and then all four of us will walk gently back to the taxi. Got it?"

"And if not, ey man?"

"Anybody runs off the track, my gun barks. He'll catch a bullet. And if you don't stop talking ey man and shit, you'll be the first. At some point I have to start killing one of you so that the others understand. I'm tired of threatening to do it and you still do what you want."

"Well, I'm with you," Eddie said. He had a feeling that this racist was deadly serious. To hide the fact that his hands were shaking slightly, the cabbie gripped the wheel tightly. His coolness had evaporated under the circumstances. "But I'll stay in the background. As a protest!"

"All right, Knut. I'll come too and follow your instructions," Konny said.

"My name is not Knut. That was a stage name. My name is Detlev!"

"Detlev, I'm in," Berti also confirmed.

The three hostages got out with weak knees. It began to snow. A light wind came up and played with the white flakes, making them dance in the air before they fell silently to the ground.

"And another warning to everyone. I'll kill anyone who even thinks about escaping! Don't do anything stupid! Forward. Let's go inside."

"Hey man, what about masks? They'll recognize us."

"No one here knows your face, Black Beauty."

"Hey man, that's the first nice sentence I've heard out of your mouth," Eddie grinned.

"Black Beauty was a horse," explained Berti, who knew the series of the same name because his older sisters idolized the horse.

Eddie suddenly lost his smile and gave Ranzinger a dirty look. "What an asshole. No one would believe I robbed a bank with a racist," he muttered, barely intelligible.

"Drive faster, you evolutionary brake!"

They crossed the street.

"Everybody in the bank. Stay in front of me. Inside the bank, stand to one side. If any of you make a sound..." the hostage-taker said nothing more. "You can put your sweatshirts on over the food in there. That's enough camouflage."

"Hey man, I've got a shirt on. Besides, it's cold. It's snowing. Can you please hurry up? I want to get back in the warm cab."

"You have the least to worry about, Eddie. The pictures on the security camera are black and white. You're unrecognizable unless you're smiling."

Eddie was seething with anger. "Do either of you have a knife in your pocket? I'm going to cut this guy's balls off," he whispered to Konny.

"Unfortunately not."

"Shut up. I'm the only one talking."

"It means only one. There is no superlative of only," Eddie improved.

"You're just as much of a smartass as the king of trivial literature. I say what I want, and anyone who doesn't get it ..."

Berti finished the sentence. "I know, he'll get a bullet between the ribs."

"Exactly."

They entered the bank. Ranzinger masked himself by pulling the collar of his turtleneck over his face. The others remained unmasked. He immediately let his eyes wander.

No customers, a counter, a cashier's room, secured with bulletproof glass. There was a camera on the ceiling, pointing toward the checkout area. Not far away is a second camera filming the exit. Everything is clear.

"We're on the air, guys," he groaned.

Berti felt worse than he had ever felt in his life. He heard his father's voice in his head. "Berti, you won't do that! If you come back, I'll punch you in the face!"

Konny's knees were weak. His stomach began to rebel. He would have liked to sink into the ground in shame. On the other hand, it was a way to draw attention to himself and their situation.

Use your brain, Konny. Come on, think, shot through his head.

Eddie didn't think about anything. He wasn't aware of any guilt. The taxi driver even hoped that the madman would pay for the ride when he stole the money from the bank. In any case, the meter was running.

A young and very attractive blonde in Bavarian dress came up to the counter. An older gentleman with glasses, suit and tie sat at the counter.

The woman greeted the four men politely. "Good morning, how can I help you?"

Eddie, Konny and Berti stood off to the side, as Ranzinger had instructed. When the man at the desk gave them a quick glance, Eddie shrugged apologetically.

Konny pulled out Rudi Radtke's business card. He imitated a telephone with his thumb and little finger and held it to his ear. At the same time, he pointed to the small card. But the banker lowered his eyes again.

When the blonde noticed that Ranzinger had a gun in his hand and his face was half covered, she knew an attack was imminent. "Help!" she cried in panic.

That was Ranzinger. "This is a robbery, darling! Get the money out, or there'll be a bang. And you, fruitcake, behind the desk, keep your fingers up. If you press the alarm button, I'll kill you! And since I don't know which finger you used to set off the alarm, I'll cut them all off! Got it?"

Mr. Wagenbauer raised his hands demonstratively. Dark spots grew under his armpits. Anxious sweat.

"We have some money in the safe. I can get it. Our machines haven't been converted. You're in luck."

"Stand up to the breast monster, you pants-wetting bastard!"

Wagenbauer held his hands up and did not lower them as he stood next to Ms. Miller.

"Please don't rape me," pleaded the bank clerk, who had noticed that Ranzinger's eyes had lingered deep in her cleavage several times.

"Don't worry doll, you'd be worth it, but I'm not in the mood right now due to an extreme incident last night."

"N-n-take the g-g-money," Wagenbauer stuttered. The safe is open. Right t-t-there in the back."

His fear mixed with the desire to rub against Frau Miller's breasts. The opportunity was good. He seized the opportunity, stood in front of the employee and moved extremely close to Anita Miller. Her breasts pressed against his back.

I am so cool.

The branch manager saw his heroic deed reported in the press. "Wagenbauer overpowers bank robber with his bare hands. The nation's lifesaver protected his employee."

His mental movie began. He lay naked in bed. Anita Miller pressed herself close to him.

At that moment, the banker took a step back. The bank manager lost contact with her breast. At the same time the mental movie faded.

Fuck! I have to do something.

If he didn't want to lose her, he had to act and take a chance. Yes, that was the secret. He had to do something to impress her. Without a second thought, he said with death-defying courage: "Leave Mrs. Miller alone!"

He would have liked to apologize to the bank robber as soon as he said it.

Was that too hard? Oh my God. He looks at me.

"Shut up, you bastard. I'm not interested in this chick. I've shagged more women than you know by first name."

The manager was speechless, Anita Miller was relieved.

Ranzinger turned to his three taxi hostages. "Do you need a special invitation? Come on, one of you go to the safe and get the money out. But no paint shit!" He looked at Wagenbauer again. "You got any paint shit in there? If you do, I'll kill you," he threatened, pointing the gun demonstratively at the branch manager's head.

This was clearly too much for the cool Albert Wagenbauer. His knees trembled and his pants turned dark at the crotch.

Ranzinger stepped back in disgust. "Man, oh man. You pissed yourself. That's disgusting. And now tell me, is the money okay?"

"Y-Y-Yes! We don't have any security packs here in the safe," came the whiny voice. He was embarrassed. It was a nightmare. Surely it was just a dream. He would wake up later and find himself in his bed at home. He took a deep breath. He closed his eyes and opened them.

No! It's real. How do I get out of the wet pants act?

Konny went to the safe. The heavy door was only ajar. He pushed it aside. "Where shall I put the money?"

Ranzinger went crazy. "Haven't you pretzel salters got anything?" He couldn't believe it. "You really are too stupid to rob a bank. I can't believe it. There are thousands of taxis in Munich and I get one with three full pickles."

"It was your idea to rob the bank, Detlev," Berti countered.

"Shut up, you coati! Don't name names."

"I'll take that," Konny called, picking up Mr. Wagenbauer's briefcase. He opened it and emptied its contents onto the desk.

There was no end to the embarrassment for the poor store manager.

That too, he thought, as a copy of the St. Pauli News landed on his desk for all to see. Headline: Fat things are there to play with!

"A customer left them lying around, I wanted to throw them away," he whispered to Ms. Miller.

Her expression was quite the opposite. She also smelled of urine. She wrinkled her nose and kept her distance. Albert Wagenbauer started to hate the bank robbers. A new headline was forming in his mind, one that would appear in tomorrow's newspapers. He closed his eyes again. He didn't want to read this headline.

Unnoticed, Konny placed the business card of the Munich police officer Radtke on Wagenbauer's desk. Ranzinger had just turned his attention to Eddie, Berti and the two bank employees. In a flash, Konny grabbed a pen and hastily scribbled a few words on the card. Call hostage! Help!

"Hurry! We're not invited to a coffee party. Besides, it's starting to smell bad in here. It smells like a train station bathroom. Only the toilets are missing. Ha ha ha," he laughed.

Wagenbauer's beautiful world collapsed like a house of cards. That was the end for Anita Miller. She would never let him touch her again. On the contrary. The mishap here at the bank was his downfall. He would become the new laughing stock of the whole community. It would certainly cost him a lot of new home loans and, on top of that, his position as mayor. His regulars' evening would probably be over as well. In the future, he would do his shopping in the county seat.

Should I sell the house and move away?

Yes, a good idea. Somewhere where he wasn't known. Those bank robbers had ruined him. He would probably offer a reward of 1,000 euros out of his own pocket for the arrest of this gang.

"I have the money," Konny called.

Ranzinger squinted at the author. "Everything?"

"Everything that was there."

"Get out!" He pointed the gun at the two bankers. "No cops, no alarms! If I see you move in the next twenty minutes, I'll come back and kill you!"

"U-understood," stammered Wagenbauer.

Anita Miller nodded.

"Well, goodbye and thanks for the money."

They hurried out of the *Raiffeisenbank* branch and walked to the taxi at a normal pace. Eddie got behind the wheel, Berti and Konny got back in the back. Ranzinger rolled down the collar of his sweater and uncovered his face. He got in on the passenger side. By now it was snowing extremely hard. The snow had already stopped, covering everything in a soft white.

"Go on, drive," Eddi was urged. "Give me the money," the bank robber demanded of Konny.

Eddie turned around and drove back to the highway. They were to continue on to Garmisch-Partenkirchen. Ranzinger took the CD from the player. He searched for a local radio station and got stuck on *Bayern 1.*

Konny handed over the booty. "Here's the money."

The bank robber put the briefcase on his lap. He opened it carefully. "You have to be very careful. There are some nasty paint bombs. When they go off, you look like you've fallen into a paint pot. And the stuff doesn't come off. I once did four years for shit like that."

He opened the bag. The snowfall took on the proportions of a blizzard. Eddie could only drive 60 mph. And it was going down.

Ranziniger groaned. He was totally disappointed. "Kids, kids, what are you doing? That's just ten big rags and some little shit."

"That's all there was," Konny defended himself.

After the robbers left the branch, Albert Wagenbauer was the first to react. "I should have knocked him out. I mean, the guy with the gun.

129

I was so close," he hissed confidently, pressing the thumb and forefinger of his right hand together. It was as if he had an imaginary bank customer sitting in front of him. He had to win this meeting. Either he would win, or he could close up shop. Wagenbauer was a winner.

Anita Miller was unimpressed. "Would you like to clean up before I call the police?"

"I don't know how he did it, but somehow he splashed me with water."

"The water smells suspiciously like urine. You don't have to make excuses. My partner and I know why we're gay. I used to be a geriatric nurse and I know what pissed pants smell like. That was one reason I retrained as a banker. There are only two things I'm afraid of. One is getting raped, and the other is horny men hitting on you and stalking you because they think they're irresistible."

"Y-y-you're l-l-lesbian?"

"Sure! Why are you stuttering? Didn't you know? I had the feeling that everyone in the village was already talking about us? Me and my girlfriend, that is."

Albert Wagenbauer's world had just completely collapsed. He changed his clothes, drank the bottle of champagne alone and thought about his future. His bubble burst with a big bang.

Anita Miller walked over to the desk. There was a business card next to the phone. She read Konny's words and was astonished. Call - Hostage! Please help!

She thought for a moment and pressed the alarm button, even though Mr. Wagenbauer signaled that it would be better to wait a few more minutes. Bravely, she picked up the phone and dialed the number on the business card.

"Radtke, Munich Police Station."

"This is Anita Miller. Our bank branch has just been robbed."

Radtke was astonished. "The display here shows a number from out of town. Why are you calling here in Munich? How did you get this number?"

"There were four guys. One with graying hair and an orange sweater, a fat guy with a Norwegian sweater, a good-looking, athletic guy, and a black guy. The one with the orange sweater had a black gun."

The plainclothesman sobered up at once. "Where exactly are they? I'll be right there!"

Rudi Radtke was digesting the most embarrassing moment of his life. He didn't care about formalities. In short, he didn't care whether Munich or some police station in the Bavarian Oberland was responsible for this reported robbery. That sewer rat from Ranzinger had almost broken his nose. A bloody piece of absorbent cotton was still stuck in his nostril.

The guy had just jumped over the desk, thrown a punch, and pulled the service pistol from the civilian investigator's holster. Laughing and cursing constantly, Ranzinger topped it off by handcuffing Radtke to the desk with his own handcuffs. Then he marched out of the office and stormed off.

Radtke was furious. It took four shots of corn, a quick beer, and an hour of trying to explain things to the boss before he finally got the phone call he needed. Nothing and no one could stop him now.

"Get the car! We're going to the country," he shouted to the young inspector Angela Adler.

She was also the one who rescued him from his predicament and promised to keep quiet among his colleagues.

"What's going on? Where are we going?"

"Our three friends and an accomplice robbed a bank."

"What do you mean, our three friends and another guy?"

Radtke laughed dirty and smug. "The two homos are supposed to be cross? They had it up to their ears."

The cop shrugged. "Don't talk so disparagingly about them just because they're a couple of men. I found them sympathetic."

"They're bank robbers!"

Angela Adler shook her head slightly. "Let's wait and see. Where are we going?"

"Towards Garmisch."

"That's no longer our territory."

Radtke stood up. "I don't give a damn! I'm going where my gun is."

The inspector grabbed the car keys. "And what does the boss say?"

"When we come back with Ranzinger and the other three bank robbers, he won't say anything."

She thought for a moment. Inspector Bro' was more inclined to refuse, but a mixture of compassion for her colleague, the thought of being able to prove Berti and Konny's innocence, and the hunting fever for Ranzinger kept her from doing so. Somewhat hesitantly, the policewoman finally agreed. "All right then! But only because I feel sorry for you. Besides, you can't drive anymore."

"Why can't I drive?"

"Because we have a 0.5 blood-alcohol limit. And I don't even want to talk about the parts per mille above that in your bloodstream."

Radtke made a dismissive gesture and tried to close his drawer as inconspicuously as possible. "Oh, 0.5 alcohol level is ridiculous. You'll get it in a minute."

"For normal people, maybe. With you, it's more like you wouldn't have to drink for three days to get to 0.5 per mille."

Radtke turned red. "Who said that?"

Bro' just pointed at the desk. "Shall I open your drawer?"

That was a low blow for the civilian investigator. He was sure no one knew about his little secret stash.

How did this stupid turkey know there were only a few bottles in there?

Well, he had exaggerated a bit in the last few days. Maybe the last few weeks too, but what she had just said was a cheek.

"What now?" asked Angela, the car key dangling from her fingers. "Shall we?"

He would take revenge for this insolence another time. This time it was 1:0 for his young colleague. Radtke gave in. "Yes, let's get out of here. We'll get this gang."

When the Munich police patrol arrived on the scene, two police cars from the local police station were already at the door. It was snowing heavily. Radtke got out, slammed the door, turned up the collar of his coat, and went into the bank. His colleague was waiting in the unmarked car. An older policeman with an oversized beer gut stood in front of Wagenbauer and took his statement. The branch manager was dressed in a jacket, shirt, tie, and sweatpants. Radtke's first thought was that the country people were crazy. "I knew the country bumpkins were all full of it," he muttered when he saw the store manager's clothes.

"Hello," Rudi said confidently to his beer-bellied colleague in uniform, waving his badge.

The big bucket-bearer turned around, recognized the document and uttered a surprised "Servus".

"Radtke, Munich Police."

"What do you want from us?"

Anita Miller's face suddenly appeared. She was sitting on a chair behind the jogger. "Radtke? Munich police? We spoke on the phone," she said loudly.

"Ah, the one on the business card?" muttered the beer-bellied policeman.

"Yes," said Mrs. Miller.

"He put it on my desk," explained Wagenbauer.

"The colleague?" asked the local policeman.

"No, one of the perpetrators."

"Oha! The perpetrator!"

"No oha, dear sir..." Rudi Radtke intervened.

"Sandlinger. Chief Constable Sandlinger from the local police station," the beer-bellied man introduced himself by name.

"I know the perpetrators," Radtke hissed unequivocally. "That's why I'm here."

Anita Miller had stood up and was now standing between Radtke, Sandlinger, and Wagenbauer. "That was somehow strange. I immediately had the feeling that something wasn't right. The one guy who had pulled his sweater over his face was the only one of the four who was armed. He had one of those black..."

"Besides, we're not talking about the gun. We know he uses a Heckler & Koch pistol."

Sandlinger was astonished. "But you comrades from the city are well informed."

Radtke ignored the patrolman's remark and probed the witness. "What was strange?"

"The other three were afraid of the actual robber. They stood off to the side, unmasked and inactive. It was as if they had to obey him."

The manager clears his throat. "One of the three went to the safe. He took the money and put it in my briefcase."

"That's right," Antia Miller confirmed. "The magazine fell out. I think it was the St. Pauli News."

"The copy was left by a customer," added Wagenbauer.

He got a dirty look from his colleague. "Oh yeah? And who pissed in their pants?"

Bright lights flashed. Someone asked several questions. The reporter from the county courier was standing behind Rudi Radtke.

Albert Wagenbauer blushed. He couldn't stand the greaser. Just last week he had happily turned down a loan application. Now he had to act. Act quickly, before something embarrassing appeared in the press. "Mr., uh ... Schemmel, is it?" Wagenbauer asked the journalist.

"Right."

The branch manager purred and grinned thinly. "I lobbied the head office on your behalf and got the green light after all. Your loan will probably be approved." No answer. The carter repeated: "I personally lobbied for it. We'll just have to talk about it again later."

Mrs. Miller intervened. Mr. Schemmel's loan application? I put it in the Schretter yesterday at your request," she wondered.

"Can we finally get on with the interrogation?" urged Radtke. "Who pissed himself, and what about the safe?"

Wagenbauer wanted to die at that moment. *Udo Jürgens'* song from *New York* came to mind. Where was his credit card? He had never been to San Francisco with ripped jeans. He didn't even own ripped jeans. Should he just leave?

Anita Miller chatted, Sergeant Sandlinger took notes, and Rudi Radtke listened. When the banker finished, the plainclothes investigator asked: "Let me get this straight. You think one guy took the other three guys hostage?"

"Yes, Mr. Commissioner."

"First Sergeant."

"First Sergeant then. It doesn't matter. The black man was the driver of the cab, the other two had to sit in the back. They drove off to the highway. I saw that from the window and called them immediately. Mr. Wagenbauer wanted us to wait with the call.

The journalist grinned, and the manager sank back in his chair.

Radke asked the pot-bellied colleague. "Is the manhunt underway?"

134

"Ongoing! But most of the patrols are tied up with accidents in this weather. It rumbles like crazy when it snows. The helicopter can't take off anyway."

"I'll find them!"

Eddie drove behind a truck. The left passing lane was deserted. It was now snowing heavily. The swirl of flakes was so thick that the speedometer needle did not exceed 20 mph.

"Golly, this is such miserable weather. Does Mother Holle have to shake out the bedding today?" grumbled Ranzinger. "Get off the highway. I have to pee."

"Hey man, the highway is ending soon anyway. In case you haven't noticed, we're about to get on the country road. It's only a few kilometers to Garmisch."

"We'll turn into a quiet side road later anyway."

"Where to?"

"Who cares? The main thing is to get off the main road. I need to piss like a bull."

"All right. And if I don't, you'll put a bullet between my ribs again, man. I know how crass your reaction is."

"Save your stupid comments, you flat-earther! I can stumble into your cab if you really want me to."

Eddie spotted a turnoff and turned on his blinker. "Don't worry. You can leave your white earthworm in there. I see a fork in the road, ey man. At least you learned how to use the flat pliers."

"Earthworm, ha ha ha," Ranzinger laughed and thought for a moment whether he should make a comparison ... No, it flashed through his mind. Because of the rumors about the colored loins, he discarded this thought and simply added: "Shut up!

The taxi driver, who was already paying extreme attention to the road conditions, slowed down even more. "Are there no plows around here? If it keeps snowing like this, we're going to get stuck. And in the middle of the road."

The Mercedes skidded as it turned onto the narrow country road.

"Watch out!" shouted Ranzinger.

"Hey, man! I'm watching out. Look at the color of my skin. I don't know how to drive on snow. There ain't no snow where I come from, man yo!"

"Please stop arguing," Konny tried to mediate. "Let the man do his business and then we'll go to Garmisch. With a little luck we'll get the bus and Mr. Ranzinger can go to his business friends."

"And I get the money for the trip."

After they passed through a village, Eddie kept following the road. Everything was white. Untouched land. Visibility was very poor. There were woods to the left and right of the road.

Ranzinger felt the pressure building in his bladder. "Into the next dirt road."

To see better, Eddie drove at a walking pace.

"You can turn in there," the bank robber said, pointing to a path he only recognized because it led directly into the forest and the trees were spaced accordingly.

Eddie turned. The Mercedes fought its way through the masses of snow. They reached the trees.

"One more piece!"

"Man yo. I'll never get out of here."

The barrel of the gun pointed at him.

"Okay, ey man. I think there's a few meters left."

After a few hundred meters, the Mercedes finally stopped mercilessly.

"Everybody out!" yelled Ranzinger.

Eddie shrugged. "Why?"

"Because I need to piss and use the phone!"

"Hey man! I don't want to watch."

Ranzinger's look was enough. Eddie opened the door and got out. Konny and Berti got out as well.

The criminal looked at his smartphone. "There's no reception here. We'll go a few meters further. Let's go! Let's go!"

As they trudged through the snow, freezing in completely inappropriate footwear, Ranzinger pondered what to do next. I urgently need to call my contacts.

The path was relatively steep, and the kidnapper hoped for better reception the higher they went.

After about twenty meters, they reached a fork in the trail. There was a sign for hikers. On the left side was the word Rundweg, on the right side most of the writing was covered by snow. Only the words: 2 hours and hut.

Ranzinger had an idea as his eyes scanned the signs. "Stop! Put all three in front of me! If one of them runs away, you know what will happen!"

"Sure man, then we'll run away and you'll pee in your pants," Eddie said, laughing out loud.

That was too much. These guys need to finally learn who is the sole announcer and who has to kowtow when I say something. Ranzinger raised his gun and squeezed the trigger.

Boom

The shot echoed through the forest several times. The echo rang ominously in the ears of the three hostages.

"Try it and I'll turn into an animal!"

Berti spoke for the first time since the robbery. The colored man's constant comments drove him into a rage. "Son of a man, Eddie! Your constant babbling and chattering is upsetting Mr. Ranzinger. It's putting us in danger. Can't you be quiet for once?"

The laughter had stopped with the shot. All three lined up in front of their captor. Konny and Berti pulled up the zippers of their winter anoraks. Then they reached into their pockets and pulled out knitted caps.

"And I didn't want to take them with me," smiled Konny.

It was cold and the snowfall was extreme. Within a few seconds, a white layer had settled on the four men. Meanwhile, Eddie danced around, freezing. He hopped from one leg to the other and flapped his arms around his chest. That was because he had gotten off the train wearing only a shirt. The jacket was in the trunk of the taxi.

"It's freezing cold. Can you hurry up? I need my jacket."

Ranzinger walked a few steps further and stood to the side of the three hostages. "Don't turn around!"

"Don't worry," Eddie shivered.

They heard a splash, a moan, another splash, another moan, and another splash, and finally a zipper.

"I hate Erna," Ranzinger muttered.

"Hey man, do you have a prostate? You're pissing in a stutter! Or is that supposed to be a rhythm or a beat?"

"Eddie," Berti poked the laughing taxi driver in the side.

"I don't say anything anymore. But when I'm scared, I have to talk all the time. I can't help it, friends."

Ranzinger did not respond to Eddie's comment. Instead he said, "Shit, still no signal.

"Hey man, what cell phone are you using?"

"Yours. That thing was in the cab! You could get something better."

"Are you crazy? I only have two euros left."

"Eddie, shut up," Berti warned again.

The ex-guru brandished his gun again. "I call who I want and what I want. And right now I'm calling my contacts. And I'm using this stupid phone. Do you mind?"

"No," came the chorus.

"Good, then shut up, all of you."

Wait.

Ranzinger took a few steps in different directions. He kept looking at the phone's display, wiped away a few snowflakes, and searched for a signal. Finally, the bar appeared faintly. He dialed. After a few anxious seconds, the call was answered. "It's me."

"Can we get a cab?" Eddie called out questioningly.

Ranzinger turned around. "Shut up! No, not you," the drug smuggler grumbled, calming his interlocutor. "I've got a couple of louts standing in front of me," he explained. "Well, I'm just outside of Garmisch... Sure, everything's fine. I even robbed a bank on the way. What? Ah, in Munich. I got away from the cops again ... How? I'll tell you later ... the fucking cops have the stuff, but like I said, after the bank job I'll have some cash with me ... Why tomorrow? ... Yeah, I know ... Well then, I'll see you tomorrow at noon," Ranzinger ended the call and hung up.

"What is it now? What happens next?" Konny asked hesitantly. The phone call had somehow sounded anything but positive.

Ranzinger's voice confirmed this with the following answer: "How can it go on? You've heard. Tomorrow is high noon. So the four of us will stay together for a while."

"Not possible! We have a hotel voucher," Berti complained. "You can't spoil our short vacation."

Ranzinger deliberately ignored the comment. "We'll take a leisurely drive back to the road. Then we'll go to the next town and check into a guesthouse. As soon as I've finished my meeting tomorrow, you can leave."

"Knut ... uh Detlev ... Mr. Ranzinger, why can't we just go to our hotel? I mean, Konny and I are just passengers anyway and just happened to be sitting ..."

In his opinion, the hostage-taker's nerves were being tested by a non-stop staccato of stupid questions that were slowly driving him to white heat. "Because I'm the boss!" he shouted loudly. "I call the shots around here, and your stupid questions are starting to get on my nerves. I'll say it again for anyone who doesn't want to understand. We stay together until noon tomorrow! That's it! We're taking a room together! Basta even more! End of announcement!"

"Hey man! No!"

The criminal was about to go crazy. "What's the matter, my chatterbox? Do you need a special declaration for tanning bed victims or what?"

Eddie's hair was completely covered in snow. He was freezing in his thin shirt. Shivering, he crossed his arms in front of his torso and still jumped up and down. "I'm not sleeping in a room with those two guys."

"Why not?" asked the hostage-taker.

"Yes, why not?" Berti also wanted to know.

"Because ... because ... damn it ...", Eddie got angry, " ... because I say so! You ain't getting my black ass!"

"Now come to your senses, friend," Konny scolded. "Berti and I are a couple. We're together and we're getting married. We're not interested in you. And anyway, what are you accusing us of?"

"That's right," Berti followed. "And don't come out with that stupid line: ... just because I'm black! You're an unbearable pain in the ass! Just like that wannabe Mafioso. If he didn't have a gun in his hand, I'd..."

"What would you call me? Fatty?"

"I've had enough. I'm freezing to death. I'm leaving now," Eddie groaned and started to run.

Berti's: "Don't call me fat" was lost in the hustle and bustle of the situation.

Events came thick and fast. The criminal raised his weapon. He aimed at the hooked black African. Eddie was quick. He moved skillfully, unconsciously jumping out of the line of fire of the gun pointed at him. He would soon be at the taxi. A strange, unprecedented feeling of fear drove him on. It was as if evil was following him into hell. He was running from man-eating zombies. They were already reaching for him. Ice cold finnails brushed across his back. If his body wasn't already covered in goose bumps from the cold, they would be popping out now from his eerie fear. Vapors bubbled out of Eddie's mouth. His lungs were pumping.

"You can shove it, chimney sweep," Ranzinger roared when he realized that Eddie was already close to the Mercedes.

wumm

The echo of the shot rang out. The bullet whizzed past Eddie and crashed into a tree. Pieces of bark and wood splinters flew at the point of impact.

"Stop right there or you'll have two assholes in a second!"

Eddie ran on undeterred. He was so close to his goal. Panting, he reached the cab. Another shot rang through the woods. The leaden core of the bullet burst through the grille, entered the engine compartment, shattered the radiator, was deflected, shredded a few wires, and remained compressed against the engine block. Hot steam hissed from the bullet hole. The snow under the car turned black from leaking oil. Eddie stood at the open driver's door and couldn't believe it. Shaking with fear and cold in equal measure, he raised his hands.

"I ... I ... just wanted to get my jacket, man ey."

Ranzinger stomped angrily towards the car and ordered Konny and Berti in front of him.

It was then that Eddie realized what had happened. Anger and despair mixed. "Hey man, what did you do? You could have hurt me."

"I'm pissed," the hostage-taker pulverized.

"My car," Eddie moaned. "You shot my cab!"

Ranzinger stood in front of Eddie. He took the gun in his left hand. His right hand clenched into a fist. Without warning, he struck. "I can't listen to this fucking whining anymore!"

Eddie took a punch to the chin. He slipped backwards, lost his balance, lay in the air like a wriggling fish for a split second, and inevitably landed in the snow.

Berti and Konny were relieved that the criminal's shot had hit the car and not Eddie. And although the situation was extremely dangerous and deadly serious, they both had to suppress a laugh. The situation was hilarious.

Ranzinger, on the other hand, was pretty much out of it. "Get up!"

Eddie jumped up immediately. He shivered like someone who had reached into a socket and gotten an electric shock. Only permanently. "I'm s-s-sorry. I'm freezing," he breathed.

Konny felt very sorry for him. "Mr. Ranzinger," he said in a slightly submissive but firm tone. He didn't want to irritate the criminal. "Detlev," he used his first name now to seem more personal and familiar. "It's winter. It's snowing and bitterly cold. Eddie has to put something on or he'll catch his death."

Berti, too, tried to calm the situation. "I would have gone to the car to get the jacket, too. It doesn't matter if I freeze to death out here or if you shoot me. Dead is dead." Then he turned to the tormented cabbie. "I'm sorry, Eddie. I didn't mean to talk down to you before. This whole situation is really getting on my nerves."

"Ey ma-ma-man, sh-sh-sh, it's okay."

Ranzinger puffed audibly. "You three bastards get in the car right now."

Berti pointed at the hood and the escaping steam. "What for? So we don't freeze to death? Gladly. But we can't go any further. The car is ruined. You've made the taxi unroadworthy. It's broken," he explained.

The kidnapper stared at the shot-out grille. His face turned bright red. "Shit! Shit! Shit!"

"And now?" Konny wanted to know. He chose a calm, slightly submissive tone again. The author was afraid of irritating the crazy drug smuggler even more.

Ranzinger put a cigarette in his mouth and lit it. He inhaled the smoke of the first puff deep into his lungs. He exhaled it again like an eruption. In the falling snow, the bluish haze drifted away like a billowing cloud of mist. The wrinkles on Ranzinger's forehead deepened. Finally he said: "They're looking for the car anyway. We'll go on foot. Bonnie and Clyde also fled into the mountains. Cool, isn't it?"

Konny thought about the weather. "Yes, cool! Really cool. I'm guessing sub-zero temperatures. And this blizzard just happened to be raging. I guess we froze to death before midnight."

"Nonsense with gravy! I know where we're going, and no one's ever frozen to death on the Latschen." Then he pointed at Berti. "And our meatball with legs certainly won't freeze so fast. He leads the way and we follow in his slipstream."

"I am strong and not a meatball," Berti replied indignantly. "These insults must stop!"

"Touret," Eddie said without stuttering.

Ranzinger flicked away his cigarette. "Follow the path."

Eddie went to the trunk of the taxi. "Can we take our things?"

The kidnapper nodded. "Fine by me. But quick! We're leaving in a minute. We go up the path and turn right. There was something about a mountain pasture. Those are the kind of inns in the mountains, or am I wrong?"

All three shrugged.

"Sorry, I'm not from here. I study in Munich and work as a taxi driver, man ey."

"A student chick," Ranzinger mimicked. "And what are you studying? Ape-logy or hash cultivation? Ha ha ha," he laughed at his joke.

"German, political science and sociology."

At first Eddie caught a look of astonishment, then Ranzinger changed the subject. "You're all wimps. You don't know anything about life, let alone the mountains. We're going to the mountain pasture. I know my way around there. In those days they used to show movies about mountain pastures. I still remember them: There's no sin on the mountain pasture.

"Don't I know you?" Eddie said dryly.

Berti joined the conversation. "Heidi and Peter lived with Grandpa on the mountain pasture. But that was a farm, not an inn."

Eddie slipped into his winter coat. What a relief. "You're talking about the black-and-white TV era, ey man." He looked at Ranzinger. "You only watched movies where you needed a handkerchief at the end anyway. But not to dry your ears."

The criminal countered: "That was back when you built houses out of elephant dung."

Konny couldn't believe it. "There's a blizzard, we're in a godforsaken wilderness, and people are looking for us. Can you two stop arguing despite all the unpleasant circumstances? I have no desire to be snowed in, or worse, to spend a night out in the open.

That was enough. Eddie and Ranzinger stared at the writer with wide eyes.

The African taxi driver opened his mouth to say something when Berti interrupted him.

"Eddie, shut up."

There was a moment of silence. Then Ranzinger began to clap. Clap, clap, clap.

"Bravo, Mr. Smarty-pants. That could be mine. All right, I agree. Let's keep the peace and go to the cabin."

Eddie took a few steps and stood behind Berti.

"Not so fast," shouted the criminal. "Would Mr. Insulted Liverwurst Taxi Driver be so kind as to carry my briefcase with the coal in it? I thought coal and your skin color go together beautifully."

"Are you crazy?" Eddie shook his head.

"Here we go again?" Konny said, annoyed.

The gun was raised. "Briefcase!" the hostage-taker grumbled.

"Come on," Berti breathed. "There's only money in it."

Eddie began to grin broadly. "But of course I'll carry the money. No problem. Give it to me."

Ranziger handed the briefcase to the cabbie. "If I see you fiddling with the clasp, I'll shoot without warning. These are my ashes."

"Sure boss," Eddie nodded.

Berti and Konny breathed a sigh of relief. They took their luggage as well. Then the unlikely quartet set off.

ai-generated-8442145_1280

Chapter 6
Hut magic

The shots had not gone unnoticed. Reinhard Schneider was an avid forester and hunter. He loved the rugged *Werdenfelser Land* with its high alpine rocky landscapes of the *Karwendel* and *Wetterstein* mountains. He also liked the *Pfaffenwinkel* upstream, a pre-alpine hilly landscape interspersed with swamps and bogs, and he was a fan of Germany's highest mountain, the *Zugspitze*. He had climbed it three times. Once with and twice without the support of the Zugspitze cable car. He felt free in nature. He cherished and cared for his territory like no other. For him, his profession was a pure calling.

When the weathermen in the media announced the onset of winter, he was already thinking one step ahead. To provide food for the wildlife, he had obtained hay from a local farmer. Schneider had been in the woods since early morning. He rattled off feeding trough after feeding trough, filling them with hay. He visited the feeding areas that could not be reached by foot with an all-terrain vehicle. He was on his way back to his ten-year-old Suzuki Jeep when he heard a loud thunderclap.

It was a gunshot, he realized immediately.

Normally, Schneider would think nothing of it. In the mountains, shots from neighboring hunters often echoed. But this time was different. He was right on the border of two hunting grounds. One belonged to him, the other to his regular hunting partner, Eberhard Faltinger. The latter, however, was in the district hospital for a scheduled operation.

"Better now than at Christmas," said Faltinger on the last evening of the regulars' table.

Schneider stopped. "Damn it! Who's shooting in my forest?" he groaned.

Was it those young, cool, rowdy guys who usually wore tight-fitting jeans that showed their underpants? Were they selling New Year's fireworks? No!

Schneider was alert. It was his forest! He was the hunter here!

145

Could poachers be up to no good?

The forester didn't want to rule that out. He would have liked to go stalking himself this morning, but feeding the game came first.

The shot had long since faded. The silence of the forest combined with the snowfall was enchanting. It was like walking through a fairy tale world. The forester mentally blocked out the incident.

Maybe it was the police. A trap shot after a wild animal accident. It happens a lot, he thought and calmed down.

Who knows what happened. Maybe it was a deer or even a wild boar. These animals also spread quickly.

Satisfied, the forester trudged on when a second shot shattered the silence once more. Again, the echo of the shot echoed through the forest several times. Now everything was clear. Clumsily, Schneider dug his cell phone out of the inside pocket of his winter parka. It showed a bar. Enough to dial the emergency number.

"Police Operations Center. Who is this and how can I help you?"

"Good morning! My name is Schneider, Reinhard Schneider. I'm a forester in the district of Garmisch-Partenkirchen," he introduced himself. He then talked about the shooting, tried to narrow down the area where the shooter must have been, and explained how to get there. At the end of the conversation, he promised not to do anything alone and promised to drive his jeep to the next street to meet a police patrol.

"How long do I have to wait?"

"I'll give you the assignment right away. Depending on how many accidents we have to deal with this winter, it could take a while."

Unsatisfied with the time given for the arrival of a police patrol, the forester made his way to his jeep. The snowfall had lost its wintry idyll.

"Damn weather," Schneider cursed, pulled his woolly hat down a bit, pulled the hood of his parka over his head, and stomped off.

When he finally reached the vehicle, he cleared the snow from the Jeep with a small hand brush. Then he got in and slammed the door shut. The engine started immediately. There was a slight clunk when first gear was engaged. The clutch pedal squeaked. The forester rolled slowly down the road. He was already thinking about his trees again.

If it keeps snowing like this, there will be a lot of snow on the ridges, he realized. Avalanche danger.

Schneider reached the fork. Although he was far and wide alone, the pedantic man set the indicator. He spoke to himself again.

"The turn signal is an important means of communication in road traffic. Even here in the forest, we don't want to let the authorities get away with it."

The forest path was completely covered with snow. Longer branches and thinner twigs were already bending under the weight of the fresh snow. Schuessler had the feeling he was walking through a hollow. He soon reached the road and the rendezvous point with the police.

An obstacle appeared dimly in front of him. Even though the forester was barely going faster than walking speed, he slowed down again. There was a car in the middle of the path.

It's been here for a while. It's completely covered in snow. Ah, a taxi, he realized.

He stopped beside the Mercedes. "Not in my forest," the forester grumbled, got out and walked around the Mercedes. Curiously, a hand moved to the driver's side door handle. "Locked," he muttered.

Back in the jeep, he dialed the emergency number a second time. The reception left much to be desired. Schneider drove backwards until a bar appeared again on the display of his cell phone. He redialed.

"Police call," he heard this time from a pleasant sounding female voice. Though the policewoman tried to speak some semblance of High German, she could not completely deny her origins. "What can I do for you?" came the unmistakable accent of the German capital.

The Upper Bavarian thought she heard laughter and whistling in the background, but she was too excited to complain. "I think I got out in the wrong state," he mumbled into his smartphone, slightly confused. "I wanted to dial 911 here in Garmisch. That's in Bavaria."

"You're right," the policewoman at the phone clarified. Her voice was sweet, calm, and extremely personable. The Berlin dialect was no longer so pronounced. She now spoke German with a slightly artificial Bavarian accent.

In the forester's mind a short film sequence played. He was a contestant in a new television show. The forester was looking for a wife. The host asked him: "Well, dear Reinhard, which of the three ladies will you take home with you? The determined Evi, who wants to steal horses with you, but doesn't like to ride? Or the clever Angelika, who

147

prefers to swim in the sea and would like to see the world with you? Or would you prefer Rosi, who loves roast pork and is a good match for you because she has enough wood in front of her hut? Make up your mind!"

He was about to choose Rosi when the policewoman spoke again. Obviously he had hesitated too long.

"Hello, are you still there?"

The forester came back to reality.

"This is Schneider again. I called you earlier."

"For what reason?"

"I reported shots fired. From my forest."

Silence for seconds, then came: "Yes, Mr. Schneider, I found the mission. I can also see that a car is already on its way to you. Is there anything else?"

"I found a Mercedes. A taxi."

Now the policewoman in the operations center became suspicious and a little more serious. "Where did you find the taxi?"

"Here in the woods, of course."

"What license plate does the vehicle have?"

"I can't read it. The car is snowed in."

"Are there people in the car?"

"Nothing to see."

"Are there any visible traces of snow?"

"Traces of snow? There are no tracks in the snow," explained the slightly know-it-all Schneider. "There are tracks in the snow, e.g. from game, or footprints and tire tracks, but there are no snow tracks as such."

"Thanks for the lesson," came the slightly scornful reply. "Do you see any tracks in the snow?"

"No! Nothing. Everything here is covered with snow."

"Are there people in the vehicle?" came the second question.

"I already said no once. If it had changed in the meantime, I would have told you. And if you want to know, the doors to the car are locked."

"Wait for us. Don't do anything. It could be the getaway car from a bank robbery."

Schneider was stunned.

"All right. I'll stay here and wait." The policewoman hung up.

The forester leaned back. "Those bastards," he muttered. "Hiding their getaway car in my forest."

Rudi Radtke was not entirely satisfied with the outcome of the conversation. He had watched the video camera footage. The witness seemed to have correctly interpreted the involvement of the four men in the crime. Ranzinger acted as the only main perpetrator with the gun, the others stood around as if forced to do so.

In the ticket office, Konrad Wels placed Radtke's business card on the desk and scribbled something on it. Then they fled in a taxi.

Does Ranzinger really have three hostages? How did he get hold of Wels and Schwartz? Would he shoot them with his service weapon in revenge for their arrest at the station?

Radtke felt an urgent need to drink. His right hand went into the inside pocket of his jacket. He always carried two or three small *Jägermeister* bottles for a snack. With a practiced grip, he pulled out a small bottle of Jägermeister, downed it, and tossed the fake bottle into the trash can in the bank's vestibule. Radtke left the building and got into the company car.

"Let's go back," his colleague urged. "The weather is terrible. It'll take us hours if it keeps snowing like this."

Radtke's conscience was getting worse. He was already mentally formulating his statement to the board of inquiry as to why he had left his area of responsibility without authorization when the radio message came.

"... in the forest... Shots fired ..."

"That's them. One hundred percent! Let's go there."

"The weather is a disaster," Angela Adler reminded her colleague once again about the onset of winter.

"Uniformed forces are not free," croaked the loudspeaker.

Radtke grabbed the radio. "We're happy to help," he announced, giving his Munich call sign.

Later there was an addition. "... Cab found ..."

Radtke regained hope. Pure hunting fever was spreading. He would catch the thief of his gun and put him in jail.

"I have no idea where to go," Angela complained.

"Turn left now, then follow the main road and turn right at the next big intersection."

The inspector was puzzled. "Do you know your way around here?"

"No, but the navigation system does. I just turned off the sound."

Angela groaned. "All right, let's go."

The drive resembled a toboggan ride. Radtke slid nervously back and forth. He was going too slowly, but he didn't say anything about the speed. When they finally reached their destination some time later, they recognized a man who was obviously waiting by the side of the road.

"That must be the communicator," Radtke muttered.

Angela Adler activated her indicator and pulled over. At the level of the person waiting, she pressed the power window button. The window lowered. "Good afternoon. Police."

"It's about time. I've been waiting for over half an hour. You can't be shot at when you're needed," it boomed at them.

Radtke saw the tire tracks of the jeep. "Is that the cab?" he asked, not answering the forester's comment.

"Uh, yeah. This is a mess. I'll..."

The policeman paid no attention to the witness, but turned to his colleague: "You talk to him. I'll take a look at the taxi."

Inspector Adler's eyes rolled. She guessed what kind of person this forester was. Meanwhile, the earwitness to the shooting went on and on. His story began at the last regulars' table, when Eberhard Faltinger had called in sick, so to speak. Angela Adler sat back patiently.

Rudi Radtke tried to open all the doors. Then he bent down. He noticed the black oil stain under the cab, took down the license number, wiped the snow off the hood, and found a bullet hole.

The ranger's jeep and the civilian patrol car rolled up. Both drivers pulled next to the cab, one behind the other.

"Have you found any clues?" Angela asked.

"Not yet," Radtke replied, walking over to the radio car, opening the door and grabbing the emergency hammer that was mounted on the center console. He stomped back to the cab, took a swing, and smashed the side window of the driver's door.

His colleague and Mr. Schneider were startled. "Rudi! What are you doing?"

"Looking for clues."

"Do you see any traces of snow?"

"No."

"Excuse me," the forester interrupted.

"Yes, please?"

"There are no snow tracks. You leave tracks in the snow, like shoe prints. But there are no snow tracks. I've already had to explain that to my colleague on the phone."

Angela Adler looked at the forester with a questioning look. She didn't like this guy right away. He had probably become a forester because he was better at talking to trees than to people.

Radtke had opened the hood. "He shot in here."

"Why?" wondered Inspector Adler.

"I don't know."

"And now?"

"Either there was a getaway car here, or they continued their escape on foot."

The earwitness spoke up. "There was no other car here when I drove to the feed mills," he remarked.

"On foot? In this weather?" wondered Angela Adler. "Where are you going? There's nothing here."

"Excuse me, but this is a very exciting and unspoiled country. You will find wild nature. Vast areas of forest invite you to walk. You can climb the rocks and mountains, walk through the swamps and marshes, or go hiking in the mountains and then stop at a mountain hut. So there's not nothing here," Mr. Schneider enthused.

"That's not what I meant."

"What did you say?" Radtke asked.

"Hiking in the mountains? Swamps?"

"No! The one with the mountain pasture."

"You can stop at a mountain hut. Only the ski huts are open now anyway. The hiking huts are closed."

"Hiking hut? Is there such a thing here?"

"Sure! Up the path ..." Schneider pointed to the fork. "Then a good two hours on foot. But as I said, the hut is closed this time of year. And in this weather it will of course take longer than two hours."

The policewoman looked at her colleague. She guessed what was going through Rudi Radtke's mind and shook her head vehemently.

"No!" she said firmly. "You can forget it. I'm not wearing the right clothes, and I don't want to go to the mountains in the worst snow."

Radtke countered. "He's looking for a place to hide. He hides there and doesn't know he's walking into a mousetrap."

The ranger cleared his throat. "May I ask whom you are following?"

"You may not," Radtke snapped at him.

The words hit Herr Schneider hard. No one had spoken to him like that since his communion. It was downright insolent. His cheeks turned red. Red with anger. "You are on my turf. I will write a report on what happened, and believe me, you ... You... You ..."

The plainclothesman smiled provocatively. "What am I supposed to believe? You know what, tree whisperer? Have a little chat with the green stuff here and let me do my job."

Schneider caught his breath.

Inspector Adler raised her hands defensively and showed Radtke her stop hand. "Stop! Rudi, I'm not doing this. I'll get in the car, announce that we've lost the trail and leave the rest to the police," she protested.

Radtke didn't believe what he was hearing. "We're very close. We can't give up now."

"Rudi, you're looking for a needle in a haystack. The weather is against us, and I don't want to get lost in this white maze and be found as a modern-day *Ötzi* after the snow melts."

Reinhard Schneider grinned. This was his chance to get back at this rude city dweller. "If I knew who or what you were looking for, I might be able to help."

Radtke was seething with anger. He wanted to catch the bank robber himself. Determined to change his colleague's mind, he tried a calmer tone. "Angela, we've come all this way and we're going to give up just short of our goal? Think about your career. If we get it now, we'll make it big."

"Without me!" The policewoman sat down in the patrol car and slammed the door. She started the engine demonstratively.

Radtke tapped on the side window. Angela rolled it down.

"At least give me your gun."

"My what?"

"Your gun, your gun."

The inspector's eyes widened. "Really now?"

"I'll take the fight. Ranzinger has hostages. It's my damned duty to free these people, and I need a gun to do it."

"He's got your gun, colleague *Jägermeister*!" she boomed.

Radtke was taken aback. "How dare you talk to me?"

"You're the Master, I'm the Inspector. I am your superior! Even if you don't want to admit it and you've been wearing that uniform since before I was born. I know you were the king of the station when I started school, but I don't care. I have the power of decision. We're breaking up!"

That did the trick.

"Who are you looking for and where are you going?" Schneider pushed his way between the arguing policemen.

"You're annoying! Can't you see we're having a conversation?" Radtke hissed at the forester.

"Well, if you know your way around here so well, I can go home," came the snarky reply from a diva.

Radtke was about to explode. "Damn it, Angela! Now give me your gun! I'm going after these assholes whether you like it or not. You can stay here and play with your Barbie dolls if you're afraid."

The young inspector sat in the car with his mouth open. This was too much. She wasn't afraid. She had never been afraid of anything in her life. Except maybe spiders. "I'm not afraid," she blurted out to her colleague.

"Then what is it? Could the snowflakes ruin your great hair?"

"What do you have against my hair?"

He put his right hand inside the car and held it out for a slap. "Compromise! You give me the gun, I'll go after Ranzinger. You go to the police station in Garmisch, send me reinforcements, call our boss and wait for me there."

"What about my hair?"

"It's fine."

"No! It's not! You said something about my hair."

The forester rolled his eyes. "Women! I know why I'm not married," he muttered.

"I heard that," Angela hissed.

Radtke tried to be polite. "Believe me, the hair is fine."

"How okay?" she asked. "Okay means they don't look like anything."

Schneider leaned down. "Why don't you get a haircut?"

Commissioner Adler had had enough. "Stay out of this, you weird ranger."

"I'll report you! I don't have to take this."

"Quiet!" shouted Radtke. He was at the end of his tether and wanted to finally go after these criminals. "Give me the gun!"

Angela Adler, startled, grabbed the gun and handed it to her colleague. "I'll wait in Garmisch and tell the boss everything."

"Send reinforcements! And have the taxi towed away!"

The window was rolled up. Reverse gear engaged, the car slowly rolled back onto the road.

"And now you."

"I'm going to report that bitch," the forester complained.

"You just called a policewoman a bitch. Now you're even!"

Schneider struggled for words. "I ... uh ..."

Radtke cut him off. "What was that about the mountain pasture?"

"Why?"

"I'm looking for a bank robber who probably has three hostages. The man's name is Ranzinger, he's armed and extremely dangerous. The taxi was the getaway car."

Schneider was agitated. His pulse beat wildly. "In my forest?"

He nodded in agreement. "Looks like it."

"And you think people will go to the mountain pasture?"

"That's a good idea, even if we don't see any snow tracks."

"You mean tracks in the snow."

"Who cares! How do I find this mountain pasture?"

"I can guide you. We won't get far by car in this weather anyway."

"Is there a shortcut?"

"Yes, there is," came the confident answer. Schneider looked at the policeman. "Don't you have a hat?"

"No! What makes you think I have a cap? The hair is real. It's not a toupee."

"I also meant headgear."

"I see. No, I don't have that either."

"There's a hat in the jeep, you can put it on if you want. It's better than nothing on your head. Your ears are free, but at least the rest is protected."

Radtke accepted the offer. Shortly thereafter, they both left.

Herbert Schwartz hadn't sweated like that since his physical fitness test. Even in the cold. He dragged the wagon behind him, making tracks in the snow. His bobble hat was pulled down low over his face, his cheeks glowing fiery red. Konny walked beside him. Eddie marched ahead. At first he had sung Bob Marley's *Buffalo Soldier* loudly, but he wasn't quite sure of the words. Later it became a hum, and for a while nothing could be heard at all. The bag of money he had to carry moved regularly from right to left and back again.

Ranzinger followed closely behind the three hostages. "Man, oh man, what the hell is this place," the bank robber cursed at regular intervals. "The stupid sign said two hours for hikers. This is pure tourist bullshit. I'm going to complain."

Berti was panting like crazy. His legs grew heavier with each step. He felt like a stranded whale, crushed by his own weight. His lungs pumped like crazy. "I can't take any more. We need to take a break," he groaned.

"Hey man, he's right. My hands are about to fall off. We're going to die in this wilderness," Eddie groaned.

"Give me the trolley, darling," Konny said, grabbing the trolley case.

"Yuck! How can you talk to someone so gay?" commented Ranzinger.

"Because we're gay, we live it, and between the two of us we've found what you'll never find. Love!" Konny replied somewhat gruffly and took the car.

The climb to the mountain pasture was anything but easy. They had started three hours ago. Despite the bad weather, they made relatively good progress at first, but the closer they got to the hut, the steeper the climb became.

The route was well suited for hikers, it wasn't a climb, but due to the extreme weather conditions, with knee-high snow drifts in places, they were making extremely slow progress.

And if it weren't for the important trail signs along the way, the group of four would have been lost long ago. Everything looked the same under the white blanket of snow.

Ranzinger stood still. He was stunned, too, but he didn't want to admit it and pretended to be strong. "All right, then. Five minute break. I'm going to smoke a cigarette."

"What are you doing?" asked Berti.

"Man, where did you come from? I eat a coffin nail, breathe adventure into my lungs, build blue clouds. Got it? I'm smoking a cigarette, you mountain gorilla."

"Must you weave an insult into every one of your sentences?" asked the corpulent detective.

Ranzinger lit a cigarette.

To avoid another argument, Konny tried to start a conversation. "Tell me something, Detlev. How did you become a criminal?" The Germanist tried to put himself in the place of the hostage-taker. Perhaps that would enable him to see through him and later to overpower him or persuade him to give up.

Ranzinger blew out the smoke and blinked. It was as if he was aiming at Konny. "What the fuck? Is this some kind of psycho trick? Like, I talk all over the bad man, then he cries and gives me the puff, or what?"

"No! For God's sake, of course not," he defended himself. "I'm only interested in it for professional reasons. Maybe one day I'll write a book about it."

Silence. Ranzinger's head rattled. It wasn't until two minutes later that an answer came. "You want to write a book about me? Sounds cool."

"Why not?"

The criminal laughed. "Me and a hero of a novel."

"No desire to be famous?"

Again, lines of thought filled the hostage-taker's forehead. "Are you crazy? I'm not stupid enough to tell you all my shameful deeds. Then the book will be on the market and the judges and prosecutors will put me in jail. I can already hear them chattering in the courtroom." He disguised his voice. "On page 23, the defendant admits to breaking into his classmates' lockers at school while they were playing sports. He is also accused of manipulating a locker in the girls' locker

156

room so that he could hide inside and watch the girls change. In chapter two, he recounts various assaults on older women whose purses he stole. On page 234, he admits to dealing heroin in no small quantity..."

Eddie was stunned. "That's cool, dude, you did all that? Hey man, you're even worse than I thought. You're even a peeing Tom. I never would have done that."

Ranzinger countered. "Of course not. It would have been a miracle. You don't have locker rooms in Africa. You go out into the desert to do gymnastics and catch antelopes on foot. That's why you're so fit and play soccer everywhere. And your women jump half naked around the campfire in the kraal. You can see your tits dancing."

Eddie shook his head. "Why do I still talk to you? You insult me every time. You racist!"

"That's not true either," Ranzinger grinned. "I'm not a racist. I even shared a cell with a black power man once."

"Look, guys. He's doing it again."

"What did I do wrong again?"

"You said the n-word."

"Is that an insult?"

"You bet it is! It means black or colored or whatever else you can say, but definitely not nigger or kaffir or half-monkey and whatever other despicable, inhuman vocabulary you use for us dark-skinned people."

Ranzinger was astonished. "You are all small-minded. I was in a cell with a Turk, a slant-eyed Vietnamese and a black man. The cumin was okay. The black guy was a real buffalo. He would have flattened us if we had insulted him. And the 16:9 guy was some kind of karate fart. I didn't insult him either. I'm not stupid."

"What is a 16:9 person?" Berti wanted to know.

"Stupid question, of course it's a gook, you wandering whoopee cushion."

Konny was seething with anger. This uncouth lout was not only insulting people of other origins, but also his Berti. He wasn't going to put up with it any longer. "Enough with the swearing and the insults. Eddie has already told you once today. It has to stop sometime."

Ranzinger grinned arrogantly and toyed with his gun. "Otherwise?" he asked.

157

"Hey man, if you got punched in the mouth for every insult, you could go to carnival as a flounder."

Ranzinger laughed. "That means carnival, you ..."

"No more swearing," Konny interrupted him.

"Well, well, well. Shakespeare plays the hero."

The writer picked up the ball and played it back. "How do you know Shakespeare?"

Eddie tried to say something too, "I wonder that too, ey man. Y-ou're usually dumber than ..."

Berti poked the taxi driver in the side. "Shut up!"

He got the hint and remained silent.

Konny continued. "How did you talk to your fellow inmates in prison? I don't mean the brawny African or the well-trained karate fighter from Asia. I mean all the other prisoners."

Ranzinger thought about it. "Stupid question, as always, of course."

"Did you insult them as well?"

"Sure! Why not?"

Konny pondered. "And you're still alive?"

Loud laughter. "I was vice president of the Aryan Brotherhood in prison. I had power and the others were afraid. With a few exceptions like blacks and asians."

"A racist after all," Eddie interjected.

"Boy, prison life is different than out here. You either fit in so-mewhere or you go down. I chose the white power and was high up in their hierarchy. Bingo," he winked.

"So you went to prison and were at the top of the Aryan Brother-hood right from the start?"

"We don't talk about the beginning."

Eddie laughed. "Ha, ha ... you started out as a pussy," he roared, pointing at the hostage-taker. "He was a prison pussy, ha ha ha."

Ranzinger pointed at the African student. "One more word and I'll save humanity from your stupidity. I'll remove you from the list of living beings and rid the globe of a parasite."

Eddie was silent. No one laughed.

Konny tried again to save the situation. "Detlev, you spoke so convincingly on the train. Where did you learn that? I mean, you al-most convinced both of us to join your sect."

"What?" Berti exclaimed. A roll of his friend's eyes was enough to alert the detective that this was a ruse to get Ranzinger's attention.

A wide smile spread across his face. "Sooo," came the lengthy reply. "Did I?"

"Yes."

"Of course," Berti agreed.

The bank robber basked in the glow of this praise. "I taught myself. In prison. I read something by Charon out of sheer boredom. He was a French Nobel Prize winner. He wrote that evolution is a drive that leads to the unity of love and shit like that. And that our power comes from a transrational source. He talked about a finality that pushes us to become one. Every holon should feel attracted to the greater. Subatomic particles are looking for connections, and our universe is a universe for everyone. For the good and the bad. So it doesn't exclude the criminals. At first I threw the magazine with the article in the trash. But at night the idea of a sect came to me. Charon enlightened me. Then I got some more cult stuff from the library. I tell you, there are a lot of crazy people in the world. Ranzinger laughed out loud. "I finally put something together myself out of all that crap. When I got laid off, I tried it out on the pedestrian mall. And sure enough, I had my first fans. It didn't take long for the first flat-earthers to follow me and give me all their money.

"It must have something to do with your charisma," added Konny, who was surprised that Ranzinger could be so intellectual. Even memorizing all the material required a certain IQ. The professional criminal was probably a schizophrenic. In normal life he was simple-minded, but when it came to committing a crime, he worked with the healthy half of his brain. This was extremely intelligent.

Ranzinger finished smoking. "Come on, guys!"

Berti crossed his arms over his chest. "I'm on strike. I'm starving and about to collapse."

"Berti, my little mouse, hang in there. Remember the concentration exercise we learned in gymnastics."

"Okay, I'll do it for you." The detective gave in. After all, he had no choice. After all, he was being threatened with a gun, and he trusted this criminal to use it without scruples.

Berti thought back to the last gymnastics program. He liked the two gymnasts because they were doing a concentration exercise that he could easily imitate. They sat on a chair and did ... nothing. They had to consciously let their blood flow, calm their pulse, put their tongue on the roof of their mouth and breathe calmly. Berti did this exercise and he actually felt better. What worked sitting down had to work standing up.

Find your inner peace, he reminded himself.

Step by step, he continued down the difficult path. His undershirt was soaked with sweat and his legs felt heavy. After this adventure, it was definitely time. He would definitely go on a diet.

At least right after the weekend at the hotel.

Berti fell into a kind of trance. He moved, but no longer felt the effort. The feeling of hunger was also gone. He was on his own personal Camino de Santiago. Thoughts came and went. Some matured. Suddenly he had just the right one.

That's it, it flowed through him.

He would wait for the right moment. At some point, Knut or Detlev, whatever this criminal's real name was, wouldn't pay attention. Then he would feel Berti's fist. Just as fearlessly as Ulf Kapaunke had attacked the Russian bouncers, Herbert Schwartz would overpower the bank robber.

There is no fear. I have no fear. Problems exist so that I can solve them. I am Herbert Schwartz, the best private detective, he repeated over and over.

Another hour had passed and the initial conversations had long since died down. Even the athletic Konny began to feel the weight of the car. He was glad that he and Berti had put on good winter shoes. Eddie and Ranzinger, on the other hand, wore normal street shoes. Their feet must have been half frozen. While the taxi driver kept complaining, the bank robber did not. After Eddie had almost given up hope of ever reaching the pasture, he recognized something large. He stopped and pointed ahead. "Hey man, guys, I see something," he shouted.

The outline of a house was in front of them.

"We're here," Berti and Konny cheered.

"Finally," Ranzinger groaned.

They had reached their goal. The alp was a simple mountain hut. Wooden railings indicated the extent of the garden, which was used in the summer. The view must be magnificent when the weather is good. They slowly approached the house.

Berti was more than relieved. He was at the end of his tether, and to reach the mountain pasture was pure relief.

"We'll go around once," Ranzinger ordered. "All together!"

There were closed wooden shutters on the windows. The door was secured with an iron bolt. A thick padlock dangled from the end of the bolt. The roof had an overhang of at least two meters. You could sit under it when it rained, and the wood stacked along the wall of the house was protected from snow and rain. There was no smoke coming out of the chimney. Not far from the simple log cabin were two small huts with heart-shaped windows in the middle of the doors.

"Outhouse toilets," Ranzinger commented. "Does anyone have to go?"

No one moved.

"It would be cold as hell ... ha ha ha," he laughed. "This finally gives meaning to the phrase 'cold as hell.'"

They had circled the mountain pasture. The hostage-taker waved his gun. "Everybody under the porch! One of you make sure the door is locked."

Konny went to the door. "The door is locked with a bolt and there's a big lock on it."

"Break it!"

"How?"

Ranzinger shook his head. "You wimps are too stupid to pick a lousy padlock. Move aside. All three of you."

The hostages stepped aside. Their captor picked up a thick log from the stack and struck the padlock twice. It popped open. "That's the way to do it, you rascals!" The professional criminal pulled the bolt back and pushed the handle down. "Shit," he cursed. "That mountain idiot locked the door too. It's like someone came here voluntarily to break in."

"Hey man, but that's what you're doing. You're breaking in."

Ranzinger couldn't believe it. "There's more brains in a piece of yellow sausage than in your head. I'm not breaking in. This is emergency protection or whatever it's called."

"Hey man, when you force your way into something that doesn't belong to you, what you're doing is called breaking and entering."

Ranzinger had two or three expletives on the tip of his tongue, but he wanted to get into the warmth. So he refrained from his usual insults. Instead, he cast a practiced glance at the door. "Beard lock. Piece of cake. Anybody got a lock pick?"

All three shook their heads.

"That was obvious. Why do I even ask?" Ranzinger looked around. His gaze lingered on the cart. "Is there a wire hanger in there?"

Konny thought for a moment. "Yes. We were going to use it to hang up our jackets."

"Give it to me, gadfly!"

Konny opened the cart. There were two wire hangers on top. He took one out of the suitcase and handed it to Ranzinger. He slipped the pistol into his coat pocket and bent the hanger apart. The former jailbird handled it skillfully. In no time at all, one end of the wire was bent into the shape of a lock pick. Smiling, he inserted the homemade picking tool into the lock. "Watch this, friends. Now you can learn something from old Detlev."

They were silent as mice. There was a metallic click. "There, that should do it."

He pushed the handle again. This time the door opened. "There you go. Get inside. Now open the shutters. I want to see you all the time. Just don't screw up."

All four men had imagined something different when they heard the word "Alm". In the restaurant, if you could call it that, there were two tables. Both on the side of the wall. In the center of the fifteen-square-meter room stood a stately tiled stove. On three sides of the tiled stove were simple wooden planks that served as benches. Only the front, where the tiled stove was heated, was uncovered.

A small counter was built into the right side of the hut. Behind it was an open, empty refrigerator and a stove. Both were gas powered. A large bottle of propane was placed under the stove.

Beyond the counter was a passageway to a small adjoining room, separated only by a curtain.

"Everybody sit down! Put the briefcase with the ashes on the table."

They sat down. Eddie put the bag of money down. Ranzinger glanced into the next room. "There's a bunk bed, nothing else. Very Spartan furnishings."

162

"Can we make a fire?" Eddie shuddered.

Each of the four men felt both the cold and the hard march. A light haze still hung in front of their mouths with every breath.

"Good idea. I'm freezing too! Somebody get some wood. Then we'll light the thing," the bank robber agreed, pointing to the tiled stove.

"I'll get the wood," Konny groaned and stood up.

"No," countered the hostage-taker. "The fat man does that!"

Berti was at the end of his rope. Only his unbridled anger and pent-up hatred for Ranzinger had prevented him from simply sitting down on the street and giving up. In a way, he was also proud of himself. He had never done anything like this in his life. He still wore his woolly hat. It was completely soaked with snow. Berti reached for his headgear and pulled it off. His hair was pressed flat against his scalp. "Don't call me Dicker! My name is Herbert Schwartz and I demand to be respectfully addressed by my name!"

Konny flinched. He had never seen his partner so angry and yet so calm.

There was also a flash in Ranzinger's eyes. The professional criminal seemed to be trying to figure out how to react. The pumped-up zero in front of him had been cowering flawlessly until now. Now he must have been in the mood to stand up.

Revolution is dangerous. He could infect the other two. I know that from prison.

Ranzinger looked around the narrow room. If they stuck together and jumped him, he could get one, two at most, with the gun. The third would lynch him. The bank robber decided to take it down a notch. "All right, Herbert. I can call you Herbert, can't I?" he replied in a surprisingly friendly manner.

Everyone was surprised. Especially Berti. "Uh ... Yes, of course," came the astonished reply. "Herbert's all right."

Detlev was back as Knut Hofmann. At least his voice sounded the same as yesterday on the train.

"So Herbert. You're the strongest of all. We're frozen and broken. Can you please get some firewood?"

Berti stood up. He didn't trust this schizophrenic, but he liked the compliment. "Sure, I'll get some wood."

163

The corpulent private detective went out onto the veranda. Thoughts of escape came. How far would he get? Would he have the strength to walk all the way back? Could he walk all the way to Garmisch and call the police? He gave himself the answer before he had finished thinking about it. It was a clear no! He was already at the end of his tether. Besides, Ranzinger or Knut or whoever else was in that madman's house could shoot Konny. Sure, Eddie was in danger too, but Konny was more important. So Berti grabbed some logs on his left arm and went back to the cabin.

"Splinters are here. Also kindling and a lighter," Konny greeted him, kneeling in front of the tiled stove.

Berti put the wood down, his friend took some smaller logs and put them in the firebox. Then he held the flame of the lighter to a kindling and placed it under the wood. It crackled. The flames slowly flickered upwards, ate into the wood and quickly began to blaze because of the draught. Konny closed the door. "We'll be warm soon."

"Like two warm brothers," Ranzinger laughed uproariously. He stood behind the counter.

"Do you have a problem with us being gay?" Konny asked in a calm voice.

"Me? Nope! Why?"

"Because you talk so disparagingly about us."

"I just said that you are fags. You are queers, aren't you?"

"I already told you. We are homosexuals. You can call it whatever you want. It's not going to change. So why are you insulting us?"

"Don't be like that. Everybody says that. You can ask blacky," Ranzinger defended himself.

Eddie sat frozen on the bench and gave Ranzinger a dirty look. The burning wood crackled. The first streams of warm air were released into the cold room.

Konny didn't want to put up with the disparaging talk. "Do you know how many people you hurt with such stupid talk? Because of people like you, young gays are afraid to come out. They're still in the closet because your words will break them. Words are sharper than blades. You should choose them carefully, because their wounds are hard to heal and leave deep scars on the soul.

Ranzinger smiled. It was as if Konny's words didn't interest him, let alone touch him in any way. Eddie, on the other hand, avoided any eye contact with Berti and his friend. He listened attentively, jerked restlessly from left to right and said: "Hey man, I feel bad because I also like to make jokes about faggots. But it's the same with us black people."

"That's right," Ranzinger said. I think everybody should have a nigger," he snorted.

"Very funny, you prison pussy," Eddie countered, immediately looking down the barrel of the gun.

Konny continued talking, unimpressed. "But that's not so bad, Eddie. We also laugh about queers and funny homos. And you already laughed at the joke about a colored man on a mountain bike, didn't you?"

Eddie turned to Konny, "Of course I screamed my head off about the chocolate crossie."

Now all four of them were laughing.

Konny stayed on the ball. "When people finally accept us as we are, always and everywhere, and when you're gay or lesbian ..."

"Or African," Eddie interjected.

"...is no longer special, only then will we have won the battle against the still widespread discrimination."

The bank robber clapped his hands. "Bravo! You should be chancellor."

Berti's anger grew to infinity again.

My time will come.

He felt a tipping point in his body. A testosterone volcano erupted. The forced march was like medicine for him. "Konny, you're great and I love you."

"Hey, hey, hey, friends of the sun! We're not at a dance. Keep your hands off each other or I'll puke."

Berti jumped up. That was too much. He wanted to stomp Ranzinger into the ground. But the attack failed in the early stages. The heavyweight's stomach caught on the table. He slid forward into a chair. It fell with a crash and right in front of Berti's legs. He got stuck and slammed down like a felled tree. Pain raced through his body like twitching lightning. They were almost as bad as Ranzinger's unmistakable laughter.

"Schwartz, you're unbelievable. I'm going to pee my pants laughing."

Except for a "Grmppff", nothing came out of Berti's lips. Now he knew how the Russian bull's neck must have felt after Kapaunke's judo throwing treatment.

Konny was scared to death. "Berti," he cried in horror and knelt down beside him.

Eddie put the chair back and adjusted the table.

Konny almost went crazy. "Blood! Oh God, he's bleeding," came the shrill cry.

Ranzinger didn't understand the commotion. "Calm down, Mother Theresa. Your bedfellow just has a nosebleed, it'll stop in a minute."

Five minutes later, Berti was sitting on the bench, pressing a damp tea towel to his neck, which Ranzinger, of all people, had given him. The handkerchief in front of his nose was reddish in places.

By now it had become pleasantly warm in the alpine hut. Konny moved two chairs closer to the tiled stove and hung his and Berti's winter jackets on them to dry.

"And now the shoes, and if the socks are wet, those too," he said.

Eddie also took off his shoes and socks. "I'm keeping my pants on, though, ey man. Don't get your hopes up."

Ranzinger agreed. "Me too."

"The pants aren't so wet that we have to take them off, you two chickenhearts," Konny laughed.

"Just because we're normal doesn't mean we're chicken, man."

"Eddie, we were just talking about that. Are we both not normal? It hasn't been ten minutes since you had a guilty conscience."

"Leave the half-monkey alone. He's right. We're normal, you're gay."

"There goes the racist again! Sometimes we hit the ho-mos, sometimes the blacks, then the Turks, the Chinese, and so on. You only have a big mouth because you've got a gun in your hand. Without the gun, you'd be scared."

"You're risking a pretty big lip right now!"

"Because you're sick. You're getting on our nerves."

Ranzinger's forehead wrinkled again.

Eddie, on the other hand, had a clear conscience. "I told you before, I can't help it when I get nervous. Then a few careless words slip out of my mouth."

Konny took a deep breath. He closed his eyes. I have to calm down, he said to himself.

Ranzinger took the floor. "Now listen, boys. I'm going to make a suggestion."

Konny opened his eyes. "I can't wait to see it."

"Me too," came Berti's nasal voice.

"Hey, man. What kind of suggestion? Do you want to pay for the taxi? It won't be cheap."

"No shit now! Watch out, you pansies." A short pause. "Sorry," the criminal added.

"Hey man, come on."

"We found a great hut here. No one will get here so fast in this snow chaos. Our snow tracks are also impossible to follow ..."

"There are no snow tracks, but tracks in the snow, and you don't follow them, you follow them."

Ranzinger raised his pistol again. The barrel pointed to the wooden ceiling. "I'd like to pull the trigger, but I want to make peace."

"What do you mean? Peace."

"Can I finally make my proposal?"

"Go ahead. We've been waiting all this time and you keep beating around the bush."

"Where was I?"

"In the hot hut," Berti mumbled.

"Hey man, whatever you think, forget it. I see two queers, uh, two homosexuals, a crazy guy with a gun in his hand, and me. I'm not going to be part of any mess. I don't like men. Do you all understand that? I'm all about women."

"Let him talk," Berti muttered, about to stick a piece of tissue up his nostril. He waited to see if there was still any blood, and was satisfied that there was none. Then he took a quick look at the edge of the table he had grabbed earlier. Damn table! How could he have missed that stupid table?

The black African looked insistently at Berti and Konny. "Can I ask you something?"

"Go ahead."

"Don't you ever fancy a woman? I mean a really hot chick?"

Berti shook his head. "No! That leaves me cold. Especially when I think of my period." He looked at the handkerchief. Disgusted, he stood up. "Can I throw it in the oven?" he asked, just in case, so as not to irritate Ranzinger.

The criminal nodded in agreement. "Sure thing, buddy. You might as well take the opportunity to fill up. After the ice march, the warmth will do you good."

"Hey man, you know nothing about women. I think you're just too chicken."

"Believe me Eddie, I tried. It wasn't the best," Konny said.

"Really?" Berti was astonished.

"I was sixteen, she was twice that age. She got me drunk, then we jumped in the box."

"And?" Eddie asked.

"And..." Konny rolled her eyes. "And nothing, of course!"

"Like nothing?"

"Earth's gravity! Everything was pointing down. For me because of the alcohol, for her because of the big breasts."

"And I was afraid you might like both," Berti was relieved.

Konny grinned, Eddie made a face and Berti sighed.

The criminal intervened. "Before things get too romantic between you lovebirds, may I make my proposal?"

Everyone agreed. "Sure thing."

"So ...", the hostage-taker tried again, "... we've got a great hut here where no one would suspect us. We have to spend the whole night here, there's no way around it."

"Hey man, we don't have to!"

"Shut up or ..."

Eddie demonstratively put his hands over his mouth.

Ranzinger continued. "I'm meeting with my people tomorrow. After that, I'll let you go. Word of honor."

"Why not before?" Konny asked.

"Because then you comedians will call the cops."

"We don't do that," Berti groaned.

"Hey man, we really don't do that," Eddie said, clapping his hands. "That's all settled then. My clothes are already dry, I'll traipse back to the cab." Eddie stood up.

"Sit down!"

It came clearly and unmistakably. Immediately, the black African's body sank back into his seat.

168

"It's clear that we're going to spend the night together in this hut. You can stand on your head and fart La Paloma! It's set in concrete."

"It's okay, we're not stupid," Konny spoke up. He wanted to prevent another stupid comment that could cause irritation.

"I could tie you up, separate you..."

"How? Ey man!"

"Easy – listen. I will put you in the right shithouse out there, the fat one in the left toilet ..."

"Which one's the ladies' room, ey man?"

"Eddie! Shut up," Berti hissed.

The taxi driver justified himself. "The way this guy has to insult people all the time, I always have to talk when I'm scared. I can't keep my mouth shut. That's just the way it is. Sorry."

"Peace," Ranzinger bellowed. "For fuck's sake, you assholes! I want to make peace for tonight. Do you understand that?"

Silence fell. No one said a word.

"There you go," Ranzinger groaned in relief. "We'll cook something tasty for dinner. I've seen canned food. Besides, they've probably got some booze stashed somewhere. We'll play cards and go to bed later." He gave Konny and Berti a warning look. "Every man for himself! And we're leaving tomorrow morning. That gives me an hour's head start. That's enough."

He looked at the men proudly. "Well, what do you think?"

Berti: "I would be hungry."

Konny: "What was that about peace?"

Eddie: "Hey man, I'm not sleeping in the same room with them."

Berti: "Asshole!"

"That's not how it works," Ranzinger interjected. "Are we making peace? Yes or no?"

They all looked at each other.

"If you do, it's on your word of honor. No one is allowed to trick anyone. Everything will be honest. I'll even put the gun away," the hostage-taker suggested.

"I agree," said Konny and nudged Berti.

"Me too."

"Hey man, but only if we..."

"Eddie too," Konny drowned out the taxi driver.

169

"Very well, but please keep your distance from me. The ride from the wild bull earlier was enough for me," Ranzinger alluded to Berti's attempted attack. "And leave the kitchen knives where they are. Even if I only have the gun in my pocket, I'm lightning fast on the draw, and when I shoot, I hit. And now, your word of honor!"

"Don't you trust us?"

"You all give me your word of honor that we will keep the peace until tomorrow morning. No one will attack the other. No one flees, which would mean death in this weather anyway, and no one ... oh fuck, you know what I mean. Just peace!"

"Word of honor," Konny raised his hand.

Berti imitated him. "Word of honor."

"Yo man, you got my word of honor and all."

"Good, then I give you my word of honor," Ranzinger confirmed and slipped Rudi Radtke's service weapon into his waistband.

"What kind of canned goods did you mean?"

"Ravioli, bean soup, Mexican stew, lentil stew, and so on. There are at least three pallets of them back there."

"Two ravioli for me," Berti ordered. "Any extra spices?"

"Cook for yourself!"

"Can you see what the bar has to offer, ey man?"

"Go ahead, Eddie," the criminal grinned and stepped aside to let the black African pass.

"Ey man, no offense?"

"We're at peace."

"Peace is a really cool act. Do they have a sound machine here?"

"I don't know, but probably not. There's no electricity."

"And when it gets dark?"

"Candles."

Berti had also gotten up and pushed past Ranzinger to inspect the kitchenette and the cans. "There's still gas in here. We have three pots. Knut has the food," he paused and looked at Ranzinger. "Should I say Knut or Detlev?"

"Never mind."

"Then I'd better say Detlev. Yesterday's song is still ringing in my ears. I already know: *Hey Knut ... la la laa laaa*".

Ranzinger waved him off. "I'm totally fine."

Berti was in a great mood, considering the hot meal that was about to be served. "So I'll take your orders. What would you like to eat?"

"Serbian bean stew," Ranzinger ordered.

"Detlev, you can take a nap in the next room," Berti suggested. "Every little bean makes a little noise."

"Texas pot," Eddie said.

"Okay, you can sleep with Detlev. You can have a fart duel."

"Better than between you two," he laughed.

Konny grinned. "Then I guess we'll both be eating ravioli after your wish earlier?"

"Yes," Berti confirmed.

The pots were on the stove in no time. It was really cozy in the chalet. It was warm, the wood crackled in the tiled stove, and it was snowing outside. After a while, the smell of warm food spread.

"I found some wine," Berti cheered, picking up a bottle. He stood behind the bar.

"After last night, I'd like some water or tea," Konny said.

Ranzinger went to Berti behind the counter and rummaged through the shelves. "I saw some tea somewhere earlier," he said. "Well, where is it?" He seemed as relaxed and at ease as when he was a cult leader on the train. He radiated happiness. "It's going to be a real proper evening at the cabin."

"You could even call it cabin magic," Berti replied, turning around. He held a wooden spoon in his left hand.

Ranzinger was standing right opposite him. The criminal grinned at Berti. "Pretty narrow here. What do you think, fat boy?"

Berti narrowed his eyes. He hated that word.

What would Magnum or Sherlock Holmes do now?

Every single insult rumbled up again. Echoing in his head. Berti saw Detlev's face in his mind. His mouth opened and insults packed in speech bubbles came out again and again. They floated up, burst and rained insults of all kinds. The detective felt an enormous inner tension. Blood rushed to his cheeks. He didn't want peace. You couldn't make peace with people like that. What had his father always said when little Berddi stood in front of him crying and wouldn't reveal who had been bullying him at school?

"Bert, you have to lie in situations. This is complicated."

The decision was made in a split second. He didn't know what Sherlock Holmes would do, but he knew what Jason Statham or Vin Diesel would do. Berti would take out the bank robber. This time it was time. There was no turning back. Ranzinger was standing right in front of him, his gun tucked into his belt. Berti's right hand clenched into a fist. The white came out at the knuckles.

"Don't always call me fat," the detective's lips came out in anger. It was like a stroke of the whip. Warning enough.

If he didn't react now and pull the gun, it would be his downfall.

Ranzinger did not react. Herbert Schwartz struck. In spite of a slightly awkward looking movement, the fist landed on Detlev Ranzinger's chin. He saw the punch coming, but was far too surprised to dodge. He took it, mumbled something about "peace" and fell over.

"Berti," Konny yelled.

"Hey man, you broke your word of honor," the taxi driver scolded.

"Eddie, we won, we're free," Berti cheered.

"Hey man, that's really cool. If that's the case, of course it's okay."

"Yes. Yea. Yea," Herbert Schwartz cheered, raising his fist in victory. For the first time in his life, he had dared to do something. If there were a personal diary, the headline would read: Berti fought back! He was the hero of the day. He had knocked out a brutal criminal, a bank robber, a drug smuggler and a swindler. He, Herbert Schwartz, the sports whistle, landed a knockout blow. At that moment he felt like Klitschko, Muhamed Ali, Joe Frazier and Mike Tyson all rolled into one. Berti the superstar! Berti the knockout, Berti the battering ram in the ring!

When Ranzinger regained consciousness, his three former hostages were sitting at the table eating together.

"Mhmmm, delicious," Konny smacked her lips. "I never knew I liked ravioli so much."

"The Texas-Can is the hit, ey man."

"That's the flair of hut magic," Berti grinned.

Ranzinger was furious. They had taped his hands and legs. He felt like a package in the mail. "You bastards! You've broken the code of honor! Schwartz, you fat pig, I'll kill you!"

"Shut up, Detlev, or your Serbian bean stew will be my dessert," the detective winked.

Ranzinger wanted to get up, but that was impossible. "I look like a Christmas package, loosen my shackles."

"We're sorry, but we didn't find anything but a Tesa package. After dinner, one of us will go down to Garmisch and call the police. We've already tried and dialed 911, but there's no reception here."

"I'm going to kill you. All three of you. You faggots."

"Hey man, I'm totally straight."

Berti stood up and put a strip of tape over Ranzinger's mouth. "Shut up, Knut, that's a good one! Great, isn't it? I just made it up. Knut do-not-good. That'll be your new nickname in prison."

The meal was a hit. A simple, unpopular canned meal was celebrated like a feast.

"I can't remember ever having such delicious ravioli," Berti blew out.

The hot meal was a boon to his body. He had reheated three cans for the two of them and had eaten a good two of them himself. He felt full. "If I eat another dumpling, I'll burst," he said, leaning back.

"The Texas pot is great! But..." Eddie didn't have to say more. The rumbling in his stomach was clearly audible.

"You should go to the house with the little hearts."

"I can't," the black African denied.

"What do you mean?"

"I can't poop in the cold."

"But you won't have a choice."

Eddie looked hopefully at the curtain that led to the next room.

"Forget it! You're going out," came Berti's voice.

Rudi Radtke and Reinhard Schneider had fought their way through the wild winter weather by stealth. While the tour was nothing special for the forester, the civilian investigator had to realize that his biological age was far ahead of his actual age. Only the will to erase the shame of the morning drove the lover of the Yeager Master forward. He made three crosses and would have loved to drink his last *Jägermeister* as a reward when they finally reached their destination, but he couldn't stand spectators. After all, he would have had to share.

So he had to wait. Completely frozen, he and Schneider crouched behind the outhouses and watched the cabin.

"They must be in the house. Smoke comes out of the chimney. The hut has been closed for two weeks," whispered the forester.

"What if the tenant is having a private party?"

"Forget it. The tenant is my cousin. He won't stay up here a day longer than he has to. His old lady is a dragon. That's another reason why I don't have a wife."

"No wife? Uh-huh."

Schneider gave Radtke a dirty look. "What does that mean?"

"Nothing. It was just something that happened."

"Oh yes, you did. You thought I was gay, didn't you?"

"No. You're not the type."

"Why am I not the type? What are you trying to say? Do you think I'm not good-looking?"

"Rubbish."

"So I look good? You just said I look good."

"I didn't!"

"You did!"

The forester's pedantic nature was annoying. "All right then. Then I just said it," Radtke hissed.

"You can find men handsome and not be gay."

"I don't look at men."

"Then why were you looking at me?"

"I wasn't."

"You were. Before we left, your eyes went up and down my body."

"I was just assessing how you would fare in battle..." Radtke was tired of talking about nonsense. "... Oh, let's leave it at that."

"I could imagine that a lot of homos like me."

"In that case, have fun."

"No, I didn't mean it like that."

"Then how?"

Schneider made a contemptuous gesture with his hand. What could this potty-mouthed big-city cop from the middle ranks of the police, or the second qualification level, as it's called in New German, possibly know? He's a worker ant without a brain, nothing more. An

174

evolutionary class below me, thought the forester and asked: "How do we proceed?"

"My colleague wanted to go to the police station in Garmisch and send reinforcements."

"Then the mountain rescue will come."

Radtke looked at his neighbor incredulously. "Why?"

"Because that's always the case here. Half of the police work as volunteers for the mountain rescue."

"And the other half?"

"The policeman?"

"No, the mountain patrol."

"Teachers, farmers and so on. Oh yes, there are also a few people from the local canine club, of course. They have top-notch trained mountain rescue dogs."

"Watch out," Radtke warned, pointing to the mountain hut.

Schneider immediately fell silent. The door had opened. A black African stepped onto the porch. His eyes went to the toilets. Radtke and Schneider immediately ducked.

"It's you! I recognized the colored man."

"That wasn't too difficult," the forester breathed.

"I'll draw my rifle, then we'll storm the mountain pasture!"

Schneider swallowed. "The mountain rescue team will be here soon. We should wait."

"For the mountain rescue?"

Schneider nodded.

"What a load of rubbish! We're going in! The taxi driver didn't look very hostage-like."

"I left my guns at home and can't help you."

"My gun is more than enough."

"I'll wait here and brief the mountain rescue team as soon as they arrive."

"Instruct them? You mean you will show the rescue team the way from the two shithouses to the hut?"

"Uh, yes. I would do that."

"Whistle."

"I'm not a whistleblower. There will be repercussions."

Radtke paid no further attention to the ranger. He was about to jump up and rush to the cabin when he heard snow crunching. He drew his gun. The cool policeman's hand shook a little. He should have drunk his last *Jägermeister.*

Has the black man seen us? Is he charging at us to overpower us? Does he belong to Ranzinger's gang? Is he not a hostage at all, but an accomplice? Or is it Stockholm Syndrome and the hostages have joined forces with Ranzinger?

While he was pondering these questions, the door of a bathroom stall was pulled open and slammed shut. Moments later he heard Eddie's voice. "Ey man ey! This is crazy. How can you take a dump in here? The jungle camp has a luxury toilet compared to this cesspool. What a load of shit! I'm used to shitting in the White House. For God's sake, I just have to get over myself and set up my island here. Then I'll be like Adolf. Me on top and just brown shit underneath. Oh man, that's disgusting."

Next came sounds that reminded both Radtke and Schneider of machine gun fire.

"Wow! I'll never eat Texas again. Horrible!"

"You hold the door, I'll storm the cabin," the plainclothesman whispered to the ranger.

"Wait, I..."

"Just sit down in front of that stupid door!"

This order was heard. Schneider crawled around the small house on all fours. He leaned against the door in a sitting position and crossed his arms demonstratively. "If anything happens to me, there will be consequences!" He wrinkled his nose. "And besides, it smells bad."

"Hey man. This is occupied, take the other throne. Who are you anyway? Konny or Berti?"

Ranzinger replied. "Shut up in there! This is the police!"

"And the forestry department," Schneider added.

Radtke stormed off.

Someone pushed open the door. "Police! Don't move!"

Ranzinger closed his eyes in shock as he recognized police chief Rudi Radtke.

Konny dropped the empty cans he was trying to stuff into a garbage bag. Berti jumped up. "Hurray! We've been saved. I couldn't have imagined this morning that I'd be happy to see your face."

The policeman saw the handcuffed robber. At the same time, Konny and Berti's torrent of words poured out of him. Outside, Eddie was banging on the toilet door, shouting something about torture and horrible smells.

Minutes later, everyone was sitting around a table in the cabin. Except for Ranzinger. The tied up bank robber was still cowering on the floor, mumbling unintelligible curses. The scene was reminiscent of the last page of an Asterix comic. Cacofonix was tied and gagged to a tree.

The forester had been fiddling with something in the next room and was the last to arrive at the table.

Radtke and Schneider's snow-soaked coats were also hanging out to dry in front of the tiled stove. They drank tea. One by one, they told the policeman about the hostage drama. Radtke had a Dictaphone running. It all sounded so crazy. A jumble of experiences. Radtke doubted it at first, because it sounded like a crazy story from a modern-day Munchausen book, but in the end he believed that everything had happened exactly as the three hostages had told it, independently of each other. In the end, he didn't care. He had achieved his goal and gathered enough evidence to put Ranzinger behind bars for many years. He had taken bitter revenge for the humiliation he had suffered, and he could already see the headlines: Munich civilian investigator brings bank robber and hostage-taker to justice.

"Is there anything solid to drink here?" he asked. "We need to celebrate. We've caught a serious criminal. The hostages are all unharmed and all the stolen money has been recovered."

"Hey man, and you got your gun back."

"What makes you think it's my gun?"

"That's what the guy said."

At that moment, Radtke decided to rethink the newspaper article and the press conference.

Journalists might ask uncomfortable questions. Maybe it was better to enjoy the success in silence.

"Hey, man. I just remembered something. About the money."

Berti was curious. "What is it, Eddie?"

"The guy shot my car, but not the meter. It should be running. That's an expensive ride."

"Charge him for it," Radtke said rather irrelevantly.

"Great, I'll take the money. That's where his money is."

Berti shook his head. "Eddie, that's stolen goods."

Radtke laughed out loud. "Did you sleep on a comedy site today, or what? That money is confiscated, effective immediately."

The cabbie watched his wages float away.

"Your colleagues and the mountain rescue are on their way," said Schneider.

"How did you get this information? There's no cell phone reception in this godforsaken wilderness."

The forester smiled superiorly. It was the sardonic smile of a loser playing a trump card. "There's a CB radio in the next room, in the back corner, under the tablecloths and towels. It always works. I radioed the guys in Garmisch and told them we were here and I ... uh," he improved, "... we ... overpowered the bank robber."

While Schneider felt like a hero, Radtke was looking for alcohol and Eddie was offended that he didn't get his money right away, Konny only had eyes for his Berti. He was proud of the hero who had knocked down the criminal with a single punch. Soon he would give him the ultimate surprise. The anticipation was immense. "Now all we have to do is get to our hotel."

"Which hotel have you booked?" Schneider asked curiously.

"Berghotel Alpentraum."

"Noble, noble. I wouldn't have thought so. Highest luxury class."

"If only we were already in Garmisch, we could take a taxi to the hotel."

"I've had enough of taxi rides," said Konny.

Schneider agreed with him. "Why take a taxi? The hotel is twenty minutes from here. The snow is gone anyway. You just have to follow the path."

"We can't even see it in this winter landscape," replied Berti, who was still smarting from the strenuous walk to the mountain pasture.

"That's not a problem," Schneider waved off. "There are signposts all along the way. The trail starts right after the pasture. You walk along the forest, make a turn, and you'll see the Berghotel Alpentraum."

Konny repeated and looked at Berti questioningly. "Sounds easy and much faster than the long way back to Garmisch".

The forester confirmed: "It's a piece of cake."

"I don't know," Berti muttered.

"It's another three-hour walk back to Garmisch. If you prefer that, then ..."

"Convinced," Berti interjected.

The forester looked at his watch. "It'll be dark in about an hour. You should get going."

Konny got up, went to the tiled stove and grabbed his jacket. "The clothes are dry and warm."

Berti got up as well. "Then let's say goodbye."

"Hey man, guys. It was nice to meet you."

"See you, Eddie!"

"Your ride..."

"...pays Ranzinger, at least that's what I thought," Berti said.

Eddie winked one eye. "You got it."

Konny had slipped into his winter coat. "Mr. Schneider, how much should we pay your cousin for the tins and the tea?"

The forester waved him off. "He has enough money. He should write up all the damage, add the cans and claim everything from the gangster boss. He was responsible for it."

While Berti got dressed, he whistled the tune of *Hey Jude* and sang softly: "*La la la la laaa ...*"

Ranzinger rolled his eyes.

Radtke was jubilant. "Here's a bottle of wine. I'll try the swill. To celebrate the day, so to speak. Anybody want another glass?"

"Hey man, you're on duty."

"It's not my area of responsibility, so I can get permission. Besides, it's none of your business."

Ranzinger mumbled something unintelligible.

Schneider said: "Should we take off his gag? Maybe he can't breathe?"

"Oh, nonsense. That would make him fidget even more," Radtke dismissed the suggestion, but thought better of it and finally agreed. "Fine by me."

"Hey man, I'd love to do that," Eddie grinned.

"Go ahead," Radtke nodded.

The cabbie walked over to the handcuffed bank robber and leaned down. "Well, Mr. Ranzinger - big mouth racist. Are we a little unshaven today and have a few too many hairs on our faces?"

179

"Hm ... hm ... mhmm," the criminal muttered.

"You want to tell me something? Wait, I'll help you," Eddie grinned, grabbed the tape and ripped it off with a vengeance.

Ranzinger's expression changed several times. Then came a scream: "Ahhhhhhhh ... Ouch ... Ahhh."

"Oh," Eddie joked. "There's still hair on it."

"I'm going to take you apart and fillet you, you cotton picker ..."

"Should I put that piece of tape over my mouth again?"

"You monkey ass in jeans. I know so many ..."

Radtke raised his thumb.

"Yes, then," Eddie sighed mockingly, and his mouth was taped shut again. "You had your chance."

Berti and Konny were ready to leave.

"Goodbye then," they waved into the living room.

"We're in Bavaria and we say *Pfiati* or *Servus*," Radtke grumbled. "The wine tastes sour. Is there anything decent here?"

Berti pointed to the bar. "The rum is on the bottom shelf."

Radtke's features relaxed. "That's tradition. When you're in an alpine hut, you drink hunter's tea. And I'm just keeping the old customs alive," he explained.

"All right," Konny grinned. „And so you really love the old custum. Wright?"

The policeman looks at the author. „Why?"

„Cause the bottle is almost empty."

Berti opens his eyes wide. „Almos empty? This bottle was full. How can it be empty?"

Radtke coughed and looked down. Then he cleared his throat and said: "I was thirsty and it was cold, so I drank enough hunter-tea. There's nothing wrong with that."

Konny answered: „You can do whatever you want. But promise me one thing. When you get home, please take a look in the mirror and see yourself. Then be honest with yourself and make the right thing of it. Now we say goodbye. The vacation begins."

Radtke nodded. "Hey man, an now have a nice holiday."

"Hello everyone."

The two friends left.

I hope I never see those two comedians again, thought Radtke, found the rum and smiled. The day was saved.

Chapter 7
Campfire romance

Silence. Except for the crunch of the snow as they walked and the sound of their own breathing, there was nothing to be heard. Not a sound. No noise. Just nature and the two of them.

Above them, mountain peaks rose into the sky, their tops piercing the dark clouds and disappearing into them completely. Below them, a belt of forest stretched along the foot of the mountain, the trees of which could only be glimpsed under the masses of snow. Now and then, the tops of conifers could be seen beneath the thick blanket of snow. The white splendor had covered the entire land like a veil. The breathtaking beauty of nature revealed itself to the two city dwellers in all its glory, inviting them to linger.

At that moment, all the fears and efforts of the strange day were forgotten. They could not stop marveling. With every step they took, they penetrated deeper into the wilderness of the mountain massif. The hut became smaller and smaller. The air was crisp and cold. They made their first tracks in an untouched winter landscape and felt like the explorers of faraway America. They felt what the old trappers must have felt when they ventured into the Rocky Mountains. The friends were free. They were adventurers. They were against the wilderness.

Delineators led the way. The tops of the poles, some as thick as an arm, had been driven into the ground in late fall, their black and red paint clearly visible against the snow. For the first time in their lives, Herbert Schwartz and Konrad Wels felt the power of nature.

Berti pulled the wagon again. Contrary to all his fears, he felt in great shape. "The ravioli gave me strength. I should eat them more often."

Konny smiled. He was just happy.

"This view makes all the effort worthwhile. I never thought it would be so beautiful here."

"It's insane. Now I can understand the crazy winter sports enthusiasts. The untouched nature is just indescribable. I feel like I'm following in the footsteps of Jack London. This strength, this view, this power and..."

Berti was a little surprised. He marched behind Konny. "What does a condom manufacturer have to do with nature here?"

The writer was horrified. "Berti! Don't you know Jack London?"

"Sure! True to feeling, sure ..."

The writer clapped his hands in front of his eyes. "No! That's a writer."

"Sorry," said Berti. "I've never heard of him."

"That can't be right. You surely know Wolf's Blood, Call of the Wild or The Sea Wolf."

"Score! I've seen them on TV."

Breathe a sigh of relief. Berti didn't grow up in an intellectual wasteland. "Thank God, I thought you were a..."

"A what?" came the startled reply. Berti stopped.

Konny stopped as well. "Oh, nothing."

"And that London guy wrote all that?"

"Around the turn of the century before last."

"I've read a lot, but I must have missed Jack London. You can't know everything. And what does this Jack have to do with the condoms?"

"The London condoms are from Durex. They bought the London Rubber Company. Jack London is a writer. They're two different shoes."

"And I always thought I knew a lot more than you."

They both laughed and walked on. The next few minutes passed in silence. Slowly, walking in the heavy fresh snow became tiring, especially when they left the sheltered part of the path. Snowdrifts piled up ahead of them, some as high as a meter.

"I am glad to leave all this behind. When we get to the hotel later, I just want to get into the bathtub and then into bed."

The cabin was finally out of sight.

"It can't be far now," Konny said happily. "We've been on the road longer than Mr. Schneider predicted."

The path, marked by delineators, led into a wooded area. The friends thought they were close to their destination and stopped paying attention to the wooden posts that pointed the way. They always chose the widest path through the trees. Eventually, the wooden signposts disappeared.

The sky closed in ominously again. It began to snow again. They looked respectfully at the sky between the treetops.

Konny didn't like it at all. "The weather is changing again."

"The forester said we could easily make it in twenty minutes. Now we've been walking for over half an hour. Once we cross the forest, we'll see the hotel for sure," Berti reassured us.

The snowflakes were getting bigger, and despite the protection of the spruce and fir trees, the visibility was quickly becoming as bad as it had been in the morning. The wind came up. It carried cold polar air. Like a big polar bear, it slapped the two hikers in the face with its icy paw. Their eyebrows turned white. Small drops had formed on the tips of their noses. It felt like the cold was tearing at their exposed skin.

"We should go back," Konny said.

Berti bravely fought his way forward. Since his victory against Ranzinger, he had never known the word "surrender". "Let's cross the forest first. First, we'll be better protected from the weather, and second, the hotel is there," he said confidently.

That was convincing enough. Konny agreed. However, they no longer walked behind each other, but next to each other. That gave them more security.

The spruce and fir trees braced themselves against the storm and formed a natural shield. Only a small uneasiness crept up in them as dusk slowly fell. It grew gradually. None of them dared to express it. They were afraid of getting lost in this wilderness. Dully, they put one foot in front of the other. Their hats were pulled down low over their faces, the hoods of their winter parkas were pulled up over their heads, and the zippers were pulled all the way up. Step by step they moved forward. Minute after minute passed. Metre by metre they penetrated deeper into the forest. It was getting darker and darker. Nightfall cast its shadow ahead. At some point Konny stopped.

"What's going on?" asked Berti. "Do you see the hotel?"

"I don't see anything. That means there are only trees and snow here." There was desperation in Konny's voice.

Berti raised his head. "Where... where is the path?" he stammered.

All eyes followed. They were gone. There were no landmarks for them to follow.

Konny said what Berti didn't want to admit. "I think we've lost our way",

Horror spread.

"That can't be right. We were on the road the whole time," Berti thought.

"That's what I thought, too," Konny replied, venting his despair. "Damn wilderness. At least in the city there are street names, the cell phone works, there are taxis and buses. But here?" he cried almost hysterically. "There's only this damned wilderness. We're going to die."

Berti tried to play the strong man, even though he wanted to cry. "Now pull yourself together! We're not going to die. We'll go back, find the path, follow it and get to the hotel soon."

Konny looked at Berti. "It's good that I have you with me. I feel safe there."

Berti was astonished, suppressed his fear and breathed a sigh of relief. Konny believed in him. That gave him strength. Without his friend he would have collapsed miserably. Now he was the strong one. "My nerves are more than tense. This journey is a journey from hell," he said.

"I think I'll write a book about it."

"A good idea. It'll be a bestseller. I can see the title now. Lost in the Wilderness of Germany!"

A branch could no longer withstand the weight of the snow and broke. The cracking and crashing startled the friends. Panic gripped them.

"Are there really wild animals here?"

Konny hesitated to answer. He was about to reassure Berti when he remembered something.

"Bears! There must be bears here." He thought for a moment and confirmed his statement. "Bears and wolves. I saw that on TV once. Damn it! We're lost. Instead of recovering in a luxury hotel, we end up as animal food."

"The forester would never have let us go alone if it was so dangerous."

Berti doubted. "Did you see his eyes?"

"No."

"Those were the eyes of a madman. He will follow our tracks, wait until the wild animals have eaten us, and then steal our valuables."

"Now you're going too far, Berti."

A certain uneasiness could not be shaken off now. They had the feeling that they were being watched all the time. When a fox successfully finished his hunt and a wild rabbit uttered its last death cry, the friends stood back to back.

"I've been thinking," Konny said. "It can't be bears."

"Why not?"

"They hibernate."

"Wolves, then?" asked Berti.

"Possibly."

"What do you suggest?"

"We should arm ourselves."

"With what?"

Konny looked around. "With wooden clubs."

"And then?"

"We'll follow our old tracks."

An owl's call echoed through the forest. Some deer jumped through the undergrowth.

"Do we have a flashlight in the car?"

Berti thought for a moment. "No."

"We should pack one for the future," Konny suggested.

"If we survive this, I'll pack two."

Konny took a brave breath. "Let's go before it gets completely dark."

For the first fifty meters it was no problem to follow their tracks, but then they became increasingly unrecognizable. Snow, and especially drifting snow, meant that soon nothing was recognizable. After another two hundred meters they stood before nothing. Snow-covered, untouched earth. And as usual for a forest, there were only trees all around, some of whose undergrowth seemed impenetrable. Dusk drew the darkness of the night behind them faster than Konny and Berti had imagined. They had underestimated the distance and overestimated themselves. They also admitted that they were lost.

"How could this happen? We are two adults."

"I don't know."

"Do you see a hidden camera somewhere? Maybe we've been tricked all day?"

Konny felt like crying, but suddenly he started to laugh out loud.

Berti was surprised. "Are you completely crazy? What's there to laugh about? We're going to die," he yelled.

"I ... I ..." the author gasped. "I feel like Stan and Olli. We're fat and stupid."

"I'm not fat!"

As soon as he said it, Berti had to laugh himself. "Hi hi hi ... of course I'm fat, but then you're stupid ... ha ha ha".

In their greatest despair, they stood in the forest and laughed. Tears welled up in their eyes. Their diaphragm burned. Stomach pains caused them to gasp for breath. Only slowly did the friends calm down. "Do you ... hi, hi ... have a handkerchief?"

"Wait a minute ... yes ... here."

Two minutes later, the laughter was over.

"Now let's think logically," the writer began to analyze their situation. "We came from the west and were going east."

"Right!"

"So we have to get our bearings from the trees. As far as I know, the moss is on the weather side. So we have to go in that direction. If we keep going straight, we'll get out of the forest."

That sounded reasonable.

"Can you pull the wagon? I'm getting tired."

"Of course."

"We must not fall asleep. I've read about it and seen it in movies. If you fall asleep, you freeze to death!"

"We're not dying, honey. We survived a hostage situation today."

"You're right. We are heroes."

They took off. If it hadn't been dusk, they wouldn't have noticed that they were only ten feet from the forest trail they were desperately searching for. By now they were armed with branches they had picked up from the ground.

"This is for our defense."

As darkness fell, it grew colder. Frost crept under the clothes of the two men. Their conversations had long since fallen silent. Sometimes they walked side by side, sometimes behind each other. Although the two unlucky men had planned to walk straight ahead, they zigzagged through the forest unnoticed. This again proved to be a stroke of luck. Eventually they made it and found themselves on a wider path. Hope grew. But also tiredness. Konny had to keep pushing his friend, because Berti had finally reached the end of his tether. The euphoria of defeating the bank robber had long since dissipated.

After what seemed like an hour, they reached the edge of the forest. In front of them was open ground again. They had made it through the forest.

"And now what?" gasped Berti, who was about to collapse.

Konny stared intently into the darkness. But it was impossible to see anything because of the snowfall. He walked a few meters further. "There's something there," he realized. He also noticed that it was much windier and snowier than they had noticed in the forest.

Berti stared into the darkness of the night, shivering. "What did you see? A wild animal?"

"Nonsense. Something stands out from the surroundings. Wait here, I'll go there and ..."

"I'm coming with you."

"Hey man, why don't you wait here and get some rest?"

"That's sweet of you, but..." he hesitated. He had noticed something. "Hey, are you copying Eddie?"

Konny laughed. "It's so catchy that you want to imitate it. But the guy really annoyed me with it."

"Me too, but he was kind of funny."

"Exactly! You could really miss him."

"Come on, let's go together."

The something took shape. It was a building whose wooden walls stood out clearly against the white snow despite the darkness.

"Looks like a cabin or something."

"We are saved."

"Careful Konny. The way things are going right now, we're definitely not saved."

"What then?"

"We are Hansel and Gretel and in front of us is the house of the wicked witch. In our case, of course, it's not a witch, it's the forester. He's waiting for us. He'll politely ask us to come in, then lock us in a cage, and at the next opportunity we'll end up as roast meat on the table."

"Don't talk rubbish like that."

"Right, I'm the roast, you're the appetizer."

"Don't be so negative about everything."

"But with my luck, it's like this. Any normal person wins a trip, goes there, and recovers. I, on the other hand, win the trip..."

"Who won it?"

"You did! But I threw in the postcard."

"Who won it?" Konny repeated, looking a little ironic.

"It doesn't matter now," Berti waved him off. "Anyway, we set off on our journey and end up in the Intercity of the Deutsche Bahn between a bunch of crazy people whose head guru is a drug dealer. We also meet a nymphomaniac who wants to eat us, only to be arrested by a drunk policeman when we arrive in Munich. As soon as we're free again, we get into a cab with a crazy guy, get kidnapped, get free again and get lost in the woods. So, my dear, what do you think? Is there a normal house waiting for us? No. It's definitely the house of a thousand horrors."

"Don't be like that. After all, with all the stupid things that have happened, nothing has happened to us. We still have the 100 euros we were going to spend on a taxi, and we even found our way out of a pitch-black forest."

Berti pondered his friend's words for a moment. "From that point of view, you're right." His eyes wandered back to the building. "All right, let's have a look at the hut."

The building was nothing more than a farmer's hayloft. The covered building was closed on three sides, while the side facing the weather was open. Inside the barn, the owner had parked a farm trailer. To the left of it was a mass of hay. It was formed into large round bales. They went inside.

"What a smell," said Konny, taking a deep breath.

It smelled like a meadow, and with it a hint of summer. Since the cold wind was kept out, they felt several degrees warmer. They also stood in the dry. Only every once in a while a few snowflakes blew in.

"It's a carport for hay bales," Berti realized, but he didn't dare go any further into the hay barn.

Konny pushed from behind. "Go on!"

"Wouldn't you rather go first?"

"My God, you're a total coward! And you want to be the coolest detective in town?"

"Konny, stop nagging me. You're scared yourself! And..."

"And what?"

"And we're not in the city either. The countryside isn't my territory," Berti tried to excuse himself.

"Then let's go in together."

"Okay."

Berti took the first step and climbed onto a rake lying on the ground. Of course, he stepped on the upward-pointing tines of the tool. They tipped forward, the wooden handle shot up and landed right in the face of the big-city investigator. Berti took the blow and was startled: "Ow!"

The pain spread in a straight line from his forehead to his nose to his mouth. The foot was lifted again and the rake tipped back. It landed on the ground with a thud.

Konny stepped aside, startled. "What's going on? Is someone there?"

Berti groaned. "Damn, that hurts."

"Did someone hit you?"

"No, I stepped on something."

"Too bad we didn't bring a flashlight."

Berti was unsure. "Should we take cover or not?"

"You're funny. We have no choice. This is our lifesaver. We're safe here. Of course we'll hide."

"If only we had at least a candle with us."

Konny was jubilant. "My God, Berti. That's it! I've got a tea light."

"A tea light? Where did you get a candle?"

"Must have come from the dining car on the train. I must have pocketed it when I was drunk."

"You stole it?"

"I didn't steal!"

"You took a tea light and I'm sure you didn't pay for it."

"Don't be like that. I was drunk as a skunk. Besides, I left a nice tip. That includes the tea light."

"I see," he said smugly. "So you can steal tea lights with a tip?"

Konny repeated. "I tipped the nymphomaniac enough. Surely a tea light is included in the price!"

"You put the check in her cleavage."

"Oh, stop it!"

"Are you mad now?"

Konny hesitated a little.

Berti rowed back. "I'm sorry."

The author relaxed a little. "That's all right. We're both at the end of our tether and have no nerves left. Besides, the tea light is of no use to us since we don't have a fire anyway. Fate of the non-smokers".

"Don't despair, ask Berti!"

Konny was irritated. "What do you mean?"

"Turrilli!" the overweight detective cheered and reached into his pocket. Since the parka hung well over his hips and covered half of his thighs, this process took some time. Berti was also a bit clumsy. When he got his hand out of his pocket, he triumphantly held something between his thumb and forefinger. "Here are some matches. Erna gave them to me. Do you remember?"

"Of course," the author said happily, digging out the candle. "That was a coincidence."

They both walked a little further into the barn. Berti moved very carefully so as not to step on anything again. Effortlessly, he let a match slide across the friction surface. The spark lit the match. Konny held the wick of the tea light into the flame. The light flickered. Konny held a hand protectively over the flat candle. A small glow illuminated the shed. It was a bit dim, but much better than before.

"It's working," Berti said happily. His first glance went to the entrance. "It was a rake."

"What?"

"The blow to my nose."

Konny also looked around. "There seems to be nothing here but hay."

"Shine a light on the side."

"On the trailer?"

"Yes. I want to see what's behind the trailer."

Konny moved slowly. He explored the rick in the dim glow of the tea light. There was a lot of wood on the trailer. It had been cut into large pieces. Suitable for fireplaces and wood-burning stoves. Behind the trailer was an old circular saw. Next to it was something covered. Berti walked over and lifted the cover a little. "That's a diesel compressor. The saw gets its power from it."

"No use for us at the moment."

"Shine a light higher."

Konny walked around the back of the trailer. The glow of the tea light traveled along the wall. Various tools were hung on hooks and nails. A few split logs lay on the floor. A strong gust of wind blew against the outside wall. It whistled and roared under the roof beams. The light flickered wildly, the flame threatening to go out.

"The candle is about to go out," Konny warned.

Berti discovered something. "There's a kerosene lamp hanging there." The detective took two steps forward and picked up the lamp. He shook it and listened. The sloshing of the kerosene could be heard. Berti placed the lamp on the crossbeam where it had been before. He carefully pushed the glass up. "Give me a hand. I can't light the matches and hold this thing up at the same time."

Konny placed the tealight on the beam next to the kerosene lamp, grabbed the lamp glass, and lifted it. Berti struck a match. He skillfully protected the flame from the wind with both hands. "Where did you learn to do that? Did you ever join the Boy Scouts?"

"No, my father taught me. He barbecued his beloved sausages several times each summer. Of course, I helped him build the fire. That's what all little boys like to do."

A bright light shone out. Konny lowered the glass, Berti controlled the height of the wick and thus the brightness with a small wheel on the side of the lamp. The candle flickered a little in the draft, then went out.

"It's actually quite cozy in here," Konny said.

"Well," his partner replied. "I always get really cold. Besides, it draws on the wall like pike soup."

"Come on, let's go over to the hay. It's probably warmer there."

There was a niche behind the first row of hay bales. It was about three meters long and two meters wide. They both sat down. They placed the lamp in the middle of the floor.

191

"There's absolutely no wind here."

"And very pleasant," Berti added. "What do you suggest?"

"There's not much we can do, Berti. We'll have to spend the night here."

"In the middle of the wilderness? Our luxury weekend vacation will turn into an absolute adventure survival vacation."

"We pick hay from the bales to cover ourselves. It might be a little itchy, but it will keep you warm."

"Are there animals in there?"

"What kind of animals?"

Berti tried to be clearer. "Little creepy-crawlies?"

"Bugs and stuff?"

"That's the stuff I'm talking about." The word stuff was emphasized.

"People have been sleeping on or in hay for thousands of years. It's actually very healthy. A hay cure doesn't come cheap."

Berti looked into his friend's eyes. Konny tilted his head to the side and smiled. "At least that's what I read once."

"That would mean that we have also found a kind of wildness luxury here."

"You see, darling, we are absolutely lucky."

"When you say 'little treasure,' I always think of Horst Schlämmer."

Konny stood up. "It's still cold. Come on, let's make ourselves comfortable."

They both began plucking hay from the compressed bales. The wind still blew around the open barn. Snowflakes were still dancing wildly around the entrance. After spreading out a considerable amount of the cut grass, the city boys looked at their work.

"Looks cozy," Berti remarked. "It's still really cold, though."

"Do you think we could have a campfire?"

"Of course. I'm a world champion at making campfires. Daddy Schwartz taught me."

As soon as he had spoken, Berti went to the trailer. He pulled down a few pieces of wood. "This is spruce. Burns well."

"It's great what you know. I'm proud of you already."

The praise spurred him on. Berti walked around the trailer. He had seen an axe earlier. He picked up the axe, went back to the logs and picked out a piece. Then he put it on another log. "Now I'm going to split the wood, make some small pieces and splinters. We'll use them to light the campfire."

Konny watched his friend. At first he was afraid that Berti might hurt himself, but the otherwise rather clumsy do-it-yourselfer handled the small axe relatively well.

"Take care."

"Sure."

Konny turned around. He went to the alcove where they had set up camp and pushed aside the hay lying on the ground. This would be the fire pit. A short scream, followed by an "Ouch!" made him turn around.

"Berti," groaned Konny, full of fear and worry.

"Ha ha," the detective laughed. "Fooled you."

Relief, a little anger and a lot of joy alternated. "Hey man, you scared the hell out of me. Don't ever do that again!"

"Should I call you Eddie from now on?"

Now they were both laughing. As annoying as the taxi driver from Africa was, they had somehow grown fond of him.

"I actually admired the way he countered that Ranzinger on the trip to Garmisch."

"My heart jumped in my pants when he ran at the VW Beetle."

"Stop it! I almost wet my pants," admitted Konny.

"Eddie is a brand in his own right."

"He'd fit right in with us."

Bertie mused. "Do you think so?"

"Why not?"

"Because Ulf would beat up Eddie and his stoner friends after a weed party."

"That's true again. Weed and kids don't go together."

They had enough wood.

"I pushed some straw aside. Do you think this is a good place for a fire?" asked Konny.

Berti looked at the spot and nodded professionally. "Actually there is a very good place. Right where we crash. It's a bit pioneer romantic. It's like the Indians in their teepees."

"Do you want something on the outside?" asked Konny. "I mean some kind of barrier."

"You mean how do we secure it? Like rocks or something?"

Konny nodded.

"Since we don't have any stones and won't find any in front of this hut, I would suggest we dig a hole in the ground. That's protection enough."

"Good idea. Were there any tools in front?"

"Sure, there's a pick and a spade."

"Here in Bavaria, the world is still in order."

"What makes you say that?"

"I think things here would have been stolen a long time ago. Here, people still seem to have respect for other people's property."

"Or fear of the police."

"Of alcohol-Radtke, for example?"

Another burst of laughter. Despite the delicate situation in which the partners found themselves, they felt safe, free and carefree. They had escaped everyday life for that moment. The stress fell away. They were no longer aware of the emergency situation they were in. They had escaped it in an eventful way.

"We are Huckleberry Finn and Tom Sawyer on an adventure."

"I told you we were lucky."

While Konny armed himself with a spade and hoe, Berti chopped up more splinters to light the fire. "We'll ask the hotel who owns the shed here and replace everything," he said.

"And then we'll put something on it. Maybe we'll give the owner a basket of food."

"Or we can invite him to our house."

A good mood spread. All the unpleasantness of the strange journey was wiped away like a wet coat taken off after a downpour. Konny drove the spade into the ground. Although he was very athletic, his movements seemed rather feminine. The blade of the spade was driven less than two centimeters into the hard earth. "I'll probably have to use the pickaxe," he groaned.

"Go ahead."

The tool crashed to the ground. The result was the same as with the spade. A thimbleful of dirt bounced to the side.

"This is concrete earth."

"Maybe the ground is frozen."

"Definitely."

"Let me try," Berti finally said, putting the axe aside and taking the tool from Konny.

He kept his distance while the bulky detective swung the pickaxe. It crashed to the ground. The success was moderate. Again, only a few small pieces of earth bounced to the side.

"We can forget about that. It's probably granite floo-ring or so-mething."

"And now?"

"You've cleared the hay away nicely. If we just make a tiny little fire, it should work."

Konny nodded confidently. He put the spade and hoe away.

"This is a huge sledge. Have you ever seen anything like it?"

"I know what sleds look like."

"No! Definitely not one of those. This is a really big one."

Berti went around the trailer. An old, big sled was leaning against the wall in the entryway. The wood had turned gray over the decades. The runners were bent way up at the front.

"This is a transportation sled. Farmers used it in the winter to bring hay or wood down to the valley. Something like this belongs in a museum."

"It's crazy what values are lying around here."

Meanwhile, the driving snow had taken on the proportions of a blizzard.

Berti had chopped up enough small and tiny splinters of wood. He carefully held a match to the splinters. The flames quickly ate their way up. The detective added larger logs. The acrid smoke danced up in the wind and drifted away. It became comfortably warm next to the fire. After a few sparks flew to the side, they pushed the hay further away.

"That should work," Berti was sure.

Konny didn't trust it. "I saw a tin bucket over there. Should we make the fire in it instead?"

"Like in the ghettos? We stand around the burning garbage can and rap? No, you. But you could put snow in the bucket."

"Why?"

"Extinguishing water! My dad always had fire water by the fire-place."

No sooner said than done. Now everything was perfect, and having been prepared for an emergency, Konny was calm. They sat around the campfire, exhausted but happy. Behind them was a bed of hay. Outside a blizzard was raging and the burning wood in the hayloft was crackling. The fire gave off a pleasant warmth. They were silent, enjoying the moment. They were free and felt like the last survivors after a great catastrophe.

"You, I think this is the right moment," Konny breathed out. His voice was very soft and calm.

"For what?"

The author cleared his throat. "Berti," he began, "we've been together for a while now. I can't imagine being with anyone else. I love you and always want to be with you."

"I feel the same way."

"Will you marry me?"

Berti was touched. "Yes. Yesa. Yes," he cheered.

Konny beamed. "I have a little present for you."

"For me?" came the astonished reply. "I didn't see anything when I was packing. What is it then? A ring?"

Konny grinned. "No. We'll pick it out together when your first money comes in."

"Or you could write a bestseller," the detective smiled.

"Your money will come earlier."

"You always give me such hope."

"It really is like that with money. That's my surprise."

Berti's ears perked up. "Now I'm really curious."

"The thing with Mr. Romer and the shoplifter."

"What about it? You know I don't like to talk about that."

"I've been thinking about it. I couldn't get your thesis about claws out of my head. You also told me about a trip and that Mr. Romer and Ms. Perla were intimate in a careless moment."

"Yes, and?"

"I wondered if they weren't both in cahoots."

"How brilliant," Berti enthused.

"Then I wondered how they were selling the stolen goods."

Berti listened intently to what his friend had to say.

"I know someone on eBay. He owed me a favor, so I contacted him. The result was that Romer has an eBay account under the name

Erotic-Dream. The turnover is considerable. And now comes the kicker. The best!"

"Come on! Don't make it so exciting," Berti bubbled with excitement.

"He's auctioning off women's lingerie of all kinds."

"No!"

"Yes!"

"Now I realize a few things. There were also some travel brochures in Romer's office," he mused. "Why are you telling me about the eBay account now? I could have told the management of the department store ..."

"Because I've already done that, my dear. I pretended to be your secretary and described the facts. One copy went to the store manager and one to the police. The evidence is overwhelming.

"Has there been a response yet?"

"Not yet, but they will fall to their knees before you."

Berti jumped up. He danced around the campfire with joy. "Yay, you're the best."

He stopped in front of Konny. "I love you so much that I want to get married right away."

"Your second case is already solved."

"What second case?"

"The millionaire mattress who shagged her tennis teacher in the luxury lavatory."

"That wasn't a case. We were just taking precautions, weren't we?" came the long answer.

"You were in the shower when Mr. Hindelang called. He was pretty upset, talking about pregnancy and impossible."

"The puke who invited me to the *All You Can Throw Up Bar-B-Q*?"

"Exactly him! His girlfriend whispered to him that she's expecting his child."

"Ow cheek!"

"Exactly! She doesn't know that Hindelang can't conceive. He never told her that he had his spermatic cords cut umpteen years ago."

"Shocking emergency!"

"For her, yes, because I sent him the sequence of our cell phone recording and a detailed report. Registered letter with return receipt!"

"And what did he say?"

"Nothing yet. I took the letter to the post office the day before yesterday."

Berti beamed. "You're really boosting my career."

"Our career, my little angel."

"We're not married yet," Berti murmured.

"But I hope to be very soon."

The campfire romance was perfect.

Brokeback Mountain - Part Three!

They talked late into the night, symbolically in seventh heaven. When they got tired, Berti put two big pieces of wood on the fire, which had almost burned down. Then they both covered themselves with a thick layer of hay. Only their heads were visible. The wind crept around the haystack. The shingles creaked, the fire crackled. The last words had long since fallen silent. Their thoughts wandered about what they had experienced. Nobody would believe what they had experienced today. Konny had met the love of his life. He didn't want to lose her anymore. Berti supported him, was funny and above all honest. He would never let him down. Conversely, Berti felt the same way about Konny. While his friend had already been through the family outing, the detective was yet to come. How would his parents take it? Berti knew his father only too well. Being gay didn't fit into his world. He was sure of it. Mother Schwartz would throw up her hands. "Oh God," he heard her call out, half asleep. His uncle Ernst appeared. He had another stupid joke in store. Berti waved him off. He didn't want to hear it. He turned around. Konny's breathing sounded regular. The best man in the world must be dreaming. Berti listened to the howling of the wind, the crackling of the fire and fell asleep.

They awoke with the rising sun. Konny blinked outside. The bright sun reflected in the fresh snow. Berti yawned, Konny sat up and pushed the hay away from him. "I haven't slept this well in a long time," he said and went outside. He stopped in front of the barn and took a deep breath.

Berti opened his eyes too. "It was really okay, but it got cold towards the end of the night."

"Look outside. The countryside is beautiful white."

Berti got up, stumbled over the ashes of the campfire and stood next to Konny in the entryway. He had never seen anything like it. "That's at least a meter of snow."

"You know what I've never done before?"

"Like what?"

"Snow angels."

Berti started to grin maliciously. "I'm first," he groaned, but Konny was ready. They both jumped into the white glory at the same time and sank into it. They turned around and lay on their backs. Then they rowed with their hands and legs. They were happy and felt great. For a brief moment, they were carefree children playing in the fresh snow.

"We're on vacation, Mr. Schwartz," Konny joked.

"No kidding, Mr. Wels."

"Tell me, what smells so funny?"

Berti sat up. "There's a lot of smoke coming from the barn."

"The campfire!" Konny shouted in horror.

"Damn, I accidentally stepped in the ashes earlier. There must have been some embers in there."

It began to smoke heavily.

"Our car," Konny shouted and ran back into the barn.

"Watch out," Berti warned and ran after him. But he stopped in front of the haystack.

Flames were flickering upwards. The smoke grew thicker and thicker. Konny coughed, but emerged with the cart in the entrance area. Meanwhile, Berti tried to pull the trailer out of the barn, but the heavily loaded vehicle wouldn't move an inch.

Konny realized that it was impossible to save the trailer. "Forget it! It's too heavy."

Berti was desperate. "What have I done?"

"It was an accident."

"What are we going to do?"

"We'll take the sled!"

Within seconds, they grabbed the big sled, put it on its runners, and pulled it out of the barn. The roof truss had caught fire.

"Get out of here," Konny said with a panicked look at the flames.

"Sit on the sledge and call the wagon. I'll push," Berti whined. His voice was a mixture of fear and guilt.

Konny sat on the horn sled, which the locals also called a horen or horner. This time, however, he was not transporting hay or wood into the valley, as he had done many years ago, but was to transport two townspeople out of harm's way.

Konny sat well and held on tight. The author clamped the cart between his knees. Berti pushed on. He gasped, struggled, put all his weight into the effort. It worked. The wagon moved. The heat of the fire was palpable. Tongues of fire shot up through the roof. The barn was ablaze in an instant.

"Quick Berti!"

There were moans and groans in response. The heat was palpable. A primal scream followed. "Ahhhhh!"

The sled was pushed forward, gliding noticeably faster over the snow. Berti had made it and let go. He immediately ran after it so that the distance wasn't too great and managed to jump on. Although his weight pushed the runners much deeper into the white ground, the vehicle did not stop. On the contrary, Berti's mass and the momentum with which he had landed on the sled caused it to gain even more speed. Snow flew upwards. A last look back. The fire was burning wildly. Heavy smoke shot into the sky.

"Someone is going to be very angry with us," Berti gushed.

Konny had other worries. "You'd better look forward," he groaned. "Does this thing have brakes?"

The two men clung to the big sled, which shot downhill with increasing speed.

The wind blew against them.

Berti tried to say something smart. "You have to steer."

Konny couldn't believe it. "Steer? How do you do that? There's no steering wheel around here for miles, you joker," he shouted in panic.

Berti felt more and more uncomfortable. "With your legs!"

"I'm holding the suitcase with them."

The heavy sledge continued to race across the fresh snow. The conditions for sledding were ideal. However, for the two involuntary winter sports enthusiasts, the descent turned into a nightmare. They were scared to death.

"Bertiiiiiiiiii ... we're going to die," cried Konny.

The detective thought about it. "Should we jump out?"

"No! We're going way too fast. It's too dangerous."

Konny couldn't believe his eyes. "We're hurtling towards an abyss," he chased his lips in panic.

Berti tried to look over the shoulder of the man in front of him. "This can't be right."

"Why not? We're in the mountains."

They had barely spoken when they suddenly took off.

"Helpeee!"

"Ahhhhh!"

They had skidded over a completely snow-covered rock that had the effect of a ski jump. The runners took off, their heavy equipment flying through the air despite their weight. Accompanied by the wild screams of the tobogganers, it landed back in the snow. The ride continued, and the next horror appeared before their eyes.

"A tree," Konny warned shrilly.

"Where?"

"Right in front of us."

"We have to go around it."

"Then do something!"

Berti put a leg in the snow. Snow flew away. The shoe slipped through the white like a fin, leaving a third deep groove beside the runners. The sled moved slightly to the left.

"That's the way to go. Yay, keep it up," Konny cheered his friend.

The second runner was pushed into the snow. Once again the sled changed direction. This time, however, they were heading straight for the large fir tree standing alone in the path.

Konny warned frantically. "The other way!"

"I can't turn around!"

"No, the one with the legs!"

Berti put both legs back on the runners.

The direction of travel remained the same. They approached the huge fir without slowing down. A long, drawn-out "Ahhhhh" followed by an "Ohhhhhh" echoed through the landscape.

As they crashed into the tree, there was a crunch and a crash. The sled broke and the two sledders were catapulted down, landing in the fresh snow. The impact caused the snow on the fir tree to thunder down and cover the two friends. Panting and trembling with excitement, they sat under the overhanging branches of the tree like two snowmen come to life.

"I'm dead," Konny whimpered.

"No, I'm dead," his friend replied.

"Are we in heaven?"

They both looked around.

"We are in the white hell. Just a moment ago it was a beautiful morning, and now the catastrophes start all over again. I can't take it anymore," Berti groaned. "The farmer will sue us, the police will come looking for me and arrest me for arson and ..."

Konny took a deep breath. He didn't feel as dead as he first thought. "Calm down," he said reassuringly. He stood up and shook off the snow with a few blows. Then he went over to Berti, held out his hand and helped him up. He smiled. "That was the coolest sled ride I've ever had. And the landing was really easy."

Berti brushed the snow off his clothes. "I can do without a repeat performance."

They looked at each other. First they smiled, then they grinned, and finally they laughed.

Konny was confident that they would find the hotel quickly. "Come on, let's keep going. I'm sure it's not far now."

"Where are we supposed to go in this godforsaken area? We are lost. There's nothing to see for miles."

"Nonsense. We are not lost. We're going straight ahead. Just downhill. Then we'll inevitably reach civilization at some point." He started.

Berti nodded. That sounded plausible. He took the cart and followed in his fiancé's footsteps. Everything was automatic. He couldn't and didn't want to think. He didn't care which way they went. The main thing was that they would find civilization. A glance up confirmed his premonition. The sky was closing in again, the sun slowly disappearing behind the next snow cloud. The first flakes trickled down. It was white above, in front of, below and behind them.

White hell, he thought.

After walking for a while, hope began to sprout. They saw the black ends of the posts again. They were like a light on the dark horizon.

"There must be a road around here. We just have to follow the posts," Konny said jubilantly.

Berti could hardly believe his luck. "We're saved. The only question is, do we go left or right?"

"Which direction do you suggest?"

Berti thought for a moment and then said firmly, "Definitely right."

"Good, then we'll go left."

The detective put his fists on his hips. "Why would you do that? If you want to go left anyway, why are you asking me?" He was slightly annoyed.

"Quite simply, if you have bad karma at the moment, all we have to do is the opposite of what you want, then everything will work out."

Berti was offended at first. The scene reminded him a bit of Asterix and Obelix when the menhir producer sulked. But then Konny's theory began to make sense. Together they trudged along the snow-covered road in the steady snowfall. Two hours later, and just before their hopes collapsed, they reached their destination.

The luxury hotel was completely snowed in and yet fantastically beautiful, enthroned like a fairytale castle in the winter landscape.

The snow glittered in the sunlight like billions of diamonds, and the crunching sound of footsteps on the frozen white was the only thing that dared to break the silent, enchanted scene.

With renewed energy, they walked the last few hundred meters through knee-deep snow. When they reached the entrance, they were happy.

"We're saved," smiled Konny.

"You were right about the karma," Berti gasped.

"We've reached our destination, that's all that matters."

An indescribable sense of victory spread. The incredible had happened. They had challenged the wilderness to a duel and won. Walking through the hotel lobby was like climbing an Olympic podium.

Inside the hotel, it was warm and inviting. A crackling fire flickered in the lobby's large fireplace, spreading a soft, golden yellow light around the room. The walls were decorated with heavy, velvety fabrics that gave the place an air of royal luxury. Huge chandeliers hung from the ceiling, causing shadows to dance on the polished marble floor.

"Konny, we're finally going on vacation.
Happiness could begin.

Chapter 8
Reunion brings joy

The doorman couldn't believe his eyes when Konny and Berti appeared out of nowhere and suddenly stood in front of him. The two guests had been expected yesterday.

Where the hell did they come from now, he wondered silently. The blizzard had raged overnight and the road to the hotel was still impassable.

The porter's eyes raced over the guests. They looked terribly tired. Anything but fit for a hotel. He would have to check their personal details carefully.

"Mr. Wels and Mr. Schwartz?" he asked politely.

On the other hand, as if they were swindlers, these people could not be exposed at random. At least not if the weather prophets were to be believed. More heavy snow and even a storm were predicted. Considerable amounts of snow were predicted. The hotel management was well prepared for an emergency. For the receptionist, Mr. Sandmann, this was nothing new. Something like this had happened before in the winter.

Sandmann, like all other hotel employees, stayed at the hotel on such days. The employees had their own rooms. His wife Traudl didn't like it at all, but there was no way around it. Her husband's safety came first. "Before you risk your life coming down to the village, you'd better stay on the mountain," she had told him in no uncertain terms.

She's a beauty, he thought.

On days like this, the porter would console himself after work with a good bottle of wine from the hotel's selection. Without the boss' knowledge, of course.

What am I going to treat myself to today?

He digressed again.

"Yes," Konny replied politely. "I'm the author Konny Wels, and this is the famous private detective Herbert Schwartz."

Sandmann had never heard that before, but he was a thoroughbred porter and the guest was king. So his reply had to be well formulated.

"I'm delighted to welcome two such prominent guests. Are you traveling incognito?" He couldn't help but make the last remark, alluding to the two guests' outfits. He looked at the screen of his PC. "Yes, I have a reservation in the name of Wels and Schwartz. The suite. We assumed Konny Wels was a woman, ... well," he cleared his throat, "... I thought you were a couple ... uhhm..."

"We are a couple," Berti emphasized, glad to have pronounced the sentence with confidence. It was good practice for back home.

"Of course," the porter stammered, making it clear that he was anything but sure that two men were checking in as a couple.

"Mr. Wels, I need your name again for verification. Preferably your ID or passport."

"I'm Konny Wels. Is there a problem?"

"Uh, no, Mr. Wels. Everything is fine. And you are Mr. Schwartz? Of course you are Mr. Schwartz, but ... surely you know ..."

Berti pushed Konny aside and stood in front of the porter. "For the record," his tone had become a bit sharper. "This is the famous writer Konny Wels. I'm Herbert Schwartz, a well-known private detective with a clientele from the highest circles."

The porter grinned covertly. "And that's why you know that I only need your passports for the registration forms. You know how it is. We're never spared this procedure. Unless you are one of our regular guests and stay at our hotel often. Then we might make an exception. Otherwise, the rules are the rules."

"Yes, of course. Of course," Berti replied, somewhat embarrassed. "Just to check," he added, pulling out his ID.

I should have known about the registration forms, he scolded himself. A private investigator of my caliber should know such things.

"Here's my ID."

Konny laid his passport on the counter as well.

After the data for the registration forms had been noted down, Sandmann returned the passports. "Suite no. 5 is reserved for you. How would you like to pay? Cash, credit card ..."

"Everything should be prepaid."

"Of course. The contest. One moment, please." That was also necessary. Sandmann wanted them to feel that they were not ordinary hotel guests.

While the concierge completed the check-in process, the friends looked around the lobby. Rural architecture was mixed with modern elements. Exposed beams and an open wood ceiling exuded rustic coziness. The masonry was roughly plastered. Oil paintings adorned bare surfaces. The motifs were varied, ranging from local hunting scenes to an abstract depiction of the Bavarian capital, recognizable only by its extremely detailed depiction of the Oktoberfest.

Konny thought the artist must have had a dramatic experience there.

"Here it is. You have booked the all-inclusive honeymoon weekend and the amount of 5,000 euros has already been credited to our account. Gentlemen, your suite is on the second floor to the left. Do you have any luggage?"

"Just this cart. We'll take it up ourselves."

"As you wish. Here is your key card. There is a bottle of champagne in the refrigerator. A welcome gift from the hotel. On the table you will find fresh fruit and some Swiss chocolates and truffles. Handmade, of course. Exclusively for our hotel. A special treat for the palate. The dining room opens in an hour. Salmon is on the menu. Of course wild caught - certified and sustainable".

Konny thanked her and took the key card. They couldn't wait to get into a warm shower. He felt terrible, too.

The hair sticking out from under their caps clung to their skin. The parkas looked tattered. There was a slight country smell about both of them, reminiscent of steaming dung heaps.

"We wear jackets for dinner here in the house," came a discreet hint from the porter.

Berti wanted to react angrily, but Konny nudged him. "Come on, leave it. We're going upstairs."

As they walked up the stairs, they could literally feel the porter's eyes on their backs.

Shaking his head, Sandmann stood behind his counter.

Typical contest winner, he thought. They are on their last legs. Dressed like second Hand Hollywood-supernumerarys. In on sentence, they are complete proletarians. That's not a ten-euro tip, I bet.

A family approached the two friends.

"Manny, I don't know if I can ski anymore. The last time I was on skis was when we didn't have children."

Manny was in his fifties, wearing a fashionable ski suit and holding an expensive camera. "It's like riding a bike, Sweety. You never forget how to do it."

Sweety had certainly looked good once. Now her former model body, with its bulging curves, was dressed in a white ski suit with a fur collar on the hood. Guaranteed real! Behind the couple, their two children skipped down the stairs. They were probably the reason why Sweety would rather win a Miss Doughnut contest than walk down a catwalk again. After the second birth, she saw no need to return to her model figure.

"Can I slide on the railing?" the junior asked.

"No!"

"But Cordula slipped yesterday, too," she replied defiantly.

"Frederick, that's enough of stupid pranks! Cordula didn't behave yesterday. That's why her dessert was taken away."

"You just ate it," Cordula grumbled. "Mom, that was mean."

Berti and Konny ignored the four snobs. Manny and Sweety, on the other hand, looked at them with a slightly arrogant look. Sweety even took a step to the side to keep her distance.

"Be careful, children, that you don't collide with the people here. I don't want you ..." she whispered the rest, "... to catch anything."

The friends ignored this remark as well.

Maybe there will be a chance to return the favor soon, Berti thought.

The hallway was wide. There were well-tended potted plants, Buddha figures, and carved wooden elephants of all sizes.

"Here it is." Konny stood in front of a massive wooden door. "It's ready," he said happily. "Our suite is waiting."

He used the key card. There was a soft click. The door opened. "Wow, I've only seen this in movies."

They entered the suite. Berti closed the door behind him. "A-wesome."

They were speechless for a moment. The friends stood in a spacious living room. A flat-screen television, reminiscent of a movie screen, hung on the wall. Next to it was a state-of-the-art hi-fi system.

White leather furniture invited them to linger. You stood on a cowhide rug. Everything was color coordinated. A large window offered a view of the Alps. But all you could see were white, dancing snowflakes.

"This is a big sliding door. We have our own terrace."

Konny corrected. "This is a balcony."

"That's right, but it's pretty big."

The showpiece of the living room was undoubtedly the open fireplace. Some wood had already been piled in the firebox to light it. More logs lay in a wicker basket next to the fireplace.

"I've had enough of open fires for the moment," Berti whispered.

"Wait until tonight. When we have a glass of wine in front of the fire, it can crackle."

The bar was housed in an inconspicuous wall closet. Small bottles of the finest brands of whiskey and cognac smiled at them. Konny opened the refrigerator below.

"Champagne, coke, mineral water, beer and even a bottle of white wine." A quick look around followed. "The red wine is stored next to the minibar in a mini wine rack so it's at the right drinking temperature. It's all so ostentatious here, I could get used to it."

Berti pushed open the bathroom door. "Three times as big as ours. And if I'm not mistaken, it's a Jacuzzi. They weren't lying in the brochure. I know what I'll do first."

"Check out the bedroom," Konny exclaimed.

In the middle of the room was an oversized canopy bed measuring 3 x 3 meters. The bed was surrounded by fluffy white flokati. The doors of a spacious wardrobe were mirrored. In the opposite corner was a bureau. The writing surface was flipped out. Stationery and writing utensils, each decorated with the hotel's emblem, were ready for use. Konny found a letter.

"This is a welcome from the hotel manager."

"Read it out loud."

"Dear guest, I would like to welcome you to my hotel. Our staff will do their best to fulfill all your wishes. If you have any special requests, please let us know. Here you are king ... blah blah blah."

"What else does it say?"

"The times for meals, when and where you can take a ski lesson, and stuff like that. Signed by the hotel management. A Mr. V.G. Ostmann."

"Stupid name."

"Seems important, though. At least he should earn his money in his sleep. This one cost a lot of ashes."

"You're already talking like Ranzinger."

"Don't give me that asshole," Konny waved him off.

As he put the welcome letter back on the secretary, he heard water running in the bathtub. He felt great. Too bad they had missed a day of vacation due to the extreme travel conditions.

"A bubble bath is wonderful. Just what you need after the rigors of travel," came the voice from the bathroom.

"It has to be, considering how much money they get for it."

"Are you coming in too?"

"Of course!"

Konny went into the bathroom. A short hesitation. "Are those really bubbles from the whirlpool?"

Berti grinned. "Of course. I'm not a methane gas factory."

"I just wanted to know for safety's sake."

After the relaxing whirlpool bath, freshly shaved and with new clothes on their bodies, they felt like they were in seventh heaven. They were ready for the 5-star hotel. Dressed in jackets, they strutted past the doorman in accordance with house rules. They literally enjoyed their victory march.

Konny heard the mouse chattering again. He immediately whispered to Berti: "I thought they were going skiing.

"They probably forgot that there's a blizzard outside."

"Now everyone is kind of doomed to stay here," the detective realized.

"Why don't they go swimming?"

"Because there's food."

"Then we'll see who else has checked in and is sharing the luxury hotel weekend with us. Maybe we'll find some clients."

"Let's go to the dining room."

"Sure. Let's see if the high society also covers their seats with towels."

Konny laughed.

The word dining room didn't quite do the room justice. In fact, it was a complete misnomer. Everything was luxuriously furnished without being too kitschy. Wooden partitions with carved ornaments separated the tables. Guests were seated in small booths, reminiscent of a mountain lodge parlor.

Fittingly, two waiters in traditional costume served the guests. One of them had a huge moustache that reminded Berti of a colonial officer in German Southwest Africa in the 19th century.

"Grüß Gott, hello and welcome, Gentlemen," they greeted politely. The waiter was unmistakably Tyrolean, but he made an effort to express himself articulately and largely without dialect. He even managed to pronounce the usual throaty "ch" clearly. "Where would you like to sit? Are you expecting other guests?"

"No, there are just two of us."

"Two people," the mustachioed man confirmed politely. "How about table no. 7 in the back corner. You'll be secluded, but you'll have a great view. A very nice place."

Berti replied: "We'll take that one."

"If you want to follow me, please."

The friends were very hungry. They hadn't eaten anything since the ravioli in the hut. Except for the chocolates in the room, of course. They sat down.

The waiter introduced himself. "My name is Mario. If you have any requests, please call me."

Berti also wanted to introduce himself by his first name, but Konny stepped lightly under the table after him, so all that came out was: "Ber ... uh, thank you very much," came from his lips.

"With pleasure. Do you gentlemen know what you would like to drink?"

"Something warm first. Maybe a cup of tea," Konny said.

"Oh yes, for me too."

"Black tea, herbal tea, lemon tea, green tea ..."

Konny took the order. "Two herbs please."

"Coming right up. As for dinner, I can recommend the menu of the day. But you are also welcome to eat à la carte."

"Thank you."

Mario withdrew. Berti opened the menu. In no time at all, he had scanned the inserted page with the menu of the day.

211

"What's on today?" Konny asked.

"What the porter said. Wild salmon with fresh herbs, served with buttered tagliatelle stuffed with porcini mushrooms and lamb's lettuce with croutons. For starters, a freshly made beef broth is served with a slice of homemade farmhouse bread. For dessert, they serve Bavarian cream."

"Yummy! I'll have that."

"I'll join you. What should we drink with it?"

"What do the guys from the hotel recommend?"

Berti read the drink suggestion. "White wine. *Custoza,* vintage 2006, dry, sparkling and light. An ideal accompaniment to fish."

"Should we have wine now? It's only noon."

"Sure! We can order a bottle of water. It's all inclusive anyway. Besides, we're on vacation."

Konny was convinced. "Bingo! Let's do it."

One by one the guests entered the dining room. The Sweety family, as Berti had named them, had changed in the meantime. Ex-Miss Runway was unmistakably annoyed.

"You've been promised a ski course and it's not taking place just because it's snowing heavily. Everyone can understand that. There's plenty of snow out there. Manny, you should sue them."

Manny was slightly annoyed. "It's all right, Sweety."

"Mom, I want Coke," her daughter whined.

"Cordula already had coke yesterday. Today it's my turn," the son complained.

"Frederick is a snitch!"

"You are!"

The visibly overwhelmed mother hissed, "Behave yourself. Manny followed, looking for help.

"Children! That's enough! Go to our table and be quiet!"

"Mom, can I play with the smartphone?" asked Frederick.

"No!"

The boy turned to his father. "Dad, can I play with the smartphone?"

"Mom already said no."

"That's why I'm asking you."

Sweety was seething with anger. "Manny, now you can finally see how I feel the whole day when the kids aren't at school. And you always say I have it so nice at home."

Cordula intervened. "Frederick has his cell phone with him."

"Tattletale!"

"That thing stays off!"

The brother's revenge followed immediately. "Cordula snooped through your make-up."

"You're a sneak," Cordula slobbered and made a horrible face.

Manny rolled his eyes. At that moment, he wondered why the weather had to be so bad today, why he had wanted children so much, and whether it wouldn't have been better to put a rubber stamp on the whole thing back then... never mind. This vacation would pass, Sweety would return to her housewife's burnout, the children would stay at boarding school and he would escape to the office.

Berti grinned. "They could be a pain in the ass."

"I bet it goes on all day. The two kids hate each other."

"Sure, they're spoiled brats, the old lady is incompetent and he's not interested in family. The guy probably hangs around the office extra long every day and then goes to a bar to come home when everyone's asleep."

Konny grinned with amusement. At the same time he saw the next guest enter the dining room. "Another one."

They both looked at the older man. "He looks like a retired parade officer," Berti said. "He walks so straight you'd think he had a cane up his ass."

The hotel guest marched past the contest winners. With a serious look on his face, he nodded in greeting, but without uttering a single word. His hair was snow-white, and only a wreath remained. A small beard, strongly reminiscent of *Adolf Hitler*, adorned the area between his nostrils and upper lip in a golden yellow.

"I didn't even know the *Führer* smoked. Grandpa wears his own personal nicotine patch under his nose," Berti muttered.

Konny had to stop himself from laughing. "God, stop it," he whispered. "I'm about to die of laughter."

The man in the traditional costume returned to the table and served tea. "Here you are, gentlemen. Two herbal teas."

213

Mario then walked two tables over to serve the elderly gentleman. "Baron von Strass, would you like this?"

Meanwhile, his fellow waiter was passing out menus at the bourgeois family's table.

"I want red and white fries," the boy said energetically.

"Frederick, look at the menu first."

"If I have to eat something else, I will play with my cell phone. I have a really cool game."

"Manny, did you hear the words the boy used?"

"Frederick," the father grumbled admonishingly.

"Yes, thats how they are, these little brats," the local waiter smiled, envying Mario's area.

More guests streamed into the dining room. Two couples sat down at the table next to Berti and Konny. Snippets of conversation drifted over. The men were talking about their business.

"I'm about to open my fourteenth butcher shop, so I need another strong partner for baked goods."

"Where?"

"Cologne-Ossendorf. Shopping center."

"Your bread rolls will come from me again," came from the obviously large baker.

"Absolutely."

Meanwhile, the wives were picking apart the latest *Let's Dance* program.

"So this former footballer is a dream man."

"He's such a great talker."

"And he's athletic, too."

Berti pointed to the back. "Good thing there are these partitions."

Konny sipped his tea. "That feels good."

After the night in the barn and the tiring walk to the hotel, the tea was a balm for the exhausted body. Although the blissful bath was fantastic, the tea was the icing on the cake of the personal wellness treatment. The aromatic taste was just spreading through the author's mouth when he suddenly jumped. "Oh dear," Konny exclaimed in astonishment.

Berti was in the process of placing his tea bag on the edge of his plate. He looked curiously at his companion. "What's the matter? Did you burn yourself?"

"No! Look who's just marching into the dining room."

Berti turned around. He couldn't believe whom he saw. "Oh my gosh, it's the old lady with the little dog named Sir Nelson, and her young lover is back too."

Konny thought about it. "Did she notice that you gave the dog something to eat at the tennis club?"

His friend waved him off. "No," he said vehemently. "Never! The most she could do is make assumptions, but she has absolutely no proof."

"Lucky you," the author breathed a sigh of relief. "They take the first table right by the entrance."

"Do they have the dog with them?"

"The bag is next to it. I can't see the mutt."

"Sir Nelson is not a mutt! He's a smart, nice, little, sweet dog."

"That's all right. I know you want a yapper like that."

Berti folded his arms across his chest, a little snubbed. "I don't think yapper is very nice either."

The rich lady's *Louis Vuitton purse* shook. The Chihuahua's head popped up. The dog stretched. The small black nose had caught something. It was a very special scent, combined with the best treat he had ever had in his short doggy life. Sir Nelson had the scent of a friend in his nose. The olfactory organ looked like a small black eraser that was being pulled back and forth as he sniffed. At the same time, the Chihuahua twitched his ears. Now its radar had picked up the voice of the best human in the world. The short-haired dog began to wag his tail automatically. He tried to climb out of his luxurious prison.

"Sir Nelson! Go back to your place," hissed the old lady. Her ringed hand shoved the dog's head back into the bag. "You've been out with the dog again, haven't you?" asked her companion, who was about thirty years younger.

He nodded. "On the balcony. You can't go outside in this weather anyway."

"Good, I don't want another mishap like that. You know what I mean."

Then he buried his face in the menu.

The children of the Sweety family could not help but notice that the sinfully expensive handbag was moving.

215

"What's that Grandma got in there?" Frederick asked boldly, so loudly that the dog's owner had to hear.

"Shh," Sweety whispered, putting her index finger to her lips. "You don't say such things. I hope she didn't hear."

The older lady's expression said that she had heard.

Frederick pointed over. "The bag is wobbling."

Cordula turned and stared at the handbag as well.

Sweety was embarrassed. "Don't look," she hissed at her children.

From the basement came the drinks. "Two lemonades, an Aperol spritzer and a pilsner."

"What's that woman got in her bag?" came out of Frederick's mouth.

Manny rolled his eyes for the second time in a few minutes. Sweety pretended she hadn't heard. The waiter glanced at the unusual couple.

The lady's young companion smiled discreetly, but his eyes remained ice-cold. "Our guard dog lives in there," he joked, beating the cellarer to the punch. "If anyone tries to steal anything from your purse, Sir Nelson will bite."

Cordula was thrilled. "Mama, I want a watchdog, too."

Sweety fought back a smile. "Excuse me. You know how children are."

"It's okay." The grin disappeared from the man's face. He whispered somethin to his companion.

Sweety took a big swig of Aperol Spritz.

Mario brought the appetizer to table no. 7 and happened to overhear Berti and Konny talking about the wondrous couple. "Does it bother you that the Schlaps have their dog with them?"

"They're married?" asked Berti in amazement.

Mario grinned. "No! They're mother and son. Ruth Schlaps has been a regular here for two years."

"Mario, what you know is quite remarkable."

The waiter leaned forward a bit. He liked the two men. They weren't as affected as some of the other patrons. "Working here, you get to see all kinds of things."

"Thanks for the information," the detective winked.

The waiter nodded. "Enjoy your meal."

216

A well-dressed gentleman entered the dining room. He went from table to table, chatting briefly with the diners. Finally, he came to the two winners of the contest.

"How do you do? My name is Viktor Gisbert Ostmann. I would like to personally welcome you to my home once again."

Konny shook the hotel owner's hand. "Wels. Konny Wels, author."

Berti remained seated. "Schwartz, private detective."

The hotelier raised an eyebrow in recognition and surprise. "Oh, a detective. A wonderful profession. *I, too, have always dreamed of being* a Hercule Poirot. I love *Death on the Nile*!"

Berti grinned. He felt honored.

"I regret to inform you that the weather situation is disastrous. Unfortunately, outdoor activities are not possible." He paused to ask them both curiously about their trip. "We're still wondering how you two managed to brave the blizzard. It must have been a life-threatening journey. How on earth did you manage the climb?"

"Oh yes, our journey was indeed life-threatening and strange. I'm thinking of writing a book about it," Konny replied.

"Due to the heavy snowfall, the road has become completely impassable. No improvement is expected in the next 24 hours. We are experiencing the heaviest snowstorm since the hotel was built. The telephone network is also down. We are completely cut off from the outside world.

"Do we have to be evacuated?" asked Berti in horror.

Konny was also shocked and feared the worst.

Mr. Ostmann reassured them. "No, gentlemen. It's more like we're snowed in. We'll be on our own for an indefinite period of time. But don't worry. Of course, we have our own power grid for such emergencies, powered by an ultra-modern and powerful diesel generator. We could go on for weeks. The oil tanks and the refrigerator are full to bursting.

"But we only have one weekend..."

The hotel manager waved us off. "Since we're in an exceptional situation, we're not charging anything extra. I owe it to my guests. I'll be happy to answer any questions you may have, and I hope you enjoy your stay."

217

Mr. Ostmann walked over to the Baron's table. Mario came out of the kitchen and started serving the menu.

The food was a dream. The dining room began to empty. The guests either went to their rooms or went downstairs to the gym, indoor pool or sauna area.

Konny and Berti did a few laps in the water after dinner. At first the pool was empty. A little later, Mrs. Schlaps and her son and the baron with the Hitler beard entered the pool. The friends swam to the edge of the pool and got out.

"It's just the thing for sore muscles."

"I hope you're not mistaken. The mountain hike and the snow hike are really getting to me," Berti groaned.

"It's great that there are bathrobes and towels here," said Konny, who didn't feel like comforting his moaning friend.

"Even in my size," Berti added with a grin.

"The blizzard is paying us back for what it got us into."

"With the extension?"

Konny smiled. "With the free extension. We could stay snowed in for three weeks for all I care."

Relaxing was the order of the day. Berti nodded off. The temperature was pleasant, the couch unbelievably comfortable. The wall was painted with jungle motifs. Sounds of nature came from several loudspeakers. Pure rainforest. Leaves rustling, birds chirping and the background sound of monkeys roaring completed the soundscape. Soothing instrumental music was interwoven. It was paradise. At least until the Sweety family arrived. Berti was immediately wide awake when he heard the voices of the horror children.

The ever-nagging son babbled on and on. "Mommy, I want my flippers."

"Frederick, you know very well that we came here to ski. We left your flippers at home."

"Then buy me some."

Now came the inevitable. The brat added her two cents. "If Frederick gets new flippers, I want a new bikini."

"Manny, why don't you say something?"

Manny rolled his eyes and grumbled: "Kids! Quiet now!"

They walked right past Konny and Berti. The detective wanted to spare himself the sight of the annoying brats and kept his eyes closed.

I hope they accidentally fall into the water and the stupid kids run back into the room crying, it went through his head.

It wasn't hard to dislike the two eternally bickering siblings.

Mrs. Ex-Catwalk tried to tame her tormentors. "Frederick and Cordula! Be considerate of the other guests."

They were at eye level with Berti and Konny when the brat said: "Dad, it stinks here."

Her brother hit the remark back like a played shuttlecock. "Whoever smelled it first crawled out of the hole."

Cordula fought back. "You stupid ass. It was you! Dad, it was Frederick!"

"No! It wasn't me. It must have been the fat man," cried Frederick.

Sweety hoped that the two men were actually asleep and hadn't heard her son's words. "Go on, children. We'll take the loungers on the other side of the pool."

The brat didn't stop berating her brother. "You already farted on the stairs."

"Cordula," drooled Sweety, whose nerves were wearing thin.

Her brother defended himself. "It wasn't me. That was Dad."

"Frederick, that's enough. One more word and you go to your room. No cell phone and the TV stays off, too," Manny grumbled.

"But this time it wasn't me. This fat guy stinks! It was either dad or the sperm whale."

A flush of anger shot up Berti's face.

I hate these snobbish kids.

Memories flickered. He was at the outdoor pool. It was the hottest summer he could remember. The first swimmers he encountered were his class teacher and his family.

"Schwartz, are you here too? Just don't jump into the water from the diving board, or we'll be left high and dry," he joked.

He, his wife and their two children laughed like idiots.

"It was a joke, Schwartz. It was just a joke! You can take a joke, can't you?" he said apologetically, interrupting the laughter.

Young Herbert nodded, but didn't find it funny. Later, when they were all in the water, he had gotten his revenge by walking over the family blanket with wet feet. He hadn't planned on slipping and falling on the basket with their food, but he considered the result a success. "Picnic with a difference. One price for everyone!"

The only bad thing was that the Möller twins had seen him commit the crime. Both boys went to the same school, two grades above him. They had Berti in their hands.

"Either you do something really cool, or we'll rat you out to your teacher," they blackmailed him.

He was in a real pickle. "And what should I do?"

The twins looked at each other. Berti knew at that moment that they were going to ask something impossible. And so it was. He had the choice between dying horribly and being killed in agony. He was only free to choose the manner of death. "Either we say it or..." it echoed in his ears again.

"I take or," he had replied.

They clapped their hands and gave each other five fingers twice. "Then watch this ..."

The situation was cruel. Berti would have preferred to run away, but on the other hand, he was able to gain something like respect. The Möller twins had the school firmly under control. Anyone who belonged to their gang was safe. Members were neither teased nor talked down to. He was convinced that this was his chance. This was his ticket. Herbert Schwartz and the Möller twins would become a team. He liked the idea right up until the moment they told him what he had to do.

"You're going up the three-meter tower."

Oh dear. This was exactly what he had feared. Berti hated diving boards.

They want a water bomb. Guaranteed.

His bottom would hurt for three days, but they would get their water bomb.

A water atomic bomb!

"All right! And how do I know that you won't continue to blackmail me or betray me afterwards?"

"Word of honor," came the chorus.

"Put your hand on it!"

"I promise, but only if you do the coolest thing ever seen in this pool."

"You mean a mega nuclear water bomb, right?"

They grinned nastily at each other. Megafies, actually. Then they had told him what the coolest act was. "No! You stand on the three-meter board and pee into the pool from up there."

This sentence had hit Berti like a hammer blow. He had closed his eyes and weighed it up.

Which was the lesser evil? Should he confess to his teacher?

In his head he heard him cursing, shouting and moaning. Berti would be the victim for the whole school year, would be questioned constantly and would end up repeating the class. And the Möller twins wouldn't leave him alone. The other evil was less severe. He would be banned from the swimming pool after the pissing incident, but that didn't matter. After that, he wouldn't be able to show his face here anyway. Otherwise, the pool attendant would cut him personally if he caught him after the pee attack.

"You mean I should pee in there?" he asked and received a demonstrative nod.

"Then we'd forget about the flat picnic basket," one of the twins reiterated.

"If you want to be cool, you have to prove it," the other grumbled.

A sideways glance fell on the teacher family's place. Pure chaos and a complete mess. His headmaster would probably put him through the gauntlet right away.

"I take your word of honor."

Astonished looks. "Will you do it?"

"Yes!"

Every step had taken effort. Berti was at the end of the line at the diving platform. Behind him, he would never forget, was Annabell Maier. She had red pigtails and her nickname was *Pipi Longstocking*. When Berti finally reached the top, he saw the Möller twins chatting with other boys. Hands were shaken. High-fives were exchanged. Glances up to the tower.

They're betting on me! If I don't make it, I'm dead! There's no turning back now.

"Do you want to go first?" he asked Pipi.

"Why? Are you afraid?"

221

"No, I just like you."

"Schwartz, you're completely crazy! Of course you're afraid!"

"I advise you to jump and then get out of the water very quickly."

"Oh, is a big ass bomb coming? All right, let me pass. And wait until I'm outside."

"I promise, but hurry."

Pipi took a running start, jumped up twice on the bouncy board, and deftly dove headfirst into the water.

"Hurry up," a boy Berti didn't know called from behind.

Berti went to the front. Meanwhile, a group of ten to twelve boys had formed at the bottom of the pool. Pipi climbed out of the water. Berti took a deep breath. He pulled his trunks down a little, closed his eyes and squeezed. It worked. There were screams. A few people laughed out loud. Insults followed. The swimmers fled the water. Wild screams. Screaming girls. Cursing boys.

A choir cheered him on: "Berti, Berti, Berti."

This was followed by: "Water bomb! Water bomb!"

He was in a frenzy of emotion. For a moment, Herbert Schwartz was the coolest kid in school. He pulled up his swim trunks and jumped in. He awkwardly pulled his knees up and crossed his arms. Then came the impact.

Splash!

The fountain splashed high into the air. The screams of the disgusted swimmers echoed through the pool.

The Möller twins had won a twenty by winning the bet. They kept their word and left Berti alone. But they did not become a team. Annabell, alias Pipi, who sat next to Berti in chemistry class, had written him off since the pool number. She was grateful for the warning. It was a good thing.

Berti had been banned from the pool for two years. He didn't care.

But what his class teacher had done was extremely unpleasant. He had come to the Schwartzs and told them everything. Of course, Berti was reprimanded for bringing the school into disrepute in public, and he had to write a five-page essay on behavior.

After that, he was prepared for all kinds of questions. Although the last weeks of the school year were hell, Berti achieved the class goal and didn't have to repeat.

Berti would have liked to take revenge for Frederick's insolence. Peeing in the pool was just one way he could do it. But he would not repeat the diving board stunt. He would have to think of something else. The boy crouched at the edge of the pool. Their eyes accidentally crossed. Berti could hardly believe that Frederick had just given him the middle finger.

"These spoiled brats. They think they're special. Did you see that? That snotty bastard just gave me the finger. I'll give him one..."

"Leave it Berti, they'll get their money's worth."

"You can count on it."

"Shall we go to the sauna?"

"Mixed?"

"I don't know."

"It's certainly better than staying here. All right then. Let's go!"

The sauna area was separated from the swimming area only by a glass door. The vestibule was empty. Berti was relieved that there were no other hotel guests here. "Look, there's a swimming pool here too. It's just much smaller than that one over there. I'll jump in quickly."

"Careful..." Konny tried to warn him, but Berti had already dropped his bathrobe and jumped into the water. "...that's the cold water pool," the author mumbled, finishing the sentence and watching his friend jump into the pool and completely submerge himself.

The many air bubbles indicated a scream from under the water. Berti shot up, like a seal-hunting killer whale, out of the water and back again. Another scream was heard. This time above the water. "Ahhh..."

Goosebumps covered the heavyweight's entire body. His face looked shocked and contorted with pain at the same time. Berti's eyes were wide open. "C-c-cold," the sauna beginner blushed. He jumped to the ladder. His hands gripped the ladder and he climbed out of the icy water. His whole body shook from the cold. His teeth chattered loudly. His fat rolls moved up and down in waves as he took a kind of gasping breath.

Konny could no longer control himself and started to laugh terribly.

"S-s-s-au-na ... sh-sh-sh-quick," Berti cackled and wrapped himself awkwardly in his bathrobe. He left his coat on the floor.

Konny took pity on him and picked up his friend's bathrobe to hang it and his own on the hooks. Then he opened the door to the Finnish sauna. They both went in. At first the heat was like medicine for Berti's hypothermic body. "Where do we sit?"

"It's hottest at the top, women like to sit at the bottom," Konny remarked.

"We're going up."

"If you're not used to it, then we'd better ..."

"We're going up!" came the more energetic reply.

"Suit yourself."

Konny took some of the birch branches provided at the entrance. The leaves were still attached. "Great service here. They freeze them in the summer so that the guests can enjoy a first-class sau-na in the winter," he guessed.

Berti looked at the branches skeptically. "What are they good for?" That was pulled out.

"Stimulates the circulation."

"So nothing porky?"

Konny shook his head. "No! No way."

Berti still seemed uncertain.

Konny helped a little. "You put the towel down and sit on it."

"You mean I take it off my body? What if someone comes along?"

"Are you embarrassed?"

"Uhhm..."

A gentle smile. "That's okay. But we're alone right now."

There was also a wooden tub of water next to the birch leaves. You could easily smell a mixture of essential oils. Konny took the ladle and poured water over the hot stones in the middle of the sauna. The temperature was electrically controlled and preset. It hissed when the water touched the heated stones. Steam dispersed. "Wonderful."

The first drops of sweat ran down Berti's forehead. "What is a sauna good for?"

"For your health, my little bacon cheek."

"Konny, I have to ask. No pet names in public."

Only two minutes later Berti's cheeks were glowing. "Don't you think it's a bit hot?"

Konny patted himself with the birch branches.

"Looks stupid," said Berti, who was not.

"It stimulates the circulation. Just copy me."

While Berti could beat the birch branches against his back, he waved them around and used them as fans. "I don't know if this is good. It's bloody hot in here," he asked: "And it's not so hot on the lower pews?"

Konny tried to introduce his friend to saunas. "At least it's not so extreme on the lower benches. By the way, saunas are a wonderful health treatment. Sweating kills germs, stimulates circulation, lowers blood pressure, and so on."

Berti pondered. "Then why doesn't anybody do it? At least the saunas I know don't."

Konny smiled. "It's becoming more and more popular here. In Finland, on the other hand, almost everyone has their own sauna."

He frowned. The wagging increased. Berti was drenched in sweat. "I don't think so."

"There are definitely more than 1.5 million saunas in Finland."

Konny stood up and went to the bucket of water. He took the ladle and made an infusion. The water evaporated with a hiss.

Berti watched with interest. "How often do you have to make such an infusion?"

"Two or three times per sauna session," the author explained and sat down again. "Isn't it wonderful here?"

"Smells like the forest."

"They have essential oils in the water. Mountain pine or something."

Someone passed the door.

That didn't suit Berti at all. He felt uncomfortable. "Damn! That's it for peace and quiet. Let's go," he whispered. "I don't like people staring at me."

"A sauna session should take a good fifteen minutes. We'll stay a little longer."

"Konny, people are coming."

"If you want to be invisible, pour a little more water on. The steam clouds everything, you little coward."

Berti didn't need to be told twice and hurried to the bucket of water. He poured several ladles over the hot stones and hurried back

225

to the benches in the thick steam. This time he sat at the bottom. Not a second too soon, he thought as the door opened.

The weighty private detective found the cool air pleasant. The two Franconian businessmen entered the sauna. For safety's sake, Berti draped one end of his towel over his lap, covering two-thirds of his genital area. He felt better that way.

"Good day," he greeted politely, looking the men in the face and avoiding the two women as much as possible.

"Hello everyone. It's steaming in here," came the reply.

Berti heard it immediately. Unmistakable Franconian roots.

You can't get rid of that dialect.

"You're from Franconia?" The detective didn't really want to start a conversation. It just slipped out spontaneously.

"Coburg, to be exact. Allow me, nobleman. Master butcher!"

"Colorful, baker! Another Franconian, he he he," laughed the second businessman.

The women actually sat down on the bench next to Berti. He was annoyed.

Why didn't I stay upstairs? Damn it! Now I'm sitting on the housewives' bench. If I get up now and go upstairs, they'll think I have something against them.

"My family comes from Franconia. You can hear the dialect everywhere. *Bratwurst* is still my father's favorite dish.

"Hopefully the good original Coburg sausages from my butcher's shop."

"In a roll from me, hey, hey, hey."

"Possibly," said Berti, doubting that his Daddy ate exactly those sausages and rolls. He always bought from the same butchers and bakers. And they made them themselves.

"You're here all alone? Where are your wives?" one of the ladies asked.

"We... We...", Berti huffed, feeling a little overwhelmed by the question.

"We belong together," Konny took over confidently.

"That's why it's so warm in here, ha ha ha" the baker laughed and continued immediately. "Just a little joke. Don't get offended. Our oldest daughter also chose the same sex. We have no problem with that."

The situation was relaxed. "I'm Konny Wels," the writer introduced himself.

"Konny Wels? Are you Konny Wels?" asked the butcher's wife.

"What do you mean?"

"Yes, darling, what do you mean?" her husband asked in astonishment.

She stared at Konny with big eyes. "Dr. Kurt Lonedale?"

"That's exactly what he is. He's always so modest in public," Berti helped a little.

"Oh my God, I always thought Konny Wels was a woman."

"Me too," the baker's wife parroted. "I love your novels."

"It's almost a woman, he he he," the master baker muttered. "I was only joking."

"Robert, please," he was gruffly addressed.

The butcher's wife gushed. "Well, your last novel was just a dream. It was much too short. Tell me, would you mind telling me something? Will Greta Schmidt's jealous sparkle manage to outdo her rival, or will Saskia win Kurt's heart after all? I can hardly wait for the sequel".

"He can't tell you that," her friend interrupted.

"But I'm so curious."

The butcher intervened. "You should know that my wife started a book publishing company six months ago. Because of taxes and all that."

"No, Honey-bunny, not because of the tax, but because there are no good books left. You can only buy that scary crap everywhere, but real romance novels are almost extinct. Charlot-te and I..."

"That's me," the baker's wife pointed out discreetly.

"...well, Charlotte and I wanted to change that."

"And we benefit from the tax," the master baker interjected.

"I'm afraid you're already under contract?" Charlotte enthused.

"He's a freelancer, and as the author, of course, he has all the rights to his character," Berti interjected. He turned to them. His towel slipped. The eyes of both women wandered over his very voluminous body and lingered suspiciously on Berti's loins.

"That's what I like to hear. Perhaps we can persuade Mr. Wels to work for us."

"Hilde! We're naked in a sauna. You don't talk business there," her husband warned.

The door opened. Cold air flowed into the sauna. Berti was shocked. Sir Nelson's mistress was standing in the doorway. Bare as a rag. Wrinkled skin, a small, plump belly, and a faded tattoo that was hard to see because of the wrinkles. Something pointed into her lap. Berti got goosebumps despite the heat. She was heavily made up for dinner. Here she was as God had made her. Only 75 years later. Pure nature! Berti had to gag. The ravages of time had long since eaten away at her breasts. The earth's gravity had struck mercilessly. The nipples seemed to be made of iron, the ground was obviously magnetic. Berti closed his eyes at the height of the tattoo. He didn't want to look any deeper.

"We're done," came from Konny at the same time. "The first round is over.

"See you again. And think about a publishing contract."

The friends left the sauna. Mrs. Schlaps sat down. Konny climbed into the ice bath. "Wonderfully cold. Come in."

Berti raised both hands. "Sorry, I know how cold it is. I'm going to take a shower."

While Konny stayed behind shaking his head, Berti strolled leisurely to the shower. The locker rooms in front were again separated by gender. You could enter the changing rooms from the pool area as well as from the sauna area. Berti could still hear Manny's familiar voice. He was talking to his son.

"You have to take a shower before you go to your room."

"Why is that? I'm clean," grumbled Frederick.

Then he was instructed. "The water is chlorinated. Take a shower, or I will revoke your permission to watch TV."

Direct hit.

"All right, I'll take a shower."

When his son was in the shower, Manny left the locker room. "And then you come into the room."

It rippled. "Sure."

Berti had an ingenious plan for revenge. No one had discovered it yet. It was perfect.

Hopefully there's enough time, he thought. A glance up followed. No cameras. Okay, that would be kind of stupid in a locker room.

When he was alone, he hurried to Frederick's place. The door of the steel cabinet was open. Everything was there. Swimming trunks, clothes, and even the hotel's large towel. Berti laughed to himself.

Revenge is a dish best served cold.

The detective quickly packed Frederick's things. He was excited. If someone caught him now, his career would be over and he would be thrown out on his ear. Berti left the locker room in quick strides. He took the way through the sauna area again. From there he scurried past the elevator and headed for the stairs. He stopped at one of the many potted plants. The perfect hiding place. Another safe look around.

Alone.

In a flash, he hid all of Frederick's utensils behind one of the many tropical plants scattered around the hallway to create a jungle feel.

You won't find them here so fast.

He was more than satisfied.

My dear little stupid buddy, that's it for you with the TV. You're either going to have to walk naked through the hotel lobby or wait for Daddy to come and get you in the shower. And if you give me the finger again, I'll take it to you! If you mess with Herbert Schwartz, you lose from the start.

In a good mood, Berti went to the stairs and up to his room.

Saunas are really healthy. I feel great.

Shortly afterwards, while standing in the shower, he began to sing. "I'm singing in the rain..."

ai-generated-8991318_1280

Chapter 9
Diavolo and Dalmore

After a long shower, Berti lay down on the white leather sofa. He wanted to relax in front of the TV, but he dozed off. About half an hour later he woke up to a noise. Konny was pacing in the suite. The refrigerator door opened and closed.

"Would you like some orange juice?"

Berti sat up. "No, thank you."

"Did you sleep well?" the author asked and continued without waiting for an answer. "I'm going to lie down again. The swimming and the sauna have made me more exhausted than I first thought."

Berti stood up. "All right."

Konny put down the empty glass. "After dinner, Hilde and Charlotte want to talk to me. I'll tell you later. I think they want to sign me."

"That's crazy. I can't wait to find out."

The author went to the bedroom and got into bed. He wanted to be fit and rested for the evening. He had been persuaded by the two publishers to go to the hotel bar later for a drink. Hilde Edelmann and Charlotte Bunt had taken the opportunity to book their favorite author. They hoped to do business with him. Like two lionesses, they stretched out their claws and snatched him up. He was their prey.

Berti reached for the remote. The screen remained black. Lettering appeared in the center. White letters in a red field. No reception. Berti turned it back on.

"Crap! The same stupid slogan on every channel. Nothing comes in. There must be something wrong with the satellite dish."

A muffled voice came from the bedroom. "It's the bad weather. And even if they had gold-plated the satellite dish on the roof here, no radio beam can get through in this driving snow." Pause. "Don't you want to lie down for a while?"

"Nope, it's too much of a waste of time. Besides, I've already had a nap on the sofa." Berti leaned back. Silence returned. He turned off the TV, put the remote control on the table and thought about what he could do. When he was sure that Konny was asleep, he got up. He was bored. He decided to walk around the hotel and look around.

Maybe I can make some contacts for my detective agency. Rich people are predestined clients for private detective agencies.

The detective was dressed casually in jeans, sturdy low shoes and a comfortable Norwegian sweater with a moose pattern. He took the key card and backed out of the room, pulling the door quietly into the lock. Berti couldn't see the chambermaid pushing her cleaning cart down the hall. He bumped into the cart with his backside. The cart tipped over. It clattered and rattled. The maid flinched, startled. Berti turned red. "I'm really sorry! I didn't see you."

The young woman slowly recovered from her fright and looked at the mishap. Then she smiled kindly and said very politely, almost humbly: "That's all right. I'll clean it up."

It was as if the hotel clerk was afraid that someone would blame her for what had just happened. She was young, slender and pretty. Even under the obligatory cleaning gown with the hotel emblem at chest height, her good figure was visible. Beneath the hotel sign was a cheesy, curlicued lettering: Facility Management.

"You should be really pissed at me right now. I walk out the door with my fat ass backwards and there's a huge ruckus."

She was unsettled. A shy smile crossed her face again. Berti scratched the back of his head in embarrassment. He reminded the chambermaid of the legendary Canadian actor *John Candy*, who unfortunately died much too young. The guest standing in front of her seemed to be very sympathetic.

The private detective noticed that the young woman was restless and suspected that it was due to some unpleasant encounters with the hotel's aristocratic guests. He wanted to ease the situation. "I'm used to a lot of things, but I've never struck so hard with my four letters. Maybe I should enter that as an Olympic discipline," he grinned. "Although... that would be sport, and sport is murder. That's out of the question for me. Highest chess or indoor halma."

Her shy grin had turned into a hearty laugh. Her coffee-brown face looked especially pretty now.

Some models could pack their bags against this young woman, Berti thought.

"But you're nice. I'll take care of it," she replied, pointing to the overturned cleaning cart.

"I'll help, of course."

"That's not necessary. If the boss sees it, there'll only be trouble."

"I am a guest and therefore king. And as king, I rule. If the boss acts up, I'll have him thrown into the dungeon," Berti grinned. "Of course I'll help."

The corpulent detective bent down and put the trolley back in place. The hotel maid put the dirty towels that had fallen out into a laundry basket.

"But you speak good German. Well, I mean, because you look so exotic."

"I was two years old when my mother and I came to Germany."

"Sounds like love or job hunting."

She smiled. "Love. My stepfather is a great guy."

Within minutes, the cleaning trolley was loaded again. The young woman looked around with satisfaction. No one had noticed anything. "Now just vacuum over it again and the mess will be cleaned up."

"Why do you look so sad?" asked Berti, who had noticed the young woman's underlying sadness.

"Just like that," came the somewhat hesitant reply.

"No, my little friend. Speak up!" Berti tapped his forehead a little exaggeratedly with the flat of his hand. "Oh, maybe I'm a scatterbrain, I forgot to introduce myself." With a small, implied bow, he said: "I am Berti. Not a gentleman, not a phrase, just Berti." The detective held out his hand in greeting.

Hesitation.

Berti thought for a moment and added, "For God's sake, I'm not one of those rich, arrogant types who think they can pick up any hotel clerk." He winked. "I'm poor as a church mouse. My boyfriend and I won a weekend in this hotel in a contest."

Now the maid laughed. "I know that."

"Like what?"

"That she's not with any girls, well, you know. The whole hotel is talking about you and your friend."

The homosexual frowned. "I only hope for good things."

"So far, actually. Except..."

"Except what?" Berti interrupted immediately.

233

"I shouldn't talk about it, I'm sworn to secrecy."

"Let's start again from the beginning." Berti cleared his throat. He stood up straight and put on his friendliest face. "Well, I'm Herbert Schwartz, private detective. But you can call me Berti and use my first name."

"Amelie Schmidt," the chambermaid replied.

"Ah, you're married?"

"No," she smiled, "my father was an aid worker in Nigeria. He met my mother there. When we came to Germany, they got married. That's why my name is Schmidt."

"Actually, I'm quite stupid. It should be normal for someone to be called Schmidt. Regardless of skin color. I'm such a plaster head."

"Berti, you're absolutely adorable."

"You ... we're on a first-name basis."

"We're not allowed to call guests by their first names."

"Thank you, as a detective, I'm curious by nature and also very mysterious." His gaze became a little more serious, but without losing the hint of a comical expression. "Who is gossiping about us and which hotel guest is giving you a hard time?"

Securing glances. They were still alone. Amelie approached Berti and lowered her voice. "The mother of the two impossible children accused me of stealing her son's bathing suit while I was cleaning. He allegedly had to wait in the changing room for over an hour until his father went to see why his little boy hadn't come to the room."

"What a cheek!" exclaimed Berti, although he was pleased with his successful swimsuit attack.

"It's settled," she softened her voice. "Halfway, at least. We found them by accident behind a plant pot. The parents think their daughter was playing a trick on the boy. She denies it, but this Frederick is convinced. He even said that he saw her running away. But no one apologized to me.

Berti was furious with the lying little bastard and his whole family. "I will take revenge on them. You can count on it!"

"The stupid family is still okay. The old woman and her son are worse. They torture poor Sir Nelson. The puppy is hardly ever allowed out of his sack. And when he does, it's only to learn tricks. Today I happened to see that the dog has to take the key card with him all the time.

Berti seethed: "Animal abusers!"

"They also get as dirty in their suite as a whole soccer team. I think they shower Sir Nelson every day, because there are always three towels lying around."

"That's really bad for the fur. I've done a lot of research on the subject. I would like to have a dog myself."

Amelie took a deep breath. "I'll be glad when the road to Garmisch is clear again and some of the guests leave. It's a disaster right now. If there are one or two persistent complainers here, oh well," she waved them off. "I'll spill the beans again."

"I like to listen."

She grabbed the cart. "I have to go."

"Can I do you a favor, Amelie?"

"You already have."

"How?"

"By just being a normal, friendly person. The other snooty types are..."

"Arrogant snooty types?"

A hidden grin. "Exactly that."

Berti liked the chambermaid. "Can I buy you a coffee?"

"We're not allowed to do that, but could I buy you one?"

"Me? I don't quite understand."

"Why don't you come to the kitchen in half an hour? The chef is always in the office at that time. There's no one there except the cook and his assistant. They are both very good and very busy. They take care of the food."

"And the other employees?"

"The waiters and the bartender are off in the afternoon, the porter is behind his counter, and we can have a good cup of coffee in the kitchen in peace."

"Isn't there a janitor here?"

Amelie laughed. "Of course we have a janitor. And a gardener and so on. Willi, that's the caretaker, is in the basement, working around each other. The gardener is only here in the summer, and Hansi, our ski instructor, is resting for tonight. He is entertaining the guests at the bar."

"How?" Berti asked curiously.

"With his charm."

"Ahhh," came the long drawn out answer. "A player?"

"Go that way." Amelie probed. "So, do you accept the invitation?"

"Very, very much so."

"Well then, Mr..."

"Berti! Friends always call me Berti."

That sympathetic smile again. "Mr. Berti, in half an hour in the kitchen."

Things were going well. The streak of bad luck finally seemed to be behind him. Berti had a new girlfriend and two new enemies. He was terribly sorry that the affair with Frederick had backfired with Amelie. She hated that mouse all the more. But something would come of it. The stupid old woman and her pomade-hair-licking son would also get their comeuppance. Berti suddenly felt an inner bond with Sir Nelson.

Let's see what happens, he thought. Maybe I'll be able to free the little dog from his handbag existence.

The Baron and another elderly gentleman, who looked as rich as his noble grandfather, were sitting in the hotel lounge. They were playing chess. The pieces were modeled after the Battle of Waterloo.

"Wellington and Blucher are attacking. Napoleon will win this time," grinned the Baron. The knight threatened his opponent's rook and queen at the same time. "Mr. Schepperlin, all your jewels won't help. You must choose a victim," he teased pointedly.

"It has nothing to do with my trinkets that Napoleon is only temporarily victorious in the third round!"

"What does that mean?"

The jeweler studied the score. His hand went neither to the queen nor to the rook. He put his bishop in position, leaned back and said: "Check, my dear! Check!"

The baron was shocked. He stared spellbound at the chessboard. "Lightning! I missed that!"

The bishop threatened both the king and the horse. To save the king, the baron would probably have to sacrifice the knight. "I always fall for the same trick."

Berti watched the two men with interest for a few minutes. They were both enjoying the game. They thought carefully about each move and commented on it with a witty, pessimistic remark.

The Baron looked at Berti. "Young man, you can learn something here. Now that we're locked in this hole, we'll have to pass the time together."

Berti replied: "I am a poor chess player. I know how to move the pieces, but that's about it."

"Then watch me," said the baron. He didn't even try to break the deadlock, but moved the king one square to the side. The check was canceled. The cost was high. His knight was captured.

Mr. Schepperlin had won the game. The inevitable followed: "Checkmate," he said, confident of victory. "And why should our spectator take notice?" he added inquiringly.

"Quite simply. Even losing has to be learned, my dear Mr. Schepperlin."

They both laughed.

"Time for my medicine. I suggest we meet again after dinner for a rematch."

"I would love to. Let's meet for dinner, then we'll play," the jeweler said as he took his leave.

Berti walked on and inspected the hotel. In front of the staff wing, a side corridor led to the hotel manager's private quarters. If you followed the corridor, you came directly to the kitchen. A glance at the clock. "Five more minutes," the detective muttered and entered the kitchen.

Amelie was already there. "Punctuality is probably one of your strong points as well," she greeted Berti.

"You do what you can. Besides, I've just seen two elderly gentlemen playing chess. When they were young, I guarantee they wore the same uniforms as the chess pieces. Early nineteenth century," he joked.

"You really are a funny guy."

The kitchen looked like one in a large restaurant. On the side of the wall were the countertops with water faucets and sinks. In the center was a large stove. Above it, many pots and pans hung on the edge of a large range hood. At the head of the kitchen was the baking area.

Everything was polished and shiny. It smelled wonderful. A young apprentice was washing lettuce. The chef was sharpening a long knife with a very narrow blade. A huge ham lay in front of him. It reminded Berti of Obelix and his beloved boar.

"Over here," Amelie led the hotel guest past a large silver door with a handle.

"Cold room?" the detective asked.

"Yes."

She maneuvered him into a small adjoining room. The furnishings were sparse but cozy. A table, a corner bench, two chairs. In the corner of the table hung a crucifix. Carved. The figure of Jesus was delicately carved.

The hotel clerk had followed her guest's gaze. "The cross is from Oberammergau. It's very close to here."

"I know it. It's where those famous passion plays always take place."

"Always is good. Every ten years."

"But then with a huge glamour."

She laughed. "That's right! But the people of Oberammergau are not only famous for the Passion Play, but also for their car-vings."

"And I've learned something new again."

There was a half-burned candle on the table. A napkin, on which some of the dripping wax had dried, served as the base. Next to the candle was a box of matches. White and blue checked curtains hung to the left and right of the window. They were not drawn, although it was already dusk. The panes of the mullioned window were frosted around the edges. The blizzard was still raging outside.

"Sit down."

"Shouldn't we be on a first-name basis? I think it's too silly for people to call each other by their first names and be on first-name terms," Berti suggested.

"It's okay here in the kitchen. I can't do it in the hotel area."

"All right, Amelie. We'll stick to that."

"What kind of coffee would you like? Espresso? Cappuccino? Latte macchiato? Would you prefer regular bean coffee or French café au lait?"

"Did you read that somewhere?"

Amelie smiled.

"What nonsense. It's part of our breakfast standard. As a qualified hotel manager, I'm not only on chambermaid duty. I also have to help in the service or at the reception. But only if one of the other employees is on vacation or sick".

"I thought you were the housekeeper here."

"Because of the Facility Management coats?" she smiled.

"That's right. And I'd like a latte."

"The smock comes in handy at work. We actually have a real cleaner here at the hotel, but Rosi is on vacation. Will it be café au lait?"

He nodded. "I'm still amazed at the enormous choice."

"You are in a luxury hotel. There has to be everything a guest could want. Normally, only people whose bank accounts have at least seven zeros after the first number stay here - on the credit side! Such people are extremely spoiled."

"Then I'll really enjoy one of those Frenchies."

"Café au Lait, oui Monsieur, served immediately!" Amelie thought for a moment. "Shall we have an aperitif with it?"

"Are you allowed to do that?"

"Actually, I could have gone home earlier. My shift is over. Of course I can have a drink."

"Where are you sleeping?"

"Mr. Ostmann is extremely generous in this regard. As an employer, he's a real bastard and thinks he's better than us, but he doesn't let us down. We have very well-equipped single rooms with bathroom and toilet in the staff wing. The pay is well above the pay scale and the co-workers are nice. We get the same food as the guests, but there are a few rules when it comes to drinks. The exclusive spirits and wines are taboo, of course, but everything else is allowed. Outside office hours, of course. If you have a flag on duty, you're out!"

"That all sounds acceptable."

"It is. If you like France," she returned to the old subject, "would you like a pastis with water?"

"Is that that aniseed schnapps stuff that looks so yellowish when diluted with water?"

"Mmmmh, yes," Amelie nodded.

"I'll take it."

A few minutes later they were clinking glasses of pastis. In front of them were two large cups of steaming coffee. The candle was burning. Amelie felt comfortable in Berti's company. He was the kind of guy you had to like. She wondered why gay men, of all people, were real women's advocates and even longed for a harmonious relationship for a moment, but Berti was definitely not her ideal of a man. She already thought of him benevolently as a great discovery and something like a male best friend.

"Your hair shines beautifully. How do you do that?"

Amelie reached into the pocket of her cleaning robe. She held a small bottle. "That's my secret. I wash it every now and then with castor oil. My mother told me to use this old household remedy. It works!"

Brilliant idea! Somewhere in the convolutions of Berti's brain, a lot of neutrons shot into the think tank. He didn't know what for, but he would like to have that little bottle. "Can you lend it to me?"

"For what?"

"To ... let's say ... try something out?"

"You're the first man I've ever talked to about something like that, you know?"

Berti was pleased by this praise.

Amelie handed him the bottle. "Here! It's almost empty anyway. It might be enough for one application. You have to wash your hair first and then massage the oil in. It's best to put a towel over your head. Castor oil is hard to get out of clothes."

Berti didn't listen at all. He had something completely different in mind.

"Tomorrow you will be completely satisfied with the result," she finished her instructions.

He looked at his future instrument of crime. "Thank you."

The oil bottle had changed hands.

"Why was it in your work coat?"

Amelie shrugged. "Encrypted? I don't remember. Maybe it was because I overslept today and rushed to the bathroom."

"It doesn't matter."

Amelie looked outside. "Are you going skiing?"

"Nope! We went sledding yesterday, but that wasn't a hit either."

The maid laughed again. "You always say such funny things."

"I'm in a good mood."

240

"You came by sleigh? Tell me about it. That's extraordinary. Usually you go downhill on a sled, not uphill."

"It was such a big machine. We found it in an old barn. But it burned down."

Amelie was astonished. "Burned down?" she asked curiously, with a hint of doubt.

"We had to spend the night there out of necessity after we got lost and made a fire."

She looked at Berti. He looked quite serious and seemed to be telling the truth. "You got lost and had to spend the night in a barn?" she asked anyway.

"Yes, after we were released as hostages, we wanted to take the shortest route to the hotel."

Amelie drank her pastis in one gulp. The glass was demonstratively and loudly put down on the table. It was a bit too much. She believed in a Munchausen story. "You're making fun of me."

Berti remained calm and shook his head slightly. "There's no reason for that. We've already exposed this Knut as a drug courier. That was the short version. Anyway, he escaped from police custody, stole a drunk cop's gun, and hijacked the taxi we were in."

The maid hung spellbound on the detective's lips. Berti just gushed out the words, recounting her experience from the beginning. "I had the whole thing under control, of course," he fibbed a little.

"Of course," she winked at him.

"Knut was suddenly called Detlev and was afraid of his backers because he ran out of coke, so we were forced to rob a bank. In other words, our kidnapper actually robbed the bank himself. We were just there."

She slapped her thighs. "I can't believe that. I heard it on the radio."

Berti sat up straight. He liked the bravado. He no longer felt like a victim. On the contrary, he was getting closer and closer to the reputation of a cool private dick. "Oh, really?"

"Yeah. It was on the news yesterday. You were the ones at the bank?"

"As I sit here."

"And then?"

"Knut Hofmann, that's Detlev Ranzinger, the real name of our kidnapper, had taken both of us and Eddie hostage."

"I can't figure it out right now. You're throwing too many names around. How many perpetrators were there? Knut, Detlev, Ranzinger and the stone thing? Were there four guys? And how big was the taxi?"

"It was all one man, really," Berti explained. "Again, slowly. The boy's name is Detlev Ranzinger." Berti calmly explained Ranzinger's alias and how they had met him.

"So that's how it was," Amelie marveled. "Where did you run off to after the robbery?"

"To a mountain pasture like this, in the middle of the wilderness."

"It's more exciting than the movies."

"I knocked him out in that cabin. I had to wait for the right time, you know. The mafioso was armed. Otherwise he might have killed us, or at least shot us and left us in the wilderness."

"Wow, I'm sitting here with a real hero."

Berti fumbled a bit. Maybe he had exaggerated a bit. He felt a little guilty towards Konny and rowed back. "I wouldn't say hero, but I wasn't far from being one."

"Would you like another pastis?"

"One more, but that's enough. We had some wine before the sauna."

"For lunch?"

"Yes."

"It's already dismantled."

Amelie filled up her drink. She didn't care if everything had happened the way Berti had told it. The story was very entertaining, exciting and funny. The fat detective made an honest impression on her. Moreover, Berti was the kind of man who didn't immediately stare at her cleavage or make stupid advances. And he was one of the rare non-snob guests here at the Berghotel Alpentraum.

A clattering sound came from the kitchen.

"Are they fighting?"

Amelie shook her head. "Pots and pans are being prepared."

"We already had a first class hot meal for lunch."

"Some guests prefer to eat hot food twice a day."

"I used to be one of them," Berti grinned and stroked his considerable belly. "You can still see the traces of it today."

"I think you look good. Your belly suits you, and there are a lot of people who like Rubens' figures."

The detective beamed. "That's nice of you to say."

The coffee was working. Berti felt invigorated and fit again. He emptied his cup with pleasure. He was about to ask Amelie about the brand of coffee when the kitchen apprentice called her.

"Amelie, do you have a moment?"

The maid stood up. "Coming!"

Berti stood up as well. "The coffee party is over anyway. I'm very curious. Can I have a closer look at the kitchen?"

"Sure. I'm sure the two boys won't mind."

Secretly, a diabolical plan was taking shape. It was even a diabolically sharp plan. He hoped to find everything he needed in the kitchen. Berti entered the kitchen behind Amelie.

The apprentice was kneading dough. The dough was sticky on both hands. "Hey, golden girl," he joked, looking at Amelie. "I need the big bowl. Can you bring it to me? I'd just get everything dirty."

"Will do." Amelie turned briefly to Berti. "This is the kitchen. The apprentice is called Klaus, the chef is Fabian Rohloff, he's about to get a star, but he's not out of order at all. They're both really okay."

"Great," Berti nodded.

"Amelie's exaggerating," the chef said. He dried his hands on a towel, set it aside and greeted Berti. "Welcome to my kingdom. It's not often that our guests take an interest in the kitchen. Or are you from the Trade Inspectorate?"

Berti stood opposite him. The cook didn't look like a star chef at all. Long hair, tied back and hidden under a chef's hat. White coat with hotel emblem, black and white che-chec pants and mules. "Would that be bad?"

"On the contrary! You can even eat off the floor in my kitchen."

"I prefer the dining room," Berti smiled.

"Are you a specialist?"

"Am I a chef?"

"Yes, a chef or a restaurant owner?"

"I may look like that, but no. Neither. I'm a private investigator."

Rohloff's face showed the famous "aha" effect. "You think of detectives differently."

"How?"

"I don't know. With a coat and a hat."

"Hollywood cliché," Berti grumbled. "I might as well walk around in a Hawaiian shirt and play with my sunglasses."

"As a cook, it's not that exciting. Here are the stoves, over there are the ovens."

Berti let himself be shown around. While Rohloff kept explaining something, the hotel guest's gaze lingered on the spice rack. "I suppose you have everything here?"

"At least I try to have everything. From ajwain, which is Indian cumin or king cumin, I have the whole range, to lemon root, which is white turmeric from Thailand. But I use it sparingly. Just like my little hell."

"Hell?" the guest rolled his eyes. "How am I supposed to understand that?"

Rohloff pointed to a row of small bottles. "Here on the bottom shelf." They were not organized by size, but by some other scheme.

"Tabasco?"

Rohloff laughed heartily. "Tabasco is a child's birthday party compared to its hot friends! Do you know how to measure heat?"

Berti was very interested. "Not really."

"To put it simply, in 1912 the pharmacologist Scoville established a scale that measures the degree of heat of capsaicin. The common sweet pepper has zero heat. So it has a Scoville rating of 0, while the purest capsaicin has a Scoville rating of about 16 million."

"But you can't eat that, can you?"

The aspiring chef shook his head. "Definitely not."

"Where's Tabasco?"

"A pepper is about 500 Scoville, Tabasco is between 2500 and 5000. Jalapenos go up to 8000 Scoville. Habaneros are between 100,000 and 350,000."

"Madness."

"Most sauces have a simple scale of 1 to 10, from mild to hot and very hot to extremely hot and inhuman. Inhuman means over 200,000 Scoville degrees and is equivalent to a heat level of 10 plus. The Tabasco you mentioned has a value of 3 to 5, depending on the type of Tabasco."

"I understand the system. What's your hottest sauce?"

"Mad Dog 357, which has a Scoville rating of 600,000 and is in the inhuman range. It should only be used very diluted, just like the Vicious Viper."

The chef pointed to the two bottles on the far right.

"And in between?" asked Berti.

"Between Tabasco and the Viper?"

Berti nodded.

Rohloff took one of the bottles off the shelf. "This is the Fire Salamander. It's between 6 and 8, which puts it in the very hot category. Would you like to try it? Would you like me to prepare something special for you tonight?"

"Thank you very much. I think Konny and I prefer the delicious ham you cut earlier. We don't need any chili sauce with it."

"A good choice. This is real Parma ham, sliced, of course. I will prepare a cold plate for you that you will never forget."

"I would love to. I'm looking forward to it."

"Klaus, note to table 7. Cold plate à lá Rohloff."

"I'll do it, boss. I just have to make the dough..."

"I'll write it down quickly," Amelie offered.

Berti was surprised that Rohloff knew his table number. But that was probably part of the service. The detective watched his new friend. She scribbled a few words on a piece of paper and pinned it to a flip-chart with a magnetic pin. Then she said goodbye. "Have fun, I'm dog-tired."

Rohloff looked at his watch. "It's that late already. Excuse me, I have to go to the wine cellar and choose some bottles. The red needs the right temperature."

"Thanks for the tour."

"You're welcome."

After the cook scurried out of the kitchen, Berti waited for the right moment. The apprentice was still working with the dough. Berti went to the blackboard where Amelie had written the note. On it was the floor plan of the dining room. All the tables were numbered and marked with the names of the guests. Berti remembered the seating plan in an instant. He now knew which table belonged to the animal abuser and her son and what would be served at the table of the horrible Sweety family when he read the notes.

Two Schnitzel Milanese with the old lady! Note: extra tender. The old lady probably doesn't want to get her teeth stuck in the Milanese schnitzel.

Sir Nelson's mistress' sauna session appeared before his eyes. A lecherous look, a limp...

A mental leap. Don't think about her!

Goose bumps covered Berti's body. The image disappeared. He returned to his task.

Your descendants must eat the same food, otherwise he will be disinherited. You old slimeball!

Then he read the food request of his first-class hotel enemies. Family *we-are-something-better*.

Berti's eyes scanned the flipchart.

A large chef's salad for Sweety, a medium steak for Manny, and the stupid kids get Wiener schnitzel with French fries.

His plan had just been finalized. The crash course in chili sauce was worth its weight in gold. After all, he didn't want to spice up the Triple A guests to the point of hospitalization, he just wanted to give them some diabolical warmth. A grin creased his cheeks. The word "chill out" had taken on a new meaning for him today.

I will light a fire under your ass!

Now he just had to know how to do it. Nothing had to fall back on the cook. Berti returned to the chili sauces. After a moment's thought, he grabbed the bottle of Fire Salamander. He spoke casually to the apprentice.

Diversionary tactics!

"Do you like it here?"

"Very well."

"What are you doing?"

"Cake batter."

"I'm off again."

"Enjoy your stay."

"Thank you."

The detective went straight to the dining room. The doorman had dozed off over a newspaper.

Perfect!

The plan of revenge began to take shape. Each table had a designer holder with vinegar, oil, salt and pepper, as well as Tabasco and Sambal Olek. Something for every taste.

A bottle of ketchup was already waiting at the table of the terribly nice family. Heinz No. 57. The avenging angel unscrewed the cap. Next, he grabbed the bottle of Tabasco from the designer spice rack. It was still about a quarter full. The detective carefully poured some of the hot sauce into the ketchup bottle. Berti thought for a moment, looked down at his work, and made a decision. "Oh no," he exclaimed and poured the rest of the Tabasco into the brand ketchup. When the Tabasco bottle was empty, he screwed the cap back on the ketchup and shook the bottle.

"Now everything is nicely spread. Enjoy your meal."

Now he took the castor oil Amelie had given him. He compared the color of the olive oil on the table with that of the natural laxative. "No one will notice," he whispered and decanted the castor oil. He shook the contents of the bottle. One last scrutinizing look. Satisfied, he returned the oil-filled bottle to its designer holder.

He hurried to Oedipus and his mother's table. What was the name of the ancient queen? Berti had read it in a history book. The historical basis of half-knowledge.

Oh yes. Her name was Iokaste! He would rename her. He thought Wrinkle Box was more appropriate.

"Oedipus and Wrinkle Box, I hope you put some Tabasco on your bland Milanese spaghetti."

Insinuating that they didn't know the difference between Tabasco and Fire Salamander, he took the full bottle of Tabasco from the table and replaced it with the empty bottle from the Sweety Family table. Satisfied, the Dinner Assassin placed the Fire Salamander next to it.

Satisfied, he returned to the kitchen. Rohloff wasn't back yet. The apprentice was filling cake tins with dough. "I forgot something," Berti said. He went to the blackboard, took a pen and wrote on the note from the folding box: Don't season the sauce, the guest wants fire salamanders on the tab-le! The hotel staff should be off the hook. The handwriting could be compared in case of a complaint. It definitely did not match the hotel staff! The work was done.

"Well, goodbye then."

The apprentice was too busy to reply.

They were all on time. German virtue was in full bloom and splendor. There was plenty of food, the seats were taken even without towels, and you could indulge yourself in expensive Schleckerland without paying a cent extra. This all-for-nothing look was etched into the faces of a cross-section of the top ten thousand.

The Bunts and the Edelmanns took their seats. They greeted Berti first. "Hello, well rested, Matlock? He, he, he," joked master baker Bunt.

Badass! Matlock was a lawyer in an 80s or 90s series, not a detective. But I have to give the self-made millionaires credit for not being too aloof despite their money, Berti thouht.

The privat detective greeted him back. To him, they were good people.

Konny received an exuberant, almost friendly greeting from Hilde and Charlotte.

"Mr. Wels, we're looking forward to the drink."

"It will be a very entertaining evening. I'm so excited."

"Sit down, girls! Mario's already dancing," purred the butcher.

Baron von Straß sat alone at his table. The nobleman with the Hitler moustache was restless. His chess opponent was late again.

The Horror family and the Oedipus clan arrived at the same time. Sir Nelson was parked on the floor this time. This was an ideal opportunity for the Chihuahua to search for his friend. The pedigree dog was sitting upright. His head was sticking out of his pocket. His eraser nose sniffed in different directions until he caught the scent of Berti. Sir Nelson jumped out of the bag and ran across the dining room to hide under Berti's table.

"The dog just ran under our table," Konny whispered to his partner.

"Sir Nelson?"

"Who else?"

They looked over at the mother and son. They were talking. The escape had gone unnoticed. Berti felt something on his leg.

"Konny, not now!"

"Huh?"

"Don't do that, you know I always get all woozy. Sir Nelson is here, my ass. Nice trick, you little philanderer," Berti winked.

"Are you out of your mind? Whatever you think I am, I'm not," the author defended himself. At the same time, he waved at the two publishers who kept staring in his direction.

"No, no," came the slightly contemptuous reply. "That's the invisible dog."

"Berti, I saw the dog very clearly. Look under the table."

"Then either the old lady or her son, the unsympathetic brain fart, would have jumped up and brought Sir Nelson back."

"You're starting to sound like Ranzinger."

"Sorry, but can you stop hitting on me under the table all the time?"

Now Konny understood what was going on. Berti had confused something. "You think I stroke your legs? Ha ha ha. Look under the table," he said laughing.

Berti carefully pushed the tablecloth aside with his left hand. Sir Nelson was sitting between his legs. The dog snuggled up to him. When he noticed that his friend reacted, he stood up on his hind legs, put his head on Berti's knee and looked up with the cutest puppy eyes in the world.

"Konny, I've just fallen in love with the dog and he's fallen in love with me. I have to have him."

"That's not possible."

Berti stroked Sir Nelson. "Good dog."

A harsh voice shattered any semblance of idyll.

"Sir Nelson! There you are! Just running up to strangers. Yikes! Off to your bag!"

"We're not strangers at all," Berti tried to counter, but the old woman's son didn't react at all.

He grabbed the Chihuahua roughly, picked it up and carried it back to the table. There he placed it in the outrageously expensive purse. "You stay here, you bitch!"

Berti was annoyed. "Strange! The guy's got a punch!"

"Don't get upset."

"Such a ..."

Konny put his index finger to his mouth to calm Berti down. "We don't talk to men who smell like *Jean Paul Gaultier* at noon and *Hugo Boss* at night. They don't have a line."

249

Berti remained silent. What his friend had said was absolutely true.

Dinner was served. Rohloff hadn't promised Berti too much. Mario put two plates on the table and placed a platter of delicious things in the middle. Parma ham, olives, sheep's cheese, goat's cheese, slices of salami, cocktail tomatoes, artichoke hearts and grilled tomatoes and peppers were draped in such a way that just looking at them made your mouth water. It was served with baguette and root bread.

"Best wishes from the kitchen. Bon appetit!"

"I'm speechless. Was this the surprise you were talking about?"

"Part 1," whispered Berti, who had told Konny in advance that there would be a surprise meal in the dining room and something funny to watch.

"And when is part 2?"

"When the others are eating."

"I'm curious."

Berti was too. He took a slice of fresh Parma ham, sliced wafer thin, placed it on a piece of root bread and took a bite. While his taste buds exploded with joy, he watched the Sweety family. Mario's colleague had just taken the last plate from the tray and wished him a good appetite. Frederick had jumped the queue for the ketchup. His sister glared at Berti, offended. She stuck her tongue out at him, angry that he had gotten the ketchup first. Manny closed his eyes in despair. Sweety poured vinegar and lots of oil over her cook's salad.

The Diavolo master hoped that the brat would finish the ketchup course before he put the first chips in his mouth.

Frederick started with the schnitzel. Cordula took the good Heinz No. 57 and poured it over her chips. A race against time began. Berti was very excited. He had to force himself not to stare at the Sweety family the whole time. The time had come. Precision landing! Pure perfectionism! At the same time, both children shoved fries dripping with ketchup into their mouths.

Berti was enchanted by the taste of the Parma ham and also enjoyed the view of his battlefield of revenge.

"A real treat," he muttered, mouth full, without taking his eyes off his victims. He tried to look over as inconspicuously as possible.

"You said it."

Direct hit! Ship sunk! The horror of the Tabasco was written all over Frederick's face. While he was still tucking into a second and third fry and a cut-off piece of schnitzel, an unpleasant sharpness spread through his mouth and throat. His sister gaped with glee, grinning broadly, then blood rushed to her cheeks.

"Take a look at the stupid kids."

Konny turned around. They were both bright red. They reached for their lemonade glasses and emptied them in one go.

"Mom, that's hot," groaned Frederick.

"I'm dying," Cordula groaned.

"I always said you eat too much ketchup," the head of the family shrugged it off. Manny wanted to enjoy his steak. "That stuff ruins your stomach."

"Manny, go complain to the waiter! Look at our children. Come on! Do something!"

Sweety's husband closed his eyes again for a moment. He took a deep breath. Berti could see a volcanic eruption brewing in his stomach, and the magma of emotions working its way up. It was about to erupt.

And it did. Manny put his foot down. He was hungry and had been looking forward to that steak all day. "That's enough for me! If you don't like it, order something else next time. I'm not a fan of French fries and ketchup anyway. My steak is excellent and I'm going to enjoy it in peace. If you're not hungry anymore, go straight to your room! Starting tomorrow, I'll be serving you cereal and milk instead of chips and cola! And if anyone talks to me before I've finished eating, I won't be allowed to watch TV or use my cell phone for the rest of the vacation!"

Boom. That did it. Both kids stared at each other with glazed eyes and fiery red heads, got up and ran out of the dining room.

Konny grinned. "I think Manny has had enough."

"One to zero for us," said Berti, enjoying his victory.

"Are you behind this?"

He grinned. "Just a little Tabasco in the ketchup."

"You rascal, what else have you cooked up?"

"I don't think Mommy will be sitting here for long today. And she'll probably prefer to be in her room in the evening instead of having a drink at the bar."

"Why?"

"She soaked her salad in castor oil."

Konny started to laugh. To avoid attracting attention, he grabbed his napkin, held it to his mouth and nose, and imitated blowing his nose.

Sweety ate the whole salad. She seemed to like the mixture of olive and castor oil. It worked faster than Berti had expected. She got up before Manny could order a second lager. "I'm going to the nursery."

"I thought we were having a cocktail at the bar? Parents' night, followed by, you know..."

"I'm sorry, I..." she broke off in mid-sentence. The rumbling in her stomach could be heard at the next table. She stalked out of the dining room, clenching her buttocks. Anyone who had ever had an acute attack of diarrhea could tell by the way she walked. Sweety's ears were flaming red with embarrassment. Her cheeks were probably red too, but they were so covered in blush that it was impossible to tell. Shortly before the door, she fell into a kind of stupor.

"Two to zero for us," the detective said triumphantly.

The observation of the desires continued. Just a slight turn of the head and he had the animal abuser faction in his sights. They raised their glasses. Berti didn't like the way the couple looked at the other guests. The glasses were put down. They picked up their silverware. Judging by the gestures, the schnitzel seemed to taste excellent. The first forkful of spaghetti followed. The chewer fell asleep. The old woman and her son wrinkled their noses at the unseasoned food. They washed down their respective bites with wine. She craned her neck, obviously looking for the waiter. He distracted her by pointing to the condiment tray on the table.

Berti breathed a sigh of relief.

He reached for the bottle of Fire Salamander. The next hurdle was ahead. Did they know the devil? The tension grew. He unscrewed the cap and poured some of the chili sauce over the spaghetti. Then he held the bottle up to his mother. She nodded and took the same portion of the infernal stuff. Berti leaned back.

"Let the final begin," he said, drawing Konny's attention to the showdown.

The Diavolo victims twisted their noodles onto their forks with seemingly enormous appetites. The concentrated loads went into their mouths. They chewed, noticing only a slight spiciness at first, and swallowed. The two contest winners could hardly believe what followed. Mother and son broke into a sweat. She was panting and fanning herself with her hands. Tears were streaming from his eyes. First they drank their glass of wine, then their bottle of mineral water. They drank and drank and drank. The son could barely speak as he ordered another bottle of water. She sat back and tried to keep her composure. The make-up ran. She was mutating into Lady Horror.

"She's showing her true colors," Konny giggled.

"That was for Sir Nelson," Berti whispered, picked up an olive and popped it into his mouth. The taste of the south, the sun and the sea spread through his mouth, while his victims had to endure the burning of an open fire or glowing coals in their throats. Berti was happy. After the successful attacks, the food tasted twice as good.

He who laughs last, laughs best.

The bar was crowded. The typical American bar sound was playing softly from the loudspeakers. Deadly dull and yet fitting. Berti didn't want to accompany Konny to the two publishers and wandered alone through the cozy room.

Schlaps, plagued by the fire salamander spice, sat a little apart. She ate dry bread and drank mineral water. He had a beer in front of him. The old woman's make-up had been reapplied and they had both changed their clothes.

Manny stood alone at the bar. He seemed to change from Mr. Hide back into Dr. Jekyll. When he ordered a whiskey, something like a smile crossed his face. "A Dalmore Quintessence." Manny knew that a bottle of this fine stuff cost a little over 1000 Euros. On the one hand, he looked as if his fortune had gone down the drain, his old lady had run off with the butler and his house had gone up in flames. On the other hand, he looked free and relaxed. When the bartender, it was Mario, poured the exclusive whiskey, the beaming face of the troubled father and husband returned. "A double in a minute," he said, gesturing with his fingers by spreading his thumb and index finger wide.

Baron von Straß was becoming increasingly worried about Mr. Schepperlin. As Berti walked past the elderly but sprightly gentleman, he was approached. "Excuse me. You also heard this afternoon that Mr. Schepperlin wanted to meet me for dinner, didn't you?

Berti stood still. "Yes, I did. Why do you ask?"

"He didn't show up. Usually my chess partner is always on time."

Berti shrugged. "Maybe he fell asleep?"

"Strange, but possible," said the Baron. "Well, then I'll have to drink my cognac alone."

Konny hadn't made it to the bar. The Bunts were at one of the bistro tables with the Edelmanns. Hilde and Charlotte had already turned their radar eyes and struck when the author appeared.

"Mr. Wels, hello," they waved, "we're here. What would you like to drink?"

Berti reached the bar and stood between Manny and a man he hadn't seen before. The stranger was chatting, laughing, and taking turns talking about his neighbor to the left and Mario.

Well, Manny the mammoth from *Ice Age*, thought Berti, turning his back on the chatterbox and nodding to Manny in a friendly way. He glanced at his drink, saw Mario put down the Dalmore and recognized a deer's head with antlers on the label. Berti snapped his fingers nonchalantly. "Mario, a double Jägermeister for me too, please."

Manny's face fell immediately. The bartender didn't understand what Berti wanted and asked: "Why, Mr. Schwartz?"

Berti pointed at Manny's glass and the bottle.

Mario grinned and winked at the guest. "This is Dalmore, not Jägermeister."

Manny interrupted. "This Dalmore is very special. It's 50 years old and has an aroma of dark forest fruits, sweet honey and jam notes and doesn't taste of 64 herbs."

Berti realized his faux pas. But he wouldn't be the eloquent Berti, and he wouldn't have come so far in life, if he didn't immediately come up with something appropriate after something like that. "I know, I was just trying to make a joke. Dalmore is just first class," he fibbed. "I noticed you were staring a little sadly in front of you. So I thought, Schwartz, why don't you stand next to this nice gentleman and share an exclusive Dalmore with him? Whiskey is better enjoyed in pairs.

Manny was confused. Mario also served Berti the fine scotch. The detective took it and raised his glass. "Cheers."

Manny's eyes read something like: "And now this!", but he toasted back. "Cheers, sir. May I introduce myself? Dr. Manfred Broederlin, member of the board of Euro Chemical Industries Ltd."

"Herbert Schwartz, private detective."

Manny's only response was a slight nod of the head in recognition. He took a small sip of the mahogany-colored drink, closed his eyes, and enjoyed the aftertaste.

Berti blinked and imitated him. It tasted terrible. The son of naive Franconian parents, in whose household the highest honor was a home-distilled plum brandy from the farmer in the next village, had absolutely no use for whiskey.

Manny, on the other hand, enjoyed the sip. "Brilliant! After a taste of the local forest, it flows smoothly into the tropics, exploding with pineapple, Daddyya, mango and juicy raisins. Ginger and licorice add a refreshing kick. Finished with the finest marzipan. This gives the whisky its body. And the finish. Medium length, blackcurrant paired with fresh orange and a little warm banana. What do you think?"

Berti suppressed a gag. "Oh yes, indeed," he moaned, making the belch sound like a "mhmm, yummy" as his brain and stomach considered whether to give the order to vomit.

"Don't you think the oak is sinking a bit?"

Berti lifted his glass and smelled the whiskey. "Do you think it's bad? Well, at this age..."

Suspicious looks. Then a short laugh. "You're joking again, aren't you?"

"Of course," Berti pushed forward. Oak fits perfectly. That stuff tastes like old wood. I'd prefer real Jägermeister.

"I almost fell for it," the whiskey connoisseur giggled and burst out laughing: "Is it ... bad ha ha ha ... with the ha ha ha age ...," he parodied Berti. "I really have to remember that. It's really good. I'll bring it up at the next board meeting." Then he ordered two more Dalmore. Berti didn't have a chance to refuse.

"You're all alone at the bar. Where's your charming companion?" Berti asked almost casually, but he wanted to savor his murderous victory.

"Sweety, my wife, isn't feeling well. Something seems to have upset her stomach. What's more, my two children have also gotten upset stomachs or heartburn from their constant bad diet. I don't care." Manny looked around and leaned over to Berti. "You know what?"

He shook his head.

"They annoy me. The kids and my wife too. I'm glad to be alone for once."

Mario placed the new glasses on two small serving trays and pushed them toward the guests.

Berti dreaded it. Eyes closed and through. "Cheers!"

A small miracle had happened. The second Dalmore tasted better. At least I didn't feel like throwing up.

Manny defrosted. "When I met my wife fifteen years ago, I wanted to suck her firm breasts and fuck her brains out."

"And now?"

"Now I think I've done quite well."

Berti roared. The atmosphere became more and more exuberant.

The unknown pompous neighbor turned to them. "Grüetzi, servus and hello, I'm Hansi."

"Berti."

"Manny," came the surprisingly relaxed and casual reply of the chairman of the supervisory board of a pharmaceutical giant.

"That's right, dear snow lovers. I'm your ski instructor, but tonight I'd like to entertain you. Since you're telling jokes..."

"We're not," Berti interjected, trying to look completely serious and a little grim.

It worked. Hansi fell silent.

The private detective pointed backwards with his thumb. "What Manny said was deadly serious. We're just solving his problems."

Hansi's eyes searched desperately for a way out. "Oh, there I see ..." he quickly pushed forward. "Excuse me, I'll be right back. I have to say hello to Professor Dr. Heberlein. I'm sure you know him. He's Europe's most renowned heart specialist."

The ski instructor disappeared. Berti saw the old woman again. She had obviously digested her encounter with the fire lamander. Her son had gotten up. He was suspiciously close to the other guests, but not talking to them. Somehow this witch and her offspring seemed strange to Berti. He watched her. Her wrinkled giraffe neck stretched

256

longer and longer. She opened the fancy bag. Sir Nelson slipped out. She whispered something in the dog's ear. The little head lifted. The cuddly nose wiggled back and forth as he sniffed. Then the Chihuahua jumped out of his luxurious home. He wanted to sprint towards his son, but Berti, who was saying goodbye to Manny at the same moment, took two steps forward at the same time. The dog slowed down and changed direction. Full of joy, he jumped up and down in front of Berti's legs.

"Sir Nelson," Berti called happily.

The old woman's face was instantly frozen. Her son turned bright red.

Berti bent down and petted the Chihuahua. "Sir Nelson, my little friend. Where are you?"

Woof.

The friends didn't last long. "There's the little runaway. Have you been running to that corpulent gentleman again?" the old woman's voice shattered the idyll. She said with a grin on her face and a cold look in her eyes: "He must have jumped out of my pocket again. I'd better take him to his room."

Berti was speechless. The old lady had just taken the dog out of the stupid *Louis Vuitton* handbag herself. He had seen it with his own eyes. The detective instinctively looked for the unsympathetic son. His eyes circled the bar. He had disappeared.

"Hop, in you go," came the command, and Sir Nelson jumped into the noble bag. The old woman staggered away. Berti suspected that something was rotten here. Very rotten indeed. He decided to drink mineral water instead of whiskey.

I'll keep an eye on them both.

Baron von Strass came to Berti at the bar. "You haven't seen Mr. Schepperlin either, have you?"

The detective shook his head briefly. "No, Baron, not yet."

He frowned. "Well, I'm very surprised."

"He'll be here soon," Berti reassured him.

"Then I'll wait a little longer." Baron von Strass turned to leave, paused, and asked: "Would you like to play a game of chess with me?"

Berti smiled. "You wouldn't like it. I'm really not much of an opponent."

Another unknown guest, who had apparently been following the conversation, approached.

"Allow me, my name is Ivan Vladimir Kurovsaltin. I am a Russian attaché and I like to play chess. May I challenge you?"

Baron von Strass studied the man in his mid-fifties standing before him.

The pattern had not escaped him. "Do you know me? Have you ever been in Russia?"

"Yes, I was in Russia once. As a very young Soldier I got as far as the outskirts of Moscow with my assault rifles, then I had to make my way back."

The Russian statesman didn't know how to react. Berti took the decision out of his hands and laughed. Humor is a good weapon.

Now the Russian also smiled.

Berti made a suggestion. "Then why don't you sit down together? You can discuss open questions and relive old times on the chessboard."

Baron von Straß clicked his heels together half-militarily. "I accept the challenge!"

The Russian was pleased. "I look forward to an exciting chess match."

The old woman was gone. Sir Nelson was gone, and so was the arrogant son of the witch. Manny was in whiskey paradise and Berti was waiting for Konny.

Mario served the mineral water. "Here you go," he said politely as always. "Enjoy your drink."

Hansi returned and joined Manny. A perfect time for Berti to leave. He took his glass and walked aimlessly through the bar. Then he found what he was looking for. The Schlaps. They had retreated to the far corner of the room and were sitting in a kind of booth. They were whispering excitedly to each other.

I wonder if Sir Nelson still has to sit in the handbag? I'll keep an eye on these animal abusers.

Konny spotted Berti. He waved. "Berti, why don't you come over here?"

Mr. Bunt and Mr. Edelmann had left their wives alone with the author and gone to the bar. Konny looked exhausted. The two women kept talking to him. He tried to get Berti's attention by winking at him to get him out of this situation.

The detective came to the table and put down his glass. "It's getting pretty late. I guess we'll be retiring."

The women frantically looked for the waiter to order something in a hurry. Konny grabbed the straw his friend handed him and yawned. "You're right. Ladies, I'm going to retire. It's been a wonderful evening."

fairy-2915532_1280

Chapter 10
Dancing Queen

When the detective awoke the next morning, he felt that he had stopped the whiskey session at just the right time.

One more drink and I'd have a terrible headache.

He got up shortly after Konny. While his friend went to the gym, Berti preferred to take a warm shower. He needed time to prepare for the big surprise. Everything had to be perfect. He had even brought the right music. To be on the safe side, it was stored on a CD, a USB flash drive and, of course, on his cell phone. He chose the CD. The remote control for the player was waiting for him in the bathroom for a perfect start. On the way to the suite's luxurious bathroom, Berti whistled the tune of *Dancing Queen*. He threw the fluffy, soft towel onto the wall hook. Of course, he missed and the towel landed on the floor. Berti bent down, picked it up and hung it on the hook provided. He climbed into the shower and closed the glass door. Berti searched in vain for the fittings. A silver strip with snaps appeared in his field of vision. He selected Tropical Summer, pressed the button, and pleasantly tempered water poured onto his bare skin from five different shower heads mounted on the sides and ceiling.

"Ahhh, that feels good," he groaned contentedly.

The detective began to sing: "*You can dance, you can jive,*" followed by humming, "*...you are the dancing queen, young and sweet, only seventeen Dancing queen. Feel the beat of the tambourine*, oh yes".

Berti switched to soft body massage. The ceiling jet was replaced by three side jets. They all had different pressure levels. Two of them also moved back and forth.

"Schwartz, you've done everything right here," the Abba fan praised himself as he let his body be sprayed by the water jets and enjoyed the massage. He switched to the hot massage. The temperature increased immediately. Steam formed.

"Uhhh, ahhh," Berti exclaimed, looking for the switch, but he couldn't find it in the haze.

"Hot," he squeezed out, jumping back and forth faster and faster. He tried to avoid the water jets, but it was impossible. The mist became so thick that he could only feel the ledge. He blindly pressed a button to start singing his favorite song again, but before he could say the word "dance," he froze. Icy water poured over his body, which had been warmed by the hot water. Goose bumps appeared. Berti's heart seemed to stop. In a blur he saw the position in the drifting steam: Iceland Shower. At the same time, his mouth formed into a scream. "Ahhhhhhh! Not again."

The outstretched index finger of an arm shivering with cold desperately searched for the tropical summer position. The icy water poured down on it incessantly.

"D-d-d-da ... is ... he j-j-yes," he stuttered from the cold and put his finger on the switch that should free him. Shivering, he expected the tropical rain from the shower heads, but he had caught the switch underneath and turned it off. The water jets stopped.

"Shit," he grumbled and angrily slapped his groin with the flat of his hand, turning on every setting for ten seconds. At first he took a deep breath in the tropical summer, but when the ice water came on again after the hot shower, he was on the verge of a heart attack. Annoyed, he got out of the shower and grabbed his towel. He wrapped it around his entire body and leaned against the pleasantly warm radiator. Five minutes later he could breathe normally again.

It was like something out of a Stephen King horror book. Shower to hell, it went through his head. Then he turned to the shower. "Are you out of a sick Stephen King novel? Asshole! I almost died!"

A thought flashed through Berti's mind. What if he sued the hotel for damages? In the USA, people have been awarded millions in compensation for far less pain and suffering. At the same moment, an imaginary headline slid across the page. Germany's dumbest detective. Berti Schwartz is too stupid to shower.

He decided not to go to court.

"But only because I don't have to pay for the hotel anyway," he said to his reflection. He looked at himself, practiced a few facial expressions from serious to humorously funny and back again, and thought his appearance in the mirror was great.

Berti dried his hair, rubbed his weighty dream body with a fragrant lotion, applied Konny's favorite cologne and was satisfied. "Man, I'm tight."

His planned surprise could begin. He would become Agnetha Fältskog. He felt like the last gentleman private detective of the good old days. He was a quick-change artist, could be the buddy Berti, could be the gentleman Berti, and could be the tough-as-nails investigator Berti.

And now I'm part of ABBA, it went through his head.

He put on his wig, made himself up discreetly and put on his briefs and suspenders.

"What should I wear as a top?" While he pondered, he danced in front of the bathroom mirror as a rehearsal.

"Nothing," he decided with great satisfaction. He thought he looked great. "I'll stay topless."

Konny would go crazy. With this outfit, the little song on her lips and a hot dance, of course the original song had to be played in the background - ambience is everything - the obligatory proposal should come a second time. This time with style. Fancy and romantic.

The door opened. Someone entered the suite.

Berti looked at himself. "Are you back already?"

"Yes."

"Don't come into the bathroom!"

Konny heard his friend's voice muffled by the closed bathroom door. "All right. I wanted to sweat it out anyway."

"Breakfast in the room?"

"Agreed. I'll go ahead and order."

Berti had made the final touches and looked at the whole work of art in the mirror. Flushes of emotion whistled through his veins, crawled under his skin and sought their way back. It was indescribable. Somehow he had stage fright. It felt like he was about to make a big entrance. The sold-out hall waited outside. The male Agnetha checked the discreetly applied make-up one last time. "Maybe a little more Ruge?" he asked his reflection.

There was a knock at the door of the suite. Berti couldn't hear it through the closed bathroom door.

Konny was surprised that room service was so quick. He got up to get breakfast. This is crazy. I called less than five minutes ago, he thought and opened the door.

Just then Berti came out of the bathroom. He pressed the remote. Music played. It was the tune of *Dancing Queen*. Konny turned around. Meanwhile, the front door was wide open. Mr. Ostmann, A-melie, Baron von Strass and the heart specialist Prof. Dr. Heberlein stood in the doorway.

They all stared at Berti, who was prancing around the hotel suite like an overweight ballerina in an Agnetha Fältskog wig, panties and suspenders, singing Dancing Queen while the original Abba song blared from the speakers of the music system in the background.

"*...you can dance, you are the Dancing Queen, young and sweet, only seventeen, Dancing Queen, feel the beat from the tambourine, oh yeah, you can dance, you can jive, having the time of your life, see that girl, watch that scene, diggin' the Dancing Queen...*"

It was not until the first chorus was completely sung that Berti noticed his audience. He felt sick. He fell silent while ABBA conti-nued to sing in the CD player. He wanted to sink into the floor. How did he get out of that situation? Which was worse? The story in the department store or the ABBA number here and now in this posh hotel where he was building his career?

Berti wanted to die right now. He closed his eyes, hoping it was a mirage, and opened them again. The people were still there. Spee-chless, their mouths agape, they stared at the half-naked man in a woman's wig.

"I'm... hmmm... I'm...uh...practicing. I have a job on Broadway. The ABBA musical is opening there soon ... so ... I'm supposed to be there as Agnetha ... My disguise is ... I'll probably have to find a new disguise ... so ..." he stammered.

Mr. Ostmann was the first to speak clearly. "You can rely on our discretion."

Baron von Strass said simply: "Ugh!"

"Ladies and gentlemen, Berti, I mean, Mr. Schwartz, as Ag-netha's double, the lady is getting on in years and has put on a few pounds," Konny explained after he had caught himself, "we don't re-ally talk about it, but as a double he prevented an assassination attempt

264

on the group ABBA. A second attack was planned for the next musical. All four former band members had planned to appear briefly on stage as guests. Herbert Schwartz is meticulously preparing for his role.

"Awesome! Just awesome," came from Amelie's lips. "You saved someone from ABBA's life?"

Berti was embarrassed. "Oh," he waved it off. "That's a bit of an exaggeration."

The hotel owner cleared his throat. "It's a good thing we have such an excellent detective in the house," he suggested. "May we come in?"

Astonished, Berti and Konny agreed. The unexpected visitors came in and sat down. The CD player was turned off. Berti scurried into the bathroom and slipped into a bathrobe to stand in front of the guests.

Mr. Ostmann came straight to the point. "We have a murder to report. The hotel is snowed in and still cut off from the outside world. You are our only hope."

Silence. Rigidity of shock. "Mo-mo-mo-murder case?" Berti stuttered.

Ostmann looked at the detective and wondered if a tough and cool investigator spoke as intermittently as a prostate patient pees. He dismissed the idea because he had no choice. This detective was the only hope for his prestigious house. "That's right! Mr. Schepperlin was murdered last night. At the insistence of Baron von Strass, we opened our guest room this morning. Prof. Dr. Heberlein could only determine that the man was dead."

Every single word that flew towards Berti had an effect. He came to his senses. The people here trusted him. He was their hope. He was no longer the silly little department store detective, he was Herbert Schwartz, private detective - their problem is my problem - investigations with a guarantee. The time had come. His life was in the workshop. It was pimped, souped up - tuned - powered up. From that moment on, everything changed. Everything! There were studied and highly intelligent people sitting there asking for his advice. He could either continue to be the little fat Berti he had always been and mess everything up, or he could make a name for himself. He looked at the guests. Amelie was his girlfriend.

Maybe she was behind this and told her boss to contact him.

Her eyes were shining. She adored him. At least she liked him. "Berti, I mean Mr. Schwartz," she corrected herself. "You'll take the case, won't you?"

Baron von Strass, who last night had found his personal revenge for the lost Russian campaign and led Napoleon's army to victory, still had some doubts whether Berti was the right man. But if the stories were true, this portly private detective in a woman's wig was a master of disguise. "If your criminal mind is on par with your camouflage skills, young man, I trust you to solve my friend's death."

Berti's eyes wandered to the next guest. He was a doctor and had examined the body. Professor Dr. Heberlein, a luminary in his field. I'm sure he could answer some questions for Berti. Uh ... do I have any questions?

"Mr. Schwartz, the honor of my hotel is at stake. I heard that you arrested a criminal during the trip. Is that true?"

"Of course it's true," he said very confidently. So confident that even Konny was surprised. "Excuse me for a moment, please. I can't work in this camouflage outfit. I'll change quickly. I feel so ... hm ... naked in my bathrobe," said Berti and scurried off to the bedroom.

The hotelier called after him. "And what is your answer?"

"Don't push him, Mr. Ostmann," Baron von Strass interjected. "If he had accepted the job at once, it wouldn't have been a good sign. All professionals think before they decide."

Berti closed the bedroom door behind him and sat down on the bed. Everything was spinning. His mind went on a merry-go-round. He had, of course, read many books on death investigations and knew almost every bestseller. Of course he would take the case. It was his ticket into the world of the rich. Herbert Schwartz stepped on the gas and put himself in the fast lane. While he was thinking, everyone else had to wait. Three minutes passed. Five minutes passed. Finally, a quarter of an hour had passed.

"Patience," Amelie advised. "It often takes me half an hour to find the right clothes."

Silence. Nervous glances. Waiting. Seconds passed like minutes, minutes seemed like hours to those who waited. When the bedroom door finally opened, the detective was holding a pen and pad. "How did it happen?"

266

Mr. Ostmann stood up. "Is that a yes?"

"Stupid question! He's in the middle of his investigation," Baron von Strass pulverized. "I like the boy. He looks normal now."

The hotelier turned to the detective. "We opened the door together."

"All of you?"

"All of us," Baron von Strass confirmed.

Berti wrote down the witnesses' names.

"What time was that exactly?"

"At 8:05," it shot out at him.

Berti noted the time and asked the next question. "What situation did you find?"

Dr. Heberlein spoke. "The body was in the bathroom. Mr. Schepperlin had probably just gotten ready for dinner. He was strangled with his own tie."

"Strangled in the bathroom with his own tie," Berti noted. "You can..." the detective hesitated and looked around the group. "You can rule out a certain sexual practice?" he finally asked bluntly.

"You pig!"

Berti defended himself with an explanation. "Baron von Strass. As a detective, I have to ask questions that you would never ask otherwise. Of course, we assume an honorable person, but asking questions clears the mind and excludes all other questions. If I don't ask questions, a journalist might ask them in public.

The older baron nodded. "I understand. Clever man. I think we've made the right decision, gentlemen."

Dr. Heberlein intervened. "No sexual practice. He was definitely strangled to death. I'd better show you on the body."

Berti pressed his lips together. "On the L-L body?" he broke, then cleared his throat to hide his nervousness. "Sorry about that. I had something stuck in my throat," he apologized. "Well, show me the body if you think it's necessary."

"The whole room has been ransacked," Ostmann added.

Berti summarized. "So a robbery-murder."

Amelie was dismayed. "Who could have done this?"

"I'll find out," Berti assured him.

Dr. Heberlein stood up. "You still need us?"

"Point 1: Who knows everything about the murder?"

"Only us," Baron von Strass replied.

"I must ask you all to maintain the strictest secrecy about this."

Berti paced the room. "Second. None of the guests are to leave the hotel."

"That's not possible anyway."

"Third, I need a list of everyone in the hotel. Guests and employees."

"You'll get it right away," the hotelier assured us.

"I can do it," Amelie suggested.

"My suite is headquarters. This is where all the threads come together. Where exactly is the crime scene?"

"Room three."

"I'd better visit the scene immediately. Mr. Ostmann and Prof. Dr. Heberlein will help me. Amelie will take care of the list. Konny will hold the fort here. Baron von Straß will sit in the foyer."

The sprightly nobleman was puzzled. "Why do I have to go to the foyer?"

"Listening post," Berti winked.

"Clever," replied Baron von Strass. "Just like in war. I'm a forward observer."

They left the suite. Each of them carried out his assigned task. The detective, the hotel owner and the doctor went to the scene of the crime. When room no. 3 was opened, Berti felt a little queasy. All three hurried into the room and the door was closed again. The room was smaller than Berti's suite, but no less luxurious.

"Shall we start right away?" he hesitated slightly. "I mean, examine the body?" the doctor asked, pointing to the bathroom door.

Berti wanted to shout *NO* and run away. Instead, the answer was: "That's probably best."

"I'll wait here," Ostmann held back.

"Don't touch anything," the detective warned, raising his index finger in warning.

Prof. Dr. Heberlein opened the bathroom door. The body lay on the floor. The arms and legs were outstretched. The arms were close to the body. The face was covered with a towel. Mr. Schepperlin was wearing a shirt and pants. He was also wearing socks and shoes.

"Is the body still in the recovery position?"

"Yes, why?"

268

"Because it's important for the investigation," Berti told the doctor. "Were there any signs of a struggle?"

Prof. Dr. Heberlein pointed at the dead man. "No, he was just lying there."

"With the cloth over his face?"

The cardiologist nodded. "With the cloth over his face," he repeated.

Berti immediately fumbled for the next question, but avoided looking at the body. "How long do you think he's been dead?"

"Well, I'm not much of a pathologist, but given the room temperature, the lividity, and the rigor mortis, I'd say death occurred between 7:00 and 9:30 last night."

"Cause of death?" the detective asked, searching his book and movie knowledge for meaningful questions.

The doctor pointed to the murdered man's neck and bent down. Then he approached, but without removing the towel from his face. "The tie is still wrapped around his neck. Can you see the marks on his neck?" he asked, tracing an imaginary line with his finger.

Berti tried to look concentrated. He was actually afraid of the corpse and found it unpleasant to be here, but he couldn't take the worst-case scenario lightly. So he knelt down beside the dead Mr. Schepperlin and followed the doctor's finger with his eyes. Now he recognized it. Discoloration was visible on the wrinkled skin. A blue-violet ring shimmered from under the tight tie. "Clear strangulation marks. You're right."

"He must have been standing in front of the mirror tying his tie when the killer approached him from behind," the doctor speculated.

Berti was surprised. "How did you know that?"

"I only suspected it because the tie is the instrument of crime."

Berti acted as if that was his conclusion as well. "I admire your criminal skills, because I assume the same modus operandi," he talked shop.

"Schepperlin must have resisted. He has bruises on the knuckles of his right hand. I think he hit the perpetrator."

"A perpetrator. Probably a man," Berti remarked. "Maybe injured."

"He was at least strong enough to slowly lower the dead Mr. Schepperlin to the ground. There are no injuries to indicate that he fell or was hit," the heart surgeon concluded his brief thesis on the course of events and stood up.

Berti stood up as well. "Thank you, Professor."

"There you go. It's the least I can do in this extraordinary situation. It's terrible enough to know that there is a murderer among us.

"Very bad indeed," Berti confirmed. "But we will hunt him down."

"Oh, what else did I want to ask you?"

"Go ahead."

"What are we going to do with the body? If it's left here, it'll probably start..." he wrinkled his nose demonstratively. "...to decompose. You know what I mean. The smell is pungent."

Ostmann's voice could be heard. "We can't leave him here. We have to get him out of here."

"Where?" asked Berti.

"A cold room would be best," suggested Heberlein.

"In the kitchen?" wondered the hotelier.

"With our food?" Berti worried.

They both stared at the doctor. He just shrugged. "We could put him on the balcony."

He shook his head. "That would only damage my company's reputation even more."

"We are in an exceptional situation," Berti raised his right index finger. "Nothing and no one will be harmed here. At least not while we have things under control."

Ostmann looked at the dead man and said: "All right, I'll put him in the cooler. We'll just have to make room and lay him out separately from the food."

"Why? Are you afraid he'll devour your supplies?" joked the doctor.

"Nonsense! This is a matter of piety." Ostmann seemed a little upset.

Berti tried to reassure him. "I also believe that the pork schnitzels don't care whether there's a dead man or a roast beef next to them."

"All right then! Then we'll take it to the kitchen refrigerator. But then the secrecy will be over."

"If we take it to the kitchen ourselves, no one will notice," the professor suggested.

The hotel owner thought for a moment. "We can get down the service stairs without being seen, but he'll be conspicuous in the cold room."

"If we put him on two or three serving tables and cover him?" said Berti.

"And the cook?"

"Tell him to keep his hands off it."

"It's at least worth a try," Dr. Heberlein agreed with the detective.

"That's how we do it," the hotelier decided.

"The body is rigid and relatively fresh. No one need be afraid to touch it," the doctor reassured him.

"I'll go first, you two carry Mr. Schepperlin," Ostmann decided.

"What if one of the guests notices something?"

"No problem either. I suppose our detective will make a speech to all hotel guests and employees sooner or later anyway. That will be brought forward."

Berti was startled. "Me?"

"Of course you are! You're in charge of the investigation."

"I mean, that was my plan, of course. I just have to think about what tactics I'm going to use," he said.

"Then think faster, before the dead man starts to smell."

"I'll take a look around the room first."

It didn't take a detective to notice that the room had been ransacked. Someone had gone through all the drawers. Most of them were still open. The victim's empty wallet lay on the bed. Nothing was missing, however, except cash. At least, nothing was known to be missing.

Berti walked around the room. The detective took photo after photo with his small digital camera. He kept making notes. As he did so, he let out an "Ah yes" or an "Ohh", but also an "I thought so".

He left his two search witnesses in the dark. Finally, he went to the balcony door. It was locked on the inside. Berti opened it and stepped out. The white splendor was untouched.

There was nothing and no one here.

"Not a trace of snow! There are definitely no traces of snow out here."

"What does that mean?"

271

"Either our dear Mr. Schepperlin let the perpetrator into the room himself, or the perpetrator forced his way in. Another alternative would be that the perpetrator or perpetrators are or were in possession of a key card."

"Good combination," Ostmann admitted. He was glad that a private investigator was among the hotel guests.

"What about the key card for room no. 3?" Berti wanted to know.

"The card is here by the door. We unlocked it with the replacement card."

"And yesterday?"

Ostmann thought about it. "Wait a minute. There was a small incident. The porter contacted me. Mr. Schepperlin spoke to him and asked him to unlock the room because he had left his card there."

"Did you open the room? And if so, when exactly?"

"I opened the door myself yesterday." Lines of thought formed on Ostmann's forehead. Embarrassed, he scratched the back of his head. "That was ... Oh yes, I remember now. It was before dinner. Mr. Schepperlin had borrowed a book on chess from the hotel library. He was holding it in his hand when he told the porter that he had accidentally left his key card in his room."

Berti made a note. "You just remembered that?"

"He was still alive then!" Ostmann defended himself. "However..."

"Did you think of anything else?"

"He told me that he was actually quite sure that he had taken the key card into the library. That's funny. Mr. Schepperlin was anything but confused. He had a crystal clear mind."

"Thank you, that's all for now."

"You don't think I...?"

Berti waved him off. "No, not that. But you may have been the last person to see the victim alive. The police will certainly have some questions about that."

"Won't they?"

"Later! For now, all hotel guests are equally suspicious."

"I have to ask," Professor Dr. Heberlein stood up.

"As a detective, I must stick to the facts. I'll check the alibis later." Berti was in his element. How often had he found himself in situations like this. Some of his favorite TV lines were rehearsed and he could fire them off as needed. "We should take care of the body."

"Should we wrap it in a sheet?"

"Good idea," Ostmann agreed and picked up the sheet. He laid it on the floor of the bathroom next to the body. Berti and Prof. Dr. Heberlein grabbed the dead man's left and right arms and rolled him onto the sheet. The sheet was then wrapped around the lifeless body, like a mummy.

"On the count of three, we lift him up."

"Good!"

"One, two, three!"

The old man didn't weigh much. Rigor mortis was complete.

"It's amazing that such a thing exists," said Berti.

"Rigor mortis?"

"Yes."

"Quite simply. Rigor mortis is a sure sign of death because it occurs post mortem. Rigor mortis is caused by the binding of myosin to actin fibers. After death, ATP is no longer regenerated from ADP. The ion pumps that keep calcium ions low in the cytoplasm of muscle cells cease to function. After death, calcium ions diffuse from the sarcoplasmic reticulum into the cytoplasm, which naturally leads to the binding of myosin to actin filaments as the calcium ions neutralize the insulating effect of troponin. In the absence of ATP, the binding is no longer interrupted, which has only one logical consequence: the onset of muscle stiffness".

Berti didn't understand a word. He stared at the doctor with his mouth open. "Sure, that's what I thought."

"Let's get Pharao down."

"Well, Professor Dr. Heberlein! I don't find the situation funny at all. How can you joke about it and call this corpse Pharaoh?" Ostmann snapped.

Berti pulled himself together. He found the doctor's comment hilarious. Heberlein is actually a very funny person. To prevent the two of them from quarreling, he said to the hotelier: "Why don't you go ahead? See if the coast is clear."

Ostmann went to the door. The hotelier looked into the hall. "You can come," he whispered.

Berti and Heberlein staggered out of the bathroom with their Pharaoh.

"I hope he doesn't break his arm," the detective breathed out.

They reached the corridor. Ostmann led the way. The hotel manager's heart was beating three times as fast as normal with excitement. He imagined the right words in case they were actually seen and asked about the strange cargo.

We're practicing for a masked ball. What a load of rubbish! I bought a new statue and we... No, that's rubbish too. Mr. Schepperlin is allergic to the sun..., that last thought wasn't good either.

Excuse me, may we come by with the body, we'll take you to the refrigerator. If we stay snowed in, dinner is guaranteed for the next few days. Nonsense! V.G. Ostmann, stop joking, he scolds himself mentally.

They reached the stairs. Step by step they went down slowly.

"I admire your manner. You really impressed me with your professionalism. You don't deal with the dead every day," Berti admitted.

"I learned everything from scratch. You know, the first time we stood in front of a corpse at the university hospital, our professor used a trick to take away our fear."

"What trick?"

"He said that the quickest way for us to lose our fear of contact was to interact with the corpse. Then he demonstratively stuck a finger up the corpse's butt, pulled it out, and licked it."

"Ugh! Disgusting."

"The best is yet to come. We students should copy that. The first four of my classmates felt sick. The professor supervised the procedure and laughed his head off. Then it was my turn. I had paid attention and did it just like the professor.

"And they didn't get sick?"

"No! There was no reason to. He stuck his index finger up the corpse's butt and licked his middle finger. Watching is half the battle, my friend!"

"That reminds me of a joke."

"Tell me."

"Why don't you say: stupid man?"

Heberlein had no idea.

"You don't say dead body either."

They both laughed.

"I've got another one up my sleeve."

"Go ahead," Berti said happily.

"Two policemen find a body in front of the high school. One of them asks: How do you spell high school? After a long pause, the other said: Let's drag him to the post office."

"Ha ha ha," Berti snorted.

"Gentlemen! I have to ask," scoffed Ostmann.

They had climbed the stairs.

"Wait here!" The hotelier went into the kitchen and was back in a flash. "Nobody's here. You can come in."

When Berti and Dr. Heberlein entered the kitchen with the wrapped body, the refrigerator was already open. Ostmann was pushing in a large serving cart.

"That's not enough!"

All three looked at the mummy. Mr. Schepperlin was leaning against a shelf where shrink-wrapped sausage and cheese products were stored.

"We could leave it here in the corner," Berti said.

"Don't go! When the rigor mortis wears off, he'll fall into us."

"Stupid!"

"I'll just use the rolling workbench. It's two meters long and 80 centimeters wide," suggested the head of the house.

No sooner said than done. The serving table was pushed out of the cold room and the mobile work table was pushed back in. They carefully placed the body on the shiny, polished silver worktop.

"Should we put a blanket over it?" asked Berti.

Dr. Heberlein was surprised. "Why is that? Do you think Mr. Schepperlin is cold?"

"Gentlemen, please remain calm," Mr. Ostmann warned.

Berti pointed at the mummy. "Of course not, Doctor, but if the cook or his assistant enter the refrigerator, they'll get a shock for life. If we put a blanket over the corpse, it might not look like a corpse. And so it won't look like a morgue."

"You mean the cook won't immediately recognize our corpse as such?"

"You could put it that way."

"Good idea," Ostmann interrupted the discussion. "You two wait here, I'll get a blanket." He had barely spoken when the hotelier ran off.

Berti and Dr. Heberlein started to freeze.

"Shall we wait in front of the door?"

No sooner said than done. Like two bouncers they guarded the entrance to the cold room. Mr. Schepperlin lay wrapped up like a mummy on the mobile kitchen worktable in the middle of the room, as far away as possible from the hotel supplies.

When Ostmann returned and they entered the cold room for the second time, the scene looked more than macabre. They quickly put the blanket over the corpse and looked at their work.

Ostmann: "Better than before.

Prof. Dr. Heberlein: "But not much difference."

Ostmann: "Still better than before."

Berti: "It's cold."

All three looked at the covered body. Their eyes met. Each nodded.

"Good," Berti spoke. "Then we consider the body safe.

"And now what?" Ostmann wanted to know. The head of the house had put up another sign: Do not touch! at the foot of the corpse, then left the cold room last and pushed the heavy door into the lock.

"We'll all meet in my suite in ten minutes," Berti suggested.

Chapter 11
The usual suspects

The team investigating the jeweler's murder had gathered in the Operations Center, as the contest winners' suite was called. Everyone was silent. Berti had been taking notes for some time.

"What is he doing there?" Ostmann whispered to Konny.

He pointed at his friend. "Leave him alone. He's combining."

Baron von Strass pointed at Berti as if he were the enemy. "When we were outside Moscow in 1941, we had to combine too. The damned winter crippled our machinery. We almost drove the Russians out of the city. Damn winter!"

"Baron von Strass, you can't compare that with our situation."

"That's right! In those days, clever minds did the thinking on the ground. But in Berlin there were only amateurs. If that Austrian corporal had been chased back to where he came from, we would have emerged victorious from the war. How could a private ..."

No one listened to the former soldier, for Berti had stood up. "We must lure him out of his shell."

"Who?"

"What reserves? We didn't have reserves back then," Baron von Strass replied, but realized that he and his stories weren't meant and commented: "I see."

Berti raised his index finger. "We must set a trap for the murderer."

Pure curiosity. Question marks seemed to circle over the heads of those present.

"And how do we do that?" Ostmann wanted to know.

Amelie had an idea and stood up. "We could say that Mr. Schepperlin is still alive. He had a cardiac arrest, but the doctor revived him. And since his body temperature has to be kept low before he can be taken to the hospital, we had to put him in the cold storage."

"Brilliant," Ostmann exclaimed euphorically.

"Complete nonsense," the doctor destroyed the plan. "Anyone who knows anything about medicine knows it's a farce."

The hotelier turned to Berti. "What does our master detective say?"

"We'll do it differently," the portly detective suggested. "First, we confront everyone in the hotel with the fact that Mr. Schepperlin is dead. Next, we'll let it slip that he didn't die of natural causes. This signals to the killer that we know about his crime. This is the first uncertainty. Step two will be to lure the killer out of his shell by making him believe that Mr. Schepperlin insisted on video surveillance of his room and that there is a recording of the murder and the search of the room."

"And how do you explain that?" asked Prof. Dr. Heberlein.

"He was a jeweler," Baron von Strass croaked.

"And jewelers use sophisticated surveillance mechanisms in their shops. We let it slip that Mr. Schepperlin had deposited a valuable diamond in the room. He therefore insisted on the installation of a miniature camera for security reasons. That sounds plausible," Berti convinced the others.

"That's good," praised Heberlein.

"And why should the killer believe us? We could confront him with the recording and ..."

"Very simple," Berti interjected. "Of course, only Mr. Schepperlin knew where the camera was. He wanted to have the sole right of access to protect his privacy. The room is locked because we're waiting for the police. As a result, both the camera with the recording stick and the diamond are still in the room. The killer must return to the room to retrieve his recording and, of course, to steal the diamond. But this time we will set a trap for him."

"Perfect," Konny beamed.

"He will be looking for both the gem and the source of the image," Ostmann rejoiced. "I'm so glad we have a professional here at the hotel. You are saving my hotel's reputation."

"We'll drop the bomb at lunch," Berti decided.

Considering that there was a corpse in the cold room, Berti had eaten with a little less appetite. At first, that is. The food was so good that he had indulged in a small second helping of each course.

After lunch, at Mr. Ostmann's request, all the guests and employees of the Berghotel Alpentraum had gathered in the dining

278

room. Only the two children of the whiskey-drinking pharmaceutical executive Dr. Manfred Broederlin were sent to their rooms.

All ten guest rooms had been rented. Berti had gone over the list with Konny and Amelie beforehand.

The single rooms were occupied by the late Mr. Schepperlin, Baron von Straß, the Russian attaché and Prof. Dr. Heberlein. The couples Bunt and Edelmann and an English couple, both well over 70 years old, had booked the double rooms. The Broederlins, Berti and Konny, and the old lady with her son and Sir Nelson occupied the three suites of the Hotel.

The staff included chambermaid Amelie, star chef Fabian Rohloff, trainee chef Klaus, ski instructor Hansi, caretaker Willi and Mr. Sandmann, the porter. Mr. Ostmann arrived with the two waiters, who were also bartenders.

"That's everyone now," he said to Berti, who had a list in his hand and was ticking off the names of the people present. No one knew what was going on yet. The atmosphere was quite relaxed.

Mr. Kurovsaltin, the Russian, sat down next to Baron von Strass. He said appreciatively: "You have given me a good lesson in chess. Can I hope for a rematch?"

"Any time! Yesterday's two games were just for Stalingrad. Anyway, I have a score to settle with your country."

The attaché refrained from a cynical remark. But his narrowed eyes were expressive enough.

Meanwhile, Berti and Konny watched the guests. Their eyes wandered from table to table.

"Who do you think is capable of murder?" asked Konny.

His friend pondered. "If I'm honest, no one."

"I feel the same way."

Berti watched the old woman and her son more closely and noticed something. The old woman's son still hadn't finished his meal. His steak stroganoff didn't seem spicy enough to him. In fact, he reached for the *Fire Salamander* bottle and poured some of the extra hot chili sauce over the meat.

"Are you paralyzed?" exclaimed the detective. "Yesterday that bastard burned his snout so badly that his eyes almost fell on his plate, and today he's spilling the devil's own stuff on his food again."

Konny looked at Schlaps Junior. "Maybe he's gotten a taste for it?" he joked.

The hotel guest shoved a piece of dripping meat into his mouth. At first he chewed with relish, then the spectacle of last night was repeated. He turned bright red, drank his glass of water and added bread. Beads of sweat ran down his forehead. His mother reacted angrily, whispering a few expletives and pointing at the bottle. Her son, now glowing bright red, just shrugged.

"If stupidity had a name, it would be his," Konny grinned. "What are their last names, anyway?"

"Schlaps. Margot and her son Eduard Schlaps. The dog's name is Sir Nelson," Berti read from the list.

"Stupidity is called Schlaps! You can't be that stupid on your own, he still has..." Konny laughed and didn't finish the sentence.

At the same time Berti stopped. Indeed, this Eduard Schlaps was behaving as if he were sitting here for the first time. The detective was puzzled, took his notepad out of his pocket and wrote something down. Konny had given him an idea.

The author nudged Berti. "You, it's time."

Mr. Ostmann had stood up and stepped into the middle of the dining room. He held a knife in his hand and struck it against the edge of a glass. The bright sound did not fail to have an effect. "Your attention, please. Ladies and gentlemen." A brief pause, then he repeated the procedure. "I ask for silence."

Berti stood up and walked over to the hotelier. He was a little nervous. Konny winked at him and secretly gave him the thumbs up. "You can do it," he whispered.

This gave Berti strength and support.

Everyone stared at the two men. "My dear guests. On a very special occasion, I would like to introduce Mr. Schwartz. Mr. Schwartz is our in-house detective and a true criminological genius," Berti was introduced. Ostmann went one better. "He is one of the best private investigators in the country, and his disguises are deceptively real. Don't be fooled by a simple appearance. Just two days ago, Mr. Schwartz unmasked a wanted criminal, personally overpowered him, and handed him over to the police."

Berti was astonished and gladly accepted the praise. He cleared his throat and remained surprisingly calm despite a certain nervousness. "Dear guests, I would like to introduce myself. My name is Herbert Schwartz and I'm a private detective," he repeated. Berti thought that repeating his name over and over would help it stick in the minds of the hotel guests.

At first there was the clatter of dishes and whispering, but then absolute silence returned. Everyone had become curious.

Berti would have liked to tell a joke and then sit down again. I could use the one about the math professor. That's a good one, he thought.

A math professor writes to his wife:

Dear Mrs,

As you know, you are already 54 years old, and I have certain needs that you can no longer satisfy. But I am still very happy when you are with me and I appreciate you as a presentable wife. I hope I am not hurting you, but right now, while you are reading this letter, I am at the Grand Hotel with my secretary of 18 years.
P.S. I'll be home before midnight.

Your husband

At home he finds a letter from his wife:

Dear husband,

At 54, you are no longer young. As you read this letter, I'm at the Sheraton Hotel with the 18-year-old mail carrier. Since you are a mathematician, you will easily realize that 18 goes into 54 much more often than 54 goes into 18. So don't wait for me.

Your wife.

When Berti looked at the faces of the hotel guests and thought of the corpse in the refrigerator, he knew he wouldn't tell the joke.

The silence was cruel to him. Everyone was waiting for the detective to speak. Schlaps-Junior drank a second bottle of water. His face was still red. That was like a spark for Berti. Now he knew how to start. He cleared his throat.

"I am not standing here to amuse you. I have a serious matter to report, but I can also offer some reassurance. There's nothing to worry about, I have everything under control."

Murmuring.

Berti now made an effort to look each guest deadly serious in the eyes. He searched for the inevitable flicker of fear in the murderer's eyes, but couldn't find it.

"Now I'm excited," said Sweety, apparently recovered from the castor oil attack.

"The jeweler Mr. Schepperlin was murdered last night."

Silence. Icy silence.

"There's a murderer among us, but I'm on to him. The handcuffs will soon click."

While everyone looked around in horror, Sweety asked unashamedly: "Who is it?"

Manny rolled his eyes.

Berti didn't even react to the aside. "I'm going to have a little chat with each of you. Please stay in your seats."

"I won't say anything without my lawyer," Manny said and was immediately kicked under the table by Sweety. "How many whiskeys did you drink last night? And why did you come into the room so late?"

Since Sweety hadn't exactly whispered, the chairman of the supervisory board was embarrassed by the situation. "Sweety! I have to ask! May I also ask where you were when I was waiting for you at the bar?"

If looks could kill. "You know," she hissed at him.

"Oh yeah, toilet paper consumption has skyrocketed. You didn't have the usual verbal diarrhea this time, but the real brisk Otto. And I don't mean our gardener."

"Not so loud!"

Manny grinned and thought. Draw.

Berti began his round of questions with Baron von Strass and the Russian attaché. "You two played chess after dinner yesterday."

"Young man," the Baron thundered. "That's right. My chessboard campaign in the East yesterday was successful."

The Russian confirmed. "We played two games. I lost both of them. You were there when we ..."

"These are routine questions. I ask every guest so that I don't compromise anyone and a possible escalation with hostage taking develops as a result."

"I see."

"How long did your two games last?"

Baron von Strass replied quickly. "Until just before eleven."

"And you were here the whole time?"

"Of course. Then I had a vodka and went to bed."

"Thank you."

"Is that all?" the baron asked.

"For now, yes."

The Russian stood and bowed slightly. "Good luck with your investigation."

Berti moved a table over. "Manny, how much longer will you be at the bar?"

Sweety made a face. "You're on a first-name basis?"

"We drank a Dalmore together at the bar."

"There were two or three," Berti improved.

Sweety's ears turned red. Her anger glowed. "Manny, I thought there weren't that many."

Berti now took a swipe at the wife of his new whiskey buddy. "Where were you while I was talking to your husband?"

Sweety winced. "Who, me?"

"No, I was talking to the wall behind you," Berti mimicked. "You, of course, who else?" he added with a serious expression.

"Manny, tell him not to talk to me like that!"

Manny leaned back. "Why don't you tell him yourself?"

Sweety's jaw dropped.

Berti continued. "Once again! Where were you last night between 8 and 11 p.m.? I'm in charge of a murder investigation here, and I'd like to point out that I'm also authorized to make arrests."

"Now you're making fun of me. You're not a cop."

283

"According to Section 127 of the Code of Criminal Procedure, you're allowed to do that. As an educated woman, you should know that," the private detective countered.

Sweety felt increasingly uncomfortable. Manny nudged his wife. He seemed to like the situation. "Now tell me where you were."

Sweety took a deep breath. "I wasn't feeling well. I was in the room with the kids."

"The whole time?"

"Of course!"

Berti had to smile secretly. He enjoyed putting the affected girl through the wringer.

"So you had a migraine?"

"Yes, you could call it that."

Manny laughed out loud.

"What's there to laugh about?" Sweety slobbered at him.

The laughter died down. "Just this," he replied. A broad grin remained. Sweety was seething with anger.

Berti took Sweety's hint and turned to the CEO. "Yes, Manny. That was a legitimate question from your wife. Why are you laughing? What's so funny?" he asked, hoping that Manny would say something embarrassing out loud.

Sweety suspected something like that. "So my medical history, and especially the migraine, is really none of your business," she interjected, fearing that her husband might tell her about the embarrassment of the spontaneous rectal eruption.

"Migraine," Manny laughed. "I'd rather call it an ass cough..." he snorted, holding his stomach. Tears welled up in his eyes. A pure flash of laughter. Vengeance could be so beautiful.

At that moment, Sweety turned bright red and glowed brighter than the wood of a blazing fire.

"Thank you, that's enough for me," Berti remarked and went to the next table. He stood in front of the Edelmanns and the Bunts. "I know you spent half the evening with Konny. That's enough for me," he said. To buy a little more time, he asked the ladies if they agreed with Konny and winked. "He seems very impressed with you."

That comment was enough to get the ladies whispering happily. The private detective walked over to the Schlaps' table and stood in front of the two strange guests. A confident "Good afternoon" came from his lips.

"Young man, may I help you?" the old woman replied very snootily.

"Have a good day," the double-fire-salamander-sauce-damaged Schlaps junior pushed hotter across his lips.

Berti stuck his finger into the sharp taste wound. "Are you not feeling well? Was it something with the food?"

"But ... yes. Everything is fine. The sauce ..." he got a little kick under the table and improved. "Uhh ... I just choked."

Berti had not missed the kick. He followed with the next question. "You were also in the bar last night after dinner?"

The old woman replied. "Yes, but not right away, a little later. My son went upstairs after dinner, and I brought our dog up to the room a little later. You must remember that. You almost stepped on the poor thing."

Berti tried to shrug off the verbal attack and remain calm. "Forgive me, but I didn't. Sir Nelson stopped and greeted me," he replied, even managing a believable smile. "You may be misinterpreting this friendly dog behavior. I'm glad I had the opportunity to clear that up." He felt great as he looked into the puzzled face of the worn-out noble saddle-breaker.

Eduard Schlaps confirmed the Dragon's details. "After my mother took the dog to the suite, we came down together and stayed at the bar until shortly before midnight. If you want to know more, here is our lawyer's card. Please contact Dr. Rehmer in the future and excuse us now," came the more than arrogant reply.

Berti slapped the flat ball back. "Oh, and your lawyer can tell me how long you were in the suite and when you left it? Is he also a guest of this hotel?"

The son's features darkened. "That's the limit. Your questions are more than inappropriate, you ... You ... blown ..." he seethed, but the old woman interrupted him.

"Your behavior is truly disastrous," she said sharply.

"I have my reasons, because I told you in confidence," Berti leaned forward a little and whispered. "I can tell you. You're both innocent, because I saw them personally yesterday at the time of the crime."

Glossy eyes and smarmy grins on both faces were the answer. The negative was pushed to the back. Mrs. Schlaps said almost politely: "Interesting."

Berti continued to whisper. "The crime was recorded. Mr. Schepperlin had a very valuable diamond with him. His insurance company required him to have video surveillance. He had to install a miniature surveillance system in his room. That's not a problem these days. As an IT specialist, I know all about it. The perpetrator probably overlooked the jewel. Mr. Schepperlin usually carries it with him or hides it in very inconspicuous places, like the fruit basket on the table. A burglar would never look there. Poor thing..." Berti lowered his eyes. "Now it's in the refrigerator in the kitchen. The camera with the memory stick is still in the room, of course. I haven't gotten around to analyzing it yet. I'll do that tomorrow morning. Assuming the mail gets through.

The grins on the faces of the Schlaps disappeared abruptly after the detective's remarks. The old woman was the first to catch herself. "What does this have to do with the post office?"

"I didn't bring my equipment. I wanted to go on vacation, not work. I ordered it. My office staff will send it here. Express delivery by courier. I'll secure all the evidence before the police arrive and take over the case. Have a nice day."

Berti left. As he asked the English couple similar questions, he could see out of the corner of his eye that mother and son were having an animated conversation. Eventually, they both got up and went to their suite. They seemed to be in a hurry.

The detective continued his round of questions. After the guests, the employees were questioned. Again, the alibis were watertight. Not a single guest or employee of the hotel was alone at the time of the crime in question. Everyone had been seen by at least two other witnesses. It was desperate. Berti ordered a large Coke with ice and lemon. He sat down next to Konny and wiped the sweat from his forehead with a handkerchief. Then he took a big sip of his drink. After putting the glass down, he took a deep breath. "The bait is set. I hope the usual suspects took the bait, but you know what?"

"Like what?"

"Every one of them has an alibi. Not a single person in this hotel was alone at the time of the crime."

Berti was faced with a riddle, and that's exactly how he looked. Question marks danced over his head again.

"And what if the doctor is wrong?" Konny put forward for discussion.

The detective began to think. "You mean if he's deliberately misleading us about the time of death?"

"It is possible."

"Then he would be the killer."

Both looked around searchingly. Professor Dr. Heberlein was standing at the bar with Ostmann. They were drinking espresso and talking.

Berti summarized. "Maybe he's in cahoots with Ostmann. After all, the hotelier noticed very late that Schepperlin had lost his key card yesterday."

"Then the hotelier would be suspect number two," whispered Konny.

"And the Schlaps aren't exactly clean either."

"But they were also at the bar all night."

Berti was at a mental dead end. "I don't know what to do anymore."

Konny leaned back. "Let the trap work."

Berti reached for the coke and took another sip. "What do you mean?"

"Someone here has to be the killer. The hotel is snowed in, no one can get in and no one can get out. That's for sure."

"That's right. There were no traces of snow either."

Konny rolled his eyes, but didn't want to correct Berti at that moment. "That's right. There are no snow tracks!"

"And you think the killer is getting insecure?"

"Definitely. First, he'll be hot for the loot, and second, he'll have to reckon with the fact that he was filmed committing the crime. He must be boiling inside by now. He's getting more and more nervous. He will make mistakes.

Baron von Strass came to the table of the two friends. Without being asked, he sat down. "I don't think much of men who live across the river, but you two are clever and cunning. I was very impressed by your performance as master detectives. We're going to catch the assassin who has my chess partner cornered. If you need any help, just contact me. I'm always willing to help."

"Thanks for the praise. I might even have a job for you."

"Job? When I hear that, I am done. Say order!"

"Mission is probably more accurate than order."

Baron von Strass whispered. "And which one?"

"We have to watch Mr. Schepperlin's room tonight."

"You mean the cold room?"

"Cold room and hotel room."

"Split me up! I will start my watch on time, as I am a retired lieutenant colonel."

"Would you take the watch from 11 p.m. to 1 a.m.?"

"In the kitchen?"

"Right there."

"I'm ready! Who will replace me?"

"Me personally," Berti assured.

"At your command, young man," the retired officer saluted. "I'm going to lie down now, so I won't be tired later on guard duty. That Russian half-monkey wanted to play another game of chess with me, but what am I to do with an opponent to whom I would give the two bishops," he said, adding. "When I asked what kind of intellectual desert he was from, the attaché replied that he was from Georgia. He's as much of a rotten scumbag as that Stalin was! I wouldn't be surprised if he came from the same clan. My God, if I could still command my soldiers from back then and use the weapons the Americans have today..." he dreamed. "I would give them a run for their money. Personally, I think this Russian had a hand in it. I don't know how he did it, but ..." the retired lieutenant colonel went into his room, muttering.

Konny breathed a sigh of relief. "I don't want him as an opponent."

"The Baron is actually quite nice, but he's still living in the past."

"Do officers get so much pension that they can afford such a luxurious hotel?"

"Mr. von Straß comes from a good family and owns a lot of agricultural and forest land. All leased very well."

Konny was astonished. "How do you know that?"

"I talked to him."

"Did you mean what you said about the guard?"

"Deadly serious! Otherwise we could have done without the trap." Berti was in his element. He was really thriving. "Come on, let's go to the control center."

"You mean the room?"

"Sure."

They went upstairs. In the suite, Berti immediately sat down on the sofa and pored over his notes. "We need a battle plan."

The author was puzzled. "You don't have it yet?"

"I've divided the list of hotel employees and guests into two parts. On one side are the people I trust 100%, on the other the rest."

Konny looked at the note. "Amelie and me? No one else?"

"The situation is too delicate. Everyone has an alibi and yet someone has to be the murderer."

Konny digressed for a moment. "By the way, I'm going to write a book. Hilde and Charlotte talked me into it. It's going to be an in-depth novel about Dr. Kurt Lonedale. If the book is a hit, there will be sequels."

"Great! And what about the fee?"

"I get a writer's contract and they pay me an advance of 5,000 Euros. In addition, I will receive the usual royalties per book sold, as well as the usual shares of the ancillary rights".

"Wow!"

"I just wanted to mention that."

"Konny, that's wonderful."

"I think so too. It's just a shame we can't celebrate it yet."

"Because of my case?"

Konny nodded.

Berti bowed his head. "I'm sorry."

"That's all right. If you can solve this case, you'll be in demand as a detective. Your fee is guaranteed to go down by one decimal place, and you'll get to solve some cases for the super-rich."

The detective was pleased with his friend's understanding. "Then let's go over everything again."

Konny sat down. "Amelie and I are the good guys."

Berti wondered if he should add someone else to the positive list, but left it at the two names. "I don't know how to put this, but there's something very wrong with the Schlaps."

"I know they are animal abusers. I saw the son whisper something to little Sir Nelson. Then the dog jumped out of the bag and ran away. I had the feeling that he had been trained to bring something.

Berti was amazed. "You mean the dog steals?"

"Exactly."

"Amelie told me something like that. The whole thing is starting to make sense," the detective groaned. "But that doesn't solve the problem of the Schlaps family's airtight alibi." Berti leaned back. He went over the conversations again and again, thinking about his perceptions and trying to put them together. "I've got to get out of here," he said suddenly. "I'm racking my brain and all I can come up with is a jumbled salad."

"Getting out is fun. The snowfall has stopped, but we're still stuck in here. Nothing works. There's at least three or four meters of snow on the roads and mountainsides."

Berti put on his parka, slipped into his winter boots, and pulled on his knit cap. "Never mind. A few minutes in the fresh air will help. That's what Daddy-Schwartz always said."

"And what should I do in the meantime?"

"You could get in touch with Amelie and make a plan for the surveillance."

"Schepperlin's room and the kitchen?"

"Bingo," Berti replied and left the suite. The hallway was surprisingly quiet. He went to the stairs. The hotel seemed eerily empty. Not a single guest was to be seen or heard. The reception desk was also deserted. The porter sat lonely behind his desk. Berti went downstairs.

How suspicious is the porter? What's his name again? Oh, yes. Sandmann.

The receptionist didn't notice the guest. He was bent over a magazine, doing a crossword puzzle. Berti watched him for a few moments, scrutinizing the man. Sandmann was about fifty years old and rather frail. As a porter, he was in charge of the room keys and knew when the guests were in their rooms and when they were out. Could this man be the killer? Mr. Sandmann reminded Berti more of a tax collector than a burglar, who didn't hesitate to take the last, icy step. No! Sandmann was definitely not capable of strangling a person. And he certainly didn't believe that this little man would calmly do crossword puzzles after killing someone. In his mind, Berti put the porter on the list of the innocent.

"Good day."

Sandmann winced. "You gave me a fright. I didn't even hear you come in."

"Excuse me. That wasn't my intention."

"That's all right," the porter waved him off. "I'm not normally jumpy either, but with the circumstances here at the moment..."

"Did you think of something else?"

Sandmann frowned. "No, not really."

"Have you ever been outside?"

The porter shook his head in the negative. "Not me, but Wil-li was outside clearing the snow from around the hotel."

"Willi?"

"The caretaker! He came in a few minutes ago and went into the kitchen. Willi wanted to make some tea with rum."

"Thank you."

Berti left the hotel. The porter took up his pen again. "European with three letters? Shit ... stupid question."

Berti stood outside the hotel. It was freezing cold and yet it felt good. The caretaker had done his best to fight the snow madness, but it was a game of unfairly dealt cards. The drifts of the last two days were piled up meters high. The course of the road could only be guessed. Berti was overcome by an uneasy feeling when he remembered that he and Konny had recently marched through this wilderness.

One more day and we would have died out there.

A shoveled path led to the garage wing. The weather side of the large carport was boarded up. In front of it, snow piled up almost to the roof. The area in front of the guest sedans had been halfway cleared with a snow blower. The machine was parked in an empty space in the carport. Berti walked over to it. He ducked his head to protect himself from the cold wind. The caretaker's footprints were barely visible.

Gone with the wind, in the leading role: Willi the caretaker, he grinned and arrived at the vehicles.

The Russian attaché's car was immediately recognizable by its license plate. The Jaguar with British license plates was also quickly identified as belonging to the English couple. The Franconian businessmen were traveling together. A Mercedes Vito with Coburg plates was parked next to the Jaguar. Berti looked inside the car.

Leather seats, he noticed. It looked like the car was fully equipped.

An SUV from Leverkusen seemed to belong to the Sweety family. Screens were mounted on the headrests for the rear passengers.

The brats watch DVDs while driving, so the old people can rest, the detective thought.

The Porsche surely belonged to the heart surgeon. Baron von Straß had arrived by taxi. The hotelier's Land Rover was emblazoned with an advertisement for the hotel. Berghotel Al-pentraum. V.G. Ostmann - a jewel of nature

"Show-off," Berti squeaked. He walked one vehicle over. "Look at that. The Schlaps drive Bentleys."

A dog sticker identified the Chihuahua owners. Again, the weighty private eye couldn't resist peeking into the car through the windows. "I think I'm crazy!" Berti muttered. A small blanket for the dog was spread out on the back seat. It was about the size of a seat.

This is Sir Nelson's domain.

There were magazines next to the dog blanket and a water bottle in the side compartment. This led to the assumption that there must have been someone in the back seat. Berti went around the luxury car. There were two cans of Coke in the front cup holders.

Both could have come from the driver, but someone could also have been sitting in the passenger seat.

Flashes of inspiration!

Did the Schlaps travel in threes? What had Amelie said? Did they need towels for three, or was it five? For Christ's sake! I'm going to have a woman's operation if there's nothing wrong here. Ma Baker and her sons, he thought.

Boney M.'s hit song became a catchy tune in his head, and he sang the chorus in silence: Ma ma ma ma ... Ma Baker

The Schlaps went to number 1 on the list of suspects and thus to the top. Berti couldn't help himself. His hand went to the doorknob. He jerked it around. Too late, he saw the sign in the side window that this car was equipped with an alarm system. Berti jumped when it suddenly began to howl loudly.

Huii huiii huiii

The beeping and screeching of the alarm system was unbearable.

"Bloody hell! Why does this have to happen to me?" the detective yelled, moving a few feet away from the Bentley. Someone ran out of the hotel. It was Sandmann. Berti reached into the snow, formed a snowball and threw it at the Mercedes Vito. Then he shouted loudly: "Get lost!"

"What happened?" shouted the doorman.

"Did you see him?" asked Berti, trying to look as innocent as possible.

The porter looked around. "Who? I didn't see anyone."

Ostmann also came running out of the hotel. Willi, the janitor, followed him.

Hui hui hui hui hui

"There was a marten. I chased it away," Berti lied, proud of his spontaneous excuse.

"There are a lot of stoats around here," Willi confirmed, shouting to drown out the shrill car alarm.

"Bastards! Willi, we have to be careful. If the stoats go after the guest cars, we can't tolerate it," Ostmann said, adding. "Since everything is fine here, I'm going back inside. It's freezing out here."

The porter was shivering too. "I'll let the Schlaps know," said Sandmann. "You must turn off the alarm. It disturbs the guests and makes everyone uneasy. He paused for a moment and looked at Berti. "Or do you think the killer wanted to steal the car to escape?"

At that moment the alarm system went silent.

Berti seized the opportunity. "That's complete nonsense. If a murderer had come from outside, which is highly unlikely, he would have left by now. But we're snowed in. It's impossible to use the road."

"He's right," said Ostmann.

"That's right," said Willi.

"It was just a thought," said Sandmann, almost apologetically.

It remained quiet. The alarm had turned itself off after three intervals. Berti saw his chance. "Why do you want to alarm the Schlaps family unnecessarily? Nothing has happened. The marten is gone."

"Ermine," Willi improved.

"Then the ermine is gone," Berti added and said to Sandmann. "I wouldn't frighten anyone over such a trifle. It would only cause more and completely unnecessary excitement among the guests," he advised, seemingly without a care in the world.

Berti received support from the caretaker. "I share Mr. Schwartz's opinion. If nothing has happened, we don't need to worry the guests unnecessarily," Willi nodded.

"If that's what everyone thinks, I'll go along with it," decided Ostmann, who was still shivering from the cold and stood next to Berti with his arms crossed. "Willi, make sure there's enough marten protection."

"I have a few ideas," replied the caretaker. "Those critters will have a field day."

They walked back to the hotel.

Berti immediately went upstairs. He had to tell Konny about his findings. The suspicion was confirmed. Berti finally had a lead.

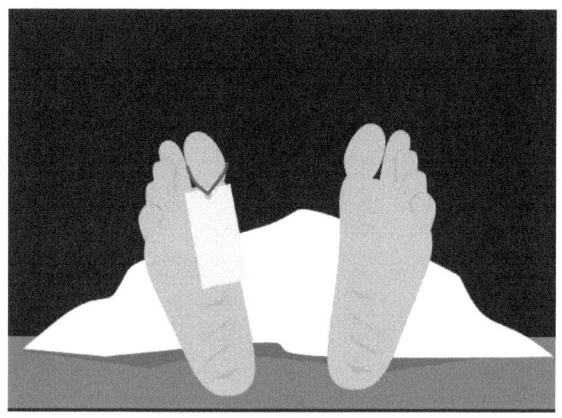

dead-7491342_1280

Chapter 12
A different kind of knuckle

After the murder was announced, the hotel guests stayed in their rooms without exception. Even the hotel's sports and swimming areas were deserted. All guests were served by room service. Amelie and the two waiters had their hands full. They had to serve dinner, wheel their carts from door to door, and deliver the gourmet meals and fine drinks that had been ordered. The staff couldn't help but notice that the hotel guests were very restless.

After each room delivery, the waiters pushed the carts downstairs. Rohloff refilled them in the kitchen.

"Master, is that really a corpse in the refrigerator?" asked the apprentice.

"Klaus, it's a piece of meat, like everything else."

"I think it's disgusting."

"Why? Maybe someone will order a knuckle of pork, then we could draw from the full ..." joked Rohloff, but was immediately interrupted by his apprentice.

"Stop it, boss, I'm getting sick."

Rohloff laughed. "A different kind of pork knuckle! You have to take it easy. As long as Grandpa stays on the table, we don't care about him. Our refrigerator is set to almost zero degrees, so the decomposition is at rest."

Klaus grew paler and paler around the nose. "That's easy for you to say. I saw Zombieland last week. I'm sure you know it. It's an old movie with Woody Harrelson. Bill Murray has a cool supporting role in it, by the way, playing himself."

The celebrity chef replied in the negative. "I don't have time for that crap."

"What are you watching? Lanz cooking? Schuhbeck alone at the stove or three super chefs saving a restaurant?"

"Cooking shows? Yuck! I'm not stupid enough to let myself be fooled by Mälzer and Co."

"They're all star chefs."

"Nobody doubts that, but what do my colleagues want to teach me? I'm a star chef myself."

"Then what are you watching?"

"I flick through the third channels. I usually get stuck on nature movies."

Klaus imitated a long yawn. "You're not that old yet."

"Don't be cheeky now!"

"I'm surprised the snobs haven't complained yet," the apprentice chef returned to the original topic.

"How do you talk about our guests?"

"You said that yourself the other day."

Rohloff laughed again. "Snooty is the right word. Just don't say it out loud, Klaus."

"The detective is different."

"You mean the other way around."

Now the apprentice laughed. "That too."

"Joking aside. I like him. Compared to the other guests, he's so ... how can I put it?"

"Normal?"

"To the point. He's completely normal."

"That's right! Schwartz is a nice guy."

"Do you think he'll expose the killer?"

"We'll see. Now get the saw out of the shed. We need pork knuckles," Rohloff grumbled.

Klaus suddenly turned white.

The star cook laughed out loud, then relented. "Okay, I'll stop with the jokes..."

"Thank you."

The mission plan was set, the tasks clearly assigned. Berti did not expect the murderer to show up before 22:00.

"Why not?" asked Konny.

"Too early. The risk of discovery is much too high."

There was a knock. Konny went to the suite door. A look through the peephole followed. "Our army is arriving."

He opened it.

"Lieutenant Colonel von Strass reporting for duty!"

Amelie stood behind the retired officer, followed by Prof. Dr. Heberlein and Herr Ostmann.

"Come in."

"I just wanted to let you know that I'm willing to stand guard in Mr. Schepperlin's room until midnight, then I'm going to bed. I won't be up all night," the heart specialist said.

"I have to get up early in the morning. I'll take over the watch with Dr. Heberlein before midnight," Ostmann offered.

"I'll take over at midnight and stay in the room until morning," Amelie said.

"But not alone. It's too dangerous. Konny, can you stay with Amelie?"

"No problem. What are you doing?"

"I'm relieving Baron von Strass in the kitchen at 01:00."

"I don't like the fact that the kitchen post is solo," the author complained.

"I may be old, but I'm still fit," Baron von Strass interjected. "After the war I marched 900 kilometers on foot. Ivan wanted to send me to Siberia, so I escaped and walked all the way home."

"Were you the guy from As Far As the Feet Carry?" asked Berti.

You shook your head and waved goodbye. "Nonsense! That was a novel by Bauer."

"I thought it was a movie," Amelie mused.

"Filmed literature. It was made into a television series in the fifties. It was street sweeping at its best. The script is based on a true story, but it had nothing to do with me. I marched from the Baltic Sea to Bavaria without anyone being interested in my story," the former Wehrmacht officer explained.

Konny urged. "Back to the main point. Berti, are you sure you can handle the post in front of the cold room alone?"

"No problem! I assume that the murderer will return to the scene of the crime anyway. That's old wisdom."

Baron von Strass stood up. "Attack! Let's get the pig!"

While the spry pensioner eagerly took up his post, hidden behind pots and pans, Ostmann uneasily unlocked the murdered man's room. "They say the ghost of a dead person haunts the room until the death is atoned for," he whispered to the doctor.

"Complete nonsense. Do you have any idea how many patients have died at my hands?" came the relatively flippant reply.

"I thought you were a specialist."

"I am now, but one is not born a luminary." The professor grimaced as if he had bitten into a lemon. "Boy, I tell you, those early days in the operating room were no picnic."

Amelie shook with disgust. "Shall we change the subject? I find it macabre to talk about death while we're waiting for a murderer."

The cardiac surgeon turned to the hotelier. "Ostmann, I hope you have enough drinks in the room. If I wait, I'll get thirsty, and if I'm thirsty, I'll want something to drink."

"The bar is full, if that's what you mean."

The doctor laughed. "Still, my dear Ostmann, it's still full. Later it will be empty and we will be full," Dr. Heberlein scoffed, patting the hotelier on the shoulder. "Don't make such a funny face. We'll celebrate a little."

"What if the murderer comes?"

A wry look. "Do you really think so?"

"I have the impression that the detective knows his trade."

"He's a big sausage, that's all."

"So far, I've had the feeling that you trust him."

Dr. Heberlein went straight to the bar. "It's better than nothing. But I can't imagine he'll be successful."

"I do."

The doctor picked up a bottle of cognac and examined it. Satisfied, he arranged two glasses and poured. "Then let's hope for the best. Cheers!"

The wait was cruel. Berti, Konny and Amelie sat in the suite. The conversations had long since ceased. Berti was reminded of his childhood. Lunch with Grandma Schwartz. Sickening. They had to sit dutifully and quietly at the dining table. You could hear the ticking of the old-fashioned wall clock that mimicked the chimes of Big Ben on the hour. Of course, the good china was laid out. White porcelain with rose patterns.

Every four weeks, Daddy Schwartz took the family to his mother's house. It was always the same meal. First, a thin soup with semolina dumplings that fell apart when you looked at them at an angle, then a dry Wiener schnitzel. The side dishes were green salad and boiled potatoes. Dessert was coffee, Kaba for Berti, of course, and a dusty, fart-dry Gugel-hupf. The spoons rattled as we stirred the coffee. Grandma always asked the same questions.

"What grade are you in now, Herbert?"

"Still in the fourth grade."

"Gell, do you want another piece of cake?"

"No, Grandma. I'm full."

A second piece of her infamous cement bundt cake was already on the plate. Back then, Berti always kept an eye on the wall clock. Although it felt like he was looking at it every quarter of an hour, only two or three minutes had passed. The only change was when the record of *Ernst Mosch* and his *Original Egerländer* was turned over. To this day, Berti can't listen to brass music and has an aversion to *Karl Moik, Florian Silbereisen* and *Stefan Mross*.

When his grandmother died, the family doctor said that she had dried up inside because she constantly drank too little. Berti, on the other hand, was convinced that his grandmother died as a result of the Sunday meal ritual. "Dry schnitzel and dusty cake until you drop. Something like that doesn't go unnoticed," he slipped out, lost in thought.

Amelie was irritated. "What did you say?"

Berti shuddered, "Sorry! I was just mentally at my grandmother's. No time passed there either."

"Visiting grandma, for God's sake," Amelie snapped. "I died. My father's old lady was a dragon. I was seventeen when she called me my little nigger doll."

"Didn't your daddy tell her that was offensive?"

"A thousand times."

"And?"

"The witch put her Nazi-era schoolbook on the table and said: That's what we learned then. The Negro as such is a subhuman."

Konny clasped his hands in front of his face. "Terrible!"

The hotel clerk got a sad look on her face. "I cried more than once."

Berti became furious as he looked at his friend's unhappy face. "I would have stuck a stick up the old woman's ass and asked her if she didn't want to ride her broom to the witch-meeting-point."

Amelie laughed. "I did something similar myself. But verbally."

Konny's ears perked up. "What exactly did you do?"

"I asked her if she would like to visit a concentration camp memorial with me. When she asked why, I told her that it would give her a chance to see her old workplace again."

"And?"

"We were never invited back! Dad decided for me and Mom."

"Very well," Berti breathed a sigh of relief.

Konny was horrified. "You poor things! I loved my grandmother. She had the heart of a person, read my every wish from my lips, and I never wanted to go home when I was with her."

Amelie beamed. "A picture book grandma. I always wanted that too."

"She absolutely was."

"Amelie, how long has that old Nazi been here?"

"You mean Baron von Strass?"

"Yes. He seems a bit strange to me."

"That's not a Nazi."

"But he looks like one and talks like one."

"Baron von Strass was an officer in World War II, just as his father was in World War I and his grandfather was in the war against France in 1870/71."

"How do you know that?"

"He has been a regular at our hotel for many years. He once told me his tale of woe."

Konny became curious. "And what was that?"

"His wife was Jewish or half Jewish. He hid her and her family in a family hunting cabin in the woods. That saved their lives. He was also part of the extended circle of resistance fighters around Staufenberg. He hated the Russians because he had witnessed too many war crimes there.

Berti frowned. "They were on both sides."

"He never really got over it, and condemned them even then. But like a lot of people, he believed in a just war. Rough sarcasm is his way of dealing with everything. He calls himself "Germany's last patriot".

Konny changed his mind about Baron von Strass. "Berti, you were right to put the Baron on the positive list."

"Detective nose," he grinned.

Another look at the clock. "As soon as you start talking a little more animatedly, the time flies."

It was close to midnight. Konny and Amelie prepared to take over from Mr. Ostmann and the slightly arrogant Prof. Dr. Heberlein.

"Take care of yourselves!"

"You too!"

The hallway was quiet. The couple scurried into Schepper-lin's room. After the agreed knock, Dr. Heberlein opened the door. He had a clear banner and spoke with a slight twang. "The relief is here. Ostmann, we can go."

The hotelier was also noticeably drunk. "Good night! I'm going ... hiccup ... to bed."

There were several empty bottles from the minibar in the room of the deceased.

"The two of them raided the whole bar."

"I'm sure Ostmann will put it on Schepperlin's bill."

"I thought it was all included."

"Not for everyone. The boss is a shrewd businessman."

"Let's sit down."

Berti could hardly wait for his turn. He checked his notes one last time. His main suspects had been narrowed down to just a few people. There were only a few final questions to be answered, but he was convinced that he was on the right track. Maybe the trap had really been set tonight. Shortly before one o'clock in the morning, he crept into the stairwell. He briefly considered listening to the doors of the other residents' rooms to see who else was awake, but decided against it. He didn't want to be discovered by some stupid coincidence right before his destination.

He walked quietly to the service stairs, scurried down, and paused at the bottom of the stairs to listen. There was a sonorous sound. It was coming from the kitchen. The detective took a deep, angry breath and exhaled. "No way, he's asleep," he muttered.

The closer Berti got to the kitchen, the clearer he could hear the blue-blooded guard snoring.

"So much for the officer and sleeping in. Now wait!"

Berti did not turn on the light. He waited until his eyes had adjusted to the darkness. Baron von Strass was sitting in front of the shelf with the chili sauces.

"I'll teach him a lesson."

Furious, the detective started to go to the cold room and open the heavy door. He felt a slight resistance. Suddenly he jumped, startled. There was a clatter and a crash behind him. Berti turned around. A hard object hit his right shin. "Ouch!"

"You bastard," the Baron roared.

The detective was about to speak when something smacked into his head. The pain shot up from his shin.

"I'm going to bash your head in, you sneaky..."

"It's me," Berti squealed, holding both hands up protectively.

"Who are you?"

The guard's voice sounded serious and a little agitated.

"Schwartz! The detective!"

Silence. A man's panting could be heard. Footsteps followed. Someone turned on a light.

Berti crouched among pots and pans. A heavy cauldron lay in front of his shin. The Baron had stretched a string and tied some pots to it. The detective had stepped on them, setting off the fatal chain reaction.

Baron von Strass held a heavy iron pan in his hands. "Why do you sneak in like a thief?"

"Because you fell asleep."

"So what? My trap worked."

"You probably woke up the whole house."

"No, not me! You woke up the whole house!"

Berti rubbed his head. "That'll give me a bump."

"You can be glad I didn't hit you with full force."

Berti had expected an apology or something like that. Nothing like that came. So he said: "Consider yourself relieved."

"If I were you, I would rebuild the pot trap."

"I'll think about it."

"Are you offended?"

Berti held out his hand. "Help me up."

„Craaaaazyyy," the old man gasped as he helped the weighty detective to his feet, "how much do you weigh?"

"More than I would like and less than some people think."

"My trap was good, wasn't it?"

Berti grinned. "Actually it was."

"You can think about reactivating it. I'm dog-tired. When shall I relieve you?"

"Go ahead and sleep. I'm fit."

"I'll come when I wake up. I usually have to go out a few times during the night."

"Cranberry Urinary." Berti hissed.

"No, the bubble."

"Cranberry Urinary advertises it."

"I see. I don't take chemicals. If I took all the pills my doctor prescribed, I would have been addicted long ago, and my body would have to be incinerated as hazardous waste after my death."

They both laughed.

The old man pointed at Berti's head. "Does it still hurt?"

The detective felt carefully over the growing lump. "It's fine."

"I'm sorry."

Then it came, the apology. Berti accepted it, of course. "It's all right, it was my own fault. I underestimated you. I only heard snoring. I didn't expect a trap."

The Baron winked. "You could still learn something from me."

"Good night."

"Good night ... and catch the bastard."

"I will," Berti replied confidently.

Baron von Strass turned and left the kitchen, stomping into the dark hallway. Berti left the light on for now and began to clear away the pots. His shins ached and his head buzzed. He could curse himself. A thought flashed through his mind.

Could the murderer have avoided the trap while the Baron was snoring? Was it possible that he was already in the cold room? He certainly wouldn't have bothered to wrap the dead Mr. Schepperlin in blankets and sheets again.

After everything was tidied up, Berti hobbled over to the light switch. He pressed it and it was suddenly dark. It gave him no peace.

No, he thought.

Click

It was light again. He had made a decision.

303

I have to look in the freezer.

The massive door acted like a magnet on the detective. It seemed like the entrance to a dungeon. An obstacle that could only be opened with a special key. The door blocked the way to a dungeon, a secret passage or a burial chamber. Yes! The refrigerator was a burial chamber. He, Herbert Schwartz, was the modern *Indiana Jones* on the hunt for the phantom. The mood changed. It settled over Berti like a shadow. It became eerie. Goose bumps covered his body.

Wasn't there a sound?

Even the last hair on his head stood up. He felt uncomfortable and kept looking around.

"Nonsense! That was probably just the Baron slamming his room door into the lock. Who would be hanging around the hotel?" he said loudly, at least to hear his own voice.

It slowly crept into my brain. Only one person would sneak through the hotel now. The murderer!

"Shit!" the detective groaned.

Berti looked around again. Everything was quiet.

"I'm driving myself crazy."

After two steps, he was standing in front of the cold room door. The light switch for the cold room was on the outside. Berti pushed it.

Why didn't they put a glass panel in the door? Then you could see through it.

He gripped the large, oblong door handle with both hands. Goose bumps still covered his entire body.

There's just a dead man lying there. It's nothing special, Berti. You open the door, look inside and that's it.

He turned the lever. It clicked loudly. The detective was able to open the dull gray, heavy door. The cold hit him. Only now did he realize how well insulated the cold room was.

"It must be soundproof," he said.

The table was in the middle of the room. Berti took a step forward. The body was still there, just as they had left it. Or was it not? Berti wanted to go back and close the door.

Coward, it flashed through his mind. This is your case. The dead man doesn't bite. You have to look closely!

"All right," he said to himself and turned around.

Berti jumped inwardly when he suddenly heard a loud gasp. Panic spread through his body like lightning. It was the same feeling he had as a child when he had to run through a dark corridor after secretly watching a horror movie. Then he felt the claws of monsters at the back of his neck.

There's someone there, he thought.

Panicked, he turned and tried to leave the cold room. A dark shadow loomed over him. Something hit his head. Stars circled. Everything went black before his eyes. A figure moved in the doorway. The detective could only make it out in a blur. It reached out a hand for help. Berti thought he heard something familiar. The door was slammed shut and the light was turned off. Berti lost consciousness.

He didn't know how long he had been lying there. It could have been a few minutes, but it could also have been an hour or more. His head hurt terribly and he was freezing. The detective's whole body was shaking. He sat up carefully.

It was pitch black, he realized, and he crawled to the door on all fours. He searched in vain for a lever.

"Bloody hell! The stupid door only opens from the outside."

Berti pounded on the cold steel. It sounded muffled. He quickly realized that everything here was indeed soundproof.

I am lost.

Herbert Schwartz was doomed to freeze to death in a refrigerated warehouse. Despair spread. What could he do?

Exercise. I must do push-ups and keep my body warm.

Berti went downstairs in a push-up position. The floor was freezing cold. No, it wasn't cold, it was the North Pole. He lay flat. It was unbearable down here. He concentrated.

Now!

He pushed his massive body up with all his strength. He didn't manage a single push-up. Desperate, the detective rolled over like a seal landing on an ice floe and sat down.

"Help! Help!"

He stopped screaming after a minute. Soundproof means soundproof. No one would hear him. Berti stood up. He started to jump, but after a short time he was out of breath.

An idea flashed through him.

A second self spoke inside him.

You know what to do!

"No, I can't do that."

Yes, do it or you'll die!

"I don't want to die," he roared.

Well then! What else is there to think about?

"I can't do it."

Then you will freeze to death!

"I want to live."

Do you know the story of the plane crash in the Andes? 1972.

"Yes!"

The survivors ate the bodies! Just to avoid dying. You manage to lie down next to Mr. Schepperlin and cover yourself. The table is wide enough.

"But I can't see anything. It's pitch black here."

No excuses! You can do it. Just do it!

Berti finally listened to his inner voice. He went to the table.

"I'm sorry, Mr. Schepperlin, but we have to share the blanket," he said to the corpse. Trembling, he sat down on the table.

Do it!

"That's all right. I don't want to freeze to death!"

Berti lifted the blanket and slid over to the body. The detective finally pulled the blanket over his head.

He was overcome with disgust. Berti imagined that the dead man beside him was a mannequin. Shivering with cold, he closed his eyes.

"I never thought I'd end up as a pork knuckle."

Berti felt miserable. He was cold and his head was throbbing. First Baron von Straß had knocked him out with an iron skillet, then Mr. Schepperlin's murderer had knocked him out. He was shamed to the bone. He had set a trap for the murderer, and now he was caught in it.

How long does it take to freeze to death? Does Mr. Schepperlin still have residual heat in his body?

Berti instinctively moved closer to the corpse, only to immediately move away again.

How long will the oxygen last in this cold room?

The detective's thoughts raced. Why did he have to go into this stupid cold room? Why hadn't he insisted on a double post?

Now, just before his breakthrough as a private detective, he suffered his biggest defeat. Despair spread.

He saw his Daddy before him. Eating a Bratwurst-Sandwich he shook his head. "Berti, Berti, Berti ... I told you to take care of yourself!"

It was cursed. Every one of the guests had an alibi. It was as if they could be in several places at once.

"If I survive, I will definitely not make this stupid mistake a second time.

That was the first spark. Berti's mind raced back. He replayed the previous evening. He let the scenes play out in front of him like a movie. Next, he flashed back to his observations at lunch yesterday, wandered to the conversations he had there, and combined that with his observations in the parking lot. He saw light at the end of the tunnel. A vague theory began to take shape. One fact followed another. Berti was convinced that he had uncovered the killer's secret.

"This has to be it!"

He was hot on his trail. Full of the will to survive and eager to fight, he wrapped himself in the blanket.

"I will survive and then I will solve the case. You've done it without Berti. Dad, you'll be proud of me!"

handcuffs-7651709_1280

Chapter 13
Exposed

The night went very smoothly for Konny and Amelie. At first they talked about various topics such as music and literature, enjoyed each other's company, and quickly started using first names. When tiredness set in and the conversations began to fade, A-melie put a game of travel backgammon on the table. "Shall we?"

Konny was delighted. "What a great idea. I love backgammon."

They played until 05:00 in the morning, then their lack of concentration due to fatigue set in. They put the board game aside and fought sleep for the last hour. At 06:00 in the morning, they gave up.

Konny stretched out his left arm so that the sleeve of his sweater slipped back. He looked at the watch on his wrist, which was exposed by this movement. "The murderer won't come back."

Amelie yawned. "I think so too. Was he with Berti?" she added.

"We would have found out by now," Konny demurred.

Amelie grinned. "I could imagine Berti sitting in the kitchen drinking coffee with Klaus and Mr. Rohloff in a good mood."

They finished their night shift. Amelie took the key card. She took a last look at the bathroom door.

"Poor Mr. Schepperlin. I feel different when I think that he was murdered there."

"Me too. Look at that," Konny said, pulling up the sleeve of his sweater on his left arm and showing his goose bumps.

"Let's go."

"I'll go to the kitchen," said the hotel clerk.

Now Konny yawned too. "I can't do that anymore. I'm going straight to our suite. Berti is probably already in bed, snoring away. Good night, Amelie."

"Sleep well," she said goodbye.

The writer shuffled the few meters to his suite. Standing in front of the door, he remembered that he didn't have his key card with him. Berti had left after him. He must have put it in his pocket. He knocked hopefully on the door of the room. Nothing moved. Konny knocked again and put his ear to the door. Silence.

"My fat friend is in the kitchen having breakfast," he whispered quietly, yawned again and turned on his heel.

The dim lights in the foyer came on. The porter rummaged around the counter. When he saw the writer coming up the stairs, he greeted him politely. "Good morning to you. You're up early."

Konny only briefly returned the greeting and scurried past the reception desk with a spartan, half-swallowed "Morning" and headed straight for the kitchen. From there a light shone into the hall. Dishes rattled. There was the smell of freshly brewed coffee. Amelie's voice could be heard. She was talking to the apprentice cook. When she saw Konny in the doorway, she waved at him.

"Berti isn't here. You were right. He's probably in bed, fast asleep."

"Guaranteed," confirmed Konny, who was extremely tired. "I knocked twice briefly. Nothing moved." He yawned again. "How do I get into the suite if the key card is inside?"

Klaus replied. "The boss can help. He's just been in and ordered a hangover breakfast. He didn't look well at all. Mr. Ostman wanted to come back and pick up the breakfast in person. Then we can talk to him about it."

"That's right," Amelie added. "He keeps all the duplicate key cards in his office."

Konny was satisfied. "Then I'll wait for him."

"How about a cup of coffee in the meantime?"

"I'd rather not. I want to go to bed and sleep as soon as possible. Coffee makes me feel unnecessarily excited."

Barely a minute later, Mr. Ostmann returned to the kitchen. Klaus had not exaggerated. The hotelier looked terrible. "Is my hangover breakfast ready?" he croaked in a deep, grating voice.

"Just a moment. I just have to get some fresh eggs from the freezer," Klaus replied, standing in front of the freezer with one hand on the lever. He pulled it down and opened the heavy door. His right hand went to the light switch. Then sheer horror gripped him. "Ahhhhh!"

The Apprentice's scream ripped through his body. He was standing in the entrance of the cold room, shaking so badly that you would have thought one of his fingers was stuck in a socket, his body receiving electric shock after electric shock.

"He's alive! The dead man is alive," Klaus shrieked.

White as a sheet, the apprentice recoiled and backed out of the cold room. Amelie spilled coffee. Konny's body hair stood on end and Ostmann grabbed his aching head.

All three pushed their way to the entrance and peered into the cold room. Mr. Schepperlin's rigid body should have been lying on the table. But whatever was under that blanket was strong and, above all, moving.

"Old Schepperlin was really bloated," said Ostmann. He felt a slight discomfort in his stomach. The urge to vomit grew.

"Rohloff said he wouldn't decompose so fast here. It must be the dead man's ghost," Klaus squeezed out in utter fear.

"We're almost there," Amelie trumpeted, confident and fearless. She squeezed between Konny and Mr. Ostmann and marched boldly into the cold room. "Let's see what's going on here," she called, more out of uncertainty than curiosity, grabbing the blanket and pulling it away with a jerk.

"Berti," came out of her mouth and Konny's at the same time.

"Mr. Schwartz," Klaus and Ostmann shouted in horror.

Konny was on the verge of fainting. The hotelier shook his head. "What are you doing to Mr. Schepperlin?"

"Mo-mo-murder-strike," stammered the chilled detective.

Amelie was the first to catch herself. "Oh my God! Berti, you must get out of here now. Come on! Over to the warmth."

Berti tried to sit up, but he couldn't.

"Now help me," the determined hotel employee hissed at the men.

Konny, Klaus and Mr. Ostmann came hesitantly to the table. Together they helped Berti up and supported him as he walked. They took the shivering mountain of meat out of the cooler, crossed the kitchen and took him directly to the small staff room.

Amelie kept track. "Klaus, you put the kettle on at once," she ordered and ran off again. "I'll get a warm blanket."

A few minutes later, a cup of steaming tea stood in front of the cold storage victim. Berti was wrapped in a blanket and recounted his experience.

311

"...and bang, another blow on the head. Then it got dark. I knew I could only survive if I covered up, so I was forced to lie down on the table with Schepperlin's remains. You know the rest."

"How terrible. Poor you," Konny comforted his friend. All the tiredness that had plagued the author until then had vanished in one fell swoop.

"The murderer wanted to strike a second time," lamented Ostmann. "I am ruined. If this gets out, I can close the hotel. I can already see the headlines. Serial killer rampages through mountain hotel!"

The detective had taken a small sip of tea and put the cup down. "Don't worry about it. I'll solve the case. Today!"

Everyone stared at Berti.

Konny shook his head, "My God, you've had a terrible time. You have to go to the hospital. You're completely hypothermic."

With trembling fingers, the detective raised the teacup to his lips. He sipped audibly, moaning with pleasure as the soothing warmth ran down his gullet and spread through his body. "Mmmmh, that feels good."

"Shall we wake Dr. Heberlein?" asked Ostmann.

"No, thank you," said Konny. "He'll look just like you. The bar was completely empty."

The hotelier then avoided direct eye contact with the writer. It had been a stupid idea to suggest the doctor's help. Especially since Konny Wels and Amelie had witnessed the little drunken orgy Ostmann had organized with the surgeon. He would have liked to sink into the ground in shame.

Berti cleared his throat. "Whales like to swim in the cold ocean. They can do that because they have enough fat. I always wanted to be slimmer, too. But tonight, my obesity has saved my life," he said, taking another sip of tea, the color returning to his face. "I am neither sick nor unable to think. I feel much better already, and I'm going to put an end to this mysterious game of death."

Mr. Sandmann hurried into the kitchen. "Boss, we've got TV reception again. The weather report looks good."

Ostmann thanked the doorman and turned to the others. "Then you'll be here at noon today."

"Who?" Konny asked.

312

"The city workers, or rather the winter service. Whenever we get snowed in, they come up from the valley with heavy equipment and clear the road up to the hotel. Now that the connections are obviously working again, I will inform the police immediately."

Berti was optimistic. "And I would ask you to invite all the hotel guests to the dining room for lunch."

A few hours of sleep and a hot spa shower worked wonders. Amelie's fabulous café au lait also drove away the last vestiges of fatigue. The two hard blows to the head had only caused a bump and a small laceration that didn't require stitches. Two painkillers eased the buzzing in his head. The important thing was that his glasses hadn't been damaged.

Berti was already sitting in the dining room with his notes when the other guests began to arrive. He was much more relaxed than he had initially feared. He deliberately looked deeply into each guest's eyes. The private detective made a note of any small mistakes, creating a general sense of insecurity. He was ready for the finale. Showdown in the dining room. The time had come for the duel. Noon was here and now. In his mind he heard the legendary theme music from the movie *Once upon a time in the west.*

Only two people were missing. Konny and Baron von Straß. They were at the hotel on a special mission for Berti.

Half an hour ago, Ostmann had told the detective that the snowplough was clearing the road to the luxury hotel. The police followed in the wake of the large catering columns and snow shovels.

As soon as the staff had arrived, Berti stood up. He ran his right hand lightly over the wound on his head. You could feel the lump. "Ladies and gentlemen," the detective began. "As you all know, an incredible crime took place in this hotel. Our dear Mr. Schepperlin was found dead in his room. Strangled to death! Treacherously murdered!"

Sweety covered her daughter's ears. "That's the limit. Man-ni, tell him to stop it. That's ... I'll ... Well, do something now!"

Manny didn't roll his eyes this time, but returned the reproachful look. Then he said in a commanding voice: "Shut up!"

Sweety's jaw dropped. She had never seen Manny like that before. She stared at her husband and remained silent. Frederick wanted to laugh at first, but the look his father gave him stopped any laughter. Cordula didn't even try.

"From today on there will be other pages. The children's pocket money will be reduced to twenty euros a month, cell phones will have parental controls, PC gaming time will be limited, and televisions will be removed from the children's rooms."

"But I..." Cordula wanted to protest, but Manny, who was in a rage, did not allow any objections.

"The children will also have to decide which sport they want to play. It will no longer be possible to be enrolled in all kinds of clubs and not go anywhere. Private tutors will be fired. If children fail in school, they will repeat the grade! They will make sure they do their homework and check it. If they fail in school, they'll spend the whole summer studying."

Sweety swallowed. "Have you had anything to drink?"

Manny deliberately ignored the question. "And you'll do more housework instead of spending hundreds of dollars on incompetent beauticians. I can't stand the cleaning lady anyway. She drinks more coffee than she cleans. She's fired!"

"And who's going to clean the house?"

"You will!"

"Manny, you must be going crazy. I'm getting a divorce, it's going to be very expensive for you."

"As far as I can remember, our marriage contract states that you will receive a settlement of 10,000 euros and not a cent more."

Sweety swallowed again. "You were joking, weren't you?"

"Do I look like I'm joking?"

"Uhh, no."

"Then do what I said. I don't have to repeat the alternatives again, do I? End of announcement and now silence. I want to hear what this detective has to say."

While Sweety and the children sat spellbound at the table, Manny leaned back and relaxed. He enjoyed the heavenly peace. It was long overdue for him to talk.

This ski vacation has really paid off, he thought contentedly.

Berti began casually. "Mrs. Schlaps, do you have your sweet dog with you?" he asked in a sweet voice.

Smiling, the old lady pointed to the luxury handbag. "Of course Sir Nelson is here!"

"Would you please let him out?"

"How dare you! I won't let you..." her son raised his voice in protest.

Berti remained cool. He narrowed his eyes and pointed at Schlaps-Junior. "You'd better take it easy, my friend!"

Uncertainty spread through the hotel guest. "You'll hear from my lawyer," he threatened.

"You have a lawyer? That's good, because you're going to need one."

The roar of heavy engines could be heard. Willi, the caretaker, called out. "I think the snowplows are here. I have to go out and brief them."

"Go ahead," Berti signaled him.

Willi went out and came back 30 seconds later, completely agitated. He was followed by two plainclothes officers and two uniforms. They stood in the doorway of the dining room and listened to Berti's explanations.

"Where was I? Oh yes, I'd like you to get Sir Nelson out of the bag, Mrs. Schlaps."

"Why?" the lady defended herself. "I don't see that at all."

"I will prove who committed the murder of Mr. Schepperlin and the attempted murder of my person. And that's why I'm asking you again to get Sir Nelson out of your handbag."

"That's ridiculous," interrupted Schlaps-Junior, looking around nervously and undoing the top button of his shirt. He felt warm. He was visibly uncomfortable.

"If you say so," the old lady relented and released the dog from the luxury prison. The Chihuahua jumped out. He immediately ran to Berti, snuggled up to his leg and finally did his little man. The detective petted the dog, leaned down and whispered to him. Sir Nelson wagged his tail happily and dashed across the dining room. He trotted straight to the table of the English coup-le. There, the key card strap was sticking out of the hotel guest's jacket. Sir Nelson did a little maneuver, grabbed the lanyard, and pulled it out of the jacket's side pocket. Then he took the card directly to Mrs. Schlaps and placed it in the *Louis Vuitton* handbag. The puppy sat down and waited for his reward.

"That's how you got Mr. Schepperlin's key card."

"You're completely crazy," Mrs. Schlaps defended herself.

Berti smiled in victory. "You trained the dog."

"Complete nonsense," Mr. Schlaps replied, taking off his jacket. Dark patches of sweat had formed under his armpits.

"I found that the dead man put up a fight. He must have inflicted an injury on the perpetrator," Professor Dr. Heberlein's voice thundered through the hall.

Mr. Schlaps' features relaxed. "You must have a problem with that, master detective," he grinned. "Neither my mother nor I have an injury anywhere on our bodies. A doctor will be happy to examine us more closely."

"I'm going to sue you for slander," Mrs. Schlaps chimed in. "That will be expensive."

Heavy cursing could be heard from the hallway. "Fucking assholes. Let me go now!"

Baron von Strass' voice drowned out the cursing. "You bastard! Just leave me alone with you for a few minutes and I'll show you what an old man can still do."

"Go on," Konny ordered.

A murmur went through the hotel guests and staff as the writer and the retired lieutenant colonel entered the dining room with a second Mr. Schlaps. The two Schlaps were like two peas in a pod.

"May I introduce you," said the author. "The Schlaps twins! That's the family trick. They check in as a couple. The other twin cheats his way into the room a little later. The dog steals the keys, one of the brothers goes to break in, while the other provides an ironclad alibi."

The uniformed policemen went to the table of the criminal family.

Berti went into overdrive. "They strangled Mr. Schepperlin!" he said firmly, pointing his index finger at the twin that Konny was holding. The detective continued. "The old man fought back and gave you a black eye."

Like at a tennis tournament, all the heads follow each other. They looked at Berti and the suspect one after the other. The murderer's eye was indeed discolored by a hematoma.

"No! I fell down," came the completely unbelievable answer.

"And when I went to check the cooler yesterday, I heard first the tap, then the whimper of Sir Nelson. You should have left him in the room. You, Mr. Schlaps No. 2, sneaked up behind me and with a club..."

"That was my brother, and he didn't have a club, he used a frying pan! At least that's what he told us when he came back into the room."

"Thanks for the tip," Berti grinned.

"You idiot," said the mother of the twins.

Berti clarified. "Besides, no one can be so stupid as to season their food twice with the fire salamander sauce in such a way that it burns their throats. That was the first time I got suspicious."

"You put my chili sauce on the table?" Rohloff interjected.

Berti winked at him. "Sorry, that was... um... that was part of my plan to catch the criminals."

"All right," the star chef grinned.

Berti stood demonstratively in front of the Schlaps family. "You've been convicted!"

The one with the black eye simply said. "What the hell! It's no use anyway. They've got us on that stupid surveillance camera anyway. I wanted to break into the jeweler's room again yesterday to steal the chip, but there were two guys in there drinking and yelling."

Ostmann and Heberlein blushed and bowed their heads.

Berti appeared. "I'm going to have to disappoint you, Mr. Schlaps, if that name is even true, I made that up about the chip and the camera."

"You fat, pompous..." was as far as he got.

"Arrest all three," the inspector's voice thundered through the dining room.

Handcuffs clicked.

"You're under arrest for joint murder, attempted murder and numerous burglaries!"

"What about the dog?" Berti asked immediately.

"He'll probably go to the pound. I expect this family to go to jail for a few years," replied one of the policemen.

"I'd keep an eye on him."

"Go ahead and take that stupid dog in. He's brought us nothing but bad luck anyway. Damn mutt," Mrs. Schlaps scolded.

The police routine followed. Employees and guests were questioned, and the perpetrators were taken away.

After all the witnesses had given their statements, Ostmann approached Berti and Konny.

"I want to thank you very much. You have saved the reputation of my house. In return, I would like to invite you both to be my guests for another week. Enjoy your stay at *Berghotel Alpenblick*. I would be delighted if you could accept the invitation."

"I would love to," Konny beamed.

Berti, holding his beloved Chihuahua in his arms, was overjoyed. "A week of real vacation. How could anyone refuse?"

Ostmann was satisfied. He owed it to his guests. I should invite this detective more often. Maybe he'll continue to be useful to me. Or I can profit from his notoriety. The hotelier retired. He needed another headache pill. Damn booze!

A familiar melody sounded. It was the ringtone of Konny's cell phone. The author took the phone from his pocket and answered the call.

"Mr. Hindelang," he greeted the caller in amazement and switched on the loudspeaker so that Berti could follow the conversation.

"I got your mail," the construction lion's voice boomed through the small speaker. That bitch ..." he scolded, but immediately became friendly again. "You did a wonderful job. Can you come to my office?"

"I'm sorry. We're in the middle of Bavaria and we just solved a murder."

Hindelang was impressed. "By golly! This Schwartz really is a first-rate detective. I have to admit, I'm really glad to be rid of that little fool of a girlfriend. Based on your evidence, I don't have to pay a single cent according to our marriage contract. This will save me at least five million euros. The whole sum is already with my lawyers".

Silence. Konny had to concentrate. What should he say? He decided on something simple: "Congratulations, Mr. Hindelang. The well-being of our customers is important to us."

"For that reason, well, and also because I'm a businessman, I have a suggestion regarding the fee. I mean, before you come to me with extrapolations of percentages of savings and so on and charge a percentage of something for which there was actually no commission ..."

Berti did a pirouette for joy, but it looked extremely awkward, so he sat down.

Konny interjected. "And what is your proposal?"

"Mr. Schwartz and you are still looking for a good office, aren't you?"

Berti nodded vigorously.

"Yes," Konny squeezed out hesitantly. "We're still looking for an office in a prestigious location."

"I've got something for you. Top location. Brand new!"

"Mr. Hindelang, you know that we..."

"Free of charge, of course. You would have to pay the service charges, but otherwise it would be rent-free."

Konny was speechless.

"Are you still there?" the construction worker asked after a few seconds of silence.

"I am."

"Now that I have saved five million and Mr. Schwartz has an excellent reputation, it is pure advertising for me to have his offices in one of my houses. I would waive the rent in exchange for the fee. Say for the next five years?"

"You mean completely free?" asked the surprised writer.

"You're a tough negotiator. So good. Completely free. I'll pay the utilities, too, but in return I'll put a big advertising sign out front. A big neon sign and then, of course, the usual brass thing. You know, like all the private investigators have in the TV crime dramas. "

Konny asked instinctively: "And who's going to pay for that?"

"Now you're getting on my nerves. Lucky for you I'm in a good mood. I'd rather deal with this in person anyway. But this is the last thing you're going to squeeze out of me. I'll pay for the stuff and the office equipment. But it's over now. You pay for the phone and all that crap yourself. What are you going to do now? Are you going to strike?"

"We're in business!"

"Great, then we'll sign the contract over a business lunch. Would you like to come to my house ..."

Berti waved him off. "Mutton testicles," he whispered.

"We prefer a restaurant for the business lunch. Then you can deduct the expense. How about an Italian restaurant?"

"You really are brilliant. Great idea. The IRS will pay for the meal. Very good! Call me as soon as you're back in town."

The "goodbye" came too late. Hindelang had already ended the call.

The two friends stared at each other.

"We made it."

"We're getting a luxury office in one of Hindelang's luxury office buildings."

"Top location!"

"Completely free!"

"What do you think that will do for the clients?"

"And we also have a week's luxury vacation ahead of us. We are in paradise."

"Not to mention we'll soon be a married couple."

"And no longer alone," Berti pointed down.

Woof, Sir Nelson barked.

"A few new rules apply to you from today, my little friend. First, you won't steal any more key cards, and second, you can completely forget about ever getting oysters from us for dinner."

They both grimaced. Sir Nelson put a paw over his little snout.

Laughter.

"And that stupid handbag is a thing of the past, too," Berti said. "You'll have a nice little apartment."

"Tell me, Berti, what did you tell the two policemen when they asked you if you knew anything about a barn fire?"

The corpulent detective shrugged. "Nothing! And you?"

Konny grinned. "After one of them mentioned a possible lightning strike, I played innocent too."

They laughed.

"A lightning strike in the middle of a blizzard."

"But we will still compensate the farmer anonymously for the damage," said Konny, who was the first to regain his composure.

"Of course we will. Hopefully I'll make enough. Although..." he thought. "Actually, I shouldn't have to do the whole detective business anymore."

"Why not?" Konny wanted to know.

Berti beamed when he said the next words. "Because you're going to be a bestselling author. Your two publishers will do so much publicity for your first Dr. Kurt Lonedale book that I could stay an amateur detective."

Konny was happy. Life suddenly seemed to smile on them. "We are two lucky children."

clover-1531035_1280

Chapter 14
Revenge is sweet an every cold has a silver lining

The friends had a wonderful week's vacation. The English couple and the Sweety family had already left the day of the arrest, while all the other guests stayed. Konny and Berti celebrated their engagement with them and the hotel staff. Ostmann willingly picked up the tab after being literally overwhelmed by a wave of bookings due to the media hype surrounding the hotel and the solved murder.

"It was pure advertising," the hotelier said on the day of their departure, even more generous than he already was.

Since the train ticket for the two friends' return trip had expired, Ostmann paid for their return flight after their week of luxury vacation. First class, of course. Berti and Konny could hardly believe it when the tickets were handed to them.

"Our caretaker Willi will act as your chauffeur and take you to the *Franz-Josef-Strauss Airport* in Munich-Erding. I would like to thank you again and hope very much to welcome you both as our guests in the future".

Shaking hands.

"If we feel drawn to the mountains again, I'd love to," Konny replied.

Munich-Erding airport was huge. The male couple had plenty of time before their flight. They made the most of it and wandered around. Hundreds of travelers hurried through the halls. A number of restaurants and shops tempted them with offers and shortened the tourists' waiting time. Every now and then you could see policemen on patrol. Suddenly, something rang in their ears. It was a greeting that had been burned into her memory.

"Hello and Servus in Bavaria!"

They jumped. In front of them was none other than Rudi Radtke, checking out two Dutch backpackers.

Berti couldn't believe it. "Now they've probably moved the old warhorse from the station to the airport."

"I don't want to know what he did with Ranzinger."

The procedure was identical to her own experience. But unlike a week ago, Radtke found nothing suspicious and let the two tourists go.

Konny and Berti had ducked into a newsstand to avoid being spotted by Radtke. Berti lingered in front of the magazine rack, while Konny stood behind a large revolving display of greeting cards, keeping a constant eye on the policeman, who liked to drink.

Hoping to find something about Chihuahuas, Berti flipped through a few dog magazines. He was engrossed in an article explaining what to look out for when bringing a four-legged friend into the house when he was bumped roughly in the side. Konny looked nervous.

"What's wrong?"

"Over there," Konny pointed to the cash register. "Rack-Romer and the Perla. You pay."

Berti was astonished. "Why aren't they in custody?"

Konny had no adequate answer. "I guess the authorities are too slow."

"Berti got angry. I still have a score to settle with them. What should we do?"

Konny thought for a moment, then said firmly: "I'll sneak up on you. You don't know me. Maybe I can find out something."

Berti nodded. "And I'll get Radtke."

When Berti returned to the newsstand with the policeman, Konny and the latest information were already waiting for them.

"You want to check in. Long-distance travel! The Romans have something like stupid police, they don't even notice that we have fake passports."

Radtke grimaced. Then he turned bright red. Pure rage. "Stupid police? I'm going to help them. This will be my first big case at the airport."

Since Konny knew where the couple was going, they hurried to the right counter. Berti walked purposefully past the line and stopped at the check-in counter. Right next to Mr. Romer, who was just handing the tickets to the Airline employee.

"Mr. Romer, how are you?" he said to his former boss.

The manager jumped back, startled. He was about to deny his identity when Ms. Perla began to chatter.

"Schwartz! What are you doing here?"

Berti grinned at the secretary. "Ms. Perla, good to see you. Did you pack enough lingerie?"

The airline lady asked. "Mr. Romer, do you have any carry-on luggage?"

"Romer? How imaginative," Berti blasphemed.

"Schwartz, you are and remain a fool. Get out of my way."

"Hello together an servus in Bavarian. Your papers, please!"

Schwartz squeezed in between Berti, Mr. Romer and Mrs. Perla. He showed his badge, put it back in his pocket and grinned broadly. "Well, it will be soon!"

Romer's forehead immediately broke into a bead of sweat. "I ... I ... this man must have me confused."

The lady at the counter looked at the line. "Mr. Romer, is there a problem?"

Radtke grinned even wider than bevor.

"I ... uh ... well."

The cop waved his handcuffs. "In order to clarify this, I'll probably have to place you under temporary arrest, Mr. Romer." He turned to the department store clerk. "You too, by the way, Ms. Perla. As far as I know, you have been ordered not to leave the country. Oh, yes, I'd like those false passports as well. You can give them to me now. That'll be another process."

Berti and Konny cheered. "Give me five."

They clapped their hands.

"Payback's a bitch," Konny grumbled, snapping a few pictures with his cell phone camera.

"That was for the ass photo in the newspaper," Berti whined to his ex-boss as he was led away.

Konny was beaming. "It couldn't have gone better."

"But Konny," Berti put on the brakes. "It could be better. I have one more thing to do."

"Like what?"

"I have to call my parents."

"Wouldn't you rather do that from home?"

Berti agreed.

The neighbors greeted us warmly. Berti and Konny stood in the hallway. Mrs. Mint had intercepted them.

"We read about it in the newspaper. There was a big report. I cut out the article," the old lady cried in the hallway.

The front door slammed shut. Hasan Özdemir came home. "Berti, Konny! Good to see you again. How was it?"

"That's a long story!"

"The Kapaunkes want to throw a welcome party," Mrs. Mint spoke again.

The next door opened. Vivien entered. She saw Sir Nelson. "What a cute dog."

They were home. They felt at home here.

"The mail's on the living room table," someone called from upstairs.

"Thank you so much. We're dog-tired for now. Let's talk tomorrow. Agreed?"

"Sure."

"Agreed."

"Good night."

When their own front door finally closed behind them, they were also mentally at home. Sir Nelson marched from room to room, sniffing around.

"Coffee?" asked Konny.

"I'd rather have some port."

"Good idea. Let's drink to everything."

While Konny filled two glasses, Berti rummaged through the mail. "Hey, there's a letter from the store."

"Open it," Konny called from the kitchen.

Berti took the A4 envelope and opened it. He scanned the first few lines.

Dear Mr. Schwartz,

We regret the premature dismissal ... Evidence ... on the basis of your investigations ... proceedings against the branch manager, Mr.

Romer, and his secretary, Ms. Perla ... Our lawyer will immediately issue an arrest warrant via the public prosecutor's office ...

Berti turned the page. "Honey, did you write to the management of the department store group?"

"Yes. It was supposed to be a surprise."

Berti continued reading on the second page.

... we offer you the opportunity to take over the management of the security departments of our nationwide stores, to restructure the system and to fill the key positions with selected specialists. Enclosed is a draft contract for your review.

"You are offering me a management position. The contract is enclosed."

"What are you paying?"

Berti read on. "It says here ... wait a minute!"

... blah blah blah, we are talking about an initial gross annual salary of 75,000 euros! If you accept the contract, please return the signed copy.

"You're in the running."

"And the detective agency?"

"You reply that you accept the assignment, but that you will remain a freelancer. Your fee for the first year will be 75,000 euros plus VAT and expenses for business trips."

Konny handed his friend the glass.

"Here, first have a sip of the delicious Porti. Here's to us."

"To us," Berti repeated.

The glasses clinked softly. The port completely washed away the worries they both had before the holiday.

"There's one more thing I have to do. I owe it to myself and to you."

"What is it, Berti?"

The private detective picked up the phone. "I have to call home and tell you everything. Especially about you."

"You mean at home? On the phone?"

"I'd rather do it now than wait a few days."

"If you feel like it, do it," Konny encouraged his friend, putting a hand on Berti's shoulder for moral support.

When he dialed the familiar number, he felt a big lump in his throat.

The bell rang. The detective wanted to hang up immediately, but he never wanted to run away from anything in his life again and stayed on the line.

"Schwartz!"

His father's voice sounded familiar and yet completely strange. Berti trembled, the palms of his hands became moist.

"Dad."

"Berti," he said happily. "Mom, Berti's on the phone!"

"Wait a second, I turn on the speaker."

"Berti, where are you?" he heard his mother asking in the background.

His father continued to speak. "You can talk son, mom can listen in."

"Good, I wanted to tell you something."

"What, you little boy?"

"I'm not alone anymore."

His father laughed, but it was a funny laugh. The laugh when Daddy Schwartz was in a good mood. "We already know that. It was done back then, you're two. Two boys."

Berti cursed inwardly. This was exactly what he wanted to avoid.

"Mom is really looking forward to it."

Berti was surprised. Completely. "What? Mom is really happy."

"Well, about our son-in-law. The Konny Wels. He's one of those novelists, right?"

"Y-yes," Berti huffed. "That's exactly what he is."

"Yay," he heard his mother scream in the background. "Konny Wels is my son-in-law! Mr. Dr. Kurt Lonedale himself. I'm going to freak out. When my friends find out. It's crazy."

"Slow down a bit. We're not even married yet."

"Then it's about time," Daddy Schwartz scolded. "You're not going to live in a sloppy relationship!"

"Dad? Is that really you?"

"Then again in slow speaking. If my son-in-law is listening, I want him to understand what I have to say! You two get married as soon as possible! I don't want my little son to live in loose relationships. Nothing beats a real marriage. Look at Mom and me. Or Uncle Ernest, who..."

"Dad," Berti interrupted his father. A tear trickled down his cheek. He had wiped the other side dry with the sleeve of his sweater.

"What is it?"

"I love you."

Then silence: "When are you coming home?"

"Visit you? How about tomorrow?"

Daddy Schwartz's voice was muffled. "Mom, you still have to cook Bratwurst. Berti and his friend are coming." Daddy Schwartz switched from Franconian dialect in normal German speech. "Does Konny understand franconia dialect?"

"I don't know."

"He has to take care of you. Boy, I'm so proud of you. We read about the murderer in the newspaper. ... the private detective Herbert Schwartz and his partner Konny Wels unmasked ..., the article begins. I've read it ten times and it hangs on the wall at the regulars' table in my favorite pub. Right next to the sheep's head cards with eight up. Just take care when you have such dangerous jobs.

"It's not always that dangerous."

"We'll talk about it tomorrow."

"See you then."

"Berti?"

"What else is there, Dad?"

"We love you too."

He hung up.

Berti held the phone for a while. He cried with happiness.

"Konny, my path hasn't always been easy, but I think we've reached our goal."

The pitch-black thread in Berti's life turned purple. The pre-alpine terrain of stumbling blocks seemed to be behind him.

Was this reality or was he slipping into a new adventure?

The author looked out of the window. "Look, it's snowing. If we take the dog for a walk, we'll leave three tracks of snow."

"I thought there were no snow tracks."

They laughed.

"We've made some really good friends," Konny said.

"Here and in Upper Bavaria."

They sat back, took a sip of port, and dreamed of their luxury hotel.

"You don't often hit the jackpot with murder," Konny said.

"I don't need it anymore," Berti smiled. "We'll go to the sea on our next vacation."

The End

Books by W. T. Wallenda

Friends with a bite
and the curse of the vampire

M. J. Wallenda, W. T. Wallenda

Friends with bite

AND
THE CURSE OF THE VAMPIRE

ISBN: 9783759767462
Print Book: 13,99 EUR

324 pages

9783759774354
E-Book: 6,99 EUR

16-year-old James Allington moves with his parents to the supposedly quiet small town of Greenfield in Massachusetts/USA. As soon as he arrives, the teenager witnesses a crime and is gradually drawn into a swamp of mysterious events.

James finds out that he lives among vampires and werewolves. His new friends Riley, Kieran and Cassie are also harboring dark secrets. The teenagers must trust each other to banish an ancient curse or Riley will die. An unequal battle against a powerful opponent and against time begins.

The novel *Friends with bite and the curse oft he vampire* an extremely exciting fantasy adventure thriller with a bit of heart and a good dash of humor and offers great entertainment.

331

Now in English – the German bestseller:

The Sniper from Stalingrad

W. T. Wallenda

THE SNIPER FROM STALINGRAD

ISBN: 978-3759720580

188 pages, 9,99 €.

*also available as an
E-Book 6,99 €*

Stalingrad, 1942 - 19-year-old Alfred Miller, a member of the 100th Panzer Division, comes to know and hate the cruel horrors of war during the fierce and costly battles for the "Red October" factory. Thanks to his marksmanship, he becomes a sniper.

After the encirclement of the 6th Army, the young Austrian wanders through the ruins of the dying city on the Volga during the coldest winter in years, both hunter and hunted. Hunger, cold, misery, death and fear are his constant companions.

The war hits hard and merciless every day. The soldiers are brutalized, the hope of salvation dies. Ultimately, there are only two ways to escape suffering and a grim fate: either get on one of the planes out of the cauldron, or die.

A true Story - without pathos, free of heroism and frighteningly close to reality.

W. T. Wallenda

Sniper at Monte Cassino:
"Sometimes I hear them still
screaming."

from the diary of a world war II veteran

ISBN: 978-3757845223

200 Pages, 11,99 €

E-Book: 6,99 €

"Sometimes I can still hear them screaming," Josef Altmann said more than 50 years after the Battle of Monte Cassino, lost in thought. He instinctively flinched, ducked to the side, apparently seeking cover from an imaginary approaching shell.

As a member of Regiment 361, the former foreign legionnaire witnessed the merciless fighting on the Gustav Line and around Monte Cassino. The war had reached an unimaginable level of cruelty, and death struck mercilessly every day.

Altmann was quickly trained as a sniper and immediately sent to the front. He recognizes the faces of his victims through the telescopic sight. His hands start to shake, his heart races. Goose bumps covered his body. Fear, misery, the loss of his closest comrades and the screams of the dying made him pull the trigger despite his initial doubts.

Josef Altmann tells his story without pathos, free of heroism and frighteningly close to reality.

This book is an unflinching factual account and should serve as a memorial against war.

A refreshing weird (crime) comedy

W. T. Wallenda & M. J. Wallenda

when grandma smokes a pipe

a totally weird comedy

ISBN: 978-3769376197

204 Pages, 10,99 €

also available as an E-Book

The three lovable scoundrels Willy, Ernest and Tommy set up a shared flat in the deepest Bavarian wilderness. The discovery of a marijuana plant turns not only their lives upside down, but also that of half the village. Grandma Huber and her women's group discover weed for themselves and are enthusiastic about this herbal medicine. When three gangsters turn up and blackmail the scoundrels, the village idyll is threatened with end.

The grandmas won't stand for that. They turn the tables and prepare for battle. When Grandma smokes a pipe - shows in a humorous way that young and old can get along excellently with each other.

This wonderfully over-the-top and refreshing weird (crime) comedy captivates its readers with humor and suspense.

YOU ENTER GERMANY ☐ was a warning to the US-Army

It was the hardest battle the US Army had ever had to endure.

W. T. Wallenda

Fields of Death
–
The Battle of
Hürtgen Forest

Information - original Photos - Novel
contemporary history of the Second World War

244 Pages
11,99 €

ISBN: 978-3769315509

also available as an
E-Book 7,99 €

Topics presented in bullet points:

-Key dates in the Battle of the Hürtgen Forest
-275th Infantry Division
-Original photos help illustrate
-The novel section reflects the events of the time from the perspective of a German sniper and a grenadier.

The five months of fighting in the Hürtgen Forest went down in history as one of the longest and bloodiest battles ever fought on German soil. It is also known as the 'Verdun of the Eifel'.
It was the biggest defeat in the history of the US Army, but it was also hell on earth for the German defenders.
The Hürtgen Forest became a killing field for soldiers on both sides.

335

The battle of Stalingrad – told coldly and without any pathos

W. T. Wallenda

STALINGRAD IN THE CROSSHAIRS

THE DUEL THE SNIPER

14,99 €
318 Pages

ISBN: 978-3759722393

also available as an E-Book

In the midst of the inhuman and brutal battle for Stalingrad, German and Russian snipers roam the ruins like angels of death, spreading fear and terror.

Katja Kalikova lost her husband to German bombs and her youngest son, Boris, to a Soviet bullet. Since then, she and her 8-year-old son, Grisha, have been fighting for their daily survival.

Major Erwin Koenig is an officer in the Wehrmacht and was stationed in Stalingrad. When his son Rolf is also sent to Stalingrad and falls victim to Russian snipers, Koenig has only one goal left. To avenge his son's death, the former sniper instructor sets his sights on living Russian sniper legend Vasily Saizev. Koenig blazes a bloody trail through dying Stalingrad, quickly turning from hunter to hunted.

When Katja and Major Koenig's paths fatefully cross, they make a pact to defeat Saizew.

The fate of the soldiers fighting in Stalingrad, as well as that of the Russian civilians forced to remain in the city, is portrayed bleakly, coldly, and without pathos.